West of North

A novel by
K.E. Hoover

ISBN:0692831746
ISBN-13: 978-0692831748

DEDICATION

This book is dedicated to the fight for federal recognition for the Five Landless Tribes of Southeast Alaska. Fifteen percent of the profits will support that purpose.

CONTENTS

ACKNOWLEDGMENTS

To my wife, Kimberly, for her continued support and to my father for his sense of adventure.

Thanks also to the Borough of Wrangell, the friendliest town in Alaska.

Special thanks to my daughter, Linnea Hoover, for designing the book cover in Adobe PhotoShop. linnea.hoover@yahoo.com

Flash Forward

The Police Chief leans forward, causing his oak chair to complain. His voice is gravel, "We are doing everything we can to solve the murders on Chief Shakes Island. I need to ensure we are thorough so we don't overlook anything.

"I hope you can appreciate we are going to ask you a lot of questions. Everything you say or do will come under close scrutiny. Before we start the questioning, we're going to need to collect the evidence on your body. We need to take samples of the blood on your hands and face."

The Chief's glare is withering. "We're confiscating your clothes as evidence. We'll inventory all your personal items and give you a receipt for them."

A weight crushes me and steals my breath. I squirm in my seat, and my left hand betrays me with a twitch.

The lamp on the Chief's desk flickers in sympathy. "Do you have any questions?"

PART 1: DISCOVERY

Chapter 1: Frigid

[Five weeks earlier]

I hit the frigid Alaskan water headfirst. My borrowed canoe rolls, driving me below the surface and soaking me in icy seawater. Upside down, I grasp for equipment spilling into cobalt waters. The extreme cold grips and squeezes; I fight to keep air in my lungs. With my legs tangled in the seat of the canoe, I scramble to get free. Perhaps I had fled too far in my effort to escape Kaeli's betrayal.

Chapter 2: Rescue

Seated at the stern of his skiff, Silver Jack snaps his raincoat closed around his neck and tucks his crush hat low on his forehead. His route faces into the rain and spray. His beard is paltry defense against the gale.

Chest-high waders and heavy raincoat protect from wind and water, while also holding in his body heat. He wears them despite the risk of falling overboard. In the water, his waders would fill with heavy liquid and suck him under. That's why he can never allow a single mistake.

Blackie lunges for the side of the skiff and begins barking at the nearby shore. The heavy wolf dog tips the boat to portside as the prospector turns and scans the dark shoreline.

About fifteen yards from the waterline, rows of entwined driftwood defend a line of dusky spruce. Pennants of witch's hair lash from the ends of heavy limbs. Nothing is dry, and there is no shelter from the punishing wind and rain.

Blackie continues barking at a bear cub along the shore. Silver Jack's about to turn away, but Blackie surges alongside him onto the rear seat of the skiff, knocking him off balance and causing the skiff to spin about on the crest of a wind-driven wave.

He yells at Blackie, "You idiot! Are you trying to capsize us?"

Blackie's throaty barks continue, "*Woof, woof, woof...*"

In the process of regaining control of the skiff, he finds he's close to the bank, and in the dim light he notices the bear cub is wearing a red vest. It's a man crawling on all fours along the beach. Shutting off his outboard motor he booms, "Hey there."

When there is no response he hollers, "Are you deaf? Do you need help?" He yells again, "Hey mister, get over here before you freeze to death."

Lurching kilter, a burly man staggers through the water to the skiff and climbs aboard. He slumps onto the forward bench, water streaming from his soaked clothing.

Silver Jack bellows over the wind, "We have to get you out of those wet clothes, or you won't make it."

He yanks on his starter rope and the outboard roars to life. Backing the skiff away from the shore, he drops the outboard's rpm, changes direction, and the skiff shoots forward into the next wave.

The man is unprepared for the lurch and falls back. He shivers repeatedly as the craft speeds past the shoreline.

Despite being patched in a number of places, the bilge holds several inches of standing water. A plastic lid between the benches seesaws as waves pummel the craft. Within two minutes Jack reenters the mouth of Crittenden Creek.

As the roar of the wind diminishes, Silver Jack addresses the man; "We'll stop the boat for a few minutes. Can you get your clothes off?"

The man provides no response as the boat is turned toward the bank and beached.

Silver Jack moves forward, "We're going to get you out of your wet clothes and into a sleeping bag for the trip back to Wrangell. Do you understand?"

The man nods. His mouth opens but no words come out. The rain assaults in waves, cold and determined.

As Silver Jack struggles to pull off the young man's soaked clothing, he introduces himself, "I'm Jack, but most folks around here call me Silver Jack." Pointing at the dog sitting in the middle of the skiff, Silver Jack proudly adds, "This is Blackie. He spotted you on the beach."

As quick as he can, he opens a sleeping bag stashed under the covered bow of the skiff and coaxes the man to crawl inside. Once settled, he calls Blackie to lie beside the man.

Within minutes Silver Jack is fighting to keep his boat on course as it plows straight into the whitecaps on the fastest line he can make across the Eastern Passage for the town of Wrangell. He hopes the young man will survive, but a lot depends on how long he was in the water, his physical condition, and if he has any health issues. In the distance at the northernmost tip of Wrangell Island is Point Highfield. The airport runway expansion project is a beacon lit up day and night. He worries about his unknown guest and wishes for a faster outboard motor.

Blackie whines and he responds, "Stay put Blackie. Hang in there and I'll fix you up later with a reward." He is grateful the dog obeys. Blackie often sits on the bench near the center of the boat to keep his big paws out of the cold water.

#

Silver Jack moves by the rhythm of the land. In his view, a man has to flow with the wind, tide, and season or need to explore new places. He'd been married seven times and in long-term relationships more times than that. Most of them fell apart because he refused to live his life by a schedule. He figured it was the natural order of things. A man and woman were made to get along, or not. So if you weren't made to travel the same trail, the sooner you parted company the better. Angry women make poor trail mates.

#

After pounding across the turbulent Eastern Passage, they round the point near the airport and turn left toward the town and port of Wrangell. With the turn, the squall pummels his right shoulder, and he is forced to steer into each approaching wave to avoid being swamped.

Under the bright construction lights, giant dump trucks trundle, carrying tons of rock to dump in the sea for the expanded runway. The construction site is noisy with activity; enough he can hear the racket over the general roar of his outboard.

Moving south, the illumination cast by the construction zone fades. When lit windows glow to port, he resolves to stop at the first house along the way. Calling for assistance will get the youngster to the hospital sooner, saving precious minutes.

He tilts up his outboard and runs the craft ashore. The tough aluminum hull grinds over the rocks as his skiff lurches to a halt.

He almost pulls away when he recognizes the home and remembers how Blackie had finished off the widow's beloved lapdog with a quick snap and toss of his powerful jaws. In Blackie's defense the little mutt should never have bounced his front paws on Blackie's shoulder. The woman's shrieks and curses still echoed.

Not excited about the upcoming confrontation with Mildred, he shuts off the outboard and climbs the bank. Tramping across the uneven rocks in the dark, he stumbles and curses, angry for not bringing his flashlight. He wallops the entry to the cottage, and within a minute, Mildred comes to the door.

"I need your help, I found a young man in the water past Babbler Point. Can you call for an ambulance while I try to get him up to the road?"

"I wouldn't lift a finger to help you, you old pervert. But no matter how much I despise you, I will do the right thing and call 9-1-1." Mildred scorches him with a schoolmarm glare. "Well go on," she snaps. "I'll make the call and come out and help you."

He lifts his gloved hand by way of thanking the old biddy and heads back to the skiff. "Stay out of the way," he tells Blackie as the dog jumps into the craft before he can stop him. The dog blocks his access, so he snarls, "Get out of the way, you big galoot."

Blackie climbs onto the central bench dropping his tail between his legs and lowering his head.

Not ready to apologize, Silver Jack is acidic, "Don't let me hurt your feelings, you wuss."

He seizes the sleeping bag and yards the man out from under the deck. Using a fireman's carry, he straightens his knees and lifts the burden. Placing each foot so as not to twist an ankle on a loose rock, he toils up the shore toward Mildred's home. Sirens in the distance announce help is coming.

As soon as he leaves the skiff behind, Blackie jumps onto the bank and follows him. The prospector hears a door slam and finds Mildred beside him, illuminating his way with a flashlight. With the aid of the lamp, he can watch sheets of rain bounce off the rocks as high as his knees. Mildred is in her bathrobe but has taken time to slip into rubber boots.

"You shouldn't be carrying him by yourself!" Mildred's tone is the same as if she were admonishing a child. "You're showing off." She marches in quickstep beside him as he staggers into her yard, grateful to find easier purchase on the turf under her fruit trees.

As he reaches the edge of the driveway, the crunch of gravel signals the ambulance turning off the blacktop. A sudden flash of light and he, Mildred, and Blackie are blinded at the same moment the sirens stop. By the time he reaches the rear door of the ambulance, the attendant has the door open and a gurney out. With everyone helping, the unconscious man is removed from his shoulder, strapped to the litter, and lifted into the aging ambulance.

Silver Jack gasps for breath and leans against the rusty fender of the vehicle. Removing his hat and gloves, he runs the fingers of both hands through his mane of silver hair. It's been a long time since he'd packed a load like this, and his legs and back scream. He puts his hat on his head, straightens, and wrings water out of his gloves. He recognizes both the ambulance driver and the attendant.

While Bill, the attendant, unzips the sleeping bag and checks for vital signs, Ed, the driver, asks, "How long was he in the water?"

"I'm not sure. When I found him he was on the bank and could walk, sort of. He looked in a pretty bad way to me."

"Do you know who he is?" Ed squints at the young man's face.

"No, but I pulled his clothes off and threw them in the boat. I'll bet his ID is there somewhere."

"Well, we can't wait. Give the information to the police." Conversation finished, Ed closes the ambulance doors and climbs into the driver's seat. "Get his name as soon as you can," Ed shouts, backing the rig uphill out of the driveway. Silver Jack and Mildred mark the ambulance's progress as it speeds away.

"Let's get out of this downpour and call the police," Mildred surprises him. "You could wait all night for them, and you must want to go home and get dried out, too. Come inside and let's get you warmed up." She hesitates, "Will Blackie be okay on the porch?"

"You make the call. I'll tie up the skiff and bring in the fella's clothes. Won't take but a moment, and Blackie will do fine on the porch. He's used to a lot worse than this."

With the need for speed behind him, he ambles to the skiff. Scooping up the young man's garb, he stuffs the items into a loose plastic bag.

Since Mildred is expecting him, he doesn't knock when he reaches her front door. He lets Blackie in first and shadows the beast inside the enclosed porch. Silver Jack ducks as Blackie sprays the porch with hard-flung beads of cold water.

A yellow bulb reveals an organized storage area, with a bench for removing boots. He peels off his raincoat and hangs it on a peg. Dropping his suspenders, he pulls off his waders and hangs them beside his raincoat. Stepping to avoid the puddles he's made, he opens the door to the living area to find Mildred waiting with a hot cup of tea and a plate of cookies.

"You might want to stand by the fire." Mildred's tone is cool as she hands him a teacup.

He notices she has changed into pants and a flannel shirt. Somehow she'd found enough time to brush her hair.

"The police will be here in thirty minutes. Would you like a bowl of halibut soup?"

"Nothing for me thanks." Silver Jack presses his lips together expecting rejection, "Do you have any kind of tidbit for Blackie? I sort of promised him a treat when I made him lie down next to the young feller in the skiff."

Mildred stiffens but for the third time surprises him, "I have moose in the freezer." She smiles and lowers her voice, "Can he eat it?"

He notices how young Mildred looks at this moment despite her being nearly sixty. He smiles, "Being frozen won't slow him much, but it would make a great perk. He's the one who spotted the man on the bank. He started barking, and I couldn't get him to shut up until I turned the boat around. I sure hope we got the young fella to town in time."

#

An hour later, he repeats his story for Detective Alex from the Wrangell Police Department. Detective Alex takes copious notes and asks lots of questions.

Silver Jack ends the dialogue, “Listen, I’ve already told you I have no information about the young man. He couldn’t talk and could barely move when I found him. The information I have is what you can find in his clothes or his wallet.”

“Most of the contents of his wallet are a watery pulp. It looks like his name is Josh Campbell, and his driver license indicates he’s from Colorado. I’m trying to find out if he has kin we can notify.” After a pause Detective Alex follows up with a different question, “Did you notice a boat?”

Silver Jack huffs. His gruff demeanor wasn’t working as planned. “It looked like there was a canoe on the beach. But I didn’t pay much attention to it, because I was focused on getting the young man into my skiff before he collapsed. I’m sorry I can’t be more help.”

“You’ve done a great job. You most likely saved the man’s life if he makes it through the night.”

Silver Jack yawns, “I’ll go up to the hospital in the morning and check in on him.”

As Detective Alex departs, Mildred stands up. “Jack, will you come by and walk me to the hospital in the morning? I want to meet this Josh Campbell and learn why Blackie watched over him.”

He smiles, “I’d be happy to stop by about daybreak.” When her eyes widen he continues, ”Thank you for the moose meat. By the way, your oatmeal cookies are the best I’ve ever tasted.”

Mildred pats him on the shoulder as he heads out to the porch. She arches one eyebrow and sternly warns him, “Don’t come before nine, I won’t be ready until then.”

Within ten minutes, Silver Jack and Blackie are back in their skiff. He sits back, determined to savor the last mile into Wrangell’s harbor. The breeze remains onshore. He enjoys the whitecaps and the windblown spray with its tangy smell of the sea.

On top of the center bench, Blackie sits peering intently ahead. The black beast blends into the darkness, and he’s difficult to make out, even though the two are less than six feet apart.

Slowing down at the entrance to the harbor, he notices a break in the clouds overhead revealing stars looming large in the

night sky. Exhausted, putting away his equipment will be a chore tonight. It has been a day filled with the unexpected. It will be a good day if the young man lives.

Chapter 3: Daycare

Anne's alarm rings at 5 a.m. She'd prefer to ignore the damn thing, but her job is the only way she can support herself and Emily. She gets up, goes to the bathroom and checks on her daughter, peacefully dreaming in her bunk. After a quick, hot shower, Anne gets dressed in her uniform and puts on makeup.

She attempts to awaken Emily and gets her ready. The girl resists, but Anne is persistent, since she has to be to work at six. At 5:45 a.m. she and her daughter are in the truck for the short hop down the hill and around the harbor to daycare.

"I hate going here," Emily declares as they near the building. "I'm old enough to take care of myself."

"We've been over this before," Anne tells her daughter. "You have to go until I can make other arrangements for you."

"I don't like it. I'm almost ten, the oldest one there," Emily pouts.

Anne sighs, she hates disappointing Emily day after day. "I know. I'm working on it."

After she checks in her daughter, Anne steers her red truck back toward town. Along the way, she passes the home she and Emily used to share with Michael. It saddens her those days are gone and will never return.

She remembers those wonderful first years. Michael had a steady job at the cannery with hope of promotion in the future. Unfortunately, Michael started to drink too much, and when they found out he was drinking on the job, he was fired.

After the cannery, Michael tried working on fishing boats.

One by one he tried them all, but lost a little more of himself every day.

About the time Emily was four years old, Anne found out Michael had a girlfriend. She'd earned herself a black eye for confronting him. She moved in with her parents and filed for divorce. She hadn't talked to Michael in five years. The last she'd heard he was a cook for a logging outfit on Prince of Wales Island, nearly a hundred miles away by boat. It sounded as if he was drinking more than ever.

Two years ago, she'd landed a job as a waitress at the café and started to work herself out of the financial hole she'd dropped into. She and Emily have a tiny apartment they call home. It isn't perfect, but it will do; and it's a damn sight better than being helpless and dependent on anyone else. She earns her own way and will never allow herself to repeat the mistake of falling for a pretty boy with no future.

With two minutes to spare, Anne parks her truck at the back of the Diamond C. As she enters the back door of the restaurant, she waves good morning to Darcy, who is the cook of the morning shift as well as owner. Darcy is busy getting the kitchen ready for the morning rush and winks back at Anne. She marvels at how chipper Darcy is, even though she opens the café at four each morning.

Anne pulls her hair back into a ponytail; smoothes out her apron with quick strokes down the front of her thighs and enters the dining room of the restaurant. She hellos two old timers sitting at the counter and pours them more coffee. They always take their coffee black and never order breakfast until they've finished at least three cups. Barry sports a curly beard and Ernie always wears a "Semper Fi" baseball cap.

As she cleans a table, the television high in a corner above and behind the counter shows the five-day weather forecast. Rainsqualls pepper the outlook.

Anne refreshes coffee to a table of fishermen in the corner. The youngest fisherman flirts. She smiles but does nothing more to encourage him. She's been caught in this trap before. No matter, he will trip all over himself running the other way once he learns about Emily.

Noticing she is low on hot coffee, Anne starts another batch brewing.

"Order up," announces Darcy from behind her at the same time the front door opens and another table of fishermen arrive.

#

Several hours later Anne overhears fishermen talking about a radio message regarding a body found floating near the Koknuk Flats in the mouth of the Stikine River. According to what he'd heard, the dead man was wearing a personal flotation device, so they were speculating he died from exposure instead of drowning. For the rest of the morning, Anne hears no other topic in the restaurant. Nearly all have lost friends or loved ones in the glacier fed waters of the inside passage.

As she continues waiting tables, she notes a lot of speculation among the diners regarding who the dead man might be. This leads to a discussion by the old timers at the counter regarding who hadn't been around in awhile. Anne hopes the dead man is a stranger. One customer reports the Coast Guard has been called in to search for the missing man's boat and to check for other survivors.

At ten o'clock, Helen, the cook for the second shift arrives. Darcy's shift as cook ends and her second shift as business owner starts. As Darcy is about to run errands, Anne whips up her courage and asks her tentatively, "Would it be okay if Emily helped me waitress during the summer? It would be fun for her and I'd watch her to keep her out of trouble."

Darcy gives her a wink and smile. "You bring your sweet girl here any day you want." Her face becomes stern, "But you tell her if she doesn't tend to business, she'll have to go back to daycare."

As her shift is about to end for the day, Anne hears a news flash. A survivor was found on Kadin Island near the mouth of the Stikine and airlifted to the hospital in Wrangell.

Her shift over, Anne counts her tips and reports them to Darcy. It has been a good day, and best of all. Her boss will let her bring Emily to work. Anne picks up her daughter and takes her along while she runs her afternoon errands. She considers the best place

to go to find fabric, intending to sew a uniform for Emily. Anne begins to hum.

Chapter 4: Mothers

I wake up disoriented because everything is unfamiliar. The room is stark white and the brightness overpowers me. Rain drums against an aluminum-frame window near my bed. The shades on the window are open, but the natural light outside is so dark it sucks light out of my room. I turn my head and spy a doorway.

Nearby, a woman speaks, "Are you awake?"

I turn my head further and take in a matron seated in a folding chair. Her dark brown eyes and the shape of her face indicate more than a little Indian ancestry. It's evident her hair was once jet black, today it's salt-and-pepper gray. It's a kind face, so I smile, even though I'm confused.

Hesitantly I ask, "Who are you?"

"My name is Mildred. Silver Jack brought you to my home, and I called the ambulance." Her speech cadence includes long pauses. She pats her hair although nothing is out of place.

I consider this for a while. I have a shadow memory of an old man and an enormous black dog. I ask, "Did he rescue me?"

"Yes, he did. He carried you up to my house wrapped in a sleeping bag. He told me he found you past Babbler Point." She shares this last bit of news as if it's a private joke between two old friends.

I weigh 190 pounds, so it's not likely one man could have carried me to her house. I must have been able to walk. I try hard to remember anything after rolling over in the canoe. All I can remember is the aching cold.

A nurse entering the room gives me a big smile. "Hi, Mr.

Campbell. How are you feeling this morning?"

She looks to be in her mid forties, short and plump, but with a wonderful, almost youthful, enthusiasm. It makes me feel better listening to her voice. I croak out, "I feel tired and hungry."

"Well that's just perfect, dearie," she says with aplomb. "It shows you're on the mend. You gave us quite a scare last night. When you came in you were in Stage Two hypothermia, but clearly you had been in Stage Three before getting help. Thank god you were found and taken care of so quick. I want to check your pulse and take your temperature. Soon we'll find something for you to eat other than saline solution."

After the nurse leaves, I turn to Mildred. "Thank you for your help. It's kind of you to come to the hospital to check on me. You didn't need to."

"I brought your clothes. I had time, so I washed them." She pauses as if carefully choosing her words, "Do you have someone we should call?"

"No, I'm new in town." I regret providing such a vague response, even if it's the truth.

She fidgets in her chair. "The police have your wallet and identification. They'll doubtless return them to you later."

I'm about to thank her again, as an old man enters the room.

"Howdy, young fella. We met last night and I'm Silver Jack." He mashes my hand, "You're looking all bright eyed and bushy tailed this morning."

I work hard at trying to remember meeting him and come away frustrated. It's obvious why he's called Silver Jack, due to the shock of ghost white hair visible under his waterproof hat and the silver beard framing his face. His white eyebrows arch out and away from his face. I don't remember anyone with eyebrows as long. His nose is long for his face, several scars and weathered skin lend a mysterious aura.

His dark brown eyes are in sharp contrast to his hair and dance with good humor. He would be considered short by any standard, but he's built like a medium sized boulder. I can tell he's a tough old man; he looks to be a picture book image of an Alaskan prospector in his dirty flannel shirt, brown leather vest, blue jeans, and boots.

Despite his cheery tone, I'm not looking or feeling energetic. "I'd like to thank you, for finding me."

"Oh, it was nothing," he defers. "Blackie, my wolf dog, spotted you and started barking. I figured you were a wild animal."

"Regardless, I owe you my life. You could have kept going and left me to fend for myself."

"You can take it up with Blackie. Here in Alaska, anybody who would abandon another person when they need help might as well be gut shot." As if to emphasize the point, he tugs on his belt with both hands.

"Thank you, regardless. My name is Josh Campbell. I'm the new science teacher at the high school."

"Josh, welcome to Wrangell." he expounds, "You'll find Alaska is full of characters." He chuckles and adds, "I'm not one of the saner ones. We're all end of the road types here, and damn proud of it. So you're a teacher. That's great. I never went to school past the eighth grade, but I try to learn something new each day."

The nurse briskly enters my room carrying a tray. "Here's hot oatmeal with bananas and cream, dearie. This has been made up, special order, just for you. You must eat everything, so you can grow up big and strong."

I wonder if she's going to pat me on the head too; but she turns and exits the room. I presume she's on her efficient way to the next patient, whoever they may be.

The old prospector says, "You weren't the only one brought in for a dip in the pond. The Coast Guard rescued a man found on an island near the mouth of the Stikine. The survivor claims his boat tangled with a log upriver, and he drifted for miles before he swam to the island. I say the whole story is a crock. You've been in the water. In fifteen minutes you're past doing anything unless you are wearing a survival suit. And he wasn't."

I have to agree with Silver Jack. After my brief and almost terminal dunking, I had been rendered incapable of taking care of myself. I knew there was no way you could drift for miles and then swim to shore.

"Tell me, son. Why were you out there in a canoe during a

storm? That was almost the last mistake you ever got to make." He pulls on his beard. "It's hard to learn if you're dead."

I feel embarrassed, but I owe him the truth. "I saw this fiberglass canoe at my landlord's home, and I asked if I could borrow it to explore the harbor. It was such a nice day I went up the shoreline past the airport. I was in the Eastern Passage when the wind came up. I wasn't aware I was in trouble until the canoe started to corkscrew in the wind and the whitecaps. I tried running with the wind but ended up in the drink before I got to shore."

"Well, it's lucky you survived. I'm glad Blackie and me was there when you needed help. Right now, I'd better head out. We have to make a run over to Crittenden Creek where we found you and try to recover your canoe and equipment."

"I can't thank you enough. I don't have any way to repay you for your kindness."

"Don't let it bother you son. I'll have your stuff at my boat down in the marina a little past the Harbormaster's office. As soon as you get well, drop on by, and we'll help you get it home."

"Thanks. I'll come by when they let me out."

After he leaves, Mildred announces she has several errands to run. "If you don't mind, maybe I'll check on you late this afternoon."

I'm sad to watch her go. As I lie in my hospital bed, I contemplate how Mildred reminds me of the mother I never had. What a concept. "I'll check on you." It implied a connection I hadn't experienced in twenty years.

My mother drowned when I was six, so growing up I had two stepmothers. The first one, died from heart failure about eight months after having heart surgery. I was ten years old and found losing a mother for the second time in my short life a mystery. She had been frail but kind and loving.

My second stepmother was a heavy drinker who enjoyed handing out stiff punishment for any infraction. She had a roundhouse slap guaranteed to rattle teeth. If I ducked, or she missed making a good connection, it made her mad, and I got worse. I followed directions to the letter, without complaining or arguing, and endured her verbal and physical abuse until the day I

left home. The one thing I can say about her, she was great preparation for a stint in the Army.

Chapter 5: Salvage

Clay Foster is leaving the marina office when David interrupts him. "Harbormaster, a raft of pilings has arrived for the new marina. Where do you want them to put the raft?"

Clay cuts, "God damn it. I've told everyone the materials for the new harbor are to be tied up to Dock Nine." Stomping away, he ignores the hurt look on his employee's face. He's being unfair to David; he'd purposely not shared his plans with his assistant.

The Harbormaster doesn't care if David, or anyone else, is unhappy. What he needs is a drink. Thankfully, the Marine Bar is nearby, hugging the entrance to the marina. He enters the darkened bar and walks to the back. The stink of stale beer, cigarette smoke, and greasy fries assaults him. Don, the bartender, notices him coming and lifts an eyebrow.

Clay orders, "Give me the usual."

Don pours him a double shot of scotch.

Clay asks, "What's going on today in this gritty little town?"

Taking no visible offense at Clay's choice of words, Don leans on the bar, "The Coast Guard found a man alive on Kadin Island. They also found an overturned boat nearby. It sounds like they're searching for another member of the boating party."

Surprised at the news, Clay takes a slug from his drink, motivated by the chance to make an easy buck. "Well, I might have to look into that." He finishes his drink in one swallow. "Here's something extra for the tip. There'll be more if I claim salvage." He hands the bartender a twenty and slides off the bar stool.

By the time he gets back to the marina office, the scotch is starting to warm his belly and crawl up his spine. Clay calls the Coast Guard and gets information on the chart location for the survivor and the overturned boat.

The dispatcher tells him, "The survivor's name is Lenn Richards. Does it ring a bell?"

Clay lies, "I've never heard of him."

Off the phone, he gathers up the keys to the marina's heavy launch. He also picks up an insulated jacket and slips a bottle into one of the pockets. Grabbing a pair of work gloves, he scans about for anything he might need on the trip.

Leaving the building, he encounters David and the scotch compels him to goad David again. The Harbormaster believes David is secretly sweet on Anne, the lovely, divorced waitress up at the Diamond C, so he asks him if he's had any luck getting a date.

David avoids making eye contact, "I haven't been over there."

Clay snorts. "David, you're a pussy. You better get it on with her before I do. A hard cock knows no conscience."

"What do you mean?" David looks as if he wants to bolt.

"It means you're not a man. You'll understand one day if you ever get balls."

David turns to leave, but Clay stops him. "I want you to clean up Dock Seven today. Don't get too far from the radio, because I might call you for help. I'm headed out for a few hours so don't try sneaking off, or I'll find out and fire your ass."

Clay gets a satisfactory glow for treating David badly. Not the first time, making the young man's life hell makes him feel better.

Speeding toward Kadin Island, Clay takes a swig from his bottle and mulls what he knows about Lenn. They'd met at the Ketchikan Regional Youth Facility when they were both teenagers. Clay spent ten months there for a series of petty thefts and delinquent behavior. Lenn had been there for a year already. The two fought once over something petty before getting along pretty well, at least as well as anyone got along in that dysfunctional place.

It was rumored Lenn had knifed a homeless man in Ketchikan. According to the rumor, Lenn figured the old man was queer when he stumbled on the broken sidewalk and lurched against the youth. Lucky for Lenn the old fart didn't die, and he only got twenty-four months for the stabbing.

One time, he got up the courage to ask Lenn why he spelled his name with an extra n. He'd wished for the words back after his friend's eyes went dead. The way he looked caused Clay to stop breathing. He held his breath until the moment passed, and Lenn's eyes returned to normal.

Lenn spat, "It's a gift from my old man."

Clay never asked him about it again, fearing for his life, because he knew Lenn kept a shiv hidden in his boot. The two of them spent hours hatching plans for great ways to get rich, once they got away from the youth facility. Clay left first and joined the Coast Guard. He'd never heard of Lenn again until today.

The launch is a fast working boat on a stable platform featuring a cable-lift hoist. He's surprised to find the overturned boat beached on the shore. The twenty-two foot aluminum jet sled would be difficult to turn over under any circumstances, especially sitting in the water, unless it were traveling at high speed and struck something.

Clay examines the hull and finds scratches but nothing consistent with a high-speed strike. He deduces the boat was overturned right there on the shore. Lenn was found a quarter mile up the shoreline of this same island. He pushes into the brush searching for clues.

#

Twenty minutes later, Clay returns to the shore of the island. He's found equipment covered by freshly cut brush. Not surprised, Lenn was too lazy to pack the equipment more than a few steps or move the boat to a different location. Lenn's deceit would have worked if Clay hadn't come along to spoil it. If his old comrade is making money from this con, he'd better cut himself in. If not, he would get a reward and recognition for turning in evidence of a crime. Clay vows to visit Lenn in the hospital and squeeze his nuts.

Clay runs a line from the launch's hoist over the hull of the overturned boat and rights the craft. He uses a boat hook to prevent a collision with his launch and jumps aboard his prize. Sure, it has scratches in the hull because of his handling, but why should he care. He attaches a towing line to the bow of the boat and the stern of the marina's launch.

Satisfied everything is ready, Clay heads for Wrangell. With a great deal of anticipation, he reviews plans for his meeting with Lenn.

Chapter 6: The Hospital

I wake and remember I'm in the hospital. I roll my shoulders forward an inch, and nothing falls apart. I lift my right arm, bringing my hand up in front of my eyes. My fingers wave at me. My left arm, hand and fingers work, too. I lift one knee and another, dragging my heels against the bed sheets until I've formed a teepee.

I hear a chuckle, and I turn my head. Mildred is seated in the guest chair beside me.

"How long was I asleep?"

"Six hours, this time," She smiles.

I consider her answer for a moment. "What time is it?"

Mildred answers, "Its five o'clock in the afternoon. Your doctor is making her rounds about six. Maybe you can find out how much longer you have to stay in the hospital."

I thank her, and we spend a pleasant hour talking about Wrangell. I learn her family has lived on Prince of Wales Island, a couple of islands west of Wrangell Island, for generations. She inherited her home from her dead husband's grandmother. It's a little inconvenient for her to live a mile out of town, but she enjoys watching the open water and being near the petroglyphs.

"Tell me about them."

"The history of the rock carvings is unknown. Scientists say the petroglyphs are three to four thousand years old. A few argue they are older. The carvings depict sea life, an owl, and faces. There are even abstract drawings. No one is sure why there are so many of them in this single location."

She invites me to come out and examine the petroglyphs for

myself. “One of them is lying in my front yard. The rest get covered up during high tide, but all of them are exposed during low tide.”

Mildred works at the post office. She doesn’t own a car, so she either walks to town or catches a ride from a friend. When I ask her about Silver Jack, she can’t tell me much. He used to be a logger, and he’s been living on a boat in the marina for at least fifteen years. He used to have another boat, but it sank while he was away prospecting on the mainland. His power was disconnected, and his bilge pumps stopped operating. There was speculation it was no accident, but evidence of foul play was never found. It cost him 2,500 dollars to have his old boat removed from the harbor after it sank. Fortunately, he’d already bought his current boat and had a place to live. He lost a lot of belongings on the sunken boat.

According to Mildred, the old prospector manages to live on only his social security plus his annual Permanent Fund allocation from the Alaskan pipeline project. “He tells me he can put two hundred dollars per month into savings. He spends most of his spare money on supplies and equipment for his prospecting expeditions.

“Blackie has been with Silver Jack for almost ten years. Everyone accepts Blackie is part wolf. The two of them make quite a sight walking along Front Street. Often the tourists from the cruise ships will stop the pair so they can take pictures of a ‘real’ prospector.

“I learned the hard way that Blackie isn’t safe to be around. Last summer they walked by my home and my little rescue dog, Sophie, ran out of my yard and up onto the edge of the road. She only weighed a little over ten pounds and Blackie ripped her throat out for no good reason.” Mildred sobs quietly before continuing, “And worse yet, he never apologized for his dog’s brutal act! All he did was scurry down the street like a bum. I haven’t talked to the man since, except last night when he showed up at my place in the storm with you in tow.”

A bit after six thirty, a tall woman in a white physician’s coat enters my room. “Hello, I’m Doctor Wilson.” She looks at my chart, “You’re a lucky man.”

“I know.”

“Yes. Well, we don’t often get a good outcome unless the

patient is removed from the water within a few minutes. In your case, you tiptoed over the line about as far as possible and still managed to make it back without complications." She flips through my chart, "There's no reason why we can't let you go home tonight; your vital signs are quite good. But I'll leave it up to you in case you want to wait until the morning."

I don't hesitate, "I'm ready to get out of here."

Doctor Wilson nods and writes in my chart. "Good. I'll have the nurse brief you and get you to sign a few forms and you can be on your way. Good luck and don't go for any more dunks in the ocean."

After she leaves, Mildred waits with me while I am lectured by the nurse. I sign more forms than I'd signed to get into the Army. Finally, I am free to go. Mildred waits outside while I dress in my hiking clothes and then she shows me the way out. From the hospital entrance I notice the harbor and smell the salty tang of the ocean. Flags and pennants in the marina flap in a breeze blowing briskly onshore. A power catamaran tiptoes into the harbor. It isn't raining, but it looks as if it might rain at any minute.

Silver Jack is waiting outside. He plays fetch with a huge dog, but he is using a plank instead of a ball. Blackie isn't the biggest dog ever, but he is pretty close. All black, he has a head shaped like a German shepherd but his body is longer and leggy. He lopes when he runs and his straight tail doesn't curl over his back.

While I watch, he rips chunks out of the plank with every move. The old prospector is wearing gloves, and he taps Blackie's face with the back of the fingers of one hand. When he says, "smile," the plank erupts in a cloud of splinters.

I feel reluctant to interrupt the two at play, but he turns and finds me with Mildred. "Howdy, let me introduce you to Blackie." With his tongue out and ears up, the animal's body language changes from wolf to dog in the blink of an eye. I'm uncertain what to do so Silver Jack instructs, "Let him smell the back of your hand."

Reluctantly, I lower my hand and extend the back of it toward Blackie. I can envision him removing it in one quick bite, but I swallow my fear and hold still. Blackie inhales and I remain frozen, until he turns his head away and blinks.

He licks his lips and the old prospector informs, "He remembers you from last night." After a quick pause he asks, "Are you ready to blow this joint?"

I am uncertain of the social norms in this remote location. In Colorado, I was never invited into the home of a local unless I knew them from work. Yet, in this frontier town, I am learning to accept strangers with a freedom I'd never experienced before. I experiment, "Yes, I am. Would you and Mildred care to come to my apartment? I'm a couple of blocks away over on Bennett Street."

I'm overjoyed when they agree to join me. As we walk, Silver Jack snaps a thick blue rope to Blackie's collar.

"What is that?" I inquire.

"I got this in the hardware store, it's a nylon rope used to lead a horse. It needs to be pretty sturdy or he breaks it."

I shake my head and try to imagine why a dog needs a leash designed to hold a horse. Considering Blackie tore the plank to shreds with his wolf-like fangs, maybe it isn't oversized after all.

Chapter 7: Invitation

Silver Jack came to Alaska years ago because it was the last great frontier. It fit him better than anywhere else. But civilization is a relentless invader. Luckily, the wild and remote regions see few travelers. They should last for his lifetime at least.

#

After visiting Josh in the hospital, he spent the better part of the day returning to the rocky shore near Crittenden Creek in his skiff and picking up Josh's equipment.

He stowed the gear in his skiff and tied the canoe so it would tow behind. It took him three attempts to get the canoe to tow properly behind the boat without corkscrewing in the water. He'd shaken his head in disgust when he confirmed his suspicion; the canoe had been designed for lakes and streams and would not be safe in an exposed sea and never should be used in bad weather.

#

Late in the day, he and Blackie return to the hospital to check in on Josh. He waits outside and when Josh and Mildred come out, he follows the pair as they stroll to the young man's apartment. He takes the opportunity to appraise Josh; it's easy to tell the brawny young man is in great shape. The ten-minute walk is uneventful, and they arrive at Josh's apartment without encountering a single drop of rain. Parked outside is a metallic green, Subaru Forester with an equipment rack and Colorado license plates.

Josh kicks one of the rear tires, "This is my rig."

"It's an interesting color." Mildred peers inside, "I don't have a car because I can't cover the expenses."

Silver Jack says, "I don't have a car because I have a boat."

Josh invites them into his apartment, so he ties Blackie's lead to the railing of the porch. Once inside, Josh asks if they'd like tea or coffee. Silver Jack asks for coffee and Mildred asks for tea. To prevent Josh from making two hot drinks, he changes his request at the same time Mildred switches to coffee. Everyone laughs, and they try again.

Josh says, "Hey, you both have done me a big favor, and the least I can do is make you something to drink. I'm going to make both."

Silver Jack settles into a chair at the kitchen table. "I found your canoe. I also found a green pack, a larger red pack and a paddle."

Mildred joins him at the table. She glances around the room. "I like your kitchen. It's small but serviceable."

Josh thanks Mildred and turns to face Silver Jack. "It sounds as if you found most of my stuff. You didn't happen to find a camera case did you?"

"No. I did walk up and down the beach for a couple of hundred yards in each direction but I didn't find anything else."

He plays with a divot in the Formica as he watches Josh prepare their drinks.

Josh turns back to the counter. Over his shoulder the young man asks, "Is everything wet?"

"You bet." The prospector leans back in his chair. "You should pick everything up tonight and hang it inside so it has a chance to dry. I've done the best I can at my place but it's a lot smaller than this."

Josh pulls out a chair for himself. "What kind of tea would you like, Mildred? I have cinnamon and licorice."

Mildred mulls this over as Josh responds to Silver Jack, "I'll be glad to come over and get my stuff. Maybe I can drive Mildred back home first."

"Cinnamon please," says Mildred.

Soon, the tea and coffee are served. As the trio finishes their hot drinks, Mildred invites the men to have dinner with her. After several feeble attempts to say no, Josh relents.

Silver Jack informs him, “Lad, never miss a chance to have Mildred’s cooking. She wins every cooking competition on the island.”

Mildred smiles at Jack’s compliment. He likes her smile a lot more than the scowls she’s recently showed him.

#

After an excellent and filling dinner at Mildred’s home, the prospector and Blackie ride back to the marina with Josh. On the way, he suggests Josh go with him to check out an unusual geological formation he’d noticed from the top of Garnet Mountain. The location is north of Wrangell in extreme terrain southeast of the Stikine.

When Josh pushes for a description of the geological formation, he responds, “It looks similar to the plume of an extinct volcano blasted out of the center of a high ridge above a creek. I’ve spent the last two summers building a trail up Crittenden Creek, and I’m close enough I can make it to there with one more camp.”

“Can I have time to think about it?” Josh asks.

He responds, “I’ll be back in about a week after running supplies for the next big trip. You can let me know later.”

When they arrive at the marina, Josh asks him about the island in the center of the harbor. It’s reached by a high walkway, and the island has several tall totem poles and a cedar plank lodge.

The prospector points at the island. “They call this Chief Shakes Island. The lodge is a tribal house and the place has a long history illustrated by the carvings on the totem poles.”

He watches Josh tilt his head back, craning to look at the top of the nearest pole. “These carvings are quite elaborate. I’m impressed by the complexity of the relief carving on the tribal house. Is anyone doing this type of carving?”

Silver Jack nods, “There are a few left. One young fella about your age named Charlie carves.”

He insists they use a couple of the two-wheeled carts from the marina to haul Josh’s gear. The schoolteacher follows Silver Jack and Blackie down the aluminum ramp to the floating dock. They pass dozens of vessels before arriving at his fiberglass-fishing boat. His craft is about thirty feet long with a cabin at the stern.

"This boat was a bow picker when I got it. As a commercial boat it used to have a drum and net in the center." Almost twenty feet of flat deck forms a sizeable work area in front of the cabin. There's a freezer as well as an anchor chain piled along one side.

Silver Jack follows Blackie onto the deck and opens the cabin door. "Come on in and I'll show you around."

Josh joins him and looks around the tiny cabin. Every corner is used to store clothing, food, equipment, and supplies. A table behind the steering wheel is a jumble of magazines, bullets, rocks, and mail. "Do you live in this year around?"

"Yes, except when I go camping on the mainland or one of the islands."

Shaking his head, Josh asks, "How do you and Blackie do it? This cabin can't be more than ten feet by twelve feet. I thought my apartment was small but this beats my situation hands down."

Silver Jack chuckles in response. "You wait until you've been out in the brush for a week. This place will look mighty good then." He helps Josh load his equipment into the carts and take them to his rig. A second trip is needed for both men to carry the canoe up to the parking lot. He helps Josh tie the canoe to the top of the Subaru. "Do you need help returning this thing?"

Josh shrugs, "Probably not. I'll leave it on my rig until morning." Josh looks down at his boots and sticks his hands into the pockets of his windbreaker. "Listen Silver Jack, I can't thank you enough for what you did for me. I'd like to find a way to make it up to you for all your help."

"What time are you going to your landlord's place?"

Josh looks up, surprised. "Why, I thought I'd get over there around eight a.m."

"Good. I'll take Blackie for a walk on Chief Shakes Island around seven thirty, and we'll be waiting for you when you come by at eight. I'll let you take me to breakfast over at the Diamond C. Afterwards you'll be able to call us even." He watches Josh smile, glad to see his whole face light up.

"I'll take the deal Silver Jack. It will be my pleasure to buy you breakfast."

The old prospector is pleased. "How about, I'll let you buy me breakfast if you start calling me Jack."

Chapter 8: New in Town

Anne loves to draw. Her earliest memories were of her father drawing pictures for her. She'd ask him to draw the same things over and over. Her favorites were a ballerina cat and a flying unicorn. She could remember sitting in church and asking him to draw them for her and making him cut them out. As soon as she was able, she started cutting out the drawings herself. When she was old enough to express herself, Anne refused to use coloring books. She wanted blank sheets of paper so she could draw her own pictures. It was wrong to even consider following someone else's lines.

Anne drew so much it presented problems at school. Her teachers thought she wasn't paying attention if she was doodling. She felt drawing allowed her to concentrate, but she learned there were consequences for drawing in class if the teacher didn't like it. This caused her to become circumspect with her art. Often, her class notes were filled with sketches of teachers, the view out the window or other students.

When Anne graduated from the eighth grade, her father moved her family to Wrangell, so he could take a job with the town operating heavy equipment. Wrangell was a big city compared to the remote area where she grew up. In the fall, when she started Wrangell High School, she discovered there were art classes. At last there was a subject in which she excelled. Anne was disappointed she could only take one class in art each year.

Her art teacher, Mrs. Johnson, was addicted to pretty art. To Mrs. Johnson, every drawing needed flourishes and an abundance of lurid color. Anne didn't care for florid art. She liked lines with rhythm, grace, and balance. She preferred using colors that accented, highlighted, or showed contrast. She would experiment with drawings using as few colors as possible. Anne's high school art classes were what kept her going to school.

In a few of her other classes, such as Math, she was a marginal student at best. She did better at English, Literature, German, History, and Social Studies. Science was tough (except when she could get extra credit for illustrations). She met Michael when she was a sophomore. He was a senior retaking a health class he'd flunked previously. Anne first noticed Michael because she could watch his profile from her desk, and it was natural to sketch it. She drew Michael at least two times each week, and by the end of the semester she could draw him in any pose. She was unprepared one day when Michael asked her to go to the prom. After their first date, she only went out with Michael.

Any spare moment when Anne wasn't studying Michael, she would daydream about going to art school. Anne got up the nerve to ask Mrs. Johnson about it when she was a junior. Mrs. Johnson laughed, "You have no idea what art school would cost. Why, the closest place to study art is Seattle. Your parents could never afford it. In addition, you haven't enough training to be competitive. There's a little matter with taking direction. No, girl, the best you can hope for is a job at the hardware store painting window signs."

Anne was crushed by her teacher's harsh assessment. She liked her art, but what did she know? She thought about getting a second opinion, but no one was available in Wrangell. When high school was over, Michael asked her to marry him. He had been working at the cannery for two years and had saved enough money to afford a car and deposit on a rental house. They were married in August at a ceremony in her family's church.

At first, Anne found time to draw. She would sketch Michael asleep or awake. Often she would walk to the bay and sketch the islands to the west or go to the marina and sketch boats or the crews at work. She liked scenes with movement, such as a soaring eagle or men carrying heavy loads. By Christmas, Anne was pregnant with Emily.

Once her daughter was born she lost all time for drawing,

and her pencils and drawing paper hibernated. When Michael started drinking, their lives became so chaotic she rarely found time for sketching. After the divorce, she had done one or two drawings, but they were lifeless and dull. She lacked inspiration. Maybe Mrs. Johnson had been right after all.

#

Anne parks her truck at the back of the restaurant and shuts off the engine. It has been daylight for several hours, even though it's not yet six. Emily looks excited sitting in the truck wearing her miniature version of the café's waitress uniform. "You have to promise to do exactly what I tell you to do, Emily."

"I will. I don't want to go back to daycare." Emily fidgets, "How do I look?"

Anne can't help but smile at her. "You look marvelous. Let's go inside, and I'll show you what to do."

Inside the café, Darcy greets both of them with a wink. "Good morning, Emily. You look ready to get started. I hope you have fun today."

She manages to blurt out, "Me, too," before Anne takes Emily's jacket and hat and hangs them in the storage closet near the back door.

Inside the restaurant Barry and Ernie sit at the counter in their usual places. Anne introduces Emily and shows her how to set up the condiment trays for one of the tables. "You check the rest of the tables."

#

Two hours later, Anne has Emily well trained at filling cups of coffee and the appropriate protocol for clearing away dishes when customers are finished.

Anne notices Silver Jack outside hooking his dog's leash to the chain-link fence separating the café from the nearest business. When he enters the dining room, Anne is surprised he has company. With him is a tall, powerfully built man. His blue eyes are piercing and she wonders if he's wearing tinted contacts. The two men settle down at one of the corner tables. She and Emily walk to their table with coffee cups and the glass coffee pot.

"Would you like coffee?" Emily stands poised with two cups.

"Yes. I would indeed little lady," Silver Jack accepts one of the cups.

"I would enjoy a cup, too," his companion adds, shifting his ball cap back on his head, exposing a freckled face.

Anne notices Silver Jack's companion has auburn hair and a nice smile. "Good morning." She asks, "Is this one of your sons?"

"Nope, only a newcomer I found wandering around lost, so I brought him in here so you could straighten him out." Silver Jack leans back in his chair with a laugh before settling forward with his elbows on the table. He points to Josh with his thumb, "His name is Josh, and he's the new teacher."

"It's nice to meet you." Anne pours coffee as Emily prepares her pad and pencil, ready to take their order. "I'm Anne and this is my daughter Emily. Emily, this is Silver Jack. What would you gentlemen like for breakfast?"

"Well, I'll have my usual. Hash browns, eggs, and toast with ham." Silver Jack hands Josh a menu. "You might need this, being as it's your first time."

Josh looks up at Anne, and she gets a full blast from his striking eyes. She feels herself flush, and it's difficult to breathe. His gaze releases her, and he turns to Emily. "Emily. I need a few minutes to look over the menu, is that okay?" He smiles and Anne notices the muscles move along his powerful jaw.

"Yes, I can wait. I don't mind." Emily is glued to her spot beside the table.

"Take your time," Anne says, "We'll come back in a few moments." Anne steers Emily back to the counter, glad for a chance to gather her composure.

"Mom, did you notice his eyes?" Emily whispers to her behind the counter. "I bet he has the most beautiful eyes ever."

Anne busies herself checking other customers. Across the room she watches Emily return to Silver Jack and Josh's table. She's glad Emily is bold enough to go take the man's order.

When the meals for their table are ready, Anne calls Emily over to help her carry the food. "You take Josh's order and I'll take

Silver Jack's and the coffee pot."

Josh thanks Emily and the old prospector thanks Anne for delivering their meals. Anne fills both coffee cups and slips away. Emily stays and talks to Josh. After watching her for a few minutes, Anne signals Emily to come to her and reminds her other customers need attention.

Later, Anne watches the men leave after the schoolteacher has paid their tab. She tries to block out how firm his butt looks striding away.

At her elbow, Emily interrupts her thoughts, "He's a hunk, Mom!"

Chapter 9: Keep me Posted

Chief Dan Ford stares past the droplets of rain clinging to the window of his office. From his chair, he can almost make out the nearest islands through the rain and fog. He wishes for the thousandth time he could be out on the water, chasing salmon as his ancestors had done. He listens with one ear as Detective Alex starts his morning report.

"Sir, there was a fight last night at the Marine Bar. Two deckhands from the *Albatross* spent the night in jail on drunk and disorderly. Officer Chak tried to set up the speed trap you requested at the city limits, but his radar unit is on the fritz again. We'll need to send it to Ketchikan for calibration."

The Chief shifts his weight. His oak and leather chair creaks when he leans forward, elbows on his desk. His glare bores into the young detective. "I thought we just got the unit back?"

"We did, sir." Alex looks uncomfortable, his square jaw shifts from side to side. Finally, he reveals the problem. "Officer Chak dropped it again."

"Damn." The Chief shakes his head, "The boy breaks more equipment than anyone I've ever known."

"He's your nephew, Chief," Detective Alex chides him, trying to hide a smile. His gray eyes flash as he inclines forward. He's poised like a linebacker ready to slant in a new direction at a moment's notice.

"Don't remind me," the Chief growls. After a moment's pause, he continues, "Send the radar gun back to Ketchikan, so we can try this again. And make sure you warn everyone not to go blabbing this time our radar is out of commission, or we'll have everyone speeding around town as if there's no tomorrow. Too bad our budget's so tight or I'd purchase a back up. What else have you got for me?"

"Well, sir. I interviewed the survivor the Coast Guard picked up. His name is Lenn Richards, and he is part of a research team working for Sealaska Corporation."

The Chief knew Sealaska Corporation is the entity created by the federal government to manage most of the land grants provided by the 1971 tribal settlement with the federal government. Five of the southeast Alaska tribes were left out of the settlement and were provided none of their ancestral lands. In an unfortunate quirky turn of events, his tribe, the one from the Wrangell area, was one of the landless tribes. "What were they doing?"

Alex refers to his notes. "The team was evaluating the potential value of land included in the outstanding claims by the five landless tribes. He says the boat capsized on the Stikine, up by Point Rothsay, when they tangled with a drifting log. I suspect they were traveling too fast and swerved at the last minute to miss it. Anyway, this guy, Richards, holds onto the capsized boat until it gets close to the island and swims for it."

"What about the others?" The Chief props his head up with one of his hands. He notices his coffee is untouched and most likely cold. He considers interrupting the Detective for a trip to the coffeemaker but defers until the briefing is over.

"Richards says once his head came up out of the water, he swam for the boat. He never saw the other two again." Alex pauses, waiting for the follow up question.

The Chief crosses his arms and leans back in his chair. "Who are they?"

"The one found by the fishing boat was Michael Jefferson. He was a surveyor. The other guy is missing. His name is Marty Ellis. He's a mineralogist." The Chief notes Detective Alex refers to the dead in the past tense while referring to the missing man in the present tense, even if it's probable he is also dead.

"What kind of condition was Richards in when they brought him to the hospital?"

"He was in pretty good shape, except for the trauma of losing his colleagues. He had no equipment to make camp but he did have waterproof matches and managed to make a fire. It couldn't have helped him much because he didn't have any way to get dry. It rained all night."

The Chief glances out the window. A gill-netter is leaving the harbor and making its way seaward. "Is the Coast Guard still searching?"

Alex draws in a breath and exhales, "I believe today is the last day."

"What about the boat?"

"The Coast Guard reported it drifted onto the shoreline of Kadin Island. The Harbormaster cruised out there, turned it over and brought it back to the marina and is claiming salvage. Would you like to inspect it?"

The Chief makes this a teachable moment, "What would you look for if you checked it out?"

"Why, I'd look for signs of foul play. I'd ask the Harbormaster to make a written statement regarding what he noticed when he found it. I'd check any equipment that is with the boat, and I'd take lots of pictures."

The Chief waits without asking a question.

Alex gets a pained look on his face. "I'd also get the boat registration and check if the boat has all the required safety equipment."

"What else?"

Alex grins. "I'd have the boat moved over to our dock until you release it."

The Chief nods his head. "It sounds as if you have a good handle on it. I'll leave this in your capable hands. When is the hospital releasing Richards?"

"They are probably letting him go tomorrow morning."

"Find out where he'll be staying, and ask him to provide you with contact information if he leaves town."

Detective Alex rises from his chair, holding his cap in his hands. "Sure, Chief. Will that be all?"

"Yes. Keep me posted. It's time I found myself a cup of hot

coffee." The Chief lurches up, a habit designed to cover a stiff knee. "Don't forget to go home for lunch. Your young bride needs to see you once in a while. You can work long hours once the baby comes. She won't miss you so much then."

"Yes, Chief, I'll be sure to remember." Detective Alex covers his balding head with his cap, turns and slips out the open door of the office.

The Chief sighs. Alex reminds him of the days when he was a young policeman. The detective is eager to please and ready to take on any assignment, no matter how mundane. He finds all the work exciting. For the hundredth time, the Chief wishes his nephew could be more like Detective Alex.

Chapter 10: Blackmail

Lenn is propped up in the hospital bed when Clay enters his room. Clay notices his old friend's signature flaming-red hair has thinned. "My, my, isn't this a cozy set up you have," he blurts out to the surprised occupant. "The next thing you know, they'll be rolling out the red carpet." In the years following their time together, Lenn has acquired a three-inch scar on his ferret face. The scar starts near the corner of his left eye, moving down and over his high cheekbone in a jagged line. Clay's assessment, the scar provides menace to an already sinister countenance.

The Harbormaster steps forward and thrusts his hand out to Lenn, who slowly takes the offered greeting with a puzzled look on his face. "What's wrong, don't you remember me? I'm Clay. We spent time together in Ketchikan when we were kids."

Lenn tilts his head and eyes Clay narrowly and nods his head. "I do remember you. We fought over a piece of toast you stole from me."

Clay grins, "I recall you stole the toast from me first. But that was years ago. I saw your name on the news, and because I live here, I figured I should drop by and say hello. So here I am." He spreads his arms as if to show ownership for the entire island.

Lenn gestures to a nearby chair. "Sit down and stay for a while. They're not letting me out until tomorrow. Tell me, what are you doing these days?"

Clay explains, "I'm the Harbormaster. Been here eight years and like it, but the pay isn't worth shit. How about you? You must be doing great working for Sealaska."

Lenn snorts. "I'm only a contractor. The pay is good, but there are no benefits. All the best jobs go to the natives, even if they aren't the most qualified. I've got plans though. I won't always be sucking hind tit."

Clay throws out his bait, "I went out and picked up your boat. It's a nice rig. The jet outboard is worth serious cash. It'll need cleaning up though, because it was upside down in the salt water."

Lenn stiffens, "Where's the boat?"

"Oh, I've got it tied up at the dock in the marina," he lies without remorse. "I was sort of hoping to get salvage or at least a finder's fee." Clay tilts the chair back and leans against the wall. Lenn is cornered, and he enjoys watching him squirm.

"You want to know something interesting?" Clay pulls on one ear. "The boat looked odd to me. It was too far up on the bank to have drifted onto the shore. It looked wrong."

Lenn twists sideways in his bed, his lank frame coiled as if ready to leap and flee. "What are you getting at?"

"I believe you know." Clay pushes the chair forward until the two front legs thump against the linoleum floor. "You turned the boat over on the bank. It must have been a tough job for one man, but with the right leverage and enough time you could do it. What I can't figure out is why you didn't move the boat to another location after you hid the equipment in the brush. I always figured you were a lot smarter than that."

Lenn snarls, "What are you going to do?"

The Harbormaster relaxes. He revels in his power; Lenn at his mercy. "I'm considering turning you in for a reward unless you can make it worth my while."

Lenn hedges, "What I'm up to is big. Big enough to make us both rich, but I'm going to need your help."

"Why should I trust you? You're probably lying." Clay pulls a flask from his pocket and takes a swig. He smiles, waiting for the alcohol to warm him up.

Lenn hunches his bony shoulders upward. "You don't have to trust me. If what I show you when I get out of this hospital don't convince you, you can turn me into the police. You won't have lost more than two days waiting to check out the cards I'm holding." He settles back and the balance of power shifts away from Clay.

"There's a bed and breakfast over on Church Street. Go there and get a room when you get out of the hospital. I'll meet you at the Marine Bar after work for a drink. You better be convincing, or I'll turn you in and get the boat for salvage. Either way, I turn a tidy profit." Clay hands Lenn his flask. "Take a drink and seal the bargain."

Chapter 11: Hope, Energy, and Enthusiasm

Awake early, I shower and enjoy a quick breakfast in my apartment. From the kitchen window, I have a partial view of the mouth of the harbor. The apartment costs more than I had hoped to pay, but the view is worth it, and it's close to school. Today at eleven, I'm scheduled to meet the Principal, Mr. Pearson, at the school. I have time to swing by the marina and check if Jack is at home.

In my Subaru, the trip to the marina takes less than two minutes. I could walk, but I don't want to work up a sweat before meeting Mr. Pearson. At the pier, I park and head for the floating dock. As I pass the harbor office, the door opens and a good-looking man walks out. He's taller by a couple of inches, making him about an inch over six feet. Older by a dozen years, his brown hair is cut short, almost a buzz cut, and I estimate he weighs 175 pounds. He looks tough enough to be a fighter.

"Excuse me. I was hoping to run into Silver Jack, has he walked by this morning?"

"Listen kid. I'm the Harbormaster, and I'm too goddamned busy to keep track of the comings and goings of every old bum in this marina. I'm afraid you're going to have to walk down to his boat to find out." He pivots on his heel, and reenters the office without waiting for a reply.

I am flabbergasted. So far, everyone I've met in Wrangell has gone out of his or her way to be nice as well as helpful. Maybe he's having a bad day.

The trip out to Jack's boat is unfruitful. He isn't home, so I walk down to the end of the dock and look at the backside of Chief Shakes Island. I watch as an eagle wheels silently overhead. The islet is deserted, standing quietly alone in the middle of the crowded harbor. I enjoy the serenity of the scene though mayhap it's the peaceful eye of the storm.

I meander back to my rig, taking my time because I hope to bump into Jack. Arriving at the marina parking lot without finding him, I give up and drive back to my apartment. On the way, I plan to fold laundry before I go to my appointment at the school.

#

Principal Jeff Pearson is tall, poised, wears glasses, and sports a shock of thick, brown hair touched with gray at the temples. He greets me at the front door and glances at his watch as if to confirm I'm respectfully five minutes early. His greeting is rapid fire, a man with a crowded schedule. "Hi. Are you Josh Campbell? Good. I'll show you around the school and get you oriented. How was your trip north? Did you have any trouble finding the school? Have you found a place to live? How can I help you?"

"I'd like a tour, if that's possible." I take a slow breath and try to recalibrate to the Principal's warp speed. I recognize his voice from the phone interview, but I find he's hard to follow in person.

"Why, of course. We're very proud of our school. For example, ninety-two percent of our graduates attend college or trade school, and the other eight percent join the military. And we get a credible graduation rate, eighty-eight percent. We accomplish this by having close personal contact with every student. We've also formed a Professional Learning Community based on DeFour's work, are you familiar with it?"

I nod, so he continues, "Here are the administrative offices." Mr. Pearson points out a bullpen with two cubicles and several private offices around the perimeter. "I'm the only one around during the summer. You may bump into teachers from time to time as they come by to get their classrooms ready. I'll introduce you to the support staff when the offices open in late August. We start the year off with a faculty and staff barbeque. You'll want to save the date on your calendar." The Principal turns and gives me a serious look. "You look to be in good physical shape. Have you ever coached football?"

I offer, "No, but I played it in high school." I hope he won't be offended at my lack of experience.

He nods his head once. "Perhaps it will be enough. We offer a two thousand dollar stipend for the assistant football coaching position and five hundred for the chess club. You have to do at least one and those are the available positions."

"How long do I have to decide?" I hope for a little time to study the pros and cons of each assignment.

"We need your choice next week since the coaching work starts August 1." The Principal shows me the teacher workroom before pointing down the hall. "Our science wing is down this hallway. Let's go there first, so I can show you what you have to work with." He charges down the hall at a pace that has me stretching my legs to keep up. He turns a corner and pivots to unlock a door. I can look past his head into a fairly traditional classroom for the physical sciences.

"This is one of our two science classrooms. It's old but it has all the basic equipment you'll need." It's obvious the place is a mess, with equipment scattered about and piles of clutter on top of every available surface.

"If we go through this door we enter the chemical supply room." Mr. Pearson grimaces but makes no comment when he faces the chaos the storage room holds. I bite my tongue; smart enough to realize you don't criticize your predecessor until you've staked out the lay of the land.

"This door leads to Mrs. Burman's classroom. She's the other science teacher and the head of the science department." We enter a well-organized, clean and neat classroom. I'm impressed with the way information is displayed. Mrs. Burman is focused on student learning.

I ask my first questions, "Mr. Pearson, have you put together a master schedule yet? What classes will I be teaching?"

I stop and wait for his reply. He turns and looks me up and down. "You have five different preps. You'll be teaching all the lower level classes and one or two middle school, while Mrs. Burman will teach all the upper level science courses. If you last past the first year, we'll reconsider your assignments in the spring. Will that be a problem?" Mr. Pearson sticks both hands into the pockets of his tan slacks as if to prepare for an unpleasant time.

I'm stunned at his direct manner, so I take a moment to respond. "Well, Mr. Pearson, I had hoped to be able to share the load. How will you know I can handle all levels if I'm working on only the lower levels? I'm not asking for the best assignments, I'm asking for a chance to show what I can do to meet the needs of all learners. I do have five years of teaching experience so it's not as if I'm a total rookie. Is there a chance we can meet and discuss this with Mrs. Burman?"

I pull out a student chair and sit down so I can diffuse the tension and give the Principal a chance to consider my proposal. I don't want to finish the tour of the school until we come to a resolution. "There was no mention of teaching middle school in the job listing."

He remains standing and takes his hands out of his pockets. "It's unusual for a new teacher to make demands about what classes they'll teach." I wait, giving him the time he needs as my gut sours. He straightens his glasses. "But it isn't as easy to find a qualified science teacher as it once was. As for the middle school classes, we're very small and specialists need to be flexible. I'd rather you teach science to middle school students than teach typing. I am willing to moderate a meeting with you and the head of the department, if you'll accept my decision regarding the classes you'll teach once the meeting is over."

I nod reluctantly, rise from my seat, and hold out my hand. "I can live with that, Mr. Pearson. I'm only asking for a chance to discuss the possibilities. I can't thank you enough for agreeing to lead this discussion."

He releases my hand and gestures to the hallway. "Let me show you the rest of the building, and I'll get you keys and orientation materials. You'll also need to stop by the district office and make arrangements to be fingerprinted and let them make a copy of your social security card."

Later, I return to my new classroom and look around. Several of the fluorescent bulbs are burned out. Paint is peeling off the walls and several linoleum tiles are missing. When I open all the storage cabinets in the classroom, I find a mess of papers or supplies behind each door.

I move into the storage room and find unlabeled chemicals, chemicals improperly stored and several broken glass containers with liquid contents spreading over the shelves. Afterwards I explore the teacher desk and find teacher guides, syllabi and lesson plans for physical science, chemistry and biology. The plans are poorly put together. Many are missing. In addition, the textbooks are more than ten years old, so I will need to find up-to-date supplemental material to help prepare students for advanced training after high school.

I track down Mr. Pearson and ask for garbage cans. He shows me where the custodians keep them, and I spend four hours cleaning up the classroom. Mostly, I dump used project materials and the piles of paper I find stuffed everywhere. Partway through the afternoon I go to one of the restrooms reserved for male staff and unlock the door. The room is long and narrow and painted institution gray. There are two stalls and two urinals.

Seated in one of the stalls, I contemplate the strange patterns in the grey paint on the floor. I wonder if others found images in pieces of flaking paint or swirls of color. I recall the strange turn of events bringing me to Wrangell.

#

I was a decent student in high school without putting in a lot of effort. On the night I graduated from high school, I fled and went to work for a construction outfit doing roadwork in Wyoming. I loved working outdoors, but by winter the work went dormant and conditions outside were extreme. Out of money and not wanting to go home or be anywhere close to my stepmother, I joined the Army.

As I entered the Army, they gave me a battery of tests to determine my aptitude for various jobs. I was sent to learn Fire Direction Control for the Artillery, because the job used a lot of math.

After advanced training at Fort Sill, Oklahoma, I was sent to Germany for thirty months and served with a self-propelled artillery unit capable of using nukes. By the time I left Germany, I had been promoted to Sergeant. I completed my last year and six months at

Fort Polk, Louisiana. While in Louisiana, I began taking college courses. Despite pressure from my unit commander to make a long-term commitment to military service, when I completed my four-year stint in the Army, I returned to Colorado.

The University of Northern Colorado at Greeley was about 250 miles from home and an inexpensive place to live and go to school on the GI Bill. My plan was to get a teaching certificate as fast as I could before my funding ran out. Because I was twenty-one, I could work in establishments serving alcohol and this helped to generate additional spending money. With my early start on college while I was in the service, I was able to complete my bachelor's degree and earn a teaching certificate in three years. I graduated from college with a BA in Education and a minor in Science when I was twenty-six.

My first job was at Summit High School in Frisco, Colorado, teaching science. I'd enjoyed working there, and I'd still be there except for Kaeli. Kaeli and I fell in lust in my third year of teaching. She was new and taught Spanish. Two years later, when our relationship cooled because I was reluctant to ask her to marry me, I caught her in bed with our Principal. She asked me to move out of her apartment, and both of them asked me to move out of the school.

I could find no reason to stay, and I had no desire to confront the complex issues of our torn relationship, so I agreed to leave. In my job search, I targeted jobs in Alaska because I wanted to go where game and fish were plentiful. It also helped that Alaska was a long way from Kaeli. This is how I ended up in a long distance phone interview with Mr. Pearson.

The Principal asked me a few basic questions and surprised me when he offered me the job over the phone before concluding the interview. I knew he had not checked any references, because there hadn't been an opportunity to offer him this information. My quick conclusion was either the Principal was desperate or Wrangell was the end of the earth.

As I considered my position, I realized I was as desperate as Mr. Pearson and everywhere on the planet was going to feel isolated without Kaeli. I accepted the teaching job without asking for time to consider it.

I sold everything that wouldn't fit in the Subaru and headed north. My route was 2,000 driving miles from Colorado to Prince Rupert, British Columbia. It took me three days of driving to get to the ocean and eleven hours on the Alaska ferry system to get to Wrangell.

I pulled my rig off the ferry at midnight and drove through town in the dark. My heart sank as I explored my new home. With a total population of slightly more than 2,000 people, the town was spread out in an area less than a square mile. I splurged and spent the night at Rooney's Roost B&B near the center of town. The host was a gem and breakfast the following morning was the welcome I needed.

#

Today I am at the end of the earth, a backwater along the Inside Passage of the Pacific Rim. The town, my school, and new job all look worn out. I had no idea I was going to live in the middle of a rainforest either. But, I'd never had it easy, why should this adventure be any different than the others? I get up from the stall and say goodbye to the paint swirl reminding me of Kaeli.

I remember educational researcher Michael Fullen, who advocated for educational leaders to bring hope, energy, and enthusiasm to their work, especially during periods of rapid change. I vow to supply my own hope, energy, and enthusiasm for my new life in Wrangell. If I bring these attitudes, they will be reflected back to me. Or so I hope.

Chapter 12: Conspiracy

The Marine Bar is raucous, full of fishermen. From the volume, Clay bets they are having a successful season. Good fish runs stimulate the taverns around town. He leads Lenn to the quietest location he can find, in one of the corners of the room, and Clay orders double shots of Scotch. Lenn orders Alaskan Amber beer.

When their drinks arrive, Lenn starts talking. "Our job was to search for valuable mineral deposits south of the Stikine. We hadn't found shit until the last day out we stumbled across a volcanic vent. It didn't look like much but near the lake at the bottom we found diamonds! The vent is in a remote section of the disputed tribal lands."

Clay asks impatiently, "So what happened next?"

"We all signed a contract when we started this job. Anything we found of value during our survey had to be reported to Sealaska. The other two guys didn't believe we'd be able to make a valid claim of our own if we had to fight it out with the corporation."

He shrugs and takes a swig from his beer. "I didn't agree with them that our find should be given over to Sealaska with no more than a thank you." Lenn gives Clay a hard stare. "Fortunately for me, the boat accident happened before they got a chance to tell anybody about our find." He smirks, "Their loss is going to be our gain."

Clay sips his scotch and leans back in his chair. "What are you proposing?"

Lenn bobs his head up and down. "I need you to file the

claim because if I file it, Sealaska will come after me. We'll be partners and split the profits fifty-fifty. I'll have to remain a silent partner of course." Lenn pulls a tiny stone out of his pocket. "I've got one sample. Marty, the mineralogist, was carrying more on him but he's at the bottom of the river."

Clay takes the pebble. It's tiny, rounded and transparent. To Clay it looks like quartz. "How can you determine this is a diamond?" he asks skeptically.

"Because Marty ran several field tests and identified them as diamonds. This chunk of rock will dull the edge of any knife or axe and never show a scratch." Lenn gets a lame look, "If you can't trust a mineralogist on this, who can you trust?"

The Harbormaster snorts. "What about a lab?" Wondering if Lenn is holding a pig in a poke, he stops a waitress passing by the table. "Delores, we'd like another round."

Lenn contributes, "We're going to need a written analysis anyway for you to file a claim."

Clay pauses while Delores delivers the scotch and another beer for Lenn. "What else do we need?"

"We're going to have to go back there with a GPS unit and get coordinates for each corner of the claim. Given the steepness of the site, we'll need a high quality device to get the size right. We go in and bring out enough diamonds to finance the startup of a full-scale mining operation."

The two men discuss and discard the idea of using a helicopter. It would expose their interest in the area near the landing site. They will wait a few days before going in to stake out a claim, because Lenn needs time to attend the funeral of his dead colleague and tie up a few loose ends.

Clay learns the boat belongs to Lenn, and he agrees to get the jet outboard repaired and the vessel ready.

"I'm in on this deal unless the claim turns out to be worthless. If that happens, I want the complete rig." Clay relishes his leverage, and he doesn't want to relinquish it prematurely. The boat and motor are worth at least fifty thousand, and he can use the money.

Clay can tell Lenn is having difficulty with his request. He stares at the Harbormaster, and Clay returns the steely gaze without blinking. After a moment, Lenn concedes. “All right, but if the going gets dirty, you can’t back out, or you lose your stake.”

Clay realizes Lenn is referring to violence when he uses the term “dirty.” He thumps the table. “I can get my hands dirty, if needed.” He polishes off the last of his scotch. “Let’s order another round. The night is young.”

Chapter 13: Company

Silver Jack sips root beer in the Marine Bar. According to the tide book, he could enter Crittenden Creek tomorrow morning about ten o'clock at a high tide of plus fourteen feet. He'd need to stay there for five days, waiting until the tide is high enough again for him to get out of the mouth of the river. It would be nip and tuck with the tide at plus eleven feet. There is enough time for him to carry several loads of gear up to Base or perhaps as far as Halfway in preparation for a push farther inland on a later trip.

Across the room, he watches the Harbormaster in conversation with another man. He doesn't trust the Harbormaster. It's his theory Clay is the one who disconnected his old boat from the power, causing the bilge pumps to stop working and resulting in his boat sinking. Clay is hiding something.

Clay's red-haired colleague shares the same secretive tendencies, casing the room with his eyes every few minutes. Both men are lean and tough looking. Clay is taller by two to three inches. The other man has very thin lips and almost no chin. He sports a scar on his face, the kind you might pick up in a knife fight.

Finished with his root beer, he leaves a tip and exits the bar. He unties Blackie's leash and releases him at the entrance to the walkway for Chief Shakes Island. "Let's go for a walk, boy."

Later, he cooks steak and sautéed onions on his gas stove. Blackie eats half of the meat. After dinner, the prospector crawls into the bunk at the back of the cabin and Blackie stretches out on the floor.

#

Blackie licking his face awakens Silver Jack. After a quick walk in the morning drizzle, they return to the boat and eat breakfast before loading the skiff with supplies. Donning his waders and rain gear he invites Blackie to board.

Meandering through the marina, he guides the skiff to the filling station, where he tops off his main and spare fuel tanks. An hour later, he finishes crossing Eastern Passage, reaches the mainland and enters the mouth of Crittenden Creek. With a good high tide, he is able to get a mile upriver before he is forced to shut off and tilt the outboard.

Slipping over the side of the skiff he wades to the bow. Using the bowline as a towrope over his shoulder, he pulls the skiff upriver for another half-mile, passing several bends in the river. As the water gets shallower, he has to be careful to find the deepest channel for the skiff. Numerous times, the craft drags along the bottom and he's forced to pull the skiff forward inch-by-inch until the water gets deep again. On these occasions, he orders Blackie out to reduce the boat's drag.

About two o'clock, he reaches his trail. Heavily forested, there is no sign from the river that muskeg covers most of the terrain above them. He secures the skiff alongside a downed tree near the riverbank. He unloads the skiff and carries the supplies up the bank where a blue tarp offers protection from the rain. After securing all the gear, he unloads the gas tanks and places them under the tarp.

He takes off his waders and hangs them upside down, so they won't hold water. He puts on rubber caulk boots and loads an army surplus packboard with gear. This trip will include a new sleeping bag inside a waterproof storage container and sixty cans of food. He locates Blackie's pack harness and straps it onto the unwilling dog. With the pack in place, he places dog food in a pouch on each side.

He shifts his own pack upright onto the bank above the trail and sits down to get his arms through the straps. Ready to go, he follows Blackie up the trail alongside the river. Four hours later, the blue and grey tarps of Base come into view. Within three minutes, he and Blackie gladly enter the sanctuary. After removing his pack, he unloads Blackie and places both bundles in the center of the shelter.

Stretching both arms over his head, he is grateful to have the weight off his back. He turns to a pile of firewood inside the shelter and selects a dry piece. Starting one of the chainsaws, he makes a cut lengthwise in the wood. By cutting with the grain instead of across it, his saw makes long shavings of the white maple. Scooping up a double handful of the shavings, he drops them in the fire pit. Carefully stacking several dry pieces of firewood around the shavings, he pours a capful of gas on the pile. He sets the pile afire with a thrown match.

The smoke lifts until it reaches a rain fly, a tarp stretched above the fire to protect the fire from rain, but set higher than the shelter tarps so the heat doesn't cause it to burn. This arrangement is effective at drawing the smoke out of the living area of the shelter.

After the fire is going well, he opens a can of dog food for Blackie and pours it into a stainless steel bowl. With an upbeat tone, "Here you go boy," he invites Blackie to partake.

He heats a can of chicken noodle soup near the edge of the fire for his dinner. Between spoonfuls he asks Blackie, "Well, you danged mutt, I suppose you want to top your meal off with summer sausage?" Blackie sits up when his master heads for a storage container near the edge of the shelter. Inside, he finds a stick of sausage and, using his hunting knife, cuts a round for Blackie plus one for himself. "Here you go boy. This is for covering my backside today. I wouldn't want any other partner in a pinch."

Blackie nods his head.

When he finishes his meal, he throws the can, the covering from the summer sausage, and the used paper towel into the fire. "Come on Blackie. Let's go to bed. We're going to have a long day tomorrow."

He removes his rubber caulks, careful to keep the sharp hobnails from ripping the tarp serving as groundcover under his sleeping bag. Crawling into the unzipped sleeping bag, his clothes damp from the muddy trail, he invites Blackie to lie down next to his legs. With the dog's body heat his pants will be dry well before morning.

As it becomes dark, he listens to the drum of the rain hitting the tarp over his head. The sounds of the river flowing by reminds him the forest is alive, even at night. He can hear the fire snapping as it fights to survive. Closing his eyes, he's asleep within minutes.

#

Five days go by in a flash. Each morning, Silver Jack cooks breakfast and does chores for a couple of hours. One day, he repairs tarps and moves gear and supplies around to keep them from getting wet and damaged. Another day, he cuts firewood and stacks it for future trips. About noon each day he heads for the skiff and returns late in the afternoon with another load of supplies. Most of the days are rainy or overcast, but the last two are dry and hot. By three o'clock in the afternoon of the last day, he returns to the skiff using high tide to help his passage out river.

Cruising into the Eastern Passage, he thinks about Josh. He wonders if the young man will join him on the mainland. It would be nice to have company in addition to Blackie.

Chapter 14: Handshake

After a packed week cleaning the classroom and chemical storage room, I've made a lot of progress. Several maintenance issues were reported to Principal Pearson, with the assurance he will turn in the necessary work orders so the repairs can be completed before the start of school.

The secondary schools have two custodians, Bert and Eunice, whom I find to be obliging. During the summer they both work the day shift on projects not able to be done with students in the way. They help me by stationing two of the rolling trash canisters in my room and drop by daily to check on my progress and roll away the full tubs.

To conserve cash until my first paycheck arrives at the end of September, I bring my own lunch every day. The faculty lounge is empty, so I retrieve my meal each day from the refrigerator and return to my room. I'm hopeful the staff room will be pleasant when it's filled with my new colleagues.

Each evening, I work on lesson plans. I start with the lower level courses as I don't want to put time and effort into classes I might not teach. Using the connection in my apartment, I go online and look for sources and resources to complement the material in the old textbooks. I am excited whenever I find an interesting way to introduce concepts.

With each lesson, I develop warm up exercises to engage students right away as class starts. I also create simple assessments. These will identify which of my students are grasping the target concept. I make notes about alternate ways to present the material if students don't understand.

On Wednesday evening, I drive to the post office and pick up my mail. In this town, going to the post office is a social ritual. I greet Mildred, and she asks me about my new work, so I describe the mess I've been working on all week. Fifteen minutes later I waive goodbye and head back to my apartment.

As I pass the Diamond C, I recall the pleasant breakfast I had there with Jack. I mull over the attractive waitress, Anne, and her equally cute daughter, Emily. Did Jack say Anne is single? I rebuke myself for not paying closer attention. I had been stunned by Anne's slender beauty. She was vulnerable and full of grit at the same time. I liked the way her short, jet-black hair curled along her neck slightly below her ears. I recall being mesmerized by her lips. Most likely, Anne has a boy friend.

About a block past the restaurant is the hardware store and one of the two grocery stores in town. As I pass them, I spy Jack and Blackie walking toward me. I stop and invite them to hop in. Jack opens the rear door for Blackie and joins me in the shotgun position. "Howdy friend. I've been in the back country for the last five days and just got back."

He's recently bathed, so I ask, "Where do you go for a shower?"

Jack points down the road toward the marina. "There's coin operated showers in the Laundromat a couple of doors from the Marine Bar."

I laugh, "Thank God. I thought maybe you took baths in the harbor." Feeling good about the progress I've made on my classroom, I want to splurge and spend a few dollars on dinner out. I hate to eat in restaurants alone, so I ask Jack, "Have you had dinner yet."

"No, Blackie and I are walking to the grocery store to get food." Jack reaches back and gives Blackie a pat on the head.

"How about we get dinner together?"

Jack recommends the Marine Bar, and I agree to try it, because I haven't been there. When we arrive, he ties Blackie to a signpost near the marina entrance, while I give the dog a pat and a scratch behind the ears. Blackie must remember me feeding him ham at the Diamond C, because he acts as if I'm supposed to give him food. Inside, we find a table in the middle of the room, and Jack orders a Kemper's root beer, while I go for a pint of Amber Ale.

When the waitress comes, Jack makes his choice, "Delores, I'd like roasted chicken and fries. By the way, this is my friend Josh."

I shake Delores' hand and marvel at Jack's propensity to view everyone as an equal. I order a burger and fries.

Jack takes a swig from his root beer. "Have you had a chance to consider my offer to take you over to the mainland? You'll get a chance to check out the country and do a little prospecting."

I'm feeling pretty good about being prepared for the start of school; after all it's almost two months away. Moreover, I'm getting tired of my solitary lifestyle. I ask, "How long would we be out."

Jack explains how the tides work in relationship to going and coming from Crittenden Creek. We must catch a high tide two days from now. We can return after eight days but no more than eleven days due to the tides. "There are no roads on the mainland and no cell phone service. You'll be cut off from civilization. Even the army couldn't find you."

It sounds intriguing to me. I relish hiking and camping. Going with Jack would be the best way to get an orientation to traveling in a rainforest with a local who knows the ropes. After a moment's reflection, I agree to go, and we shake hands.

I feel the thrill of anticipation and a shimmer of trepidation. What adventures will I find in this remote section of Alaska? What might go wrong?

Jack goes over logistics and the type of gear I'll need. Required equipment includes rain gear, a backpack, several pairs of wool socks, and mosquito repellant.

As we'll be hiking through muskeg part of the time, I will bring two pairs of boots. One pair will be leather-hiking boots, well oiled and I'll also carry rubber boots for the muskeg. I ask, "I suppose I need a sleeping bag."

Jack pauses. "No, I have a new spare sleeping bag in Base you can use." Jack rolls up our chicken bones into several paper napkins, "This is for Blackie. He inhales fried chicken."

Outside, Jack feeds Blackie the remnants of his meal. "Come

by my boat tomorrow afternoon with your gear, and we'll check what you have and make a list of what we need to get before we go."

We settle on a time, and I hop into my rig for the short drive back to my apartment. It has been a long week, and I look forward to something interesting. I hadn't planned on a vacation this summer, because funds would be tight, but going to the mainland with Jack sounds as if it would be a great adventure at low cost. Other than food and supplies, there would be no spending at restaurants, gas stations, or motels.

Chapter 15: Lying

Clay is having a bad day. So far, not a thing has gone well. When he stops by the marina, he scans for David. Unfortunately, David has the day off. When he goes to the police department to get Lenn's boat released from police custody, it takes two hours of paperwork before Clay gets permission. Later, he tries loading the boat on a borrowed boat trailer only to find it doesn't fit.

He brings another boat trailer to the boat ramp and successfully loads Lenn's craft. Being careful to secure the boat on the trailer, Clay tows it to the Bay Company, a marine motor repair shop on Front Street.

Inside, he discusses the repairs with Clarence, the marine mechanic.

"I recommend replacing most of the electrical components. I'd also disassemble, clean, and lubricate all parts to prevent corrosion."

"What's your estimate?" Clay braces himself for the shock.

Clarence scratches his head. "This is a top of the line motor. I'd say it could easily run you two to three thousand. I can't provide a better estimate until I find out which parts need to be replaced. If it looks like it will run you more, I will call you."

He rages silently at Lenn. How did the fool sink his talons into Clay's wallet so fast? It's nearly impossible to go up the Stikine in a craft with a standard outboard motor because the propellers foul up in the shallow mud and silt of the river. The advantage of the jet outboard is a jet of water is used to propel the craft. He and Lenn will need to travel nearly twelve miles upriver before turning up one of the tributaries to get close to the diamonds. He asks the question that really matters. “How long will it take you?”

“I should get going right away. I’ll dip the motor in a tank of fresh water until I can get to it. It stops the corrosion and flushes out the salt water. I can be done in a week.” Clarence starts to fill out an estimate for Clay to sign.

Clay hesitates. “A week is Okay, but don’t take any longer. I want to be ready to go out fishing in ten days.” He isn’t ashamed of lying to Clarence, because the mechanic often misses deadlines. “Fly the damn parts in if you need any.”

Clay charges out of the shop, climbing into his pickup. Tomorrow will be better he realizes. David will be back.

Chapter 16: Concerned

It's another rainy, overcast day as Anne watches Emily greet a table of fisherman and take their order. She's amazed at the confidence Emily has gained from one week working in the cafe. Emily knows all the menu items and isn't thrown off by substitutions either. She's overcome her fear of the old timers, despite their gruff voices, and begun to banter a bit with the regulars. Anne has trained her daughter to pour coffee safely, away from the table, so she won't burn anyone.

Ever since starting work, Anne has been frugal with spending and recently celebrated paying off her truck. This milestone is significant, because she can put money into savings with her next paycheck. Until recently, monthly bills consumed all of her money. Six months ago, she started working extra days and shifts at the café. She used what little extra she could save to pay off her truck early, thus eliminating payments and the high interest rate on the debt. Her priority is to have funds set aside for a financial emergency. Perhaps, when she reaches her goal, she can save money for Emily's college.

About 7 a.m., Silver Jack and Josh enter the café. The old prospector looks unchanged, while his young companion arrives in a wool fedora, dark blue sweater, blue jeans, and rubber boots. Anne remains surprised at the unusual partnership.

As far back as she can remember, the old prospector always arrived and departed alone except when one of his sons was in town for a visit. Anne remembers Josh is a schoolteacher, so when she brings coffee to the table she calls him by name and asks if he's been to the school yet. Emily arrives, hands out menus, and stands ready with an order pad.

Josh responds by tipping back his hat and leaning back in his chair. "Oh yes. I've been cleaning up at the school for a week. The classroom was a mess."

Josh's smile is engaging, but she doesn't stumble, "What do you teach?" She waves the coffee pot, and when she gets nods from each man she fills their cups.

"I teach science. The exact classes I'll be teaching aren't finalized yet." Josh reaches for cream, adds a dollop, and uses a spoon to stir his coffee. He glances at Anne to catch her reaction.

"That sounds interesting. I wasn't good at math or science when I was in high school. Have you been teaching long?" She worries her conversation is too predictable and gently bites her lip to prevent herself from talking more.

"I taught for five years in Colorado, and I love it." He turns to her daughter, "Emily, do you like school?" He radiates confidence. Anne is jealous. Her lack of confidence often makes every interaction difficult.

Emily nods, "My favorite subject is math. I'm getting lots of practice adding up bills for customers." Realizing she has not completed her task, she asks, "Can I take your order?"

Later, when the two men have finished their breakfast, Anne returns with the bill for the table. Josh reaches for it, saying, "This is on me." He adds, "Jack is taking me over to the mainland for a hike and won't let me pay for any of the supplies, so I'd better cover this." He smiles, and this time she smiles back, against her better judgment.

Anne is concerned. Silver Jack goes into a remote area the locals won't travel into because the terrain is too difficult and bear infested. She glances at the old man and relaxes. If he can go out there by himself at his age, the two men together should be safe.

Silver Jack laughs, "We'll be over on Crittenden Creek for at least eight days, maybe as long as eleven. If we're not here for breakfast on the twelfth day, call in the marines. We may need their help." He scoots his chair back from the table. "We should get going, if we want to go upriver at high tide."

Josh pays the bill with cash. Anne watches them don their raincoats and go, her concern returning. She and Emily pick up the dirty plates, and she notices the newcomer has left a nice tip. She watches as they go outside in the drizzle and feed Blackie leftover ham from the old prospector's breakfast. Anne glances at the calendar on the wall, twelve days from today is July 7. She makes a mental note to remember the date and find a way not to worry about Josh.

Chapter 17: Wits

We pass Point Highfield and enter the Eastern Passage. With a westerly breeze pushing us from behind as well as a flood tide, we make good time as we pass tiny Simonof Island and head toward Babbler Point. Simonof Island looks to be less than a hundred feet across and boasts two trees and a lot of underbrush. I remember passing close by it on the ill-fated day when I capsized the canoe.

Silver Jack points and shouts to be heard, “This is where Chinese workers were allowed to bury their dead.” He looks directly at me, “Prejudice can be a mean thing. There’s no dirt on this island, only rocks.”

“Why were the Chinese here?” Josh asks.

The old prospector shakes his head, “Not sure. It was well before I arrived. My guess is they worked in the canneries mostly.”

A moment later dolphins breach portside and Silver Jack booms, “Those are Dall’s porpoises.”

I watch as the pair easily overtake the boat and ride our bow wave. The porpoises are black with a striking white patch on their bellies and flanks. They have horizontal tail flukes, with the trailing edges of the flukes trimmed in white.

Their dorsal fins are small, and their heads slope steeply to a short, indistinct beak. I remember reading that one major difference between dolphins and porpoises is dolphins have pointed teeth while porpoises have shovel-shaped teeth.

The creatures entrance me. I’ve never been this close to any marine mammal and watch in fascination as they play with the boat for five minutes. Finally, as we pass Babbler Point, the pair break off and streak away to the south. I watch them leave with a tinge of regret.

We pass the shoreline where I waded ashore after capsizing the canoe. Sitting dry and warm in Jack's skiff, it doesn't look remote or deadly. I am not fooled. The water is frigid due to glacial runoff, and I want no rematch with its icy embrace.

I have a few moments to dwell on how this lonely shoreline could have been my final resting place as we pass by it on our way to the mouth of the river. As soon as we arrive, my attention is drawn to the pristine waterway. I lean over the gunwale and peer into the clear water.

The river curves and twists, as it claws its way almost due north, deep into the mainland. I note an eagle at the top of one of the tall spruce trees lining the riverbank. It's easy to identify by its pure white head and matching tail feathers. Jack gradually slows our speed as the waterway gets narrower and the noise of the engine reduces to a steady hum. The sky is overcast, and occasionally raindrops pelt us as we move upriver.

If we could travel east, we'd arrive at the border of British Columbia. I ask Jack how long it would take to cover the distance.

"On foot, it would take two weeks to go twenty-five miles." He wrinkles his nose, "You'd have to cross three major drainages and mountain ridges along the way. It would be tough going, that's for sure. There are no roads between Canada and the panhandle of Alaska except way up north near Haines. The terrain is so difficult, the cost is prohibitive."

Jack steers to the middle of the watercourse, where the channel is deepest. After several bends in the river, Jack slows so we are barely making headway. "Watch for rocks coming up close to the surface, we don't want to hit them with the propeller."

I peer into the water and can make out house-sized boulders. I spy several, which almost break the surface, and point to them. Without a word, Jack steers around them.

We travel for twenty minutes, with me occasionally suggesting a course change to miss a boulder. Eventually, it looks as if we have nowhere left to go. Jack tells me, "This is where we get out and start towing the skiff." He shuts off the motor and tilts it up, as I swing my legs overboard and stand beside the boat.

Before we left Wrangell, Jack prevailed upon me to wear a pair of his chest-high waders. It's easy to understand why they are needed. "Grab the bowline and tow the boat up the deepest channel," he instructs. He slips over the side and joins me in the shallow river. Through the thick rubber of my waders the cold is distant.

We pull the skiff upriver. At times we are forced to drag the boat over rocks. When we get to these spots, Jack orders Blackie out of the skiff. We must pull together to budge the craft. When I miss the rhythm and pull alone, nothing happens except I wear myself out. I imagine the old prospector doing this job by himself. After an hour I am amazed he could have made this trip once, let alone dozens of times. I ask, "Why do you bring the skiff so far upriver?"

"If a higher tide comes in while the skiff is tied up, or if heavy rains cause the river to rise it could lift the skiff and flip it over. I had it happen once, and it caused the motor to be unusable for days. We want to avoid getting stranded over here." We pass another bend in the river and Jack points ahead. "See the blue tarp along the western side of the riverbank? That's where we leave the skiff."

My initial excitement fades; as the river remains so shallow we are forced to drag the skiff over rocks almost the entire distance to the tarp. Thirty minutes go by before we get to a downed tree, forming a partial safe-harbor for mooring the skiff.

"This is it," Jack announces. "We tie the boat here and take the gear up the bank and put it under the tarp."

Twenty minutes later, we've stowed our gear and changed from waders into boots. Because we'll be walking through muskeg today, I'm wearing black rubber muck boots I bought at the local hardware store in Wrangell. Jack is wearing rubber caulks. These are the same boots worn by loggers, which have short spikes protruding from the tread to allow them to walk on logs without slipping. The rubber version of the boot is waterproof, allowing Jack to walk through the muskeg without getting his feet wet. My muck boots are waterproof, but they won't offer the support or traction his caulks provide.

Fortunately, I have a much better backpack than Jack. I've

brought along my internal-frame pack with adjustable hip belt. He's using a World War II Army surplus packboard. It's not contoured to fit his body and the flat nylon straps offer no cushion. In addition, all the weight of his load will be carried on his shoulders, because there is no hip belt.

Jack organizes our supplies into packs. He is fast and efficient, and within fifteen minutes the loads are ready. He hefts each one. "These are both between fifty and sixty pounds. We'd have to carry more, if we didn't already have a stash at Base." He loads Blackie's pack with dog food. "I make him carry his own food. Even so, he hates this pack."

Because of the drizzle, I opt to wear my rain pants and rain jacket. Thankfully, my wool fedora is doped with water repellent. We take turns sitting on the ground and helping each other with our straps before lurching to stand upright with our loads. Jack hands me his rifle, "Here, you carry this. You can shoot a rifle can't you?"

I nod my head. The rifle is a bolt action with open sights.

Jack pauses. "If a bear gets close, stick the muzzle in his mouth and pull the trigger." He grimaces, "You only get one chance, so don't forget to take the safety off."

I hold the rifle to my shoulder and sight down the barrel. The rear sight is folded down, so I reach forward and lift it into position.

"It has a weak spring. You'll want to make sure it's up before you shoot." Jack turns and picks up his chainsaw with one hand. Using his other hand, he picks up two jugs; one container has gas and the other bar oil. Both are needed for the ongoing operation of the chainsaw. He looks at me quizzically, "Are you ready?"

Again I nod my head, and Jack turns and starts walking on the trail along the river. At first, the going is easy and the trail is flat, side hilling the steep bank along the river. I recognize sword ferns and vine maple trees under the tall spruce. I ask Jack about one leathery-leaved shrub along the trail.

He stops. "It's salal. The berries are mildly sweet and mix well with the tart berries of the Oregon grape. Unfortunately, Oregon grape doesn't grow this far north."

At one point, we go downhill until we reach a small tributary and cross it. On the other side, we climb a steep bank and stop to rest and catch our breath. When we stop, I ease my load so the weight on my shoulders gets a little relief. I'm grateful we have a trail to follow. I ask, "Jack, how long has this trail been here?"

"I started working on it three years ago. It's in better shape on this end. I brought along a new chainsaw, so we can use it to buck logs out of the trail when we go past Halfway, our second campsite. I like to leave one in each bivouac if I can."

I hear a thunderous roar from the river, "What is it?"

"There's a waterfall over there. The river drops twenty-five feet, so my trail goes up here to the first muskeg and bypasses the falls."

We pause three or four more times to catch our breath before we get to the top of the hill and enter the muskeg. At this point, the flora changes dramatically. We had been walking through arboreal forest with tall spruce and hemlock mixed with deciduous alder trees. The salal, ferns, and vine maple stop where the muskeg begins. The trees in the muskeg are stunted, thin, and many are dead. "What kind of trees are these?"

"In the muskeg you'll find mostly white pine with a few stunted spruce trees thrown in. It takes them three to four hundred years to get this size." He gives me a hard look. "There are dangerous sink holes here. Watch where I walk and step there too. You don't want to sink out of sight."

Within a few steps, I recognize hiking will be difficult. For one thing, the footing is not firm; walking on the muskeg is like walking on a sponge. When I believe the ground is supporting my weight, my boot sinks farther and adds an extra strain. Frequently I must take an extra long stride to reach the root or log Jack has selected for a foothold. These stretches tax my legs, because they're awkward and my load is heavy. Within a hundred yards I'm sweating profusely, so I unbutton my raincoat to let body heat escape. Blackie has little trouble with the swamp; his extra-beamy paws allow him to travel with little effort.

Our path does not follow a straight line, but instead weaves back and forth, avoiding the dark pools of brackish water. Even with his load, Jack flows over the trail with ease, while I labor to keep up. I wonder how he is able to take such long steps with his short legs.

He must be in incredible shape. I consider the hiking machine this guy must have been fifty years earlier.

The muskeg is dotted with spring flowers. The vegetation is stunted and shows amazing color diversity. The groundcover is sphagnum peat moss, which can hold fifteen to thirty times its own weight in water. The muskeg is made up of dead plants in various stages of decomposition; therefore the bog smells like rotted vegetation. Tiny gnats form dark clouds above the pools of water.

Among the stunted trees, I can see farther, almost twenty yards. Jack has felled pine trees along the trail and cut the logs into short lengths. These are thrown across the trail to create stepping-stones. Periodically, the trail enters areas with no trees, and it widens so we are stepping on moss never trod on before.

In the muskeg, time loses it's meaning. If it weren't for my wristwatch, I'm not sure I would have been able to say how long we'd been marching. We aren't going uphill so we travel roughly thirty minutes between breaks. When we stop, we use a fallen log wedged three feet off the ground as a place to sit.

Blackie lies down and Jack helps him with his pack. "The cans of dog food press against his ribs and he can't get comfortable, so I have to pull off his pack while he is lying down."

I raid my water bottle for several slugs of tepid water.

Jack points at a plant near our rest area. It has slightly elliptical, thick and glossy leaves. "This plant is used to make muskeg tea."

After the first break, it's my turn to pack the chainsaw and jugs of oil and gas. Jack carries the rifle. Each arm must be carrying fifteen extra pounds and there is no way to cradle the objects in your arm like you can the rifle. I'm grateful when we take another break, and I carry the rifle. Approximately four hours after entering the muskeg, we reach firm ground and stop for another rest. I sit on a wet log, "How much farther is it to camp?"

"It takes about twenty minutes from this point. Base is my code for the first camp." Jack shifts his pack trying to find an angle where he can get relief from the weight.

I remove my hat letting more heat escape. Sagging against my pack straps, I'm grateful for the momentary respite. "I know I'll be glad to get there."

The trail turns east toward the river. When we reach the riverbank, it bends north and follows the shoreline. All the fallen logs are bucked so we don't have to climb over them. Based on the number we walk past, it must have taken Jack days to cut all these logs and clear the trail. We stop and he drinks from a brook. I rinse my hands but drink from my treated water bottle. While I wait, I wonder how long before I give up on my plan to drink water I've treated with iodine. For now, the thought of catching the parasite, Giardia, is enough to keep me away from untreated water.

As we walk along the river, I hear a rapid-fire *rattle*.

Jack and Blackie pause, "It's a Kingfisher. A bird with a long beak designed for snatching minnows out of the water. With luck we may get to see it as we walk along the trail."

Before long, Jack points out a bright blue bird perched on a limb hanging over the river, "Notice the large, crested head and long sharp beak. This one has a red and white chest. The added red color indicates it's a female. One of the rare cases among birds where the female is more colorful than the male."

I listen as; once again, the Kingfisher's distinctive *rattle*-song vibrates the air. The bird launches off her perch, swoops low over the water, and wings swiftly away upriver.

A few minutes later, we round a bend in the riverbank and Base is a short distance ahead. The trail leads under several teal blue tarps. We walk inside the shelter and set down the items we are carrying and shed our packs. Blackie stands, waiting for Jack to remove his pack, too.

I look around, fascinated by the piles of equipment and supplies. It looks as if there's enough to live comfortably for a month. The site is on a level bench eight to ten feet higher than the river. I look around and count six huge tarps neatly hung to create a sizeable shelter. One tarp above all the others is arranged to protect the fire pit from rain. The center of the retreat is spotted with rounds cut from logs turned on end. Similar to end tables in an apartment, these rounds are used to stack supplies, equipment, or waterproof containers.

On the edge of our camp I spot a fiberglass canoe turned

upside down. “What is this for?” I ask.

“Tomorrow we’re going to load it with gear and paddle upriver to Halfway.” Jack stretches, “We’ll have to portage around a couple of spots along the river, but it sure beats walking.”

I consider the canoe for a moment. It looks to be twenty feet long and almost certainly weighs 250 pounds. “How did the canoe get here?”

Jack snorts, “It took me a month to drag it over the falls and up the river to this spot. I didn’t do it all in one trip though.”

I’m stunned into silence. I’ve traveled half a day with a load of fifty pounds plus whatever I was carrying in my arms. At this point I’m pretty exhausted, wet, and hungry. Jack had obviously hauled a ton of gear and equipment to this retreat plus drug a heavy canoe across formidable terrain. He’s accomplished all this, spending days alone in this remote location, with only Blackie as company. Maybe it’s time I reevaluate the tenacity and capacity of my new traveling companion. I shake my head. I wouldn’t buy it if I hadn’t seen it for myself.

Jack heads for the fire pit. “I’ll get a fire started. Why don’t you take this water jug down to the river and get us fresh water? How about fried potatoes and onions for dinner?”

When I return, Jack asks me to peel two bulging russet potatoes. Meanwhile, he pulls a cast-iron skillet from a nail hammered into a tree near the fire and covers the bottom with cooking oil. He deftly cuts up an onion while holding it in the palm of one hand. Following his instructions, I slice each potato lengthwise and cut up the remaining pieces into thin slices.

Once he has everything in the pan, he creates a flat space on top of two logs at the edge of his fire. He adds salt and pepper and covers the dish. Wearing gloves so the heat from the cast-iron doesn’t burn his hands, he turns the potatoes every few minutes until he declares the dinner ready.

Removing the skillet from the fire, he instructs me, “Grab a couple of paper plates and silverware from the bin over there.” When I’ve retrieved the supplies, he scoops half the dinner onto each plate. With his spatula, he points at one of the chairs, “Make yourself comfortable. There’s ketchup here if you want some.”

I remove my rain pants and settle into one of the folding chairs, making sure I'm positioned to get heat from the fire to dry out my wet jeans. I'm famished, and the hot meal is excellent. "Wow, this is good," I manage to get out between bites.

As I eat, the pace of the day slows. Unlike when we were hiking or dragging the skiff up the river, I no longer have to work to get to a destination. I have arrived, and it feels good after a long day of arduous activity to rest and let my body recover. I pay attention to small things around me I'd failed to note, when I was busy helping to get the meal ready. I can hear the forest breathe. We are remote; it would take a day to return to Wrangell, because we couldn't travel at night through the muskeg.

After we finish eating dinner, the old prospector pours water into the skillet, covers it with a lid, and puts it on the fire. "When the food remnants in the frying pan are soft, it will be easier to clean it." We sit near the fire and soak up the heat. Jack finds a summer sausage in his gear and cuts a piece for Blackie. "Ah, poor baby," he tells the giant dog in a singsong voice, patting him gently on the shoulder. Later, he pours the steaming water out of his skillet and uses a paper towel to wipe out the pan. When he finishes, the paper towel goes in the fire and the pot is hung on a nearby tree.

Following Jack's lead, I wipe off my fork with a paper towel. I pull dry clothes out of my backpack and change into dry pants and socks. Jack helps me rig a rope over the fire to dry my damp clothing.

He offers me summer sausage, and I take one piece. We sit by the fire and talk. Jack tells me stories from his life as a logger. I'm fascinated, so I keep asking questions. He tells me story after story of the early days, when he'd learned to climb trees, top them, and rig them for spar poles. Many times his stories include a fight. By all accounts, Jack has led a colorful life. Jack lives by a strict unwritten code. Break one of his rules, and he moves on without you.

Finally, Jack stands and stretches, "I'm going to turn in because we need an early start in the morning. Let me find your sleeping bag, and we'll get you set up." He goes to a storage tub and removes the lid. Inside is a heavy, full-size sleeping bag. Jack hands it to me, and I estimate it must weigh between ten and fifteen pounds.

"Why not use a mummy bag?" I ask in a surprised voice.

"I like the standard type better." Jack straightens, "We go this way to the sleeping area." At the back of the shelter he pulls back a tarp lying on the ground. Underneath is Jack's sleeping bag, which is on top of another tarp. "Spread out your bag here. The top tarp is to keep dew and moisture off the bedding.

Jack arranges his rifle and a flashlight near the head of both sleeping bags. "If a bear comes into the tent at night, the first one who wakes up grabs the gun." I watch him climb into his sleeping bag and invite Blackie to join him.

I pull off my pants and wool socks and crawl into my bed. I use my pants for a pillow. Lying there, rain drips on the tarp and the fire crackles. I worry a bear might enter our shelter but am reassured by the rifle not far from my head. I can hear the river rustling, and I remember Kaeli. Tomorrow, if I'm lucky, I will put one more day between us. With this thought, I drift off into exhausted sleep.

#

In the morning I eat an inch thick pancake, the full size of Jack's cast iron skillet. Because of his earlier trips packing gear, we have margarine, strawberry jam, and syrup. I joke with him. "I'm going to write a book about you. I'm going to call it, *Cooking With Your Gloves On*."

After breakfast is cleaned up, we slide the canoe to the river and load it. We need equipment to build Jump Off, the next camp after Halfway, so Jack loads the canoe as full as he dares. He will be wearing waders, as we'll need to pull or push the canoe through the shallowest parts of the river.

With me in the bow, Blackie on top of the gear in the center, and Jack in the stern, we push off and enter the current of the river. I experience a moment of panic as the canoe settles in the water to within three inches of the gunwale. I quick stroke and find the canoe is responsive, even if it's a little sluggish from the heavy weight and deep draft.

By the time we've paddled past the first bend, I start to gain confidence in our ability to keep the canoe from rolling and capsizing. I relax and look closely at the surroundings. It's beautiful and peaceful. The river is roughly sixty feet across in most places. The depth of the water varies from four feet in the shallow areas to twenty feet in the deeper pools. Along the riverbank grow salmon berries, alder, and spruce trees. Thick grasses and underbrush drape over the bank and reach for the river's edge.

Our journey upriver is slow but steady. At one point, we dig in and paddle with rapid strokes to make it through a narrow, swiftly running section of the river. On two occasions, we detour around overturned trees crossing the river and find a narrow channel near the bank wide enough to accept the canoe. One time, we get out and chop through roots and dirt with an axe until we open a way past the root ball of a fallen tree.

About noon, we arrive at a tangle of logs blocking the river and Jack steers the canoe to the west bank. He holds the craft steady for me, "This is where we portage. I've made a trail around this logjam. Let's unload the canoe and carry the supplies to the upriver side."

Together, we haul the canoe onto a low spot in the bank and unload the gear. Jack leads the way as we carry our backpacks along the trail. A bit more than 300 feet away, we arrive above the logjam and find a suitable place where we can launch the canoe.

The following two hours are backbreaking. Hauling gear along the trail is the easy part, because we can carry the gear and equipment in manageable loads. The difficult work begins when we drag the canoe up the bank and along the trail. Like the skiff, moving the canoe works best when you are in perfect timing with your partner. The canoe slides easily along the ground, but every turn, tree, log, or root increases the difficulty. Silver Jack was persistent to do this alone more than once. Dragging the canoe for miles to Base takes on a whole new meaning.

After we complete the portage, we eat nuts and jerky before reloading the canoe. We take our places and shove off. The sun comes out, and the journey along the river is pleasant. Ahead, to the west of the river, a ragged, steep ridge dwarfs us.

From behind me, Jack says, "That ridge leads up to Garnet Mountain. The river bends around the point of the ridge in a huge semicircle. Where we are headed is north from here, straight past the point of the ridge."

An hour later, we enter an area where the river is punctuated with sandbars, and several fallen trees present barriers to our passage. Bowing across the river, the logs are nearly head height, held off the ground by giant limbs thrust into the sand bar. Jack exits the canoe and pulls out a chainsaw. With a quick crank, he starts it up and holding the chainsaw over his head, cuts the fallen trees into chunks six feet long. He manages to cut the logs without getting his saw stuck. The short lengths are shoved to one side to allow passage of the canoe.

Once on the other side of the sandbars, we resume our trip for several more turns of the river. Finally, Jack gets out of the canoe, and wading ahead, pulls the craft between two half-sunken logs, following their length to the east side of the river. "Get out here, Halfway is just ahead, fifty yards from the river."

We each grab a load from the canoe, and the old prospector leads the way up the bank and along another trail. We arrive at Halfway, but it looks like a disaster befell it. There is one tarp hanging from a rope between two trees, but all the additional ropes have come undone. At first I suspect a grizzly has torn up the place, and I check the safety on the rifle. But Jack announces, "It looks like the river flooded through here during the winter or maybe the spring melt, carrying away a lot of the supplies. We'll have to rebuild."

At Jack's suggestion, we move forty yards farther from the river. The elevation gain is slight, perhaps a few feet, but the old site will flood again at some point. The new campsite is near the edge of the muskeg where the old man points out several snags with the potential to make good firewood.

We spend the afternoon re-hanging the tarp, ferrying supplies from the canoe, cutting firewood, and setting up shelter. Fortunately, we have carried two sleeping bags with us for use at Jump Off and we use them to replace the soggy ones we find at Halfway. Before the new sleeping bags go on the ground, Silver Jack uses his saw to cut long shavings from our firewood. He has me layer the shavings to create a soft mattress for our sleeping bags. To prevent the bags from drawing dampness out of the wet ground, we lay a tarp as ground cover over the shavings and fold it in half so it will cover over the sleeping bags while we are in them.

The work is tedious and several hours pass before we are set up for the night. By the time we finish, only weak light filters through the clouds as this overcast day starts to wane.

After setting up shelter, Jack builds a fire in the middle of an old stump and places four cans of soup near the edge of the fire. Each can has been carefully vented along the top edge. Supplies surviving the flooding are salvaged if possible. These include frying pans and pots hanging from nails in a nearby tree, an axe, shovel and saw oil.

We spot an unspoiled can of spam sitting on a stump. "It must have drifted onto the stump as the water receded. We'll feed this to Blackie." He opens the spam and cuts it into chunks and drops them into the dog's stainless steel bowl. Jack finds a percolating coffee pot in the brush, "I'll make us coffee. It will help revive us."

I notice several mosquitoes buzzing around the old prospector's head and look for my mosquito repellant. I spray my clothing and Jack's too. He informs me, "These aren't mosquitoes, but the repellent will help anyway."

I look closely at the buzzing insects, "They sure look like mosquitoes."

Jack settles his hat back on his head; "There's a white stripe on their hind legs. We call them white socks. They are black flies and they bite. The bites can get infected, and an allergic reaction is possible. When hundreds are after you at the same time it's darn hard not to get lots of bites."

I swat periodically at the white socks and when the soup cans are steaming, Jack hands me leather gloves, an open can of hot soup, and a ladle. "Here, try this. I buy them when they are on sale at City Market and the labels came off long ago, so this is chef's surprise."

I settle into one of the folding chairs near the fire and try the soup. Mine is chicken noodle, and the hot, salty liquid is delicious. As we eat, I watch sparks from the fire jump high into the darkness. "How far are we from the skiff?"

Jack ponders this a moment, "We're not as far as you'd think. Nothing we've done in the last two days has been in a straight line. In addition, the pace in the muskeg is almost glacial. I've looked at a map and my best guess is we're only three or four miles away at this point." The coffee starts to perk, so he pulls it back from the edge of the fire.

Needless to say, I'm dumbfounded. Two days of difficult travel and we've covered no more than three or four miles. "Based on how my body feels, I'd say we've traveled at least twelve."

"Wait until tomorrow lad. The loads will get heavier, and we have to gain elevation to make it to Jump Off." There's a twinkle in Jack's eyes, "We'll have to pack a chainsaw with us, as the logs aren't cut out of the trail, and we'll need it to cut firewood at Jump Off." He pours us each a cup of coffee and sits back in his chair.

I groan, remembering what a pain carrying the chainsaw is while weighted down with a heavy pack. I change into dry clothing and set up another drying line above the fire for my wet clothes. I comment to Jack, "The trip today gave my feet a chance to rest, although they are sore."

Jack takes a drink from his coffee cup. "Take care of your feet, and they'll take care of you."

I sip my coffee. Alaska is a rough frontier, and it takes tough men to cope with the weather, the lack of basic amenities, and the isolation. After two days on the trail, and my own close call not long ago, it's easy to understand why emergencies occur every season.

I review our situation. We have the supplies for making fire and shelter. We don't have a way for immediate communication in case of an emergency, but we have each other and our wits. Like Jack has always done, we can find a way if we have to. I am comforted that I'm on the trail with experienced travelers, Jack and Blackie.

Maybe tomorrow won't be as bad as it sounds. I go to bed with sore arms and shoulders matching the soreness my legs gained from our first day's trek. I lie in the warm sleeping bag, with netting draped over my head to keep the white socks and mosquitoes away, and evaluate the hours between Wrangell and me. I consider what I have allowed myself to get into by agreeing to come prospecting with Jack. Next time, I vow, I'll be sure to ask more questions before making a decision like this one. I really need to remember this lesson when I get back to the comforts of Wrangell.

Blackie lies between our sleeping bags, and his nearness reassures me. In the last two days, my status with Blackie has improved. He views me as a member of his pack. Blackie is also our best alarm system. He will provide advance notice if any creature invades our roost in the middle of the night. As I become drowsy, I reach out and touch the rifle butt.

Chapter 18: Exploration

Silver Jack wakes to Josh leaving his sleeping bag. It's early, but there is enough daylight for him to tell the fire has nearly burned out during the night. A few embers remain, so it will be easy to get the fire started again. He stretches and runs his fingers through his hair.

Nearby, Blackie is lying on a corner of his sleeping bag. His golden brown eyes are fixed on him, waiting for the signal to start another day. "Alright, you poor baby, I'll get up and get you something to eat." He reaches for his boots.

Josh returns from the bushes wearing a sweatshirt and boxers, his feet stuck into his unlaced boots. Silver Jack reaches for his hat and directs a question at Josh, "Are you ready to get up? We've got a long day. It'll definitely be late by the time we make billet."

Josh shakes his head and mimics propping open the eyelids of his right eye with his fingers. "I'm ready to go when you are," he flops onto his sleeping bag.

Silver Jack snorts, "Come on hotshot. If this old man can get out of bed, so can you."

With a little groaning and good-natured bantering, the two men rise and prepare breakfast. The prospector makes pancakes, and Josh finds condiments. Silver Jack fries a package of bacon in another pan. "I brought this along for a special treat. Without refrigeration we need to use it up today. Trust me; you'll burn enough calories before the day is over to more than make up for the bacon."

After breakfast, Silver Jack considers what is needed for

Jump Off and beyond. He suggests making a pile of the necessary supplies and equipment, so they can assess what must be carried. This time, the packs will include a number of heavy items. For example, they will pack two iron skillets, a hatchet, several cooking pots, bowls, lots of canned food, potatoes, onions, syrup, pancake mix, salt, pepper, two heavy sleeping bags in waterproof storage containers, plus three tarps. When the pile is complete, he tells Josh, "We have choices. We can try to take everything in one load or make two trips." He waits as Josh considers the pile.

Josh asks uncertainly, "How far is it?"

The prospector responds, "It's roughly two miles with an elevation gain of about one thousand feet. The last half-mile will be uphill through an open muskeg." He slaps at a white sock trying to land on his exposed neck. "It will take us four or five hours to get there. It will take longer, if we try to make it in one trip. Once we get there, we'll have a shelter to set up. If we take two trips, we'll probably spend tomorrow getting the second load."

The young man nods his head. Josh replies, "I'd rather take a heavier load and get everything up to Jump Off today. This way we'll be able to push on and get to our objective tomorrow."

The prospector laughs, "You may regret this before the day is over. But I like your spunk." He directs the loading of the packs. His packboard can accommodate unusual sizes, so he puts denser items into Josh's pack. He likes the advantages of the young man's internal frame pack. The center of gravity for Josh's load will be higher, which will be easier to carry. Josh's pack also has lots of straps, making it easy to attach a shovel and axe to the outside. When packing is completed, he hefts each load. "They weigh eighty pounds, plus or minus five pounds. You'll need to wear the leather gloves I gave you, and we'll take turns hacking our way through the underbrush."

Silver Jack loads Blackie with a case of his dog food. The two men put on their rain gear and take turns helping the other lift his pack onto the top of a nearby stack of firewood. The prospector straightens, and lets the load settle. "You'll need to be cautious walking today. If you fall with this load you'll have a good chance of getting hurt." He reaches over and picks up the rifle and his US Army surplus machete. “You take the chainsaw plus the gas and oil. We’ll swap in a little bit.”

In an earlier trip Silver Jack followed the waterway and found a labyrinth of fallen trees blocking the way. Later he’d reconnoitered a way around the mess and marked the trail with ribbons.

At first, the trail skirts the edge of the muskeg east of the river. The undergrowth is drenched, and the ground is mucky. In the lowest areas, he steps from one skunk cabbage plant to another to keep from sinking too far into the soft muck. With his machete, he cuts away the wet underbrush and clears the path so future trips will be easier. The forest is spruce and hemlock. Occasionally, old growth stumps rear high above the underbrush, creating a multigenerational aspect. The trail crosses a runnel before following it, climbing gently uphill. The going is slow, requiring several cuts with the machete for each step.

The prospector notices Josh has stopped behind him, and he turns to find out if the young man has a problem. Josh points, “What is the name of this plant? It’s armed to the teeth.” The plant is covered with long, sharp spines even on the veins in the leaves. Maple leaf shaped leaves are attached to a dead-looking, club shaped growth sporting even more thorns.

He laughs at Josh’s description, “It’s devil’s club. The new growth is green, but the older part of the plant is yellow and shaped like a club. Watch out for the thorns, if they get imbedded in your skin you’ll likely get an infection. We’ll be going through places where it will be taller than your head.”

Thankfully, he had cut the bigger logs the previous summer. This helps, as the men don’t have to crawl over them with their heavy loads. After an hour, he gives Josh a turn at the two-foot long machete. “Be careful to angle your cuts away from your body. The momentum of the blow can easily be redirected toward you if you strike something hard with a glancing blow. Follow the blue ribbons along the stream bed.”

Another hour passes and Silver Jack swaps the saw and accessories for the rifle and machete. “The trail turns here. We follow this dry creek bed downhill to the northwest.” The two men continue following ribbons. Because they are walking on river rock, there is no underbrush for several hundred yards.

They leave the dry creek bed and follow a swale flowing north. To the east, a timbered ridge rises gently away. To the west, the land is flat but many of the trees are blown down crisscross, creating an impenetrable barrier. After cutting their way through the underbrush for 200 yards, the two men hear the sound of rushing water ahead. Several minutes later they come to another creek running from east to west.

The water is deeper than their boot tops, so he finds a spot where a log spans it. The log has lost its bark and is slick and wet. "I can cross this with my caulk boots, but you'll have a devil of a time. Wait here, and I'll drop a pole alongside the log and you can walk on it and use the bigger log for a handrail."

He crosses to a rock-strewn bar, while Blackie wades through without a second thought. The prospector spots a windfall lying parallel to the creek twenty feet from the water. Finding a likely spot next to a tree, he sits on the log to remove his pack. With his load leaning against the tree, so it won't fall over, he returns with a long pole and lays it beside the log, spanning the run. Josh crosses without incident.

With his load off, Silver Jack feels weightless. He walks into the water, stoops, and drinks deeply of the cold liquid until his thirst is quenched. An interesting stone catches his eye so he picks it up. The stone is periwinkle grey with black patches, looking almost like freckles across its surface. It isn't valuable, so he chucks the stone to one side. He suggests, "Let's take a longer break. From this point on, it's uphill all the way to Jump Off." He digs a Hershey bar out of his jacket pocket and offers a piece to Josh. "Let's snack on jerky and nuts too. The protein and fat will help provide stamina for the climb."

While they rest, he tells Josh he hasn't had a chance to pan this waterway yet. "I've spent more time making trail, hauling gear, and setting up camp than I've spent prospecting. It takes a lot of time to get here."

After the break, he lets Josh take the lead. "Follow the ribbons up this ridge. When you come to a log, wait for me to buck a chunk out of it."

The underbrush continues to be thick, obstinate, and when devil's club isn't present, crammed with huckleberry bushes. Blackie follows Josh; face tight up against the back of his legs, so the branches don't whip him in the face. Josh is forced to use the machete to clear the trail. Away from the creek, they encounter the first blowdown. The log is two feet in diameter, but the top is roughly four feet above the ground making it impossible to cross with a load. Josh steps aside and Silver Jack starts the chainsaw and makes two cuts, being careful not to pinch the bar when the log drops. He makes another cut to free up the chunk he wants to remove.

Again, Josh takes the lead, cutting away the underbrush until they encounter another blowdown. Silver Jack cuts away a length of the log and rolls it out of the way. They rest before resuming. This process is repeated dozens of times, while the steepness of the ridge increases.

By one o'clock, they reach the edge of the muskeg. This bog is different than the ones down by the river. For one thing, it looks more like a meadow, with open spaces extending for hundreds of yards. For another, it's pretty steep. In addition, there are more flowers in bloom at this higher elevation. One of the most common is stark white with miniscule flowers in bunches, shaped so they remind him of tiny orchids. A bright yellow flower, thrusting several inches higher than the grasses around, is prominent. He remembers his granddaughter, an artist, telling him yellow is the first color we notice.

Like the earlier muskegs, the walking is spongy, making it difficult to carry a heavy load. Silver Jack takes the lead, as the machete is no longer needed. He leans forward into the climb and picks the firmest route he can find on the spongy surface. The trail parallels a ridgeline. Every once in a while, one of the short trees dotting the muskeg is tagged with a ribbon. The climb is tedious, and there are no logs available on which to lean their packs.

When his legs tire, he stops and rests in place, hiking his pack high on his back to take the tension off his shoulders. By finding the right balance point, even his leg muscles get a break. Josh and Blackie stop also. Sweat is running down Josh's face from the exertion. The prospector wipes his own sweaty face. "I'm glad it's rainy and overcast. Climbing uphill on a sunny day would be a lot worse."

Josh points at the chainsaw, "My turn to carry it."

It's torture to carry the chainsaw and accessories. The dead weight must be carried off to one side to avoid bumping against your legs; and, because it pulls at the end of your arms, it helps cut the circulation to your hands. You also can't use your hands to shift your load into a comfortable position unless you stop and put the gear down. The weight in your other hand isn't pleasant either. The gas and oil jug together weigh sixteen pounds, as each holds approximately a gallon of fluid. Each jug has a short nylon rope through the handle, and this is looped around your wrist. Due to their soft sides, at least when the jugs bump against your legs, they don't leave bruises.

He is pleased Josh wants to carry his share of the load, even if the work is difficult or unpleasant. The young man has the makings of a good trail-mate. At least he might if he can talk him into returning to the wilderness with him after this trip.

The prospector swaps gear with Josh and resumes his climb north through the open muskeg. The ridgeline becomes more prominent and starts to boast a stand of trees and underbrush. They keep to the open area nearest the tree line.

Two hours later, they reach the end of the muskeg, where a great ridge cuts across their path, descending gradually from east to west. Ahead, the ground becomes sheer and timbered. The ridgeline they have been following reaches it's highest point and begins to descend before it joins the larger, higher ridge directly ahead.

Silver Jack points, "There's a rivulet over there ahead of us. We're going to make Jump Off at the high point of this ridgeline. Let's take our packs off and find a place in the center of the brush pile for our shelter." He carries the saw, gas, and oil. Josh brings the axe, shovel, machete, and rifle. Near the highpoint of the ridgeline they have been following is a stand of dead snags.

The prospector finds two snags thirty feet apart, with a level area between them. "I'll cut the huckleberry brush with the saw, and you throw it in a pile over there out of the way." It isn't easy to use the saw to cut underbrush. The fast moving chain tends to whip the brush, slapping the operator; and if the chain comes loose, it can cut badly before it stops moving. The trick is to connect with the brush close to the ground where it's stiff.

Within twenty minutes the area is clear. Blackie gets into the spirit of the occasion and snaps at the brush with his powerful jaws. Silver Jack indicates the sleeping area. "Take the machete and cut the brush stumps as low as you can. We don't want them poking us when we are sleeping."

When the task is completed, the two men, followed by Blackie, cut a trail through the underbrush back to their packs and return with the rest of their gear. Silver Jack has a coil of rope used by halibut fisherman. It's incredibly strong and doesn't stretch, making it ideal rope for securing tarps. He cuts a length of the rope long enough to fit between the two snags; and this is tightened, lifting the main tarp high into the air. Shorter lengths of rope are cut and attached to grommets along the edge of the tarp then secured to trees, roots, and logs so the tarp is stretched tight. After the main tarp is set, he directs the hanging of another tarp at one end. This tarp is higher and covers the fire pit.

"Let's cut firewood." He picks up his chainsaw and points at one of the snags, "I'll fall this one next to our shelter so we won't have to pack the wood more than a few steps. Snags make better firewood, because they are drier. Anything touching the ground sucks up water like a sponge." Within a few minutes, the snag is down, and he cuts up the log, while Josh carries the pieces and stacks them inside the tarp. A drizzle begins and gets heavier as the afternoon wears on.

When he finishes bucking the log into firewood, he fills his saw with gas and oil and uses it to cut shavings to put under their sleeping bags. In the process, he rips a few planks one inch thick. By the time he is finished, Josh has carried all the wood and stacked it. The prospector points to the shavings. "You spread these, and I'll start us a fire."

Once the sleeping area is prepared with a ground tarp and the sleeping bags are in place, Silver Jack grabs a water jug, several pans and the coffee pot. "Let's get water." Pushing their way through the brush, about 200 feet downhill they find water running between the big ridge and camp. They fill up their containers with water and backtrack through the brush, trying carefully not to spill. “I’ll put on coffee while you finish unpacking our supplies.”

The drizzle becomes a steady downpour, and Silver Jack is grateful their shelter is finished. Josh hangs a drying line near the fire and changes into dry clothes. The prospector suggests potatoes and onions for dinner. Josh agrees with great enthusiasm.

After dinner, the two men share hunting and fishing stories. Mosquitoes and black socks invade as dusk arrives; so repellant is applied to their clothing. When the conversation turns to women, he learns about Josh’s breakup with his girlfriend. “I can’t give you much advice when it comes to women.” He shares his own dysfunctional history with wives and girlfriends. He laughs, “You don’t want to pick one you have to roll over in bed with a peavey.”

Josh has never heard of a peavey so he explains it was a tool used by loggers to move logs by rolling them. Peaveys feature a pointed, wooden handle with a sharp metal hook attached to it so the hook can pivot and bite into the bark, thus using leverage to roll the log. Explaining the joke to Josh makes it a lot less funny. Sadly, it might be a long time before he finds anyone to appreciate his joke.

Josh revives a bit after dinner. Both men are tired and sore from three days of travel and go to bed. An early start will be needed to gain the ridge top with time for exploration. Because of the mosquitoes, Josh uses netting, while the prospector covers his head with his sleeping bag. Blackie lies next to him and stretches out on his side. A steady rain and wind are the last things he notices before he falls asleep.

#

At five o’clock, an hour after first light, he starts the fire, while Josh gets the coffee pot ready. They start with a hot cup of coffee and pancakes. The sun is peaking through patches of clouds, and the men can look southwest and spy the bluffs of the steep ridge, which forces Crittenden Creek in a wide arc. From this vantage point they can look due west to its headwaters.

When breakfast is over, Josh asks, “Are we climbing up the high ridge to our north?”

He considers. "I haven't been past the spot where we filled our water jug last night. I thought we'd follow the rivulet uphill and find our way up to the top of the ridge. We'll return here tonight, so we won't be packing much. According to the map, we'll climb two thousand feet to get to the saddle of the ridge above us."

In the end, they settle on using Josh's daypack to carry lunch plus a first aid kit, repellant, fire starter, GPS, and waterproof matches. At the last minute, he adds two cans of soup. "These are in case we don't make it back before dark." He carries the remaining coil of their rope slung over one shoulder. Josh looks everywhere but can find only one glove.

Silver Jack shakes his head; "It probably dropped off the line last night and fell into the fire. Do you have anything else you can wear on your hands?"

Josh digs through his pack and brings out a box of latex gloves. "I brought these along in case we were working in water. They're better than nothing." He puts a pair on and slips on the remaining leather glove. "It's just my luck. I'm right-handed, so I'm missing the one for my right hand."

Josh changes from rubber boots to his leather-hiking boots. The men don their rain gear, and Josh shoulders the daypack. He hands the young man the rifle, and he keeps the machete.

Silver Jack looks at his watch. It's a few minutes past six. He gives Josh a roll of fluorescent red ribbon. "Let's mark our trail as we go." The prospector hacks a path to the waterhole and up the other side of the draw. Thick patches of devil's club guard the spring, making the going slow and difficult. As the timbered ground gets steeper, the devil's club and underbrush fade away. The steepness of the climb slows the ascent until the two men and Blackie are moving at a snail's pace, required to knock toeholds into the tough soil. The men are sweaty and black flies and mosquitoes plague them as they climb.

They come to a narrow pitch between two rock outcroppings. Slowly, because Blackie has no ability to kick toeholds for himself, the men wedge his body between the hillside and their legs. Moving in leapfrog fashion, so the dog always has one of them for leverage, the trio pull themselves carefully up the steep incline until they pass the rocks.

After they pass the outcroppings, Blackie's attitude toward Josh visibly improves. The steepness of the hillside lessens; but thick, nearly impenetrable huckleberry bushes bar their way. Hacking and pulling themselves uphill through the wet underbrush, the men continue climbing. As they gain elevation, the trees grow shorter.

At intervals, the men cross patches of muskeg. Surrounding each bog is often a thick fringe of devil's club. Even though the going is spongy, the open areas are a welcome relief from cutting their way through the brush. As they climb, the vegetation gets wetter and wilder. Grasses stand head-high along the waterways, and huckleberry brush grows as tall as he can reach with his machete. Signs of bear activity--digging in the bogs, claw marks on tree trunks, and piles of fresh bear scat–are everywhere.

He watches Josh slip repeatedly on the wet vegetation. His boots are not adequate on the steep, wet hillside. They begin to encounter patches of snow.

During one break, Josh asks, "What direction is this, Jack?" With the machete, he indicates the course the men had been following for the last fifteen minutes.

He laughs, "You've noticed I've changed the angle of our ascent a little to the left. I'd say we're headed west of north."

Josh has a puzzled look, "What's that?"

Swatting at a white sock buzzing his head, he responds, "On the compass, it's a point a little to the west of due north. It's a vector not far enough westerly to be called northwest. For me, west of north has always symbolized being headed in an important direction. When you leave Seattle, you go west of north to get to Alaska. Because of this, for many Alaskans, going 'west of north,' means more than a point on the compass."

Josh nods his head but does not reply. Silver Jack swaps the machete for the rifle and lets Josh take the lead. Blackie promptly takes up the center position with his face pressed into the back of Josh's legs. The young man hacks his way uphill through the huckleberry bushes following the new heading.

#

By noon, the clouds thicken, and it starts to rain in sheets. Not long afterwards, Josh rounds a corner of the hill and stops. When Silver Jack catches up with him he finds a nearly unbroken snowpack stretching ahead of them. This must be the toe of the glacier that fills the ravine climbing to the northeast. There's enough visibility to discern a saddle in the ridge. Below it, and to their left, is the mouth of a massive vertical hole. The upper edges of the hole thrust higher than the surrounding terrain, forming a neat perimeter wall. It looks as if the hole has been created by a gigantic underground blast.

"This is it." He steps forward and points west and up to the tallest peak. "I was on top of Garnet Mountain when I saw this vent. It's taken me three years to get here, and I've made it with your help, young fella!" Enthusiastically, he thumps Josh on his back. "Let's explore."

Chapter 19: Worry

Anne and Emily work at the local food bank on one of their days off. The Salvation Army is hidden in an old church beside the Zimovia Highway. Because the weekend is busiest and brings in the best tips, Anne works at the café Wednesday through Sunday, with Monday and Tuesday off. On those days, unless she is working an extra shift, she often devotes one to doing chores and errands and the other to working at the food bank for three hours before a planned event with Emily. Several times they walked along the docks looking at boats. Once they went north of town and traced images of the petroglyphs. Later today, she has plans to do their favorite activity, going to the library so they can return books and perhaps find new ones to read.

The food bank is crowded with regulars. Many of the customers are reclusive and want to remain unnoticed. Others are eager to say hello and thank the volunteers for their help. Anne remembers when she used to rely upon the food bank for basic food supplies. This was during the time before she kicked Michael out and returned to live with her parents.

Earlier, Anne allowed Emily to do her favorite job at the food bank, stacking cans of food on the take out shelves. Anne watches her daughter carefully turn labels to face the customer, making it easy to see the contents. She builds precise pyramids with the cans.

Anne also likes working at the food bank, because she feels she is repaying for the times when she needed assistance from others. It makes her feel good to help people in need. Each week, Emily and she go through their cabinets seeking enough items to fill a grocery bag. If they don't find enough, Anne stops at the City Market to pick out items on sale. The food bank has greater purchasing power, and would prefer cash, but it's satisfying to bring in bags of rice or beans.

When the food bank closes, the two of them stay to help with cleanup. Almost everyone is a volunteer, and the one paid director, Dorothy, receives so little compensation, she might as well be one, too. The cleanup doesn't take long, and Dorothy has instructions for those who will return the following day. Anne signs the log and volunteers for next week.

As she leaves, Dorothy stops her, "Anne, do you have a second?"

Anne is worried Dorothy will ask her to stop bringing Emily. Had she been inappropriate? Despite her anxiety, she responds in a calm voice, "Why, of course. What do you need?"

"We are preparing to start our summer food drive, and we hoped you will let us feature Emily as one of our volunteers. It's so good of you to bring her with you. It helps to instill community service at an early age. Will you allow it?"

Relieved, Anne assures Dorothy she would approve the idea. She adds, "You should ask Emily."

As Anne predicted, her daughter is thrilled to be asked. She has her own ideas for the article. "You can show me stacking cans."

#

The Irene Ingle Public Library is on Second Street. The new facility is the pride of the community. Wrangell's library is not part of a regional library system, so it does not have the ability to borrow books from other libraries in southeast Alaska. Anne parks her truck by a neatly tended flowerbed. She and Emily dash to the entry to avoid being soaked in the heavy rain. They enter the building, each carrying a stack of books, and go straight to the book return. Once their items are deposited, Emily disappears among the bookshelves, and Anne heads for the nonfiction section. She's looking for art books.

An hour later she has a pile of books to take home. She has found books on still life, landscapes, portraits, perspectives, and wildlife. She even found a book on drawing eyes. She thinks of Josh. She frowns in concentration and is not surprised when Josh's jay-blue eyes are easily visualized. One of the attributes of being an avid drawer is she retains detail.

As she waits for Emily to finish selecting her books, she continues to worry about Josh. An accident might happen to him while he's on the mainland with Silver Jack. She's aware the old prospector camps out often, but he's an old man and risking his neck is his own business. Josh is a different matter entirely. Not only is he new to Alaska, he's not used to the hardships of the wild. To make matters worse, Silver Jack doesn't carry any modern communication equipment to call for help if it's needed.

She vows, "If Josh isn't back on time, I will call the Coast Guard myself." Anne makes a mental note to put the projected return date on her calendar.

Anne feels less helpless because she has a plan. She looks for Emily and finds her snuggled into a soft chair reading a book. "What are you reading, dear?"

"Oh, mommy, I've found the best book. There's a girl who'd rather be friends with dragons than marry a prince."

Chapter 20: Dud

I'm soaked through, despite my rain gear. My gloveless right hand is raw from hacking my way through the brush with the machete. The latex glove I'd started with, hangs from my wrist in ribbons. My hand throbs in a dozen locations from devil's club thorns imbedded deep in my flesh. I'm thirsty, hungry, tired, and cold. Looking at my watch, I find the crystal is fogged from moisture, but I can read the time. It's almost noon, so we've been climbing and hacking our way uphill for six hours.

I feel blisters on my toes and feet. My leather-hiking boots failed me hours earlier when the continuous rain and soggy ground turned them into cold, misshapen lakes in which my feet are submerged. Worse, the rubber soles of my boots lack sufficient traction to cling to the wet plants and brush, and I slip constantly as I walk. I've fallen to my knees dozens of times and taken a ride on my butt twice. During one of these wet slides, I had been holding the machete and quick thinking prompted me to loft the deadly weapon away from my body. While plunging downhill, I probably looked much like an attacking crusader running at full speed with sword held to the ready. Had I slid against the sharp blade, I'd have been quite likely to cut an artery, which would have been the fast end of me.

I find myself standing on a field of compressed snow that is sucking all the heat out of my body. Jack is thumping me on my back because of the great hole in the ground before us. He plunges ahead across the whiteness with Blackie close behind. I follow, unsure what else to do. I would prefer to stop and make a fire, but in this downpour there hasn't been a dry spot in the last two hours. One might find shelter under a stunted spruce, but I don't think it likely.

As I walk along, I observe the hard-packed snowfield is a series of cupped depressions. I assume this pattern is caused by the melting action of the glacier, but I realize this is an untested theory. In any case, the going is slow as we are walking on a slope and neither one of us wants to make a wild, unchecked slide down the hill and into the gaping hole below. Jack and Blackie are leading when we come to a fault in the earth. It traverses the slope at a shallower angle than our path, and thus we merge with it from above as we near the great hole. The fault is twenty feet across and nearly the same depth. Strangely, it's so even it looks man-made.

Jack, Blackie, and I enter the fault and follow it into the abyss. As we near the perimeter, the fault twists, so the lower wall becomes a ledge on which we can walk. Above our heads, the other wall of the fault is a ceiling of stone above us. The walking isn't easy, because sections of the rock have fallen onto the ledge. The schist is dull black and steel grey with veins of midnight black shot through in wide bands. We follow the ledge for twenty minutes, and it widens as we near the midline of the cliff. Far below, I spy a lake at the bottom of the rock formation. All in all, I get the distinct impression I'm inside the vent of an extinct volcano where one-third of the mountain top has vaporized, representing the open area through which I can look at the headwaters of Crittenden Creek, to the southwest.

Jack finds a dry area between several boulders and stops. "Let's take a break here and eat. As long as the wind doesn't blow the rain inside this fault, we should have protection from it."

I remove the daypack, and we do our best to make ourselves comfortable. Looking at my watch, it's almost one o'clock. "How long can we stay before we have to head back so we can get to Jump Off before dark?"

Jack looks as if he's considering the question carefully. "In the summer we have really long days. It doesn't get dark until past ten. I figure we can make it downhill in half the time it took us to go uphill, especially if we don't take time to cut brush as we go. Meaning we need to leave here no later than six thirty. I'd say we give ourselves at least an hour buffer to be sure. If we want to make this climb again tomorrow, I'd rather leave here at four o'clock and give us time to rest and have a nice dinner before we turn in. So, we'll regroup at four and decide what we want to do. What do you say?"

I consider it as we divvy up two apples, pieces of summer sausage, and cut slices from a brick of extra sharp cheddar cheese. I'm wet and cold, but we've hiked for the better part of four days to get to this isolated spot. There's no reason to leave without checking it out thoroughly. I sigh, "Let's compare notes at four o'clock."

After we finish eating, Jack pulls his rock pick out of my pack and uses it to break away sections of sable rock running in thick seams through the bedrock. I move ahead along the ledge and look for anything unusual. Within minutes I hear him calling my name, so I return to our break site. My voice shows my excitement, "What have you found?"

"I'm not sure. But this layer is sprinkled with hard stones. It kind of reminds me of garnets, except there aren't any faceted sides, and the color isn't red." He dumps several chunks of black rock into my hand. "It would be easier to tell, if we could find stones bigger than a pin head to look at. I may have to dig out my magnifier. It has a light and is useful for getting a close up look."

The stratum Jack is working on runs vertically across the fault so it climbs away from us uphill. Above our heads a section of the vein is missing. Searching for broken pieces among the rocks on the ledge, I soon find the missing section thanks to its jet color. I carry it to the old prospector. "Try this."

Accepting the rock, Jack props one end of the eight-inch-thick rock against the wall of stone. With his rock pick, he strikes the center and the rock collapses, broken neatly in two. I watch as Jack tilts the edge of the stone, and we each notice a shiny stone the size of my little fingernail protruding from its edge. Jack looks at me, shakes his head, and carefully chips away a section of rock with the pick. He holds up our specimen, it's clear, with rounded edges. His voice trembles as he speaks, "Maybe I'll break out the magnifier and we'll take a closer look."

After looking at the stone, Jack offers me a look. "Look

through the lens with the lighted end held against the surface of the stone."

I take the magnifier and look at the stone. Under magnification, it looks transparent, and the outer surface is irregular, except where the edges are rounded. "I don't know what I'm looking for," I shrug apologetically.

"When we get back to Jump Off, we'll test it for hardness. Meanwhile, you break out the GPS and get a fix on our location while I look for more specimens." Jack turns and hacks at a chunk of rock, which likely had fallen from the ceiling of the fault.

When I've completed getting a location from the GPS, I save it as a waypoint, and copy the information into a notepad I've kept safely tucked away from the wet inside my shirt pocket. By the time I've finished, Jack has found two more specimens. One is larger than the first. He pulls a zip-lock bag out of a pocket and drops the three stones inside before returning the bag to his shirt.

Jack points along the ledge, "Let's go a bit farther. Maybe we can find more like these."

The way gets more difficult as the ledge narrows and sections of it are missing. We are wary, making sure the ledge will hold before we commit our weight to each section. Before long, the ledge ends in a gap forty yards across. We peer down and ten feet below us the ledge continues across the gap.

He uncoils his rope, and ties it around a boulder on the ledge. "I'll tie a few knots and loops in this rope so we'll have easy handholds and footholds for getting up and down." With the task completed, the rope is hung in place. Jack commands Blackie to lie down and wait, and we lower ourselves down leaving the rifle and machete on the ledge above us.

Jack spots a shiny stone protruding from black rock. Using great care, he chips it loose and places it in the zip-lock bag with his other specimens. We check nearby veins and find another stone. I wish I had a way to tell if we were finding anything valuable. It feels like we are stumbling around, as likely to overlook something of importance while we focus on worthless items.

Blackie whines periodically as he waits. Fortunately, we remain close to the drop in the trail, and he doesn't get too anxious. I record another waypoint with the GPS. I'm able to help Jack, breaking the bigger pieces of rock into smaller pieces by dropping them on boulders in the trail. I find one or two stones using this crude method. By four o'clock we have nearly a dozen stones. Jack calls an end to the day's search. "If we want to come back tomorrow, we're going to have to leave."

I agree, and so we pack our supplies into the daypack. I climb the rope first and Jack follows. Blackie greets me with a lick on my face as I clamber up. I ruffle his fur, and he slaps me with a paw. I take it he's glad not to be left behind. I gather up the rifle, while my partner takes the machete, and we retrace our way to the edge of the vent.

Jack asks me to make another waypoint. We leave our rock pick and any uneaten food at the ledge but cover the food with rocks to discourage scavengers. Even though the combined weight we leave behind is only a few pounds, it makes no sense to pack it up the hill again.

As we step out into the open, we encounter a driving rain. Fortunately, we can keep our backs to the wind as we retrace our steps uphill over the snowpack. We find our marked trail, where we enter the thick brush.

The trip downhill is faster and easier than the trip up. It's hard on my legs because I'm using a different set of muscles. I can feel my feet slipping inside my boots and I can tell from the sharp pain I've rubbed my feet raw in places. Following the trail is easy, as its well marked with ribbons, and the brush has been thrown out of the way. As we travel downhill, I feel a strain in my knees as I attempt to keep from sliding on the wet brush. The rain pelts our raingear and cascades from the rim of my fedora. The strain becomes more intense as the hours wear on, and my leg muscles tremble as I make my way downhill.

It's almost six by the time we near the cliffs in the timber. We climb through the narrow chute and make our way through the steepest section, leapfrogging again to provide Blackie with scaffolding for his descent. Because the rain hasn't let up all day, the chute is a torrent. This makes it difficult to find footholds and handholds for our climb down. At one point, when I'm hanging on a root, the sleeve of my raincoat dips in the water, and I get a cold bath running down my sleeve and into my armpit, before I manage to let go and shut off the supply.

In the steep timber below the cliffs, we move warily because any slide would go unchecked for a hundred feet. By the time we get to Jump Off it's seven. I am exhausted. Blackie flops down near Jack's sleeping bag with his tongue lolling out of his mouth.

Without conversation, we take care of chores. I fetch water while Jack starts a fire. As I cool down, my muscles tighten and stiffen. For dinner, the old man cooks fettuccine noodles and heats up Alfredo mix. He uses a can of chicken noodle soup with the mix. Chopping up a whole onion, he adds it to the sauce. I start a pot of coffee.

Locating the clothes I dried out the previous night, I pull off my wet ones and hang them near the fire. Instead of putting on dry socks, I leave my feet bare because I want to tend to them later. I keep my feet clean by sitting on one of the upright rounds of wood and placing my bare feet on one of the planks Jack had made the day before.

When dinner is ready, he piles my plate with noodles and pours sauce over all. I find pepper and sprinkle it generously.

"This is excellent," I mumble around the hot food in my mouth. "I could eat a dead horse by myself."

"You can eat as much as you want." Jack gestures with the ladle. "We burned at least four thousand calories today, hiking up and down this mountain."

After dinner, we pour ourselves hot coffee, and I retrieve a bottle of "new skin" and use it to patch up the blisters on my feet, as well as the cuts in my hand. My feet are in terrible shape, with patches of skin missing the size of quarters. The product stings for a bit when it's applied to raw flesh. Better to sting than to get infected. I use a needle to dig out the more obvious thorns left in my hands by the devil's club. When I'm done, I put on clean, dry, wool socks and the rubber boots I dried out the evening before.

After cleaning up our cooking utensils, Jack sits on a nearby round and pulls a box out of his supplies. "This kit's for testing the hardness of stones. Every mineral is unique, and this test helps with identification. If these are diamonds, they'll have a hardness of ten, the highest reading on the scale. If they are garnets, they'll have a scale reading between seven and eight."

I offer, "The Mohs ten-point hardness scale was named after its creator, Frederick Mohs. He was a German mineralogist. He died in the early nineteenth century, sometime before our Civil War started."

Jack's hardness kit consists of a series of metal tips attached to tiny handles. Each handle holds two tips, one on each end, and they are marked with their numeric hardness. He selects a tool and shows it to me. He points out, "The hardest tool in the set is marked nine."

I contribute, "To be a hardness of ten it would need to be a diamond. This tip is probably edged with Corundum, the second hardest mineral."

Using the tip, Jack attempts to scratch one of the specimens. Neither of us can tell if there is a scratch on the stone. I suggest, "Why don't you look at it through your magnifier again?"

Jack examines it before giving me a turn. Neither of us can find a scratch, so we try to scratch it again, choosing an obvious rough spot on the stone so we can use this as a landmark when we peer at it through the lighted magnifier. Again, we can't observe any scratches.

After several attempts on other stones, Jack looks at me, and a big smile spreads across his face. There's a twinkle in each of his dancing, brown eyes. "We might have something here, partner! Do you feel up to climbing the mountain again tomorrow?"

I forget my tired legs, sore feet, and stiff muscles. Instead, my face breaks into a grin bigger than Jack's. "Count me in. I'll climb up there if you will."

We talk for an hour, sitting near the fire and soaking up the heat and the unusual feeling of being dry and warm. As the light wanes, Blackie sits up and growls, ears forward, his face alerted to the muskeg. He shifts his head back and forth to catch the slightest sound and his nose is held high. Jack whispers to me, "He smells something." After a pause he suggests, "Step outside with the rifle and fire a round into one of the snags. That way we won't have a bear bumping into us by accident."

I ask, "Are you sure?" He nods his head, so I pick up the rifle and stand outside the tarp, despite the steady rain. I make sure the rear sight is in the up position, push the safety forward and take aim at a spot twenty feet up on a nearby snag. I hold my breath, and release it partway while I slowly squeeze the trigger. I remember a line from a movie, "Aim small; miss small."

"*Click*," the sound of the firing pin striking the shell is loud, audible even to Jack sitting ten feet away. My heart stops, surprised by the unexpected dud shell.

Jack doesn't miss a beat, "Put another round in the chamber. Some of those shells are pretty old, and if they draw dampness, they misfire."

I eject the dud shell onto the ground and chamber another. I repeat my firing sequence, and this time a long flame leaps out of the muzzle of the rifle when the shell explodes. I don't notice the quick kick of the rifle, but watch as a chunk of the snag spins away as it falls into the brush. The roar of the rifle echoes off the ridge behind me. I chamber another round and reset the safety.

Reaching down, I pick up and toss the ejected dud into the brush so there is no chance it can end up in the fire. Inside, I locate Jack's belt with two cartridge packs and his hunting knife. "I should reload the clip."

Blackie settles down near where I sit, as if the firing of the rifle was the end of the event. I'm a little less certain, but as time goes by and the woods return to their deep silence, broken only by the steady thrum of raindrops, I too relax. I reach down and scratch Blackie behind the ears. He accepts my attention and enjoys it. I cut off a piece of summer sausage and reward him.

We agree on an early start, so we can maximize our time at the claim site. Later I pack my daypack with all the supplies we will need.

Jack explains mining claims to me. "This would be a lode claim. Federal statute limits the size to fifteen hundred feet long by six hundred feet wide. If the ends are parallel, then the claim extends vertically at a depth beyond the boundaries of the claim. If we set waypoints on top of the ridge tomorrow before we go in the hole, we'll have a few of the corners we need for our claims. Given the size of this vent, we should try to mark two claims so we can each file on part of it and cover more territory."

I can't find any fault with Jack's logic, so I agree with his plan. By the time I go to bed, it's after dark, 10:25 p.m. I berate myself for not getting to bed earlier so I can be rested for tomorrow's hike. Covering my head with mosquito netting, I find a comfortable position and fall asleep.

#

The following day goes well. I choose to wear my rubber boots, not wanting to repeat yesterday's painful trip using my leather hikers. We get an early start and reach the top of the ridge by ten thirty. As we walk on the glacier near the giant vent, the clouds break open and blue sky wins out for the first time in more than two days. Jack picks out a straight line perpendicular to the center of the vent and has me take readings every one hundred feet along the ridge above the perimeter of the hole. He walks off the distance between points. "We won't know which ones we'll need so we'll take lots of readings and pick the best for the corners of the claim."

Blackie assumes we are playing a game, so he joins in, racing back and forth between us, as his master walks ahead to find each waypoint. He reminds me of a big kid, grinning from ear to ear, playing tag.

Around the great hole, there is a series of rock outcroppings thrust up around the perimeter of the vent. On one rock outcropping, we find wolf scat. It's apparent, even to my untrained eye; the feces are not fresh. Blackie sniffs the scat briefly before feigning indifference. I stop and take a picture of Jack and Blackie using my digital camera.

After taking fifteen readings along the ridge, we return to the cache we left the previous afternoon at the edge of the hole. Jack points downhill from the fault. "Let's move farther down this ridge along the vent's perimeter. Maybe we can find another way. We have a good idea already of what we can find if we take yesterday's route."

I follow Jack along the southeast perimeter of the hole. The ground gets steeper and snow gives way to rocks covered with lichen of many different shades of brown, ocher, and green. Continuing downhill, we encounter another fault and follow it into the vent. This one is ten feet across and it also twists to create a ledge for us to follow. The fault is tilted at a steeper angle so we descend rapidly as we follow the ledge. One hundred yards in, we again encounter midnight seams in the schist. The fourth vein looks mottled and knobby so we stop and use the rock pick. Jack whoops, "Yea-hah," as our first piece yields three specimens similar to the ones we found yesterday.

We spend a couple of hours in the surrounding area and find more specimens. It's slow going because the rock is so hard. Unless pieces are already knocked loose, it's difficult to break the stratum open to get at the stones. We eventually resume our way along the ledge as it moves down toward the center of the vent. At one point, we look to be seventy-five feet above the talus slope running down to the surface of the lake.

I indicate the lake; "We're going to need to go down to the lake edge so we can set the corners for the claims."

Jack nods his head. "It looks like this ledge keeps descending until it reaches the base. Let's hope there aren't any gaps."

We follow the shelf, with Blackie between us. The going is slow, but there are no gaps wide enough to stop us.

When we reach the talus slope we climb down to the lake. It is surprisingly shallow. I offer to hike along the beach and make waypoints, while Jack looks for diamonds.

When I am finished, I return to the ledge and find him sitting on a boulder, counting specimens. "In addition to the eleven we found yesterday, we've found fourteen today. The ones near the bottom are bigger than the ones higher up. To bad we can't be sure these are diamonds." He pauses and gives me one of his piercing gazes, "We won't until they've been examined, but it's exhilarating to have something to show for all our hard work."

We eat a late lunch and share with Blackie. He likes the summer sausage and cheese, watching intently for any indication of an offering. I look up toward the top of the vent high above us. "How far to the top, Jack?"

He looks at the massive wall looming above. "Well, it must be at least six hundred vertical feet, maybe more. Why do you ask?"

"The GPS shows it's nearly eight hundred feet higher on top of the ridge. Is it possible we could follow the lakeshore and cut across the side of the hill until we get to our trail? If we could find a decent path, it would save us a lot of climbing."

Jack considers my question. "It might be possible. How much of a gambler are you?"

I realize the unexplored hillside could be steep and difficult. But not climbing hundreds of feet each day would save us much work. "I say we give it a try."

"Then let's get started young fella." We might need all the daylight we've got left to get back to Jump Off." Jack looks at his two bags of specimens. "We've done well for one day and can spend a little time making an easier trail for tomorrow."

Three hours later, we stumble across the trail from Jump Off to the top of the ridge. It hasn't been easy going, cutting through the thick brush on the steep hillside, but we have a trail to the claim site bringing us out by the lake. As a bonus, we'd found an excellent spot for a camp near the lake's outlet. The two trails connect slightly above the spot where our original route snakes through the steep rocky chute between the outcroppings. This evening, the chute is dry and our trip back to Jump Off is uneventful.

After dinner, Jack suggests, "Let's go up for one more day before we head back to Wrangell. We can take more GPS readings, if our calculations tonight show we need additional waypoints."

I use the charting feature on the GPS to calculate horizontal distances between waypoints. With these calculations, I attempt to pick waypoints to describe two adjacent rectangles of 1,500 feet by 600 feet. I'm surprised by my findings. Because of the vertical drop from the top of the ridge to the lake, I misjudged how far we had traveled horizontally. "We need to go to the far side of the lake to get nearer to the fifteen hundred feet in length."

Jack's response is to state the obvious. "If you've learned anything, it's how difficult it's to judge distance in this country."

What have I learned on this trip? We've traveled over tough

country in lousy weather and relied upon our own devices for food, shelter, and medical care. I've learned this eighty-year-old prospector is tougher than old saddle leather and as full of adventure as any twenty-year-old. Even Blackie, who is as fierce as any wolf, also has simple needs, like companionship. Oh, I've learned a few things on this trip in addition to the more obvious ones. Perhaps, Kaeli dumping me in Colorado wasn't the end of the wonderful part of my life after all. If Jack bounces back time after time at his age, why there's hope for me, too.

Chapter 21: Sissy

His coworkers believe Clay is in Ketchikan for a much-needed sojourn with the prostitutes for whom the town is famous. Clay and Lenn detour to Kadin Island to retrieve the hidden supplies. It takes them two sweaty hours to lug the equipment from its hiding place in the brush to the boat. A light mist keeps the brush wet but doesn't slow down the work in any way. Using the hidden equipment saves them a big cash outlay, but they run the risk of creating suspicion if they show up with the gear in Wrangell. To eliminate the risk, the two men will use the island as a stash on their return.

Shortly after leaving the island, the ocean changes color to creamy milk, evidence of the silt being pushed inevitably seaward by the Stikine. The river is dangerous as the silt beds are within inches of the surface. Over time the silt drifts, forming transient islands, known locally as the Koknuk flats, ringing the mouth of the river.

With its shallow draft and no propellers, the jet outboard pushes the boat upriver without difficulty. To the east the two men make out the shoulders of Garnet Mountain, the top obscured by heavy clouds. The steep, forested hillside on the east side of the river looks raw and difficult.

Five miles upriver, Clay removes his raincoat when they catch a break in the cloud cover. He wonders where Lenn staged the accident killing his two partners. He realizes the shifty redhead dealt with the two men as soon as they showed any sign of not cooperating. Lenn is capable of doing the same to him, if necessary. Despite the risk, he isn't afraid of Lenn. Lenn needs him to file a claim. Once he learns where the diamonds are, Lenn will be equally as vulnerable, because Clay can finish him off any time he wants. Clay pats the 9mm pistol in his shoulder holster, finding its weight reassuring.

Upriver, Lenn pilots the boat toward the eastern shore and into a narrow channel beside Cottonwood Island. He follows the channel between tall cottonwood trees for two more miles before turning into Government Creek. The aluminum sled is tough and the boat is capable of traveling in four-inch-deep water. They encounter a lake and cross it. The branch turns southward before they enter another lake. This one is long and narrow, cupped between two ridges rising magnificently ahead of them. They enter a darkly overcast area. Soon, it drizzles, and Clay slips into his rain gear.

They are able to travel another half mile before they come to the end of the lake. Lenn shuts off the motor and the boat glides until it touches the shore. "This is it for the boat. From this point on, we walk. There's a good camping spot four hours hike upstream. From there, we can make it to the claim in less than a day."

The two men are well equipped with the latest in lightweight equipment. Even their food supplies are light, using dehydrated or freeze-dried technology. In addition, they each carry a rifle and pistol. Lenn takes the lead, and Clay lets him guide. He warns himself not to allow Lenn to get behind him on the trail.

At dusk, the two men circle up on a flat, sandy bench above the creek. They use a portable stove to heat food and water. Clay sets up a two-person tent while Lenn cooks dinner. After the meal is finished, the Harbormaster gets out his flask, and the two men take turns drinking scotch. They drag a couple of logs over to the stove, and use them as seats. Clay is glad for the fire in his belly from the alcohol, it helps to make up for the lack of a campfire.

Clay wants to know about the route. "I've noticed the canyon ahead gets narrow and steep. Are we going to stick with the waterway or move up onto one of the ridges?"

Lenn takes a slug from the flask. "We climb to the west, going up the point of the ridge behind us. When the ridge starts to flatten out, we turn south and climb on an easy grade uphill until we cross a saddle. The diamonds are inside a deep vent on the other side."

Scratching his ear, Clay takes another drink. "Is there much brush to deal with?"

Lenn slaps at a white sock buzzing around his head. "We have to go through a few patches, but mostly we'll be hiking on bare rock or over muskeg."

The alcohol reminds Clay of old times with Lenn, together in Ketchikan. "This scotch tastes a damn site better than the stuff we drank at the Youth Facility. You never told me where you got it."

Lenn snorts, "Do you remember the prick who was the counselor?"

Clay shifts his butt, trying to find a comfortable spot on the log. "You mean, Mr. Spencer, I bet."

"Yeah, he's the one. I found it in his desk. He couldn't report it lost, because no one was supposed to have liquor. It might have been cheap whiskey, but I don't remember you complaining." Lenn passes the flask back to Clay.

He takes another swig and is compelled to push another of Lenn's buttons. "Since we're partners, how come you spell your name the way you do?"

Lenn glares, but when he notices the Harbormaster isn't backing down, he sighs. "I told you I got it from my old man. It's partially true. At the Youth Facility I was required to sign everything with my middle initial, so I simply added the "n" as a lowercase letter to my first name." He stops talking and takes another drink from the flask.

Clay ponders Lenn's answer for a moment. "It doesn't make sense you'd go through the cover up for nothing. What does the N stand for?"

Lenn looks as if he doesn't want to respond, so Clay prods him, "We're associates. I should know the name of the man I'm thrown in with."

Lenn looks away and swallows, his Adam's apple breaches up and down. "Alright, god damn it, my middle name is Nancy. It comes from my grandmother's maiden name. Her family was proud of this name, as there's a city in France named after a long-dead ancestor. He done it to make his mother happy."

Clay is shocked into silence. He looks at the slender, wiry

Lenn in a new light. He can't imagine the tough youth he knew from juvenile hall with a sissy moniker like Nancy. Clay can't find the right thing to say, the awkward moment lingers until he snaps out of it and silently hands Lenn the flask.

Chapter 22: Competitors

Silver Jack and Blackie rest in the shade near the lake's outlet. Dark clouds in the south threaten but for now sunshine prevails. Their last day at the claim has been fruitful, and Josh is setting the last of the waypoints along the side of the lake away from the vent. The young man is invaluable, since he can use the GPS to calculate distances between points. From the sketches Josh shared with the prospector, it looks as if he is getting the claim corners placed with a level of precision Jack could never have matched.

#

The two of them had spent a long day working on the lower part of the vent near the lake. Josh had found a way using three or four nails and the hatchet to break out sections of the vein. This allowed Silver Jack to spend his time breaking these chunks into pieces, thus exposing more diamonds. When they stopped for lunch, he remembered today was his eightieth birthday. He mentioned it to his partner, and the two men celebrated by eating a can of kipper snacks Josh had carried up the mountain.

While they worked, Josh came up with two or three ideas to speed up the process for getting the stones out of the stratifications. Twice during the day, Silver Jack combed through the debris and found specimens he'd missed earlier. One of these was strange. When he'd first spotted it, the prospector was sure it looked green. When he held it up in the light, the color changed to golden. He puzzled over this stone more than all the rest. He had always heard the most valuable diamonds were colorless, but he was no expert on diamonds.

As excited as the men were, they realized their find could be worthless. They must wait until the stones are examined to know for sure. Silver Jack had once overheard a jeweler tell a customer about the difference between a jeweler, gemologist, and appraiser. From what he could remember of the conversation, he would need a gemologist appraiser to look at the stones. Hopefully, he will find a qualified appraiser in Ketchikan and get the analysis needed for filing the claims.

Because it was their last day at the claim site, the two men stayed longer than usual to find as many specimens as they could. When they stopped at the end of the day, the prospector estimated they had thirty specimens from today's work alone. Josh established several more waypoints, where they'd found the most diamonds, before trudging around the lake to get his final readings.

#

It's almost seven; it will be nearly ten o'clock by the time they can get to their shelter. The prospector is making a mental list of gear to pack out and equipment to leave at Jump Off, when he hears a great slap, followed closely by the far off *boom* of a rifle. He jerks his head around to find Josh face down near the water's edge. From the sound of it, he can tell a rifle was fired from the top of the ridge above the vent.

He crawls forward to get behind a fallen tree and rests the rifle over the log. Two men are near the top of the ridge as Josh is scrambling to his feet. To provide cover for Josh, he fires at a boulder twenty feet to the left of the men. He must sight above his target to compensate for the extra drop of a bullet travelling uphill. He is satisfied when a puff of pulverized rock marks his bullet striking the desired location.

As he reloads to fire another warning shot, he yells at Josh, "For god's sake, get out of the open!"

Another bullet bounces off the rocks on the shoreline and pings as it passes over his head. Josh is running toward him, and the prospector fires his next shot into the open space separating the two men on the ridge. He watches them dive for cover at the same time Josh rushes past him into the woods. Blackie leaves his side and rapidly follows Josh. He reloads but holds his ground behind the fallen log. He suspects whoever is shooting from the top of the ridge must have a scope on his rifle and, therefore, has a serious advantage. After a moment, he crawls away into the woods, sticking to the brushiest areas.

Thirty yards back, he stands up and spots Josh standing behind a tree. Blackie is seated at Josh's feet. Approaching Josh, he doesn't notice blood. "Are you hit?"

Josh is ashen. His voice trembles, "No. But I sure got the crap scared out of me."

"You're lucky. Those guys are amateurs when it comes to shooting at a living target. They overshot you, because they didn't account for the fact they were aiming downhill at a steep angle."

"What are we going to do?" Josh peered around the side of the tree toward the top of the ridge.

"Well, for one thing, we're going to get to where they can't see us. I don't want to give them a chance to hit us with a lucky shot."

Silver Jack and Josh duck low and jog around the hill until they are out of the direct line of sight from above the lake. Blackie remains attentive and close to his master.

Stopping, Silver Jack asks, "Okay, let's take stock. Did you leave anything by the lake?"

"No, I was wearing the daypack and I'm holding the GPS unit."

Silver Jack adds two shells to the clip in the rifle and wipes his forehead. "I left the machete where I was sitting. But I have the specimens we acquired today in my pocket. The ones we found the last two days are in Jump Off."

Josh looks toward the lake, "Do you want to go back for the machete?"

"No, we don't need it to get out of here, and if they miss finding it, it will be here when we get back. We should head back to Jump Off. It will take them at least an hour, maybe longer, to climb down from the top of the ridge to the lake. An hour or two later, they'll be halfway to Jump Off when darkness catches up with them. I wouldn't want to be stumbling around on this steep ground among the cliffs in the dark, and we know the trail." He slaps at a white sock on his arm. "The damn thing got me right through my shirt."

He can tell Josh is troubled. Finally Josh asks the obvious question, "Why did they shoot at us?"

"I'm wondering the same thing. They wouldn't have shot at us simply because they ran into us out in the brush, unless they were hiding or protecting something. I suppose it's possible these guys have already staked a claim and are trying to protect it. But if that were true, we'd have noticed claim markings." He pauses and both men look up at the treetops as a stiff wind bends all the trees on the hillside. "No, it's unlikely they've filed, so my guess is they were trying to scare us off so they can have it to themselves, while they set up their claim."

Silver Jack walks uphill through the brush, searching for their trail back to Jump Off. Another gust of heavy wind pushes against the hillside and a few raindrops splatter the men.

Josh and Blackie follow. In a few minutes, they find their trail. The young man removes his pack, and they don their raingear before continuing. Silver Jack uses a belt knife to cut away any ribbons he encounters so it will be more difficult for them to be followed. As dark clouds overtake them, the sporadic rain becomes a steady drizzle and turns the underbrush wet in a flash.

Josh breaks the silence; "Jack is it true the party who files a claim first gets the claim?"

"Pretty much that's true. If they haven't filed yet, our best hope is to hightail it out of here and get filed before those guys get done staking their claim. If we get there and they've beat us, we'll have nothing to show for it but the specimens we found on this trip."

Walking determinedly through the steady rain, he recalls the years and the hard miles he's spent with Blackie and Josh to get to this volcanic vent. It's unusual to have competitors for the same claim. He can only shrug; Alaska has always been full of strange coincidences and even stranger stories. He needs to put forth his best effort. Nothing less will do.

Despite his sore muscles and the steepness of the hillside,

he picks up the pace. The trail will become more slick and difficult as the rain continues. Jump Off is three hours away.

PART 2: THE RACE

Chapter 23: Claim Jumpers

After hours of climbing uphill, traversing a long open ridge, Clay and Lenn pass through a saddle with hard-packed snow and a series of deep faults and cracks. The faults create strange valleys between outcroppings of solid rock, split the earth across their path, and give the terrain a surreal look. If it weren't for the lichen on the rock and the clouds overhead, they could be on Mars. Once through the saddle, they start a gentle descent over terraces of stone and soon begin to glimpse a lake far below at the bottom of a natural, cylinder-shaped hole.

Lenn points at the giant crater, "It looks like a perfect circle if you imagine the area below the lake wasn't missing. Marty, the mineralogist called this feature a diamond pipe. The dark rock is called Kimberlite. Apparently, the Kimberlite was pushed upward from deep below the surface and carried diamonds with it. Tremendous pressure and high temperatures are needed to create diamonds."

They climb down from one terrace of rock to another. As the ground becomes steeper, Clay is uncertain how they will find a way to descend safely. Abruptly, Lenn swears, drops his backpack and lifts his rifle to his shoulder, firing downhill. Clay has no time to register what is happening, when the face of a boulder twenty feet to his right explodes, and he hears the *thunder* of a rifle from below. He takes three or four steps forward. A man is running for the woods beyond the lake. Lenn's rifle barks, and as Clay begins to confront him, the ground erupts between them, spraying them with mud and debris. Instinctively, he dives behind a low boulder.

Clay is furious. He spits mud. On his belly, in a half-inch of ice-cold water, his forearms are scraped, stinging and obviously bleeding. His pack has shifted forward, the weight of it pressing his head toward the puddle. He notices his rifle, clenched tightly in his fists, drips water and slime. He slaps away a wad of muck from his rear sight and contemplates using the weapon on Lenn, his so-called partner.

Clay turns and glares at Lenn, who is also down in a depression on the terrace. Clay's heart is pounding. "What, in hell, was that?"

Lenn shimmies forward on his belly. He peers down the barrel of his rifle before glancing over his shoulder at Clay. "You dimwit, somebody else has found the diamonds. If we don't stop them, we get nothing. After what I've gone through so far, I'm not going to let that happen."

Clay's fury subsides. He removes his pack and slides forward until he can peer around his boulder. A short juniper bush, strategically between his position and the lake, provides him with additional cover. A brook leading downhill into trees empties the lake. "Have you any idea where the shots came from?"

"Maybe, because of the slope of this hill, they must be past the lake, or they wouldn't be able to see us. I suspect someone is behind the big log running up and down the hillside. Whoever it is, he must be a mighty fine marksman as his second shot nearly hit me. They have to be almost five hundred yards away. I wouldn't be surprised if they have a scope and are looking at us right now."

Clay notices ominous clouds advancing from the south. "It looks as if it's going to start to rain in a few minutes. What do you want to do?"

When Lenn doesn't answer right away, Clay shifts his gaze from the lake to the face of his partner.

Lenn gives him a steady look, "Let's crawl backwards until we get out of the line of sight. Then we can move over to the west and descend down toward the lake. We should be able to get almost to the lake before we have to show ourselves."

Feeling like a fly on the wall, complete with a flyswatter hovering overhead ready to smash him flat before he can move, Clay crawls uphill, dragging his pack. It takes twenty minutes and starts to rain before they get far enough back to be out of view from the edge of the lake. Tentatively they stand and reconsider their plan.

Lenn points left and right. "We can go east and down or west and down. These guys didn't get here by coming up Government Creek or we'd have crossed their trail. They either came in by chopper or came in from the south. What's the terrain south of here?"

Clay shakes his head, "I've never been anywhere you can't get to by boat. But if you look south, you can spy Wrangell Island from here. It doesn't look as if it's more than four or five miles to the water."

Looking around carefully, Lenn takes charge, "You go east and I'll go west. Watch for any sign of their trail. Let's meet at the south end of the lake, in say, ninety minutes, where the rocky point sticks out. If shooting starts, try to come up behind them if you can."

Clay hesitates, "Do we take our packs or leave them up here?"

"Let's take them with us. We wouldn't want to climb back up here to get them, if the trail leads us in another direction."

Clay nods and picks up his pack. He can tell from the steepness of the ground to his left he will have to climb uphill first to get to the crest of the ridge. From there, he must circle around the bluffs before he can climb down to the lake. It doesn't look far around, so he hopes it won't take him much walking to get to a point where he can descend.

Within fifteen minutes of starting his climb around the rock bluffs, Clay finds himself engulfed in a thick bank of clouds. The rain thickens, and his visibility constricts to less than a hundred feet. Fortunately, a fault on the ridge top circles close above the bluff and makes for easy going. He walks in a great arc around the hole in the ground. The fault is filled with hard-packed snow, but he finds no evidence anyone has trod here before his arrival. He checks his watch when he emerges onto a hillside full of loose rock and brush. Forty-five minutes have elapsed.

Clay checks his rifle to ensure it's ready and moves downhill. He must go slowly, as the hillside is treacherous. He encounters underbrush so thick it's difficult to force his way through it. Periodically, he comes to steep ravines plunging down the hillside toward the lake, and he is forced to search for a safe way to cross. Finally, Clay emerges from the brush into a grassy opening fifty yards uphill from the lake. He moves downhill until he gets to the water's edge and finds a narrow strip near the water where it's easy to walk. The rocks are wet from the ongoing rain and slippery. He turns left and follows the lake, heading toward the rocky point he and Lenn had spotted from the top of the ridge.

The trip around the lake takes longer than Clay would have estimated, because he makes sure he remains close to the underbrush. He considers pushing his way through the thick brush but rejects it as too difficult. He's vulnerable in the open, but no shots are fired. When he reaches the point, he looks around for Lenn.

Finding no evidence of the other man, Clay turns and scans the high cliffs forming a bowl around the lake. The cliffs are sheer, with no vegetation at all for three-fourths of the distance around the lake. From his observation point, there are great faults in the solid rock and many vertical, dark fissures traversing the cliffs. At the bottom of the cliffs are patches of snow and a slope of jumbled rocks.

Clay's thoughts drift, and he daydreams. Claire is the beautiful, but spoiled heir, to a major logging company. She had married young, attracted to a man with education and position, plus a tidy inheritance from a grandfather, who had been one of the original investors in the local cannery. Fifteen years later she began looking for a real man, and Clay had found himself to be in the right place at the right time to make her his mistress.

Clay hears a crunch of loose rock behind him, and spins hastily around with his rifle at the ready. He relaxes when he finds Lenn twenty feet away. "Find anyone?"

Lenn grimaces, "Nobody so far. I just got here. Have you come across a trail yet?" When Clay shakes his head, Lenn continues, "Let's spread out and head toward the woods. Whistle, if you find any sign."

The two men spread out, and Clay watches Lenn check

alongside the fallen tree they had noticed previously. Lenn holds up an empty brass cartridge. Clay keeps Lenn in sight through the brush and woods as the two men curve away from the lake in a long arc. When they are ready to turn back, Clay spots an area where the brush has been trimmed by a machete. He whistles for Lenn, and waits for him to arrive.

Lenn takes one look at the cut underbrush. “This must be part of their trail. Let’s follow it for a little way and make sure.” Lenn looks at his watch. “It’s almost nine. We’re going to have to set up our tent soon, before it gets dark.”

Clay follows Lenn as he ferrets out the trail used by the others. Within five minutes, they realize it will be slow work following the trail around the steep hillside, especially with everything soaked and slippery.

Lenn stops and shrugs his head. “Let’s go back to the lake and set up shelter. We’ll return to this trail at first light, when we can see what we’re walking into. We need to catch these guys, and finish them off, if it’s the last thing we do!”

Chapter 24: Dry Camp

I slip on the steep hillside and manage to stop myself from sliding away by grabbing a handful of huckleberry brush with my gloved left hand. Jack is setting a fast pace, so I resume following him and Blackie along the trail spur connecting with the lake. Jack is packing the rifle. I feel naked, without even the machete as defense.

The adrenaline in my blood assails me, I'm jittery, and it's difficult to walk. I stumble often and can't concentrate. Time slows down, I look at my watch; twenty minutes since the shots were fired but it feels like it just happened.

The terrain changes as we leave the slope leading to the lake and pass around the first sharp ridge. The timber gets smaller and is clumped in scattered patches. The underbrush is thicker; and at the wettest places in between sharp ridges we are forced to crawl between mountain alder. These trees are particularly difficult to travel through. Their trunks follow the slope downward for a distance of six to eight feet before the trees bend upwards. They grow thickly, and the horizontal trunks make a challenging barrier. Even where our trail passes through the mountain alder, the going is difficult, since we have not yet had time to cut all of them.

We reach the end of the spur trail as it merges with our route up from Jump Off more than ninety minutes after leaving the lake. The trail is mushy from the steady downpour, and I wonder if we will have to wade through water again when we get to the rocky outcroppings and steepest ground. Jack doesn't pause, and we continue our fast-paced march along the trail. I'm exhausted, tired, and sore from traveling up and down the steep terrain between

Jump Off and the claim site for three days in a row. Jack isn't bothered by the hard labor, so I keep going without complaint, ignoring my sore feet and stiff muscles.

Stumbling into Jump Off after ten o'clock, in the semi-darkness we load our packs for a fast start in the morning. We agree to have a 'dry' camp with no fire and no lights so we will not provide a potential guide for uninvited guests. I laugh at "dry" as a description, because all of us are soaked. I can at least change into the clothes I'd dried out the previous evening.

Jack tells me, "We need to push through all the way to the skiff by four p.m. tomorrow. If we make it, we can get out on the high tide. It won't be easy, because the tide isn't robust, but we can make it if we're willing to drag the boat."

I try repairing the blisters on my feet with new skin. Jack runs through the list of items to leave behind and those to take. "We'll leave the tarps lying on the ground so the site will be harder to find, they might miss it in this thick brush, if it isn't visible from a distance. Tonight we'll hide the cooking gear and equipment under one of the downed trees away from camp. We'll take the sleeping bags and most of the food. We don't want to leave anything here that will make it easy for whoever might follow us."

Jack creates caches of supplies in multiple locations away from our shelter. It's well after dark when we get ready for bed.

I crawl into my sleeping bag, cover my head with mosquito netting, and try to fall asleep. The events of the day keep replaying in my head until I am dizzy. One minute I'm noting the coordinates of the last waypoint into my notepad, and the next minute I'm face down in the rocks watching as pebbles kicked up by a speeding rifle bullet slowly come to a tumbling halt. Each time, it crosses my mind I am carrying no rifle, so I can't fight back. I break out in a cold sweat and begin an endless run toward the far away woods.

Chapter 25: Recognized

Clay awakens when Lenn calls his name. Inside their two-man tent, it's easy to tell the darkness isn't waning outside.

Lenn sits up in his mummy bag. "It's stopped raining."

Slowly, Clay sits up too and pulls on his pants. "It's nearly midnight. I thought we were going to wait until morning? Are we going to leave our equipment here?"

Lenn rearranges a wool cap on his head. "The guys we are following should have a camp within a few hours hike of this location, and I'll bet they headed there last night. If they had a bivouac here by the lake, we'd have found it. We need to try to get to them before they leave it in the morning. We've got to travel tonight. I'd recommend we leave the heavy stuff here so we travel fast. We'll return here before tomorrow is over. We've got to get our hands on more diamonds and get the information we need to file our claim."

Lenn turns on a miniature flashlight, and the two men finish getting ready. Clay loads a daypack with ammunition, water, and first aid equipment. He checks his rifle and pistol to ensure they are loaded and ready. He watches Lenn do the same. Both men have flashlights, so they use them to find their way to the trail and follow it.

Clay follows Lenn as he doesn't want him behind his back. In the darkness, the moving flashlights cast shadows, making it difficult to walk and Clay trips frequently. They don't lose much time searching; as the underbrush is so thick the path of least resistance is usually the correct way to go. Slightly past two, the men find themselves at a junction. To the right the trail descends, and to the left the trail climbs.

Lenn stops and follows the trail for fifty feet uphill. He returns and points up the ridge. “I suspect this trail takes you to the top of the crater. I’ll bet their encampment is the other way.”

Shortly after heading downhill, the trail ends in a series of rock outcroppings. The ground is so steep it isn’t possible anyone would make a trail through this area. A few feet away, Clay can almost touch the tops of tall spruce trees, their trunks disappearing into the darkness below.

After twenty minutes of searching for the trail, Lenn calls Clay over and flashes his light down a ravine. “I bet they went down this chute between these two outcroppings. There’s flattened mud and leaves by that rock.”

Clay looks carefully. He doesn’t like how steep and unprotected the trail looks. He has to admit, it could be the path taken by the men they are following. He goads Lenn, for the fun of it, “If those guys can do it, so can we. I’m sure it’s not as bad as it looks.”

Lenn gives Clay a hard stare, but obviously can’t see Clay’s face in the darkness. “All right, don’t follow too close behind me. I don’t want you sliding into me and knocking me off the mountain.”

Clay stands and holds his flashlight, so Lenn can descend. The man starts by lying on the outcropping and lowering his legs over the side, seeking purchase for his feet. After finding a place to stand, he cautiously slides over the drop and makes his deliberate way down the chute. Fifteen feet from the first outcropping, the chute turns. As Lenn nears the turn, Clay commences his own descent, cursing to himself.

Making it to the turn, Clay scowls to find the ravine continues for another fifty yards. Slowly, painfully, the two men make their way through the steep stretch of rock outcroppings. Clay slips once, when the muddy ground gives way under his weight. He grabs a nearby tree root and scrambles for a couple of seconds, until he finds secure footing. Below the rocky chute, the ground is sheer and dangerous. Here, the timber is thicker and the underbrush thins out, making it harder for them to find the trail. At one point, they have to climb back uphill to find the correct path.

Dawn comes while they are in the deep timber. With an open sky and no clouds in sight, the dim light provides much needed help with finding their way. The trail stops traversing the steep hillside and descends a ridge. This section is steep, but vine maple and huckleberry brush dot the way, and this helps them because the trail is easy to follow where a machete has been used to cut away the brush.

Following the ridge, the men hear a freshet off to their right. At one point, the trail leads them into the runnel, and they stop for a much needed drink. Continuing on, Lenn indicates they should shut off their flashlights. The vine maple and huckleberry brush give way to devil's club as the terrain flattens and gets wetter. The trail crosses a series of rotten logs and meanders into a draw.

An hour after dawn the men find a place where the trail crosses a brook. Ahead of them, a knob protrudes and the terrain flows downhill both to the left and right. Lenn holds up a finger for silence. He points at a trampled spot that has been used for gathering water.

Pointing ahead, Lenn shakes two fingers to indicate a cautious approach. Clay releases the safety on his rifle and removes the safety strap on his pistol. He anticipates finding the men they are hunting blissfully asleep in their sleeping bags. He wills it to be this easy.

It takes them thirty minutes to creep along the brushy trail. For one thing, there is so much downed vegetation; it's almost impossible to step without creating noise. Eventually, Clay notices sawdust, where a snag has been cut up for firewood, and a flash of blue tarp. Sensing their prey is near, Lenn signals him to charge.

As soon as Clay reaches the opening it's apparent the place is deserted. Tarps are lying on the ground and the fire pit is cold. Clay turns to Lenn in disgust. "I was hoping to catch them sleeping in bed. Now what do we do?"

Lenn removes his wool cap and considers their situation. "If they are ahead of us, we may never catch them before they make it out. Let's look around. Perhaps we can figure out who they are."

Lifting one of the tarps, Clay checks out the cut firewood and the shavings used for bedding. "Whoever was here, they planned on staying for awhile. You don't pack a chainsaw if you're hiking around the country."

Lenn calls to him from thirty yards away. "I've found supplies under this log. Check in the brush around the shelter."

Thirty minutes later, the two men compare their findings. Clay has found an old coffee pot, and Lenn has found a stash of dog food cans.

Clay ponders the dog food. Out of the blue, the answer comes to him. "I have an idea who this might be. In fact, it fits perfectly. I'm surprised I didn't remember it sooner."

"What are you jabbering about?"

Clay straightens, "Why I'd say our prospector is a well known character with a dog. He lives on a boat in my marina. His name is Silver Jack, and he's been prospecting without finding anything for so long I'd forgotten him."

Lenn sits on a block of wood and stretches his legs. "I'm sore, and we've got a three or four hour hike back to our tent. I propose we finish getting what we need to make a claim. We can deal with the old prospector when we get back to town. If he files first, he'll regret it. Nothing is going to stop me from getting my share of the diamonds, especially not a dimwit prospector. If we have to take him to court, who's going to credit the stories of an old unemployed bum of a prospector against the Harbormaster for the port of Wrangell?" Lenn pauses and an odd look flits across his face. "That is, assuming he gets a chance to have his say in court or anywhere else."

Chapter 26: Improbable

Silver Jack wakes in darkness. He shifts in his sleeping bag and disturbs Blackie, lying against his legs. The rain has stopped and the night is quiet.

He considers their options. They must stay ahead of their pursuers or risk getting killed. He doubts any pursuer could track him faster than he can travel. If the men who shot at them yesterday had trailed them all night, it's possible they could be closing in.

Although he considers such a possibility improbable, he must admit it could happen. Indeed, the odds anyone would be after their claim site at precisely this time is also a long shot. For him, the whole thing boils down to one fact: this is Alaska, and strange things happen too often to ignore.

Understanding returning to sleep might lead to their ruin, he throws the sleeping bag off of his body. He twists around and reaches over to Josh's sleeping bag. Tugging on a corner, he wakes the young man. He speaks low, so his voice won't carry, "Let's get going. We don't want them other guys finding us here. We'll stop and eat later along the trail."

Within ten minutes the two men are dressed and ready to go. Both men move their packs outside the shelter. Silver Jack reaches up with a hunting knife and cuts the rope holding the center of the main tarp. With several more slashes, the tarp protecting the fire pit is down too. Silently, the men pick up their packs and load up with the rifle, chainsaw, gas, and oil. Moving quietly, the prospector leads the way through the near dark, following the trail down through the underbrush until it breaks out into the muskeg.

In the open, it's easier to find their way. Without a word, they turn and follow the muskeg downhill. Silver Jack wishes there could be a way to avoid making an obvious trail in the mushy ground. He considers a false trail into the woods headed east but rejects the idea when he realizes their original trail uphill, made four days earlier is visible to anyone trained to look for it. At best, a false trail would slow down their pursuers. At worst, it might slow them down more than the men who were following them. Considering the alternatives, he sticks with his original plan, outdistance the men behind them with a combination of persistence and prior knowledge of where to go. Once they reach their canoe and start their journey down the river, there will be no way anyone following them can keep up. After all, there is only one canoe.

Chapter 27: Civilization

I follow Jack and Blackie as we descend through the open muskeg. The weak light creates an eerie effect. Ground fog fills the lowest places. As we reach the first steep stretch, I glance uphill, in the hazy predawn light I cannot make out any sign we spent nearly four days here. Behind the campsite, the steep ridge rises dark and ominous above the serene picture of the meadow-like muskeg. I consider the trail between the lake and Jump Off and wonder if the men who shot at me are nearby.

By the time we reach the tree line at the bottom of the muskeg, there is enough light to find our way along the trail in the woods. Jack signals for me to stop and remove the first blue ribbon. We agree whoever is packing the rifle will be the one to take down the ribbons as we come to them.

The old prospector sets a steady pace, and I'm grateful it's not raining for once. We take turns every thirty minutes or so carrying the chainsaw. Daylight is firmly established when we reach the creek with the pole crossing. We take off our packs and rest them on the same windfall we used on the way up the mountain. I wade and suck up great gulps of the cold water. I push the thoughts of waterborne parasites to the back of my mind and enjoy the refreshment offered by the pure liquid.

Blackie joins me and is up to his chest lapping water. When he emerges, he shakes his coat, giving me a shower. His master laughs, and breaks the tension for a wonderful moment.

We return to our packs and dig out food to replace our lost breakfast. The white socks skirmish, so we escalate to chemical warfare. I break out jerky and offer a piece to Jack. He shares chocolate with me.

After five minutes of resting, I can tell he is starting to get nervous. So I bundle up my gear and slip my arms through the straps on my pack. We continue to follow the trail between Jump Off and Halfway. Jack removes blue ribbons despite the fact anyone who follows us this far won't have much difficulty because of all the brush and logs we've cut to make the trail passable.

At eight thirty in the morning, we reach Halfway. In this location, we spend twenty minutes storing the rest of our gear and food so it will remain safe until our return. For the trip out, we need our packs, clothing, rain gear and the rifle. I am overjoyed when I notice Jack storing the chainsaw and accessories beneath a nearby log. We'll have a lot less to carry later. He takes off his caulk boots and climbs into his waders.

Either because we are on the edge of the muskeg or in the damp area near the river, we are plagued by mosquitoes and white socks. We turn the canoe upright and drag it from its storage location on the bank, down to the water's edge, swatting bugs the entire time.

The water level has dropped at least six inches. We load the canoe and Jack bids me to climb in and move forward into the bow. Blackie jumps aboard midships and Silver Jack pushes us off from the bank. He wades alongside until we are deep enough for him to climb in, while I hold us steady with a paddle jammed into the sandy bottom. Once he is aboard, we test stroke with our paddles and the canoe responds as if alive. A lighter canoe is much easier to move through the water. In addition, we are moving with the current, so we travel fast.

After the first bend in the river, I relax when I realize it's impossible for the people who shot at us to catch us. I look at the thick brush along the bank and remember how difficult it can be. We glide swiftly past with little effort. The sun remains out, and we keep a steady pace. We do not feel the need to race, but we also must not tarry if we intend to make it out on schedule.

We fight our way through the shallow section of the river with its exposed sand bars. As the water level is lower, the rock bars are longer. But the canoe is lighter, so we get through them with relative ease.

Forty minutes later, we arrive at the logjam, and again we must portage the canoe and our gear around it. This time, we make one trip to carry all the equipment. On our second trip we drag the canoe. As I push on the canoe, Jack pulls and Blackie watches us from a safe distance. We complete our portage in thirty minutes. Without stopping, we reload the canoe and enter the final stretch of river.

We reach Base close to noon, and by this time the sun is out and the woods along the river are steamy with humidity. After unloading the craft, we drag it up the bank and return it to its storage space near the tent. Because the bank is steep and muddy, it takes all our strength and perfect timing to inch the canoe. The paddles are stored inside the upturned canoe for safekeeping.

We open several food containers. Jack prepares a can of dog food for Blackie and finds baked beans for us. He opens one can each, and we eat them cold, using spoons from his array of utensils. The sweet, smoky flavored beans make a gourmet meal. The old prospector takes out slices of bread and spreads mustard-relish on each slice. He hands one to me, and I wolf it down, glad to get the calories.

It doesn't occur to me to comment on the strange fare, because I'm too hungry to care. I realize Jack has no refrigeration, so foods with high sugar content are good candidates for his supply list. We wash the food down with water from the river and pick up our packs.

Jack leads the way south along the river. I'm grateful my pack is light. There is only an empty frame with a daypack, one change of dirty clothes, my rain gear, my useless hiking boots, a digital camera and a few first aid supplies. In addition, we are able to take turns carrying the rifle, as it's the sole hand-carried item on this leg of the trip.

We enter the muskeg. As I slog through the muck, my thoughts turn to Wrangell and Anne. I wonder if I can talk her into going out with me. I realize I'm a little fearful of rejection, but I'd felt a connection the first time we met. At our second meeting, she was showing more than casual interest. I recall the way her jet-black hair contrasts with her green eyes.

Walking through the spongy muskeg is slow, hot, and awkward work. I sweat and swat my way through the hot afternoon, more than ready to have this part be over. I daydream of Anne, and this helps get me through the bog.

As we near the end of the muskeg, I hear the roar of the falls to our east. I call to Jack so he will stop, and I do a little dance on a hummock of roots and brush.

He leans against a pole and asks, “Have you gone crazy?

“No,” I reply. “The falls mark the edge of civilization, that’s all.” We both laugh at my nonsense and return to slogging our way through the muck.

When the muskeg ends, vine maple and salal dominate as we move onto firm ground under the tall spruce near the river. It’s cooler here, and we make faster time on the hard ground. My legs and feet are sore, and I walk gingerly, trying to protect my feet from additional bruises or blisters.

At four o’clock, we come into sight of the shelter near the skiff. I’m enthused with the prospect of getting a chance to rest. Jack stops and points. I step past him, and I’m appalled to find the skiff resting upside down in the water.

“What happened?” I ask. I’m alarmed. I wonder if this event will prevent us from getting back to Wrangell tonight.

Jack hands me one of the waders. “It looks as if the gunwale of the skiff must have caught and the water level rose enough to flip the boat over. We’ll have to turn it over and bail it out before we can load our gear.”

It takes us thirty minutes to get this done. Jack assures me it will take several hours to clean up the motor so it will operate. He suggests we take the skiff down to the mouth of the river, so we can get out on the high tide, before stopping to work on the motor. Fortunately, all of our gas tanks, flotation devices, and paddles were stored high and dry, under the tarp. If our gas had become contaminated, we’d have no hope to fix the motor before heading for home.

With the gear loaded, and Blackie out of the skiff, we

commence the arduous task of dragging the boat downriver. As we discovered earlier, the river is running lower than it had been on our upriver passage. Also, the tide is not as high. Because of this, we must drag the skiff for two hours through the shallows. Blackie wades with us, careful to ensure he's not left behind.

Along the way, we stumble past signs of Humpies, or Pink Salmon, spawning in the shallow water. We watch as one of the female Pink Salmon turns sideways in one spot and digs her redd, or spawning space. The number of eagles along the river has doubled since we made the trip in, and Jack tells me they congregate when the fish runs arrive.

Once we begin paddling, our progress improves. I find the skiff awkward and difficult to push through the water. For one thing, the shape makes it hard to get comfortable and I'm forced to lean over the gunwale to keep from banging my hands against the side of the craft. We figure out the best way to work together, with me on one side near the bow and Jack on the other side near the stern.

With the mouth of the river a half mile ahead, Jack informs me we are ninety minutes past high tide. "That's why we had to drag the skiff a lot farther this time. At least we were going with the current."

It's hushed and beautiful in the estuary. Both of us are exhausted, so we pause often to look at the wildlife. I notice a blue heron near the shore and point it out to Jack. Later, we encounter a family of mallard ducks. The indignant hen herds her brood away from us and into the tall grass at water's edge.

Finally, we reach the mouth of the river and can look out into the Eastern Passage. Jack points down the beach in the general area where I landed with my capsized canoe. "It looks like we might be in luck, Josh. Maybe we can get help from whoever is in that boat."

Chapter 28: Help

Katie pushes the throttle full open and listens with satisfaction to the roar of the outboard as it responds to her command. With a quick surge, her fiberglass boat planes on top of the water and reaches a speed of almost thirty knots. Standing, so her head and chest are exposed above the windshield, she revels in the wind pushing against her.

She cherishes the kind of freedom she has. After two years of temporary, seasonal work with the Alaska Department of Fish and Game, last month she received a promotion to a permanent job as a Fishery Biologist. As far as she is concerned, this is as good as it gets.

The last two days have been spent making the seventy-five mile trip around Wrangell Island, familiarizing herself with the salmon bearing streams in the vicinity. Today, she woke up in Fool's Inlet on the southeast corner of the island. After spending the morning exploring the inlet she began working her way around the island's eastern side, up Blake Channel and through the narrows to the Eastern Passage. Both the island side and the mainland side of the channel contain a number of salmon bearing streams, and Katie wanted a first hand look at each. Whenever possible, she travels upstream far enough to identify the species currently using the waterway for spawning and to make notes regarding the overall condition of the spawning areas.

She checks her chart and is glad she has only one stop left before returning to Wrangell. It has been a long two days on the water, and she can't wait to get back to town and take a shower and clean up. She feels gritty and more than a little wind burned. She slows her boat as she approaches the shore, careful not to let her wake wash over the stern of her boat when it drops off its planing position and settles deeper into the water. Using her trolling motor, she enters the mouth of the river and works her way unhurriedly upriver.

Katie peers into the water. Beneath the boat, there's evidence salmon are entering the estuary. According to her chart, this is Crittenden Creek, and it should experience moderately sized runs of Pink and Coho. Her predecessor's notes indicate the waterway also carries trout and Dolly Varden. She enjoys eating Dolly Varden; although they are from the char family, the pink color of their meat and their taste remind her of Eastern Brook trout.

Katie sees boulders in the water that almost break the surface. She is aware the tide is going out, so she turns down current and drifts back to the mouth of the estuary. As she nears the opening to the river, Katie spots a sea otter playing in the tall grass along the bank. She tries to get closer by shutting off her engine and letting the boat drift. She moves slowly, and by remaining still, she passes the creature within ten yards. It's electrifying for her to discover a pup playing alongside its mother.

After Katie drifts past the pair, they roll onto their backs and peer at her intently. When she is well past them, they swim away from shore and dive. She turns to watch the surface hoping to see them again. After waiting five minutes, she gives up. Either the pair can hold their breath longer than she'd thought, or she had been unable to notice them surface.

Ready to start her motor, she spots a skiff coming down the river toward her. Two men are paddling the craft and this action strikes her as odd, so she waits to find out if they need help. At the very least, she can ask them about conditions upriver.

As the skiff gets closer, Katie can make out two men and a big black dog. One of the men has a silver beard and the other reddish brown hair. She straightens, cups her hands around her mouth, and calls out, "Do you need help?"

The younger man in the front of the skiff calls back, "Yes."

Katie starts her trolling motor and turns her boat around to close the distance between the two boats. “Where are you headed?”

The older man answers, “We’re headed for Wrangell. Our motor won’t start. Is there any chance you can give us a tow?”

Katie puts her boat in neutral and throws the men a line. “I’m headed to Wrangell, too. Tie this to the bow of your boat and come alongside. We’ll make better time if everyone rides with me.”

She holds the gunwale on their skiff to keep it from tipping as the two men and the dog climb aboard. She straightens and holds out her hand to the old man. “Hi. My name is Katie Stevens and as you can see painted on my boat, I work for the Department of Fish and Game.”

The man shakes her hand. “I’m Silver Jack, and this is my dog Blackie. We’re mighty obliged to you for helping us out.”

“It’s my pleasure. I’m glad I was here at the right time.”

Katie turns to the younger man and shakes hands. She notices he is well built, with blue eyes and a pleasant smile. His unshaven face gives him a rugged look she finds attractive.

“Hi, Katie, my name is Josh Campbell. I’m a science teacher at Wrangell High School. I’d like to add my thanks to Jack’s. I sure wasn’t looking forward to paddling all the way back to Wrangell.”

Katie is curious, “My notes indicate there are falls approximately two miles upriver, but no one has been that far in years to confirm this fact. Have you ever been there? Is there a falls?”

Silver Jack and Josh look at each other and burst out laughing. Katie feels the spontaneity of their laughter and can’t help but join them. “What’s so funny?”

Josh is the first to stop. “We’ve been upriver for seven days. When we got back to where we could hear the falls, I did a little dance as I thought it marked the edge of civilization. You tell me no one has been to the falls in many years. That’s why I thought it was so funny.”

Katie beams at the man, “Well, my friend. I believe you erred when you thought the falls was such a landmark. But, my boat will count, so let me be the first to welcome you back.” She flashes Josh a brilliant smile and notes with satisfaction when it has the intended affect. Josh’s nostrils flare, and she turns to the wheel of her boat to hide her pleasure. "Please be seated gentlemen, while I prepare us for takeoff."

She shuts off the trolling motor and starts the outboard. Once the engine warms and runs at idle, she shifts into forward and pulls away until the skiff follows. Gradually, she increases speed until both craft are planing on top of the water. She checks her occupants to ensure they are settled and concentrates on driving the boat efficiently.

She is in her element, even better than having a fast boat is having someone who needs help. As she jets along, she occasionally turns her head to make sure she's not going too fast and threatening to swamp the skiff being towed behind her. At one point, she is sure Josh is watching her. She can't help but wonder if the man is interested in her.

The ride to Wrangell is uneventful and quick. Katie recalls her recent escape from Juneau and her clingy boyfriend, Warren. Warren had smothered her by watching her every move. She couldn't even go shopping without Warren inviting himself along. In the end, she was grateful her promotion gave her an excuse to leave town and end her relationship with him.

She had learned about herself in the process. She needed freedom, and she was going to have to work hard to maintain it. Oh yes, there would be room in her life for men, but they would have to accept her on her own terms. How it was all going to work out was hard for her to imagine at this point. She knew she didn't want any more clingy relationships.

When Katie slows down for the harbor entrance, she gets a chance to ask the men where they'd like to be dropped off.

Silver Jack replies, "I live on a boat in the inner harbor. If you can take me there, it will save me a lot of trouble."

She agrees and follows his directions. Once alongside the dock, she drops fenders over the side to protect her craft from bumping or rubbing. Securing her vessel with lines fore and aft, she helps the men unload the skiff.

She hands Josh one of her business cards and flashes another trademark smile. "The department has lots of educational programs. I'd love to come and share what we're doing with your students. My cell phone and email address are both on the card." She waits, feeling anxious for his reaction. "I'll be in Wrangell every other week for the rest of the summer keeping track of the salmon runs."

Josh takes her hand and gives it a firm shake. "It was my pleasure getting to meet you Katie. You saved me from paddling all night and made my transition to civilization a lot more pleasant than I ever expected. I'll be sure to give you a call. At the very least, I owe you a dinner for helping us out."

Katie finds herself saying, "I'd like that." Before anything else blurts out of her mouth, she walks back to her boat and climbs in. She allows Josh to untie her lines and toss them to her.

Smiling broadly, Katie waves goodbye and pulls away from the dock. She steers the craft over to the marina station so her boat will be fueled up and ready to go in the morning. Her first summer she learned you have to take care of your boat and your equipment before you take care of yourself. After two days away from town, she is eager for a hot shower. After spending seven days upriver Josh will likely appreciate a shower that much more. She gives herself a shake. Imagining Josh in a shower is too much distraction.

Chapter 29: Division

Clay's sides burn. The climb back up the steep ridge from Silver Jack's camp has been brutal. It took the two men more than two hours to make it to the top of the chute between the rocky outcroppings.

To make matters worse, the white socks had found them in the timber and had stuck with them without letup as they climbed the steep hillside. With no repellant, they cut switches from a cedar limb and spent every step slapping their bodies to keep the black flies from landing on them and biting through their clothing. Clay had several painful lumps, and he knew each would be difficult to live with when they began to itch.

Clay hurries to catch up with Lenn. Fortunately, the trail begins to side hill the ridge instead of climbing it. The sun hangs hot overhead, causing him to sweat. After ninety minutes, the two men begin the gentle descent to the lake and their tent. Clay looks at his watch; it's late morning, nearly eleven. The two men have been on the trail for almost twelve hours. When they reach their tent, Clay lays his rifle against a nearby tree and digs through his pack for mosquito repellant and food supplies.

Clay asserts his leadership, feeling this is a crucial point in his delicate relationship with Lenn. "We need to get out of here as fast as possible. I'm going to suggest we divide our tasks. You can collect the diamonds, I hope."

Lenn nods, "Yes. I helped Marty dig for the diamonds after he'd found the first specimens. I can do that while you take the GPS and get readings so we can make a claim. Let me tell you how I'd do it." Lenn points out areas around the lake he believes would be approximate locations for the corners to the claim site. "Try to center the claim on the point across the lake where the cliff has a horseshoe shaped divot in it. That's where I'll be digging."

Clay spots the landmark Lenn describes. "What size did you say we could have for a claim?"

Lenn scowls and responds, "Six hundred feet by fifteen hundred feet. Weren't you paying attention?"

Shaking his head, Clay retorts, "Steady, I want to make sure I do it right. I'll get started as soon as I finish eating. I'm going to have to take my first reading near where you'll be working so I can make sure I center the claim."

While eating dehydrated fruit and jerky, Clay familiarizes himself with the GPS unit. Fortunately, he's used it before and has the instructions. He sets a waypoint for the tent and records this information. By the time he is ready to go, Lenn has prepared a daypack with the items he will need, and the two men set out around the lake.

Soon the hillside gets steeper and the boulder field below the cliffs makes traveling slow and difficult. Lenn angles uphill and aims for the divot. They trudge through a patch of packed snow and come up against the scarp.

Lenn points above their heads. "Check out this fault. It runs the opposite way from all the other faults on this rock face. Marty climbed up to the first ledge to find the diamonds."

The two men climb eight feet to reach the first part of the ledge. Once on the shelf, they follow it for thirty feet until they reach the edge of the divot.

At this point, Clay spots black veins in the rock. Lenn turns around and smiles. "This is it. The digging is slow due to the hardness of the rocks. If you center on this point, you should be fine. The trick is which way to make the long part on the claim. Perhaps the long side should run north-south, but I'll leave it to you to figure out."

Clay stops and sets a waypoint, then calculates the distance to the waypoint near their tent. When he finds it's nearly 700 feet, he is not surprised. At this point, he realizes calculating exact locations for the corners of their claim will be more difficult and time consuming than he'd first thought.

Clay turns to his partner, "Hey, this is going to take me awhile. I'll meet you back at the tent, a bit before dark."

Clay climbs down the cliff to the boulder field and retraces his steps back to the lake and around it, until he gets to the shoulder of the escarpment. He finds it difficult to retrace his steps uphill. At several points, he is forced to pull his way upward using the thick brush. Climbing the hill is hot work, and he is grateful when he breaks out on the ridge above the vent.

He follows yesterday's route through the fault above the cliff and walks in a great arc around the hole in the ground. Using the GPS unit, he watches the display and keeps walking until he forms a straight line with the previous two waypoints. He stops and makes a new waypoint before checking the distance to the center of the claim. Clay discovers he is roughly 500 feet, horizontally, from Lenn. He looks at the terrain perpendicular to the line he has just created. If he moves a hundred feet farther away from Lenn, he will be centered on the saddle of the ridge. From there he could travel 300 feet in either direction, perpendicular to his current line, and establish the two northern corners for the claim. The resulting rectangle would be 600 feet by 1,200 feet. Smaller than the dimensions Lenn specified, but it would save him hours of hard work on steep hillsides.

This will be good enough. An hour later, he records the location of the second of the two northern waypoints and marks the location with a tiny pyramid of rocks. He turns and looks south, he must return to their tent and find waypoints to the east and west to finish his work. From his vantage point high on the eastern shoulder of the saddle, the easiest route is to follow his track back to the lake.

By six, Clay reaches the tent. He checks the visual display on his GPS, and walks east, keeping track of the distance covered. At 300 feet, he sets another waypoint and uses his knife to blaze a nearby tree on all sides. Heading back to camp he repeats the process to create the final corner of the claim, to the west.

It's almost seven thirty. It will be dark in a little over two hours and he needs to hook up with Lenn. He hikes out of the woods to the lake and scans the cliff face for his partner. Finding him, crouched low in the divot, he considers his options.

He could try moving their tent closer to Lenn's location. The big problem with this idea is he did not recall a level spot alongside the lake where they could pitch their tent.

Clay stretches out and watches for Lenn's return aware of the pain from infected white sock bites. He drags a log to use for a headrest to a grassy spot where he can watch for his partner. Lying in the warm sunshine, he removes his pistol from his holster and holds it on his lap, out of sight under his jacket. He relaxes and listens to a gentle breeze rustling the leaves of the willows alongside the brook. Within minutes he falls asleep.

Chapter 30: Gambling

I carefully tuck Katie's business card in my pocket and watch her motor away. What a pretty woman. I can't help but be attracted to her infectious smile. On a physical level, Katie is major eye candy. With her wavy blonde hair, trim athletic body, sparkly eyes,, and brilliant smile, she is easy to notice. She's probably a couple of years out of college. Her skin has a healthy bronzed look, and it's obvious the outdoor work suits her well.

I turn back to the task at hand and help Jack unload the rest of our equipment and put it away. He asks me to take apart the rifle and oil it, so it won't pit or rust. While we work, I ask, "What are next steps for filing a claim. Where do you have to go?"

"I need to go to Ketchikan. As soon as we get the equipment cleaned up, we should check the ferry schedule. Can you run me over to the terminal?"

I'm exhausted, but I don't hesitate. "Sure. I'd be glad to."

When we are finished putting away Jack's equipment, he gets what he needs so he can take a shower at the Laundromat. I gather up my pack and dirty clothing, while Jack attaches Blackie's leash. We walk up the dock toward the marina. Blackie bristles at every dog on the dock, and each one moves out of his way or stays as far away as possible.

Because I left my Subaru parked at my apartment, we walk there first. It isn't far from the marina, but both of us walk at a snail's pace due to our sore muscles and tired feet. The route is uphill the last two blocks, and it is tough. When we reach my place, I leave Jack and Blackie outside, while I go in and retrieve my car keys. I open the passenger door for them. "Let's go and check out the schedule."

I drive through Wrangell to the ferry terminal. In the last week the town has grown in my eyes. At the terminal, I get out of the vehicle with Jack, and we check out the schedules posted on the bulletin board. Finding the southbound schedules, I look up Wrangell and discover there are three boats stopping at the harbor each week. "There's one tonight at eleven fifteen."

Jack smiles, "This works out great. It's almost eight thirty. I've got time to shower and get a bite to eat before I go. Will you give me a ride back over here later?"

"Of course, why don't you buy your ticket, and I'll drop you at the Laundromat."

Jack shuffles his feet, "Josh, I'm going to need your help on a couple of things."

It's my turn to feel awkward, "What do you need?"

Jack looks directly into my eyes, "First, I'm going to need you to watch Blackie for a few days until I return. He can't travel with me on the ferry, unless he's in a dog kennel on the car deck. I'd rather not put him through it if I can help it."

I nod my head, "I'll be glad to do it. What else?"

Jack coughs, "You're going to have to gamble on our find. I'll need one hundred thirty-five dollars to file a claim for you. I've done it before, and this amount covers the recording, one year of maintenance, and the location fee. We can fill out the forms tonight, and you can sign them before I leave."

I laugh at Jack, "It isn't gambling. Not when I've been shot at. I'd be crazy not to spend the money after all the work we've put into this."

With the funding issue settled, Jack goes inside the terminal to purchase a ticket, while I hop in my jeep to stay with Blackie. The dog greets me with a sniff and enjoys it when I scratch him behind the ears. As fierce as the dog looks and behaves, he warms to you when you are part of his pack. When Jack returns, I drive through town to the Laundromat near the marina.

On the way past the Diamond C, I'm reminded of Anne and her daughter. I wonder if she'll be working the next time I stop by for breakfast. I've thought of Anne every day. It crosses my mind I am afraid to ask her for a date. Perhaps being burned by Kaeli has ruined my confidence, but I can come up with lots of reasons why Anne might say no and few reasons why she'd say yes. I remember the same fear paralyzing me when I was twenty years old. Given the extra years and experience, I'm going to have to ask her and take my chances. My odds of getting a yes from her will not improve with more time and exposure, either she's interested or she's not.

I'm so deep in thought I almost drive past the Laundromat. I drop off Jack and Blackie, and we agree to meet in forty-five minutes at the Marine Bar for dinner. I drive two blocks to my apartment and go inside. The first order of business is to strip out of my filthy clothing and take a hot shower.

Shampooing my hair twice, I let the water run down my back and legs until the temperature fades to warm. Toweling off, I comb my hair and dress as fast as I can. I write a check to give Jack for the claim application, gather my notes from the GPS and lock up my apartment.

Blackie is tied up to the sign by the bar, so Jack is ahead of me. Inside, I find him drinking a root beer. His hair is damp, and he sports a clean flannel shirt and jeans.

While we wait for our meals, Jack drags out the claim applications, and we fill them out. I supply basic personal information as well as fill in the longitude and latitude data for the corners of each claim. I give Jack his money and ask him if he needs me to do anything while he's gone.

"Could you check on my boat every day?" He hands me two zip-lock bags. "These are most of the specimens we found. One of the bags has two that are a different color from the rest. Also, they change color when you expose them to light. I don't want to take them all. Why don't you go to the local bank tomorrow and get a safe deposit box."

Perhaps Jack is being a little melodramatic, but I remember being shot at and nod my head in agreement. I take the stones and drop them into my pocket to keep them out of sight.

The food is wonderful; the jo-jos hot and tender. I load them up with salt and cocktail sauce, and I'm as satisfied as if I'd been eating at the finest restaurant in Denver. We sit back and enjoy our root beer. My belly is full, I'm warm and clean, and it's a long way from Jump Off where our day began.

After I pay for dinner, we walk to Jack's boat and get the pack he will use for traveling. He entrusts me with the key to his boat. Back in my apartment I search the Internet for a gemologist in Ketchikan and also find the address for the mining claim office.

Loading up, we drive through town to the ferry terminal. Along the way, Jack points out the incoming ferry. "All the state ferry's have navy blue hulls with a gold stripe," he says. "You can spot them five miles away."

Once we get to the terminal, Jack looks at his watch. "Our timing is good; the ferry will leave in thirty minutes. I plan to get one of the reclining chairs on the observation deck and be asleep before we leave dock. I'll try my best to be back in three days, but a lot will depend on the ferry schedule."

I shake Jack's hand. "Good luck. I wish I could go with you, but one of us has to stay here and take care of Blackie. If you get back and don't find me at my apartment, try the high school."

Jack points at my rig, "Don't wait here for me, you're tired and need rest. I'll be all right."

When Jack enters the terminal, I return to my jeep. Blackie whines and watches for his master as we pull out of the parking lot. I urge him to move up into the passenger seat and reassure him with a pat and a scratch behind the ears.

Back at my apartment, I take Blackie for a short walk, so he can do his business before bringing him inside. I get two stainless steel bowls out of my kitchen and fill one with water and open a can of dog food. Despite eating earlier, he has no trouble downing the contents of the extra-large can.

I get ready for sleep, and Blackie lies down on the floor near my bed. He looks at me and whines. He's worried about Jack.

I reach down and pat Blackie on the neck. "Let's go to sleep, partner. It won't do us any good to worry. He'll be back in a few days."

Chapter 31: No Questions

A boot step on loose rock jolts Clay awake. He opens his eyes; through his eyelashes he watches Lenn striding toward him along the bar. He slips the safety of his pistol to the fire position. Nonchalantly, he stretches his other arm over his head. He doesn't want to give Lenn the idea he'd been deep asleep. He wants Lenn to believe he has been patiently waiting for his return.

Clay can tell Lenn is tired by the set of his shoulders and his stride. He identifies with the man's exhaustion as well as his fierce determination. When Lenn is twenty feet away, he rises to his feet and deliberately holsters his pistol so Lenn can watch him do it. "Well, how did it go?"

"Frankly, it hasn't gone well at all. I spent all afternoon breaking rocks, and found two specimens. I can't figure it out. When Marty did it, he didn't have as much trouble breaking the rocks apart as I did."

Clay screws up his face, "How many diamonds do you need to file a claim?"

Lenn shrugs his shoulders. "Only one, but it would be nice to walk out of here with a dozen or so. To my way of thinking, we need to make this trip worth the trouble, and what happens if these specimens don't have any commercial value. I'd hate to lose all this work over a technicality."

Clay contemplates for a minute, "Let's go make our meal while we consider our options. I'm starving."

As they walk back to their tent, Clay assumes Lenn is lying regarding the number of diamonds he's found. He wouldn't put it past the bastard to lie, if he thought he could get away with it and pocket a few diamonds for himself.

Back at the tent, the two men set up their portable cooking stove and boil water to make beef stroganoff. Clay removes two packages. He laughs at the advertising on the container claiming it will satisfy two hikers. With a dry weight of less than five ounces per package, they're more appetizers than meals.

While the water is boiling, Clay presses for more information, "So, what are our options?"

Lenn hands Clay a spoon, "We could hike out tonight, although we may be too tired to pull another all-nighter. The other option is we sleep until daylight. In the morning, we get up and take our gear with us partway around the lake so we don't have to backtrack. We work for two or three hours in the morning and get as many diamonds as we can. Afterward, we push all the way out to the jet sled. From there, we run our way back to Wrangell. It'll be way after dark when we get there."

Clay considers their choices. "Is it possible the other guys might be getting back to Wrangell tonight?"

Lenn shrugs his shoulders. "I suppose it's possible. How old is this prospector?"

Clay sneers, "Silver Jack has got to be pushing eighty. My bet is he can't cover the ground very fast. We might be able to beat him if we get back to Wrangell early enough tomorrow we can charter a plane to fly us to Ketchikan. He doesn't have the kind of money it would take to pay for a plane. Most likely he'll use the ferry and it takes nearly seven hours to get there, plus he might have to wait as long as thirty hours for one going south." Clay pauses, "We've got a decent chance of beating him if we go now."

He waits until the water boils before Clay adds a measure into each of the two packages of beef stroganoff. He hands Lenn one of the packages and keeps one. Following the instructions on the package, he seals the bag for three minutes, and stirs. He takes a bite and chews slowly. "I hate to say it, but we should hike out to the sled tonight. We could be in Wrangell by noon tomorrow. It would allow us to file our claim tomorrow afternoon."

Lenn doesn't look happy. Abruptly, he jams a stick in the

ground, "You're right. We need to hike out tonight. As soon as we finish eating, we'll climb up to the saddle. It would be nice to be finished with the uphill part by the time it gets dark."

Clay and Lenn complete their meal and pack their gear. Lenn groans picking up his pack. "We could save ourselves ten pounds apiece if we didn't have to pack out all our food. We don't want to leave anything here though, because the claim jumpers might find it. I suggest we unload the food when we've passed through the saddle."

Following Lenn, Clay falls into the familiar pattern they have used since leaving the sled. They climb the steep hill beside the great hole in the ground and pass through the saddle before it gets dark. Fortunately, a solid meal has revived them enough they make it up the hill without major difficulty. With the saddle behind them, they stop and remove their food and bury it under a pile of rocks near an outcropping. They also get out their flashlights and prepare for another night of stumbling through the Alaskan wilderness.

Even though the two men must go slowly due to the darkness, they make better time going downhill than they did on their way into the claim site. They stagger into the place where they stayed beside Government Creek slightly before two in the morning. Clay is glad to get to their old camp but is discouraged when he realizes it's four hours until they reach their boat.

At four o'clock, first light teases them before becoming strong enough to help them. With daylight, their speed increases hardly at all, because both men are at the end of their endurance. At six in the morning, they arrive at their jet sled and collapse.

With a final burst of energy, they push the sled into the water and turn it around. Both men get their feet wet. Within minutes they are headed across the lake and downstream. Lenn pilots the sled while Clay plots.

He gets Lenn's attention and shares his plan, "We need to stop at Kadin Island and stash the equipment. When we get to Wrangell, I'll take the GPS, our notes, and the diamonds and arrange for a flight to Ketchikan. I know an acquaintance who won't ask any questions and who can be trusted to keep quiet." He gloats. "It surely pays to have leverage over other people. I've been waiting a

long while to call in this little favor, and this is the perfect time."

Chapter 32: Waiting

Silver Jack slings his pack over one shoulder and walks down the ramp and onto the ferry dock in Ketchikan. He isn't surprised to find it raining, because this part of Alaska averages 160 inches of rain each year. It's six o'clock, and he has three hours to walk two miles to the main part of town and get breakfast along the way. He strides into the terminal and purchases a return ticket on the next ferry headed north. The ferry departs in two days, at 1:10 p.m.

Instead of getting a taxi, he walks south along Tongass Avenue. The city has an unusual layout; it isn't a harbor but instead is a narrow passage between two islands. On the west side of the passage is Gravina Island, which hosts the airport. To get to the city from the airport, travelers must take a water taxi. Fortunately for him, the ferry terminal is on Revillagigedo Island, where the town of Ketchikan trims the east side of the narrow passage.

Across the street from the ferry terminal, he takes his time over breakfast, as he is certain the jewelry store won't open until at least nine o'clock. The cinnamon roll is excellent and as big as the waitress promised. He leaves change for a tip near his plate, pays his bill at the counter, and heads out into the steady drizzle.

He hikes south for a mile and the street changes its name, aptly, to Water Street. He spots a Super 8 motel down a side street, marking it for later use. Another half-mile brings him to city center. Here a series of streets run at an obtuse angle to his course along the waterway. Where Water Street turns away from the shoreline, it changes its name, becoming one of the angled streets. At this intersection, Front Street continues south, parallel to the water.

Keeping out of the rain as much as possible, he crosses Dock Street and Mission Street. On the west side of Front Street, he can count three cruise ships tied up at the dock. They are tall and wide, far too big to stop in Wrangell. Nearly every store holds Alaskan or Native jewelry.

His route follows the street as it curves left and becomes Mill Street. From the middle of the block, he spots the jewelry store on his list, at the corner of Main Street.

After crossing at the light, he can read the jewelry store hours. Today is Friday, so he has roughly an hour to kill until the shop opens. He decides to look for the Federal Building. Finding it should save him time after he finishes with the jeweler.

Walking north on Main Street for a block, he turns right on Mission Street. The street bends southeast, and he follows it past St. John's Mission. He finds the Federal Building wedged between Mission Street and Mill Street. The signs at the entrance indicate the building holds the headquarters of the US Forest Service for the Tongass National Forest, the US General Services Administration, plus the US Bureau of Land Management. Signs near the entrance show the building is open until five.

He strolls past the Federal Building until three streets converge, just before crossing Ketchikan Creek. Hanging over downtown, the rocky, forested foothills are dotted with two and three story buildings, each one topped with a steeply pitched roof to shed rain and snow. He is used to the wet and low hanging, dark clouds. Even so, it feels as if Ketchikan is engulfed in a dank fogbank.

On the other side of the next street is Ketchikan Creek. The branch is powerful and swift, contained by the hard, black rock serving as the base for the entire city. Across and upstream, is the famous Ketchikan Creek boardwalk. With most of the businesses built out over the edge of the torrent, the scene is rustic and charming at the same time. It's a famous stop for the crowds of tourists pouring off the cruise ships.

Turning, he follows Mill Street two blocks to get back to the jewelry store. He arrives there ten minutes before the store opens, so he kills time by window shopping, keeping to areas under overhanging roofs and awnings to avoid the rain. Everything is too expensive, especially the jewelry.

He waits while a young woman with colorful tattoos unlocks the store doors. He follows her inside and asks her about the gemologist. She frowns, "No. He's not in yet. He usually gets here at ten. Can I help you?"

Silver Jack shrugs, "I need an appraisal for some rough diamonds."

The clerk looks surprised, but doesn't falter. "You'll want to meet with Mr. Boggs. If you'd like to wait, I can fix you up with coffee as soon as I get it brewed." The young woman points to one of the back rooms. "Why don't you follow me back to our break area? You might be more comfortable waiting there."

The break room is clean. He sits at a small table with a stack of newspapers. The young lady starts a pot of coffee and directs him to help himself when it's finished brewing. "There are clean coffee cups above the sink."

The strong, black coffee hits the spot. With the mug in his hand, he browses a recent copy of the local newspaper. He skims the classifieds looking in the marine section for boats and outboard motors. He has been researching a replacement skiff for a long time. His review of the ads is casual, because there is no way he would buy one in Ketchikan; it's too far to run the craft to Wrangell and too costly to ship.

Chapter 33: Courage

I get up late in the morning and find Blackie patiently waiting for me. It's easy to tell the big dog needs a trip outside to relieve his bladder. I dress and attach Blackie's leash to his collar. Outside, he pulls me down the street, relieving himself on every landmark bush or post. I'm amused at the dog's capacity to mark territory.

Nearly two blocks from my apartment, a dog waits in the middle of the street. This dog is dirty white with an ear torn to ribbons, giving him an intimidating aspect. Blackie ignores him, and I'm surprised at this reaction. Not wanting a dogfight, I pull Blackie around and walk in the opposite direction. Without warning, I hear a snarl, and I turn too slow to stop the white dog rushing to attack Blackie. I jump to one side, prepared to deliver a swift kick if necessary to break things up but find myself off balance.

Blackie chooses this moment to lunge at the attacking dog, and I fall on my hands and knees in the street, losing my grip on Blackie's leash. He strikes the other dog squarely in the chest with his massive shoulder and knocks the dog to the ground. In a blink of the eye, Blackie has the other dog's throat in his powerful jaws.

I get to my feet; mortified at the thought Blackie will kill the white dog. Before I can take a step, I realize the white dog and Blackie are not moving. Blackie withholds the killing strike. Instead, he growls from deep inside his chest. This is a low, short growl, full of menace and portent. The white dog licks his lips, lowers his head and whines in a simpering fashion. With another short growl, Blackie releases the throat of the white dog and lifts his head a few inches. Manifest power is on display. His lips are pulled back and his gleaming fangs are exposed. The white dog licks his lips again and slowly, carefully, slinks away.

After the white dog retreats into a poorly fenced yard, I walk over and pick up Blackie's leash. I pat him on the neck and gently scratch him behind the ears. He looks up and our eyes lock. He smiles, and I find the reaction to be contagious. I hoot in jubilation and relief, "Blackie, you are the alpha male."

Later, after eating ham and eggs for breakfast, Blackie watches while I do laundry in my apartment. My clothes and equipment reek of smoke. I wash my raingear, backpack and other gear in my kitchen sink to remove the pungent odor.

I choose to keep my backcountry beard for a day or two longer. With my washer and dryer loaded, my plan is to go to Stikine Bank and deposit the specimens in a safe deposit box. I'm not sure how the safe deposit box process will work, so I find a medium sized envelope among my stationery and drop the two bags of stones inside. I envision myself placing the envelope in the safe deposit box under the watchful eyes of the branch officer. Unloading the envelope, I count the specimens twice. Both times I come up with fifty-two stones. I mark this number on the inside of the envelope and add the date so I can use this in the future as a ledger, in case we withdraw any of the stones.

I load Blackie into my Subaru, crack the windows to keep the vehicle from getting stuffy, and drive downtown. Leaving Blackie in my rig, I go inside the bank.

While I am waiting for the bank officer, a woman entering catches my eye. I watch her walk across the lobby, and I can't keep my eyes off her. Curvaceous, shapely, voluptuous, are some of the terms leaping into my brain.

The mystery woman strides into the lobby as if it's her personal mansion. The swing of her hips makes my groin tighten. Her clothes are designed to enhance her figure; a low-cut, cream color, silk blouse reveals as much as it conceals. Her navy wool skirt stops well above the knee and accentuates her slim waist and muscular thighs. Dark sienna hair bursts loosely from her head to her shoulders, striking the perfect balance between looking completely natural and difficult to achieve at the same time. Her outfit, hairdo, accessories, pearl earrings, and necklace shout money: scads of money.

I resist the impulse to let my head follow her across the room. Instead I study her with my peripheral vision. When she stops, she leans forward to place her purse on the counter. One high-heeled pump is left on point, behind the heel of the other shoe. This action leverages calf muscles, thigh muscles, her butt, and the small of her back into angles defying imagination.

I find myself fighting the urge to act showy so I can attract her attention. I beat this urge away with all the self-will I can muster. After a tough moment, I'm in control of my body, outwardly calm, and patiently waiting to be helped.

On her way out, she pauses three steps in front of me, searching in her purse. Finally, she pulls out dark red lipstick and touches up her lips. She turns to examine me, rolling her lips to spread the lipstick and giving me a sly smile. Without speaking, she arches one eyebrow, parts her lips, exposing the tip of her tongue, and slides it along her top lip from one corner of her mouth to the center, before pivoting away and striding out of the building.

I'm left flushed, excited, and a little weak in the knees. I resist the compulsion to run after her, but I find it impossible to ban the image of her curvaceous figure from my memory. I'm in a state of confusion, when I hear a cough at my elbow. "Excuse me, sir. Are you waiting for help?"

I turn and face a thin, middle-aged gentleman in a three-piece suit. I haven't seen one worn, except in old movies, so I'm a little unprepared to face one in real life. I stand and hold out my hand, doing my best to recover my composure, while I try to forget the way the mystery woman's skirt moved as she walked away. "Yes, my name is Josh Campbell, and I'd like to make arrangements for a safe deposit box."

His grip is firm and fast. Directly he continues, "My name is John Cuthbert. I'm the manager here. You've noticed Claire. Her grandfather started this bank almost fifty years ago. Why don't you come over to my desk, and I'll help you set up an account for your deposit box."

I follow him to his desk in a corner of the lobby. Once seated, he describes the various plans, sizes, and features of their safe deposit boxes. I select a size that will fit and arrange for the monthly rental to be taken out of my bank account. In addition, Jack is authorized to access the safe deposit box. When it comes to "identify a beneficiary", I'm at a loss. There is no one I can list so I leave this question unanswered.

With the specimens in safekeeping, I head outside and take Blackie for a ride south, down Zimovia Highway. I roll down the window, so Blackie can enjoy the scents along the winding and scenic two-lane road following the western shore of Wrangell Island.

Five miles south of town, we come to the marina at Shoemaker Bay. This marina is bustling with activity, filled with fishing boats and a number of yachts. Adjacent to the marina is a recreation park with picnic tables, shelters, tennis courts and a playground. I notice the recreation area also includes spaces for tent and RV campers.

I pull over along the highway past the marina and spot a sign indicating the clearing is a cleanup project by the Alaska Department of Environmental Conservation. From the sign, I also learn this was formerly the site of the Wrangell Institute, which is currently owned by the City of Wrangell. I've always been excited by history and this site interests me. What was the Wrangell Institute? Why is it no longer here? Why is it a cleanup site? I find a notepad and make a note to research this topic as soon as I can.

Satisfied I will not forget to look into this mystery, I switch to considering Anne. I am pretty sure showing up at the café frequently isn't a workable strategy for getting a date. For starters, lots of guys have walked into the café and flirted with Anne. If I'm going to stand out, I'm going to have to do the unexpected.

I drive back to Wrangell and the café, aiming to find out when Anne gets off work. The town is an interesting mix of houses. For the most part, bright colors dominate the exteriors; vibrant, steeply pitched metal roofs also add to the festive display. I assume the brilliant tones are chosen to overcome the dull sameness of the gray weather. I follow a side street and pull around to the back corner of the cafe. It's apparent this is the loading dock and entrance for employees. I hang around and come up with an idea.

Gathering my courage, I approach the back door and knock. Within twenty seconds, a gray haired woman answers the door. “May I help you?”

“Yes. Ma’am, I was hoping to talk to Anne. Could you help me out and tell me what time she gets off? I’d also be mighty obliged if you keep my being here a secret.”

The lady cackles with delight, “Isn’t this interesting. Tell me your name, pretty boy.”

“I’ll tell you mine if you tell me yours.”

She cackles again, “You’re kind of cheeky aren’t you, young man. Well, my name is Helen, and I cook the second shift here. You come in, and I’ll fatten you up a bit.”

“Helen. It’s nice to meet you. My name is Josh Campbell. I’ve been in before, and the food is excellent.”

Helen’s face splits into a huge smile, “I have food on the grill, and so I have to run. Anne gets off at two. Her red pickup is over there. I’m not sure it will help you any sneaking up on her. She’s been down on men for a spell, and I reckon she can handle the likes of you, same as all the others.”

“Thank you for the advice, Helen. I’ll keep it in mind.” I step back from the porch and feel foolish. At least I had the information I wanted. Now it depends on timing, and luck.

Back at the jeep, I look at my watch and find I have almost two hours until Anne gets off work. I give Blackie a pat on the neck, and we head off to my apartment to do research.

#

Forty-five minutes later, I’ve learned the Wrangell Institute was a boarding school for First Nation children built in the 1930s by the Bureau of Indian Affairs. Like all Native boarding schools, pulling children out of their homes and taking away their language was controversial. Most of the schools, including this one, punished the young students if they spoke their language. I found several reports indicating the children were beaten with razor straps if they spoke even one word. During World War II, the site had been a relocation camp for the Aleut people while the Aleutian Islands were under attack by the Japanese. The boarding school program ended in the

1970s.

Later, the Forest Service used the site for the Young Adult Conservation Corps. In 1995, the property was transferred to the City of Wrangell. When polluted soils were found on the property, a site assessment was performed, and the buildings were torn down in 2001. The Alaska Department of Environmental Conservation is scheduled to start its cleanup of the petroleum-contaminated soils this year, 2007.

After I complete my review of the conservation website, I web search for "Wrangell Institute" and find many pages of links to stories by individuals who attended the boarding school, a study of the impacts of Alaskan boarding school policies on the tribes and the culture of the region, plus photographs of the Institute during the time of the Aleutian relocation.

I sit back and consider what I've learned. Not five miles away is a landmark to eighty years of local and national history. It even has environmental science thrown in to spice things up a little bit. Can I find a way to follow my curriculum and make use of this nearby learning opportunity?

Abruptly, I realize it's almost two o'clock. I grab Blackie's leash, hook him up and we spring for the jeep. After making a fool of myself in front of Helen, I don't want to miss my opportunity to link up with Anne. Maybe my crazy idea will work.

Chapter 34: Threats

Clay uses his cell phone as soon as they reach the edge of the cell reception area for Wrangell and arranges for the pilot, Hennessey, to be waiting for him. They make a fast job hiding the boat equipment on Kadin Island and reach town near noon. Clay regrets losing the time to hide the equipment, but it wouldn't do to have equipment from Sealaska Corporation show up in their boat. This could initiate questions they did not want to answer. Following the sketchy plan they contrived on the way to Wrangell, Lenn would deal with putting away the rest of their equipment and find a room in town.

On the way to the airport, Clay curses at Lenn for his bull-headedness. The two men had fought over Clay taking the diamonds. In the end, Clay had been forced to threaten Lenn with turning him in before he would part with the stones. He was more convinced than ever Lenn had found more and was keeping them to himself.

On the short flight to Ketchikan, the conversation is limited to weather and politics. This is the way Clay prefers; he'd warned Hennessey there were to be no questions. Upon landing at the Ketchikan airport, he tells Hennessey. "I'll be back in three hours. I'll look for you in the bar." Acerbically he adds, "This time, be sober enough to fly."

From the airport, Clay catches the water taxi to the city, and hails a cab to take him downtown to the Federal Building. Once inside the building, he finds his way to the mining claim office. He glances at the clock on the wall. It's ten minutes after 2 p.m.

Chapter 35: Piece of the Action

Silver Jack gives up on the gemologist after waiting several hours. He returns to the showroom, standing near one of the display cases until the young woman with the tattoos isn't busy with a customer. He asks, "Are you sure he's coming in today?"

"Oh, yes. He always comes in, although there are days he comes in later than others. But it's possible he had an appointment or meeting this morning. If you don't want to wait, I could get your phone number and he could call you later today."

Silver Jack remains and returns to the break room. Forty minutes past noon, he is elated when a medium height, balding man in a sweater and slacks enters the break room and thrusts out his hand, "Hello Sir. My name is Boggs. I'm a Graduate Gemologist. How can I help you?"

The prospector stands and shakes Boggs' hand. "My name is Jack Hunter." When he catches a whiff of whiskey on the man's breath he almost walks out of the building. "I have specimens I believe are rough diamonds. I want to file a mining claim, and I need written confirmation. Can you help me?"

Boggs steps back, the fingers on his left hand idly strum the nearby counter top, twice, before he answers. "Are you hoping to sell your specimens to me?"

He swings his head back and forth, "No. I only need written confirmation so I can file a claim."

Boggs relaxes, "Okay. Well, I have experience with rough diamonds, and I've taken a couple of courses, so I can confirm if they are real. I can also give you an indication if they would be industrial grade or commercial grade. I'd have to send them away to get them evaluated for you, if you wanted to get specific information on their value. Will that be good enough?"

Silver Jack responds, "It will have to do for today. Where would you like me to show you my specimens?"

Boggs considers the question, "I'm kind of busy; can you leave your specimens with me and come back tomorrow?"

He feels anxious. He is uncertain if he is ahead of his competitors and fearful they might file before he does. In addition, as nice as Boggs presents himself, he wouldn't trust the man to keep his diamonds without a way to confirm he would get the originals back. He fudges, "I need to get my claim filed today since the claims office will be closed for the weekend."

"Let's go into my office," Boggs turns and leads the way to another room. It's piled high with boxes, tools and a wide variety of jewelry projects. "I do repairs, and restore heirlooms in addition to making jewelry of my own." He rummages among his tools. "First, I'll run these to find out if they show up as diamonds on the tester, then I'll look at the stones with a magnifier."

Silver Jack pulls a zip-lock bag out of his pocket and hands two stones to Boggs.

The gemologist lofts the two stones in his hand. "Well the weight is right and they look like rough diamonds. Let's check them with the tester." Boggs picks up a rectangular instrument half the size of a pack of cigarettes with a pencil shaped probe on one end. "This uses thermal conductivity and also measures the reflectivity of the stone to determine if it's a diamond."

With the stones lying on top of a felt rectangle, the gemologist touches the probe to one of the stones. Within a few seconds, a green LED glows. Boggs shifts to the second stone with the same result. He puts his tool down and looks at the prospector. "Green means your stones are diamonds Mr. Hunter. Congratulations!" Boggs smile is authentic. "I'll examine them with my loupe and check for clarity, orientation and inclusions. I'm no expert, but I should be able to tell you if these are better than industrial grade. This may take me a few moments, so please be patient."

The prospector settles back into his chair. He realizes, belatedly, he had been holding his breath during the first test. He watches Boggs carefully examine the first stone. The gemologist holds the monocular close to his right eye and the diamond in his left hand one inch below the lens. Slowly he turns the diamond back and forth, examining it from every angle. Boggs repeats the process with the second diamond.

He sets them both on velvet and leans back in his chair. "I can't observe anything that would eliminate them from being considered commercial grade. A definitive appraisal would have to wait until these have been sent to a lab. I can do it for you and send you a report. My estimate is it will cost two hundred dollars to get analyses from a lab. Are you interested?"

Silver Jack remains focused on his first priority, "Can you fix me up with something in writing I can use for filing my claim?"

Boggs pulls out a sheet of paper with the letterhead for his business. "I'll take care of it. I need to charge you twenty-five dollars for the appraisal. I'm sorry I have to charge for this, but I won't make a living if I give my time away for free."

He pulls out his wallet and extracts two bills and passes them to Boggs. "Would you like me to make a deposit on sending the diamonds to a lab or do you want me to pay when the work is done?"

Boggs shrugs, his forehead crinkling into deep lines. "If you give me a deposit, I can mail you the results as soon as they come in, it will shorten your wait."

"Okay. I'll give you two hundred in exchange for a receipt."

Mr. Boggs folds his hands and places his elbows on his desk. "That will be fine. I'll refund the difference if the cost comes in under the amount deposited."

The prospector hesitates and asks his final question, "Would you look at one more stone for me? It's different from the others because it changes color when exposed to light."

Boggs freezes then tilts his head. "Why, I'd be happy to look at another stone for you."

He hands Boggs his final specimen and anxiously watches as the gemologist tests and examines the stone. After careful review,

Boggs drops the diamond on the velvet. "I'm not sure. It could be worthless or it could be extremely valuable. The only way to find out is to let me send it to the lab for analysis. I recommend you get it analyzed."

He considers Boggs' recommendation. "How do I safeguard myself so I get these stones back?"

"I'll take magnification photographs of the rough diamonds and sign I've received them from you. Each diamond is unique so you'll be able to prove the ones you get back are the same as the ones you left with me. I'll keep a set of the photos for my records. I always do this when I send gems to a lab."

Worried about time, he doesn't hesitate, "Good. Here's cash for the lab work."

Boggs completes invoices for the written report to be used with filing the claim and the lab analyses of the three rough diamonds. Boggs adds blown up pictures of each diamond and initials these are the specimens deposited by Silver Jack. Finally, he hands the prospector his statement indicating the stones are diamonds and have commercial value. "I'm going to need a way to contact you Mr. Hunter. Where do you live?"

The prospector responds, "I live on a boat in the Wrangell marina. I'll write down my General Delivery address plus my phone number for you. I don't check the messages on my cell phone, so please don't leave a message."

Boggs leans back in his chair, "I must ask. Are you interested in selling any of your diamonds, if I come up with a good offer for them?"

"I'll need to consider it. I'd like to keep as many as possible so I can show them to a company interested in buying a share of my claim."

Boggs leans forward, one elbow on the desk. The prospector can tell the man is anxious to find a way to get a piece of the action. "How many stones do you have, are there any more similar to the one that changes color?"

Silver Jack is reluctant to be candid, at least with this stranger. "Oh, I probably have a dozen additional stones. I may have one more that's a color changer." He pushes back his chair and rises. He offers his hand to Boggs, "Thank you for your help. I'll be sure to come back if I need more assistance with getting additional appraisals. I look forward to getting the analyses, so I can raise enough funds to develop my claim."

He turns and leaves Boggs' workshop in the early afternoon. He waives goodbye to the shop girl, thanks her for the coffee, and exits the jewelry store. Within five minutes, he enters the Federal Building.

Chapter 36: Chameleons

Jason Boggs returns to his desk and the three rough diamonds. He sits down and carefully notes the color of the third diamond; it has changed to a bright yellow while being exposed to the light in his workshop. When he first was handed the gem, straight out of the darkness of the old prospector's pocket, he remembers noting its color as green. He looks at the size of the specimen and estimates a three-carat diamond might be resident in this stone. He realizes much depends on the lab analysis and the skill of the diamond cutter, but he could be holding a chameleon diamond. This stone could be worth well over one hundred thousand dollars.

He puts the stone down on the piece of velvet and cradles his forehead against the knuckles of his hands. With his thumbs, he gently massages his throbbing temples. He sighs. A man could solve a lot of problems with that kind of money. God knows, he has his share of financial troubles. His excessive drinking is more difficult to control in Alaska than anywhere he had ever lived. The continuously wet and dreary weather, lasting days and months on end, took a toll on his ability to cope with life's little problems. Recently, he had started gambling in addition to drinking. Last night was a good example; he'd started playing a game of high-stakes poker, and like most nights recently, his luck had been strong during the early evening. At 5 a.m., they woke him and gave him an invoice.

With twenty-four hours to come up with nearly twenty-three thousand dollars, paying up will bust his savings, take his entire supply of cash, and require him to sell off part of his inventory. When his wife finds out all their savings are gone, there will be hell to pay. It's pretty certain she will take the kids and fly back to Oregon, leaving him in this dump to straighten out the mess.

Jason reaches in his desk and pulls out a bottle of whiskey. He uncorks it and takes a pull from the bottle. The whiskey no longer burns going down. Sadly, it takes more and more alcohol to get him feeling good. There are times he feels bad no matter how much he drinks. He finds his future prospects gloomy, and he refuses to think about them.

He takes another swallow from the bottle. All his bad luck could be attributed to a string of events from two years ago. At first, everything he touched made money. He had started the jewelry business in Ketchikan ten years earlier, using funds from his wife's inheritance. At roughly the same time they started their shop, cruises to Alaska increased in popularity so their investment paid off handsomely. Pretty soon, Jason had to find ways to invest their extra cash and profit. He began to buy shares in local crab boats, finding those needing cash to upgrade their equipment. Occasionally for fifty thousand dollars he could buy majority interest. He used an attorney to write airtight contracts leaving him with guaranteed returns and little risk. At this point he owned the majority share in fifteen boats with a total value, on paper, of five million dollars.

Then, his bad luck started. Two years ago, one of his boats hit a reef and sank with all hands lost. Angry relatives sued when it came to light the boat lacked basic safety equipment and the Captain was drunk.

He found out his airtight contracts were not unassailable after all. The law is very clear; you can't sign away liability in a contract. After spending 150 thousand dollars in legal fees, a year ago he was forced to settle with family members for over 600 thousand dollars before his insurance kicked in and took care of the remainder. To make matters worse, his insurance company jacked the rates up on his remaining boats. When he tried to find another insurance company, no one would talk to him. He had no sooner paid up the insurance than diesel prices jumped before the season opened. They continued to climb during every day of the season. Hemorrhaging cash, his Captains got together and demanded greater returns for their crews. Unfortunately, the crab season turned out to be a bust, and they all came out of the season deep in debt.

In Ketchikan, this year's cruise ship season was in a slump due to a weak national economy. This translated into sluggish sales in his jewelry store, when he needed cash more than anything. He had hidden most of the bad news from his wife, but he knew she was starting to get suspicious. As a family, they hadn't cut back on spending while their resources faded. His wife had gotten used to spas, luxury cars, designer clothes and charitable giving. Recently, she came home in tears when one of their credit cards had been confiscated at a local retail store.

Jason gulps another shot of whiskey and wracks his memories of Wrangell. He knows the city from his survey of the region three years ago. He had considered setting up a satellite business there, but the future growth predictions showed no hope the community would grow any time soon. Anyway, only the smaller cruise ships stopped in Wrangell, as there were no amenities to attract tourists. Nobody wants to spend money to visit quaint towns with quaint harbors. He remembers the sleepy harbor a short walk from the center of town. It will not be too difficult to find Jack's boat, if he needs to do so.

Unable to stand the tension any longer, Jason shoves his bottle back inside the desk drawer. He picks up the phone and dials his brother in San Francisco. Without saying hello, Jason cuts directly to the purpose of the phone call as soon as the connection is made. "This is what I want you to do."

Chapter 37: Miracles

Anne frets waiting for Josh and Silver Jack to return. By Friday morning of the eighth day, she has resigned herself to a constant state of anxiety. She prays for news of Josh's safe return.

Their shift ends at two o'clock. As she is putting things away, Emily comes running to where she is standing behind the cash register. Her arms akimbo and her face flushed, Emily blurts out, "Mom, Josh is outside!" Emily darts away to stand near the back door, waiting for Anne to join her. Anne closes her eyes and offers a silent prayer of thanks. She opens her eyes and walks to Emily's side at the back door. Josh is sitting in his jeep.

Anne is struck by a moment of panic. Is Josh showing an interest in her by waiting outside the café or is this a coincidence? She realizes there is one way to find out. She will have to go outside, face her fears, and find out if he is waiting for her. Perhaps this guy hasn't been scared off by the fact she is the mother of a ten-year-old.

After putting away her things, and waiving goodbye to Helen, she and Emily go outside and walk up to Josh's jeep. She notes with surprise his new beard. The rugged look makes him more handsome, not that he needs help in this department.

Anne nonchalantly gestures at the café, "Didn't you feel like coming in?"

Josh smiles and leans forward, one arm on the steering wheel. "I knew you were due to get off soon, so I thought I'd hang out here and ask if you wanted to go for a walk with Blackie. It sure is good to see you both." Part of his smile is directed to Emily. "I haven't talked to anyone except Jack and Blackie in over a week, and I don't mind admitting I'm desperate for company." Josh winks at Emily.

Both Emily and Anne laugh at his pitiful expression. Anne nudges Emily, "What do you say; do you want to put him out of his misery?"

"You bet. Can I hold Blackie's leash?"

Josh opens the vehicle door and steps down, placing Blackie's leash in Emily's hand. He encourages Blackie to jump out of the jeep, and they walk past one of the town's grocery stores toward the nearby shoreline. Holding Blackie's leash, Emily is pulled ahead.

Anne is concerned, so she hangs back with Josh. With Emily concentrating on Blackie, she whispers, "Is Silver Jack alright? I've never heard of him and Blackie being separated."

Josh grins, "No, he's okay. He had to go to Ketchikan to file a claim on interesting minerals we found, and he left Blackie with me for safekeeping. He should be back in a couple of days."

Anne glances around, checking if they are being watched. Finding no one is paying attention to the trio with the dog, she asks, "So, the two of you went prospecting?"

"We sure did. We didn't find any gold, but we did find something unusual. We also covered a lot of territory. We came back last night and Jack caught the late ferry to Ketchikan."

Blackie stops, lifts his leg and urinates on a rock pile along the pathway. Embarrassed, Josh looks sheepish as Emily giggles. Anne can tell he is searching for the right words. Finally, he asks, "Did anything happen in Wrangell while I was gone?"

Anne laughs, "Oh, we had a party every night. Didn't we, Emily?"

Emily is confused, and then laughs, too. "Yes. We also had a parade with elephants and dancing flamingos."

Josh puts both hands in the air, "Okay, I surrender. I'm glad to hear it was business as usual around here. I'll make sure I check the town's social calendar before I leave again."

Anne notices all the scratches and cuts on Josh's hands and forearms. "It looks like you've tangled with a bear."

It's Josh's turn to laugh, "No, I got into a fight with devil's club, and the plant won. Next time I fight it, I want a machete and thick leather gloves."

Anne gets concerned again. "You should be careful, devil's club thorns tend to get infected easily. You'll need to keep an eye on these." She pulls Josh's arms and hands close for inspection. She gives him a glare when she finds redness around several of the cuts. "Many of these are inflamed. Do you have any iodine?"

"No."

Anne takes charge, "You're coming over to my apartment tonight and get these fixed. When can you come over?"

"I have to go to check up on Jack's boat, and then I could drop by, if you'll tell me where you live." Josh's smile melts her anger.

"I'll be expecting you, kind sir. And don't you dare skip out on this, just because it will hurt." Anne almost takes back her invitation but bites her tongue. She turns away, blinking back tears threatening to overrun her eyes. It has been a long time since she's talked to any man, except customers at the café or long-term acquaintances of her father or mother.

They walk along the shore toward the cannery, and Anne notices a crabber leaving the harbor, the deck stacked high with empty crab pots. The wind is damp and fresh with a salty tang. It isn't unusual for fishermen to leave any time of day or night as they unload at the cannery when their holds are full. Anne wants to sketch the scene, but can't because her drawing supplies are at home.

No one talks as the foursome makes its way past the waterfront museum in the Nolan Center and along the dry dock area operated by the port. Several boats are up on blocks with For Sale signs, while others are obviously in various stages of repair. This part of the shoreline is near the mouth of the harbor and is not sheltered by Point Shekeski, which forms a natural sanctuary protecting the harbor marina from the prevailing, westerly breeze.

Emily shivers, "*Brrr*. I'm cold."

In response, Josh removes his hooded sweatshirt and pulls it over Emily's head. Anne has to laugh because his sweatshirt overwhelms Emily. The waist reaches her knees and the sleeves have to be pulled up so she can hold Blackie's leash. At this point, they reach a chain-link fence bordering the cannery. Reluctantly, the group turns and heads back toward the café.

At one point, they climb down close to the water's edge, and Josh shows Emily how to skip stones. She listens intently to his instructions. "The objective is for the stone to strike the water at high speed at an acute angle, it also helps if it's spinning." He adds, "Let me show you. When I place my forefinger along the edge of the stone, I can get it to spin as I throw it." He spins a stone at the water and laughs when it goes plunk instead of skipping. "It also helps if your stone is flat, and the water is calm."

As they walk past the Nolan Center, Josh spots a bicycle locked into a bike rack. He announces, "I like bike rides. Would you girls like to go riding?"

This is an overture. Josh is searching for a way to fit in with her and Emily. She smiles sadly, "I'm sure it would be fun, Josh. But Emily has never learned to ride a bike. I'm afraid we'll have to come up with another idea." Anne can tell Emily is embarrassed. She hopes Emily's feelings are not hurt by her mother's revelation.

"That's not a problem at all," Josh announces. "I happen to be licensed in every western state as a certified bike instructor. I can teach you to ride a bike in three easy lessons. If you sign me on as your private tutor, I'll have you winning races in a month."

Stopping to look up at Josh, Emily responds enthusiastically, "Could you? I've wanted to ride a bike my whole life."

Anne is struck by this revelation. As far as she knew, Emily had never mentioned wanting to ride a bike. Perhaps she didn't know her daughter as thoroughly as she'd thought.

"You can count on me," Josh salutes Emily and holds his salute until Emily cheerfully returns the gesture.

Anne, watching the scene from a few steps away, can sense the profound impact this assurance has on her daughter. Hoping Josh is as sincere as his word, Anne realizes Emily has been set-up for major disappointment if the young man does not follow through. It will be a test of his character no one can help him with, she concludes fearfully.

When they return to their cars, Anne pulls a pad out of her

glove compartment. Flushed, she writes down her address and adds her phone number and hands it to Josh. Silently praying for strength, so she won't stumble over the words. She says, "We're expecting you in an hour. I've added my phone number in case you get lost." Without waiting for a reply, she lifts Emily into the truck and hops in herself. Waving, so she won't have to say goodbye, Anne puts the truck in gear and drives out of the parking lot.

As soon as she can, Anne turns the heat on in the truck. She realizes Emily has Josh's sweatshirt. This causes her to smile. Maybe miracles do happen when you least expect them. She'll get to spend more time with Josh.

Chapter 38: Mutual Understanding

Clay eagerly approaches the counter of the mining claims office. He notices, with growing satisfaction, there is no line.

The clerk at the counter listens to his request and hands him forms and a clipboard. "Do you need a pen?" He indicates a jar on the counter stuffed with writing utensils. "The required information is marked with an asterisk. If you need help, come find me."

Choosing a corner in the lobby, Clay fills out the forms. It takes him twenty minutes to answer the questions and five minutes to provide information on the claim's location. When Clay gets to the questions about the minerals on the site and an assessment of their value, he writes 'diamonds of commercial value' in the space provided.

When he is finished, Clay returns to the counter and the clerk accepts his paperwork and stamps it with the time. "We're going to need cash or a cashier's check for one hundred thirty-five dollars to cover all the filing fees. Also, you need to submit documentation the minerals have sufficient value before the claim can be finalized. You have ninety days to supply this information. If you fail to provide the required information within the time limit, your claim will be null and void." The clerk pauses and gives Clay a funny look. "This is interesting, I've never had a claim filed for diamonds before today, and now I have three of them. Where did you say this claim is located?"

Clay responds tersely, "I didn't say, but north of Wrangell."

The clerk pauses and looks as if he's trying to remember a different conversation. "It sounds like the claims I processed less than an hour ago. I'd better double-check. Excuse me while I go check your claim location against the earlier ones."

The clerk walks into a back room, and Clay stands nervously at the counter, feeling sick to his stomach. He berates himself for not having had Lenn drop him in Wrangell instead of stopping at Kadin Island to hide the equipment. Those two hours might have made the difference.

The clerk returns with another man. He is wearing a jacket and tie. To Clay he's young and inexperienced. "Hi. My name is David Bergvald. I'm the unit supervisor. It looks like two other claims have been filed earlier today on the same location. We can accept your claim, but you are advised it cannot be finalized for ninety days, while we research your case. You cannot touch the claim site until we notify you in writing you can move ahead. It's possible we might invalidate the earlier claims, or your claim location is partially different from the other claims."

Clay swallows his anger, barely, "Did you say claims? Can I have a copy so I can adjust my claim if necessary?" Clay seethes. It's apparent he and Lenn are holding an empty bag. His main concern now is to clarify where they stand, so they can formulate a new plan.

The unit supervisor straightens his tie. "I can't give you a copy of the claim documents, but I can give you the location as well as the name of the individuals who filed claims. It will take me five minutes."

The unit supervisor leaves, and Clay sits down in one of the soft chairs in the waiting area. Tired, dirty, and disappointed, Clay cannot come up with an acceptable plan of action before the unit supervisor returns with an envelope. "I've copied the site map and written description of the location for each claim as well as the names and addresses of the two men who filed earlier today. In a couple of days, we'll be sending letters warning you and the other two men no one can work the site until our review process is complete. If the claims of the other two men hold up, we'll notify you your claim is invalid. If their claims are invalidated, we'll complete the processing of your claim, and we'll need an assay or lab analysis to quantify the value of the minerals. Do you have any questions?"

Clay stands and looks down at the unit supervisor. He leans

forward bringing his face within inches of the younger man's, grasping the lapel of the man's jacket with one big fist. "I comprehend, you snotty little shit. But I might not need your help. It's likely me and these other guys will come to a mutual understanding in a few days." Clay watches fear spread across the face of the preppy unit supervisor, as if the man expects him to knife him right there in the Federal Building. Satisfied, Clay spins on his heel and leaves the lobby.

PART 3: THE DANCE

Chapter 39: Balance

I drive to the marina. While Blackie and I walk down the dock to check on Jack's boat, I bask in the warm glow of success. I can't get over my luck with Anne and Emily. It was so natural spending time with them along the waterfront. I wish it could have lasted longer, but I am not disappointed. After all, I have an invitation to visit their apartment. True, I couldn't call her offer to help a date; yet, I wouldn't call it a failure either. Besides, if Anne had been unavailable, she'd brush me off.

At Jack's boat I unlock the padlock and check the bilge pump, to make sure the boat isn't slowly filling up with water. Everything is fine. I take the opportunity to check out Blackie's dog food supply and make a mental note to buy more.

I don't need to take Blackie for a walk, so I drive down Front Street to the clothing and sporting goods store. Inside, I rent a girl's bike and helmet for a week. I choose a size I hope will fit Emily. I consider training wheels and discard the idea. At her size, training wheels would be difficult.

Back in my Subaru with Blackie, I pull out Anne's address, but I don't recognize the street name. I go back to my apartment, and I search the net to find directions to her home.

I don't want to show up at Anne's home empty handed. This causes me to go into a panic regarding what to bring. Should I bring traditional items like wine or flowers? I reject these ideas outright as too formal for a first meeting, especially one that isn't a date. In desperation, I remember a box of chocolates from the Rocky Mountain Chocolate Factory I'd picked up from the outlet store in

Silverthorne before I left Colorado. I've been saving it for a rainy day when I am feeling down, but this would be a far better use. It's my hope both Emily and Anne will find the chocolates to their liking.

By the time I find the chocolates and get Blackie loaded in the SUV, I worry I'll arrive late. Fortunately, her apartment is only a few minutes away, so I end up there, more or less, on time. I crank the Subaru windows down halfway so Blackie can get lots of air. Low clouds are a blessing, as Blackie will not overheat in the vehicle while I'm inside.

Anne lives in a townhouse. As I knock on her door, I spot a knot of interested neighbors watching me from the other half of the duplex. I waive casually, hoping none of them is going to be one of my students. At this point, I've not yet become recognizable, and I'm hoping to maintain this anonymity for a while longer. Once folks figure out I teach at the high school, everything I do in public will come under scrutiny. I don't mind the special attention, but I have learned it pays to be careful in public places.

I ring the doorbell, and Emily opens the door. "Hi, Emily, I've brought a gift for you and your mother for being so nice to me."

Emily accepts the chocolates solemnly. I can tell she is uncertain what to do with the box, so I suggest she give it to her mother. Not losing all her poise, Emily invites me in and closes the door behind me. "Would you like a glass of water or milk?"

"Thank you. Water will be fine."

Emily turns and leads me to a tiny kitchen. I watch as she sets down the chocolates on the kitchen table and retrieves a glass from the cupboard above the sink. She is forced to stand on her tiptoes and stretch to reach the glass. "Would you care for ice?" When I nod, she fills the glass with ice cubes and water from the dispenser in the refrigerator and hands it to me.

I indicate one of the chairs at the kitchen table, "May I sit down?"

"Sure." Emily pulls out a chair, too. "Mom will be right down. She's fixing her hair."

I smile at this revelation and take a sip from my glass. "Tell me. What has your mother planned for the cuts on my hands and arms?"

Emily's eyes grow big with concern, "This is going to hurt. A lot. She has to dig the thorns out with a needle. When she's done, she'll have to put iodine on the scratches. I sure wouldn't want to be you."

I look at my hands. Sure, a few of the scratches are red, but I doubt this process is going to be tough.

Anne enters the kitchen. She has pulled her hair back on one side behind her ear and pinned it in place. She's changed into a blue and white pinstripe, short-sleeved blouse with jeans. The combination makes her look younger, but I can't explain why. "Welcome to our home. I wasn't sure you would come. Maybe you don't understand what you're in for."

I force a smile, "Hi, I'm glad to see you, too. Isn't it premature to torture a newcomer until the drifting snow has trapped them here? I might run away."

Anne laughs, "Oh. You'll wish you had run away all right. But this is the standard test we give to all newcomers who play with porcupines or devil's club."

I give Anne my best, "I'm not convinced" look. "I spent four years in the Army. I can handle torture."

Anne smiles, sweetly, "Then you'll pass this test with flying colors." She takes me to the sink and has me scrub my hands and arms all the way past my elbows with hot soapy water. Next, Anne scrubs the entire area with Betadine, an over-the-counter providone-iodine, and topical antiseptic.

Emily hands Anne my gift, "Mom, Josh brought us chocolates. Can I have one?"

Anne looks at the box and smiles at Emily. "Yes dear, you may choose one, but you'll have to wait until after dinner to have another." Anne turns to me, "Thank you for the chocolates, you didn't need to bring anything."

"It wouldn't be right to take your help without bringing a token." Turning, I head for my chair.

Back at the table, I watch as Anne scorches a needle with a lighted match. I understand this is being done to kill any germs on the surface of the needle.

With her light on and angled to provide the most

illumination, Anne looks expectantly at me. I give her my left hand. Watching Emily while her mother digs the tip of the needle into the first welt, I ask, “Did you know devil’s club plants take eighteen months to two years to germinate? Any plant living out its whole life in one year’s growing season is called an annual. Plants going for two years are called biennials, and plants living for a number of years are perennials.” I pause as Anne holds up her needle to the light, showing off a shiny piece of thorn.

Anne tilts her head to one side, “Devil’s club must be a perennial.” She opens tincture of iodine and smears it liberally on my cut.

“Why?” I ask, trying hard to embrace the sharp sting of the iodine.

“Because it grows at the edge of our backyard and we cut it back every year, it just keeps growing.” She turns my hand over and commences work on another welt.

I’m curious. “I wonder if the stinging is caused by the iodine or the alcohol?”

Anne looks at me closely, “It could be both.”

We all laugh. Anne is efficient and thorough. When Emily is finished eating her chocolate, I ask her if she has a favorite card game. She leaves and returns within a couple of minutes with a deck of cards, and we play Concentration while Anne continues to dig out thorns. When Anne is finished, she covers my welts with bandages.

I focus on Anne, “Thank you very much. I have to admit, you’re pretty good with a needle.”

“It was my pleasure. I wouldn’t want you to end up in the hospital with blood poisoning.”

I look toward Emily, “Anne, I wonder if you’d let me start Emily on her first bike lesson this afternoon.”

“Where were you planning to give the lesson?”

Anne is wary so I jump to reassure her, “I was hoping your backyard might work. I need a grassy area with a slight slope.”

Anne nods. “The yard in back should do. You’ll want to start up by the devil’s club. I’ll show you.”

Anne and Emily take me through the apartment to a sliding door. Fortunately, the yard is deep and shaped like a bowl with a slight depression in the center.

"This will be perfect," I announce. "Can I have an hour of Emily's time this afternoon?"

Getting a nod from Anne and Emily, I head around the end of the duplex to retrieve the bike.

#

Thirty minutes later, Emily is struggling, and I'm feeling frustrated. Emily is frightened of falling over and getting hurt, so I'm forced to run behind the bike with my hand on the bike seat. As soon as Emily gains speed, moving downhill into the depression, she stops pedaling and coasts. This produces insufficient speed for a novice to control balance. Once she senses she is out of control, Emily puts her feet down, terminating any chance of getting her balance.

While I'm catching my breath, I come up with a plan to break down the skills needed into basic components and teach them individually. First, I get Emily to chant the phrase, "peddle for power," with me over and over. I explain to Emily the importance of bike speed, or momentum, in maintaining her center of balance while on the bike.

"What does "peddle for power" mean, Emily?"

"I have to keep peddling, so I don't fall down."

"Okay, let's try it two times, while I hold onto the back of the bike, until we get all the way across the backyard." We chant, "peddle for power," over and over again, while Emily peddles across the yard. When we get to the end, I ask Emily to stop. I reinforce her effort, while I pick the bike up and turn her around for another try. "Let's do it again, but faster this time."

At the end of the run, I'm forced to sprint as fast as I can. I feel pleased with Emily. "Yes, that's good. What do you do if you feel out of balance?"

Emily looks puzzled, "Do I put my foot down?"

I laugh, "No, that's what you've been doing. What I want you to try is steering the bike, a tiny bit, in the direction you feel it will fall. Can you do it while peddling for power?"

Emily looks at me with big brown eyes, "I think I can."

On the next pass, I focus Emily on peddling and steering,

allowing myself to catch her as she loses her balance in the middle of the run. I don't want to ruin her progress with a bad crash. I praise her for keeping the power up and learning how to steer the bike to help her gain control. "Emily there is one last thing to practice. I want you to drop your shoulder and tilt your head the opposite direction from the way you feel you're falling." I describe how her head can act as a counterbalance to her body. "Let's practice. I'll push you on one arm, so you'll feel as if you will fall over. You drop the closest shoulder and tilt your head."

We practice this three times with Emily sitting on the bike. "Okay, if you're feeling like you will fall over, what two things are you going to do?"

Emily responds, "I'll steer into the fall and tilt my head the opposite way. Really I will do three things since I have to also peddle for power."

"Good girl. Let's try putting all these elements together." Chanting together "peddle for power" we start out near the apartment and run toward the depression in the yard. I let go of Emily's seat and watch in satisfaction as she sails up the slight incline in the backyard. Thirty feet from the edge of the grass, Emily starts to shriek when she realizes I am no longer alongside her and the blackberry bushes, nettles, and devil's club are rushing at her. Emily stops peddling, and as the bike slows, she leans far to the left and puts her left foot down on the ground. This causes the bike to swerve toward the wooden fence separating the two apartments. When her foot hits the ground, she is forced to make one or two hops before the bike spins out of her grasp to go crashing into the bushes at the edge of the yard.

Before Emily can realize she has safely dismounted from the bike without grievous injury, I've caught up with her, and I swing her high into the air. "Hooray, you did it Emily. You rode a bike for the first time."

Emily whoops and cheers, as I put her feet back on the grass. I watch as she does a jig in a circle around me. I get a sense of accomplishment reminiscent of those times in my classroom when everyone masters a concept after much effort and difficulty.

I extract the bike from the bushes without getting any more

thorns in my skin. "Let's call it a day Emily and go tell your mom how well you did."

We troop toward the back door. I prop the rented bike by the slider and go inside, while Emily recounts the wonder of her first bike ride to Anne. I ask for a glass of water and listen, trying to catch my breath. On the coffee table in the living room I spy a sketchbook so I walk over and check it out. Neatly drawn, is a sketch of Emily and me. I'm running behind the bike, while Emily is peddling furiously toward the viewer.

I turn to Anne in surprise, "Hey, this is excellent. Where did you study?"

It's Anne's turn to look defensive. "I didn't want you to look at it, it's doodling." Anne places one hand at the pit of her stomach.

"Are you kidding? I've a bit of art training, and it's challenging to capture motion and make it look natural like this." I study the efficiency of her lines, noting faint traces of construction lines used to assure alignment and balance. The detail is amazing, and she captured the emotion of the moment, when Emily started to realize she could control the bike. I look at my likeness and observe pride and joy in my expression. I look up at Anne, "Surely, you've had training?"

Anne shakes her head, "No. I took a few classes in high school from Ms. Johnson. She told me I wasn't good enough to get accepted into a college level art program. More importantly, my parents couldn't help me with the expenses."

I can tell from the tone in Anne's voice I've reawakened a painful experience she would rather forget, so I try a different tack, "Do you have more sketches? I'd like to see them if you'll let me."

Anne looks reluctant, so I try again in as sincere a tone as I can manage. "My best friend in college was an artist. I spent a lot of time with him, while he worked on his projects. I'm not an expert, but after three years of spending time going to art shows, exhibits, lectures, and stuff, I can recognize college-level work. This is better than anything I saw when I went to college." I walk over and look directly into her green eyes. Her face is lovely and her deep dimples capture me. I wonder; how did I miss them? Do they come out only when she's perplexed? "I'd like to look at more."

She relents and returns in a couple of minutes with a dozen sketchpads. I sit down on the sofa with Emily on one side and Anne on the other and work my way through her portfolio. I appreciate all her work, but I'm particularly impressed with the scenes from the harbor. Again, Anne is adept at putting together detail with motion in ways evoking strong emotion. I want to go to the harbor and view this scene to find out what happens. I spend forty-five minutes looking at her sketches. When I finish I turn to Anne, "This work is amazing. Have you done anything in other media?"

Smiling whimsically, she responds, "I have pictures I've done in pastels and a few in oils. But I don't have time to show you today. I have errands to run with Emily before dinner."

I take this as a cue it's time for me to go. I stand and thank Anne for tending my wounds. "Can I have this sketch? It will inspire me to come back and complete the lessons."

Anne is pleased at my request. She pulls the page from her book, places it inside a transparency, and hands it to me with a smile. "Thank you for teaching Emily how to ride a bike. Apparently she's always wanted to, but I never knew."

"When can I return and give Emily another lesson? I've got to return the bike in a week, so I hope you'll invite me back." I smile when I realize I have a reason to return without having to ask her for a date. We walk through the kitchen toward the front door.

"How about tomorrow afternoon, say three thirty?" One dimple tantalizes.

I smile and turn as I cross the threshold. I'm sorry our time has come to an end. "That's perfect. I'll start with teaching her how to stop the bike." I pause, looking for an opening to connect with Anne, "Maybe I can look at more of your work tomorrow?"

Both of Anne's dimples pop into sight. "I will be happy to let you look at them."

I turn and go out to my rig, while Anne closes the door behind me. Mindful the folks next door are probably watching me, I wait until I'm in the Subaru and a block down the highway, before I whoop with exultation. "Yee Haw!" Blackie gives me a concerned look, so I scratch him behind the ear as I hum contentedly. I will send Anne's sketch to my artist friend in the admissions office at the

Rocky Mountain College of Art and Design in Denver. I want his professional perspective on her talent and hope his assessment is as positive as mine.

If I'm right, Anne will be surprised to find out Ms. Johnson had given her bad advice. I realize it may make a difference in what Anne chooses to do with the rest of her life. This fact makes me consider again the oft-repeated theory teachers have too much influence over students' lives. Every comment a teacher makes can either enrich or devastate. The potential unintended consequences posed by my every word frighten me.

As I stop in the driveway of my apartment, I belatedly remember Blackie needs more dog food. As I back out of the driveway, I give him a gentle shake. "You're falling down on the job, Blackie. It was your responsibility to remind me."

Chapter 40: Adultery

Clay seethes all the way back to Wrangell. Unable to check his anger, he imagines slow and exotic ways to get rid of his incompetent partner. He relives every word spoken at the mining claims office, hoping to find a way to reverse the turn of events.

At the end of his flight, one piece of information troubles him. Although he's learned Silver Jack's sidekick is Josh Campbell, he has no idea who the man might be. In addition, the address provided is useless because it's a post office box number. By the time Clay lands in Wrangell, he is assigning all blame for arriving late to Lenn. If his partner had offered to go back to Kadin Island and hide the equipment by himself, he would have arrived at the claims office before the old prospector. Instead of sucking hind tit, he and Lenn would be celebrating.

At the airport, Clay retrieves his pickup from the parking lot and drives back to town. His mood blackens, and he jerks the steering wheel through the curves as if he's chopping down weeds in an overrun lawn. Entering the north end of town, he spots Blackie tied to the flagpole in front of the post office. Guessing Silver Jack's partner may be inside, he waits patiently in his truck until a young man exits the building and goes to the dog. Clay climbs out of his truck and walks up to the man. As he nears, he calls out a greeting to Blackie. In response, the beast crouches low, bares his teeth, and growls throatily.

Clay makes sure he doesn't get within reach of Blackie's jaws. "Hello. My name is Clay, and I'm the Harbormaster. Looks like Blackie isn't in a good mood today."

The young man goes to one knee and pets the big dog on the shoulder while turning to face Clay. “Blackie is out of sorts because Jack isn’t here. My name is Josh. I’m the new science teacher at the high school.”

Clay keeps his face neutral, rejoicing at his good luck in finding Silver Jack’s partner within minutes of returning to Wrangell. “Nice to meet you. I’m not aware Blackie has ever gone with anyone but Jack. Is Jack ill or hurt?” Clay feigns concern.

Josh’s response is casual, “No. He’s fine. He asked me to watch Blackie for him so he could go to Ketchikan and take care of business. He’ll be back in a couple of days.”

The beast turns his head away from Clay, repeating his threatening growl as Josh rises to his feet.

Clay likes to use his height, when he can, to intimidate other men, but he notices Josh isn’t put off by his slight height advantage. The young man is strong, like a body builder. Not the kind of person you should goad into a fight.

“Well. It was nice meeting you. If you ever need anything, my office is at the marina.” Clay turns away and ambles into the Post Office as if he has to check on his mail.

After Josh and Blackie climb into a jeep, Clay returns to his truck and follows Josh from a distance. When Josh’s vehicle penetrates a dead end street, he turns into another street to avoid being noticed. Later, he cruises down the road and spots the SUV parked at the far end of an apartment complex.

Clay goes to his apartment. While he is cleaning up, he picks up his phone and listens to his voice mail. One of the calls is from Claire trying to arrange a meeting. He returns her call first and sets up a midnight rendezvous. Afterwards he calls Lenn and arranges to meet in an hour at the Marine Bar.

Clay arrives at the bar fifteen minutes late to ensure Lenn is forced to wait for him. Lenn is sitting in the darkest corner. The Harbormaster orders a drink. When it arrives, he orders another round before downing his drink in one gulp. He wipes his mouth, “We were too late. Silver Jack and another guy filed claims minutes ahead of us. We’re shit out of luck! I learned one thing though; the old coot is in Ketchikan. He probably won’t get back for a couple of days until the next northbound ferry arrives."

Lenn leans forward, his chin buzzing the tabletop. "I told you before. There ain't nobody who's going to get any diamonds out of the claim except us. Didn't you say the old prospector lived on a boat in your marina?"

Clay leans forward, mimicking Lenn. "Yes. That's right. Usually a big black dog protects his boat, but his partner is a new guy in town, and he's got the animal at his apartment several blocks away. I ran into them at the Post Office. We could sneak onto his boat tonight and take a look around with nobody the wiser."

Clay agrees to meet Lenn outside the marina office at 2 a.m. Not only is the time right for their covert trip to Silver Jack's boat, but it will allow him time to rendezvous with the Principal's wife.

#

Nearly midnight, Clay coasts his darkened pickup to a stop, a hundred feet from Claire's backyard. He lights a cigarette, killing time until her arrival. Claire waits until her husband falls asleep before slipping out the back door to meet him. His cab light is disconnected, so when Claire enters his rig, the light will not go on and reveal their late night meeting.

On a few occasions, Claire hadn't been able to rendezvous, as her husband hadn't followed his usual pattern of falling into a sound sleep. Clay hated the nights when she failed to show up but chocked these few episodes up to fate. Conversely, every tryst had been better than the last. Fooling around with another man's wife is dangerous, but he concedes Claire has much more at risk in this affair than he.

Within a few minutes, he spots Claire's silhouette in his rearview mirror. He isn't surprised when she opens his passenger door and climbs into the cab. Clay turns and pulls her roughly to his side, seeking her upturned lips in a bruising kiss. The sweetness of her quickened breath, her searching hand, and the smooth feel of her silk pajamas against his rough skin ignite his passion.

Without waiting for permission, he pulls her pajama bottoms and panty down over her knees and casts them aside. Locked in a passionate kiss, Clay pushes Claire's torso down onto the seat with his heavy chest. Her filmy silk pajama top outlines the twin mounds made by her upturned breasts. Inspired, he unbuttons her top as Claire unzips his pants. Finished, she parts her legs and rises to meet him.

Clay experiences the ultimate thrill. Conquest and pleasure mix to create unequaled lust. He braces his left hand against the dashboard to sustain his position over her on the narrow seat.

Deliberately, he slows his cadence, recognizing Claire is urging him faster to meet her needs. Not willing to let her set the pace, he kisses her neck and savors every thrust and sensation. After all, Lenn won't mind waiting.

Chapter 41: Ransacked

Early in the morning, Katie is loading equipment into her boat. It's nearly six o'clock and the dawn light should be strong; however, an overcast sky makes it feel like first light. Low clouds and mist create long streamers obscuring the trees and foothills surrounding the harbor.

Across the way, Katie spots Josh and Blackie walking down the floating dock. She starts her trolling motor, casts off, and heads over to the marina. Matching pace with Josh and Blackie, Katie calls out, "Howdy stranger. Do you need a ride?"

Josh laughs. He is freshly shaven and wearing an army fatigue jacket and jeans with a dark blue stocking cap. He looks at home in the Alaskan setting. Josh stops, "Throw me your line, and I'll secure your boat to the dock. If you've got a few minutes, you can join Blackie and me as we check up on Jack's boat."

Katie speedily joins the pair. On the dock, she points at Blackie's heavy nylon leash. "Why does he use a lead built for a horse? Wouldn't your basic anchor chain do?" Katie is pleased to get a chuckle out of Josh.

He turns and gives her a smile and his blue eyes penetrate as if he can peer directly into her thoughts. She blushes, and his smile becomes a grin.

"An anchor chain might be an improvement. With his fangs I wouldn't want to wager against him if he goes after this nylon rope."

They walk down the dock, making small talk and enjoying the sights. Josh thanks her again for her assistance two days earlier. She listens intently when he tells her why he came to Alaska. She is elated to realize from his story he has yet to form a new attachment. Deliberately, because it will signal her availability, she reciprocates by telling him about ending her relationship and moving away from Juneau.

Too soon, as far as Katie is concerned, they reach Silver Jack's boat. A flock of ravens is fighting over items on his deck. One is on the dock, gulping chunks of partially thawed hamburger. As they come alongside the boat, Josh expresses surprise when he notices the cabin door is ajar. They rush aboard the old fishing boat, scattering the ravens, and enter the cabin to find it torn apart. The flooring has been lifted out of place to reveal the motor compartment below the cabin. The bunks are ripped to shreds and the contents of the cabin are strewn everywhere.

Katie surveys the wreckage, "Why would anyone want to damage his boat? Who would want to hurt that nice old man?" She becomes angry, "What could he possibly have that anyone would want? He's just an old prospector, for pity sake."

Josh looks at Katie, "It might have been claim jumpers." He reaches for her hands, becoming solemn. "We were shot at when we were in the back country. We got out of there as fast as we could, and Jack went to Ketchikan to file our claims. This indicates whoever shot at us knows it was Jack."

Katie, liking the warmth of his strong hands holding hers, hesitates before releasing his grip. "Shouldn't you report this to the police?"

Chapter 42: Awkward

Katie is beautiful, standing in the cabin of Jack's boat, obviously concerned for the old man's safety. Her blonde, curly hair must be natural. I doubt any girl working as a fishery biologist would have curled her hair before going out in the dampness, where it would go flat.

When she isn't flashing her smiles; this girl is serious, smart and passionate. She is wearing tan cargo pants, a flannel shirt under a navy, fleece vest, and a navy baseball cap with white trim. I almost take her in my arms to reassure her everything will turn out okay, although I'm not sure how I can reassure anyone on that account. The moment passes, so I recover by turning to the door, "Let's go outside, there's nothing we can do here requiring immediate attention. I'll report this to the police and spend the morning cleaning up the worst of the mess."

Katie gives me a funny look and ducks her head, as she steps over the threshold and passes through the cabin doorway. As I watch her leave, I'm reminded I need to follow up on yesterday's conversation. I step through the doorway, close behind her. "Katie, I owe you a dinner. Are you free this evening?"

She spins around, beaming. Because we are so close, I steady her and find myself with both hands on her trim waist. Her hands rest lightly on my arms. I inhale and smell her breath and the faint aroma of shampoo in her hair. Her eyelashes are translucent, and her blue eyes are bigger than they should be. Her lips part, and my feet are frozen to the deck of the boat.

With a quick, light laugh, Katie dances away, creating a stir among the ravens roosting above the cabin. "It's a great idea. I must warn you, I'll smell like fish. I usually do after a day on the water."

"What time is good for you?" I ask.

Katie frowns, "I should get in around seven p.m. What if you pick me up at the Sourdough Lodge at eight? It's where I'm staying."

It's my turn to frown, "The Sourdough Lodge. Where is it?"

"Turn around and I'll show you."

I turn, and Katie steps up close beside me. She points, "We're looking west across the marina to the peninsula protecting the harbor. If you follow the harbor shoreline to its most southern point you can see a boat launch. Right behind is the Sourdough Lodge." She smiles at me, "Can you can find it?"

I smile back because I find smiling to be contagious around Katie. "You bet. I'll be there at eight on the dot."

Katie laughs, "Great. I need to take off, if I'm going to be back on time. Are you sure you don't need help with cleaning up Jack's boat?"

"No, I can handle it. Don't forget, I have Blackie."

Blackie and I watch as Katie walks down the floating dock to her boat. When she is out of sight, I turn to Blackie, "Do you believe that close encounter was planned or an accident?" In response, the dog tilts his head to one side. I laugh and give Blackie a hug, feeling the warmth of his body through his thick, black fur. "My assessment exactly, it was definitely not an accident."

I spot one of Jack's chainsaws sitting on the deck near his freezer. I go inside the cabin and peer around wondering if anything valuable is missing. The flooring section covering the motor compartment is leaning against the dining table.

His fishing poles hang above his top bunk near the rear of the cabin. The plastic caps covering the base end of the poles have been cut away or removed. I check the corner behind the steering wheel and find his rifle standing propped up, undisturbed. I certainly don't have any idea if he had any valuables or cash in his boat, but this mess doesn't add up to burglary, not with the rifle and chainsaw left behind.

I try calling 9-1-1 and get no signal. I make a mental note to try Jack later in the day from my apartment, where the reception is better.

The first step in the cleanup is for me to find garbage bags. If I go up to the police station, I can file a report and pick up trash bags at the grocery store.

Jack keeps a chest freezer on the deck of the boat, and whoever had ransacked it had strewn most of the contents on the deck. With a quick glance, I can tell every package has been ripped open by the voracious ravens. Not wanting to leave the semi-frozen food to attract more unwanted pests, I find an empty five-gallon bucket and fill it with ruined hamburger, steak and fish.

Rounding up Blackie's leash and closing the door to Jack's cabin, I head up the floating dock toward the Harbormaster's office lugging my hoard of spoiling meat. Trailing in my wake, ravens fly from boat to boat, marking my progress with raucous cries. At the top of the pier, near the marina office, I dump my load of trash into the dumpster. I make sure the lid is closed so the ravens won't be able to get in and make another mess.

It rains as Blackie and I go into the marina office. I find a slender man with curly brown hair behind the counter. "Hi, my name is Josh, and I'm watching Silver Jack's boat and taking care of Blackie for a couple of days, while he is out of town. I went down to check on his boat, and it's been broken into. The entire boat is a mess."

"Hello. I'm David. I'm sorry to hear of the trouble. We've haven't had a report of a break-in for months. I sure hope Jack didn't lose anything valuable. He doesn't have much money." David pulls at the wispy beard that does a poor job of covering his weak chin.

"I'm going up to the police station to file a report. Can you find out if anyone on the dock heard or saw anything suspicious last night?"

David shakes his head, "No, but I can put a note on the message board. In addition, I can ask the folks moored near Jack's boat."

"Thank you, David. I appreciate it."

I exit the marina office, with Blackie in tow, headed for my rig. As I walk away in the steady drizzle, I notice the ravens are lurking near the dumpster, waiting for the lid to be left open.

I recall bumping into the Harbormaster, the man I met yesterday in front of the post office, in this exact location before my trip to the mainland with Jack. He had been nasty in our first meeting, and I was surprised he failed to recognize me. Blackie hates the man; I'd never observed him react so viscerally to anyone. My assessment, Blackie has him pegged correctly. Unlike David, the Harbormaster is not to be trusted.

Forty-five minutes later, I return with a box of trash bags and a new padlock for the door to the boat. I'm not surprised to find the ravens at the dumpster busy at work, ripping packages of meat apart.

With a bright sun peaking through the clouds overhead, Blackie and I take a stroll over the boardwalk to Chief Shakes Island, where I turn him loose to run free and do his business. When he is finished, I return to my SUV and retrieve the trash bags and the five-gallon bucket. I carry my load to the boat and begin clean up.

Climbing down into the engine compartment, I pick up the items dropped below. Many of his belongings can be cleaned up, while a few are ruined after spending hours in the oily water at the bottom of the bilge. I stuff ruined items into a trash bag. Cleanable items are dropped into the bucket.

I'm below deck when I hear Blackie barking and growling. As fast as I can, I climb up and step out onto the boat's deck. Standing on the floating dock are two men. One is David, and he introduces the other man as Detective Alex.

The detective boards and David heads back up the dock. I make sure Blackie is well out of the detective's way near the bow of the boat. Detective Alex opens a notepad and goes inside the cabin, standing inside for a few moments, taking notes. Returning to the deck, he asks if I took any pictures of the boat before I started cleaning up. When he gets my negative response, he purses his lips and writes in his notebook. He picks up and examines Jack's padlock, noting it has been cut with bolt cutters.

After fifteen minutes of checking out the boat from every possible angle, he asks me a series of questions aimed at pinpointing when Jack left, when I visited the boat last and the time I found the boat this morning. I gather the detective suspects Jack's boat may have been broken into by an individual looking for drugs. It's the logical explanation for looking inside every small container on the boat.

I keep our recent trip to the mainland or the reason for Jack's trip to Ketchikan to myself. I get the impression Detective Alex senses I'm withholding pertinent information. I can't overcome his suspicion without telling a lie and opt for keeping my mouth shut. He gets my identification, address, and contact information. As the detective is preparing to leave, I promise to have Jack stop by the police station when he returns.

It rains again so I go inside the cabin. By noon, I have the worst of the mess cleaned up. Jack will need a new sleeping bag and pillow, and he'll need to replace several items of clothing taken out of the bilge. Everything else can be cleaned up or repaired as needed. I lock up the cabin with the new padlock, and Blackie and I head up the floating dock in bright sunlight with two bags of garbage slung over my shoulder.

Blackie and I climb the ramp to the stationary loading pier. Because the tide is quite low, the incline is steep, so I climb the left hand side with aluminum treads bolted to the grating to prevent slippage. At extreme high tide the ramp will have a modest incline.

After a quick lunch, I take a long, hot shower and clean up. At three o'clock, I load up Blackie in the Subaru and drive to the hardware store to buy a gift. After looking around for a bit with a growing sense of desperation, I stumble into a section of art supplies. Wasting no time, I pick out a box of colored pencils, charcoal of various sizes, and kneaded art erasers. We drive to Anne's apartment to give Emily her second bike-riding lesson.

The girls are waiting for me when I arrive. We sit down at their kitchen table for cookies and milk. I hold up my glass, "Here's to cold milk and warm peanut-butter cookies, there can't be anything better in the whole world."

Emily laughs. "Nothing beats it, except chocolates from the Rocky Mountain Chocolate Factory; right, mom?"

Anne blushes, so I surmise yesterday's gift has been a hit. She reaches across the table, "Show me your hands and arms. I'd like to check if anything is inflamed. It's the best way to find out if I missed something yesterday."

I get a clean bill of health from Anne's inspection, at least for today. I give the girls their gifts, and we chitchat while we drink our milk. I learn it has been a slow day at the café. Apparently, many of the fishermen were after fish runs on the west side of Prince of Wales Island, too far away to come back to Wrangell every night. A slow day at the café is a slow day for tips, too. I eat three of the home-baked cookies before I ask Emily if she is ready for her lesson.

"You bet."

Outside, I go over the basics from yesterday. When I'm convinced Emily remembers the essentials, I go over the technique for stopping the bike. Fortunately, the rental bike has hand brakes, so I teach her how to use the rear brake to stop her forward momentum. "When the bike has slowed almost to a stop, lay the bike over on its side and put one foot on the ground."

We practice this technique several times at slow speed, with me running alongside. When I'm sure she has the technique down pat, I allow Emily to peddle across the yard and stop by herself.

At the far end of the yard, Emily stops easily, and turns the bike around. Wearing a big smile, Emily speeds across the yard and stops directly in front of me. "Yeah, I can do it. I can do it all by myself."

I work with Emily for an hour, showing her how to improve her posture and balance. It drizzles, so we go inside, and I find Anne sketching. This time she's using charcoal as contrast to fine, light green pencil lines. The perspective is from ground level, in front of and to one side of the bike. From this angle, the sole of Emily's shoe is about to crash into the viewer.

Despite the sharp perspective, the determination on Emily's face is the dominant aspect of the piece. For context, her bike has been transformed into an airborne mountain bike, jumping head first down a steep mountain trail. Emily's bike helmet has morphed into the kind worn by an extreme sport contestant. Anne has also added kneepads and gloves; completing the impression this is a dangerous ride.

After absorbing the emotion of the sketch, I look up to find Anne holding her breath, waiting for my assessment. I smile and comment, "This piece is better than yesterday's." I tease her a little bit more, "Did you sneak a lesson while I was gone?"

Anne blushes, "This is similar to stuff I watch on television. When I saw the look on Emily's face, it reminded me of the young woman in the race. From there, it took care of itself."

Studying the picture again, although my mind is screaming duck, to avoid an imminent collision, the look on Emily's face is one of absolute control. This girl will land precisely where she intends. There's no fear on her face or in the way she holds herself on the bucking mountain bike. The scene is absolute confidence layered atop supreme skill, a winning combination in any field.

I remind Anne she'd agreed to show me more of her art. She evaporates upstairs and returns in a few minutes with several framed pictures and a sheath of pictures inside transparent portfolio sleeves. "I don't have many. The materials are too expensive."

It strikes me Anne has not had much in the way of money in her life. Her tiny apartment is clean and tastefully decorated, but everything looks as if it were purchased used or gifted by friends or relatives.

We go through her pastels and oils. I'm impressed. Without training, this woman has mastered techniques often requiring years of specialized study. A common theme is emotion and the range of sentiments is unusual. In her pieces I find joy, fear, malice, loathing, reverence, shyness, anger, and innocence. I ask Anne, "Have you ever failed at capturing the emotion you're after in your sketch?"

"No, but I've not tried them all." Anne smiles, and I try not to notice how her deep dimples enhance the beauty of her green eyes.

I hesitate before asking, "Could you change the emotion of your last drawing? For example, could you redraw it with Emily showing great fear?"

"Oh, yes, easily. The bike would be out of control too."

I nod my head, "Anne, I have to repeat what I said yesterday. Your work is impressive."

Anne smiles at me. This time dimples sustain. Perhaps other emotions educe one or two of them to appear. I might like to find out the answer, if I can.

There is an awkward moment when Anne invites me to stay

for dinner, and I have to make up an excuse so I can say no. After all, I have a date with Katie I don't feel comfortable revealing. I counter with an invitation to take her to dinner the following day. I feel relief, along with guilt, when this strategy works but Anne asks to skip a day and go on Monday since it's one of her days off from work.

Anne and Emily wave goodbye from the porch, as Blackie and I drive away in the rain.

Chapter 43: Next Time

Katie circles Zarembo Island counterclockwise. At every major salmon-bearing stream, she stops to review spawning and water conditions. She takes water PH and temperature readings and records her observations by location in her daily log.

Continuing southward, Katie enters Steamer Bay on the west coast of Etolin Island and goes ashore for a bathroom break. She chooses a beach on the west side of the bay because of its open, grassy, low bank. After relieving herself near the boat, she walks up the beach to stretch her legs. Above high water mark, she spots a pile of bones in a rocky low spot and stops to investigate.

She finds a skull and realizes it's from a bear. The black tufts of fur attached to the bones indicate it was a black bear. Looking over her shoulder toward the bay, she guesses the bear was shot from a boat. She will take the skull with her to Wrangell; perhaps Josh can use it in his science class.

Back in her boat, Katie follows Steamer Bay to its source, Porcupine Creek. The rivulet meanders over rocky flats covered by water at high tide. She nods her head in satisfaction, the spawning conditions here look excellent and must support a sizeable salmon run.

Turning north, Katie speeds back to Wrangell. She slows down to three miles per hour as she enters the harbor and stops to refuel before heading to the lodge. The fishery biologist stows her gear in a lockable storage compartment and hurries to her room to get ready for dinner. She glances at her watch; she has forty-five minutes.

After a quick shower, she blows her hair dry, thanking her parents for the genetics supplying her with naturally wavy hair. She dresses in a knit sweater, blue jeans, warm socks, and boots for the evening. Carefully, she applies lipstick, blusher, mascara, and a slight trace of eye shadow. With one last check in the mirror to assure herself everything is in order, she picks up a clutch and heads downstairs.

In the lobby Katie finds Josh reading a brochure on Stikine River tours. Realizing he isn't aware of her arrival, she watches him from across the room. He's changed outfits since this morning, and his auburn hair frames his face. She crosses the room and as she nears him, he senses her and turns. "Hi, Josh. How do I look?" She smiles and is satisfied when his grin greets her.

Josh's eyes twinkle, "You look great and very much worth the wait. For a while there I thought you forgot our date."

Katie protests, "Its not even five minutes past eight."

Josh looks down at her, "It felt like an eternity to me."

To mask her reaction, Katie takes his hand and pulls him through the entrance of the lodge. "Where are we going?"

Blackie is in the back seat of a green Subaru, and she surmises it must be Josh's vehicle. When she notices his out of state license plates she asks, "Are you from Colorado?"

Josh chuckles, "I need to get my plates changed. Yes, I've lived there my whole life, not counting the time I spent in the army. It's quite a change to leave the high desert and come to the Alaskan rain forest." He opens the passenger door of his jeep for her. "By the way, if you're hungry, we can go straight to dinner, but if you feel up to a short walk, I'd like to show you a local treasure first."

Katie is starving after an entire day out on the open water. Despite this, she likes the idea of spending time with Josh. "I can hold off on dinner, so long as it isn't too late. I do have to work tomorrow."

Josh closes her door and walks around the jeep. As he climbs into the vehicle he asks, "How was your day?"

"Oh, the day was wonderful, but the weather was bipolar. It alternated all day between cold rain and baking sun. I took my raingear off and put it on so many times I didn't get much else done." Katie fastens her seatbelt, "By the way, I have a gift for you. I found it today. Remind me when we come back after dinner."

Josh looks curious, but starts his vehicle without a word. He pulls away from the lodge, headed toward town. "We've had weather extremes today, too. But I missed a lot of it since I was inside for big chunks of the day."

Passing through town, Josh questions her, "Have you ever eaten at the Stikine Inn?"

Katie considers for a moment, "I've heard of it, but I haven't eaten there. Usually I cook in my room. The state per-diem isn't generous."

Josh drives her nearly a mile north of town to the public access for the beach. Instead of pulling into the gravel lot, they park in the next driveway, near an old white house. "I'd like to introduce you to a friend of mine."

Josh, Katie, and Blackie reach the small dwelling. Josh knocks on the door. When it opens, Josh introduces them, "Katie, this is my friend Mildred. Mildred, this is Katie. She's a fishery biologist with the State of Alaska. She gave Jack and me a tow back to Wrangell when our outboard motor wasn't working." Josh straightens, and adds, "Mildred helped me after Jack found me suffering from exposure. Her beach is full of petroglyphs. I thought you might like to look at them before we go to dinner."

Finding Mildred's high cheekbones, dark brown eyes, and raven hair dusted with gray to be exotic, Katie is glad Mildred isn't competition. Mildred offers to take them on tour, but Josh declines her offer. "It will be fun to discover them on our own. We'll come back if we need help."

Josh leads Katie to the first petroglyph at the edge of Mildred's lawn. This one is a killer whale, and the illustration is simple, yet powerful, in its depiction of the magnificent sea mammal. Josh releases Blackie, and Katie enjoys a wonderful half-hour searching for and finding the rest of the petroglyphs. Almost all of them are below the high-tide mark, and Katie marvels they can last so long despite being exposed to the water twice a day.

At the end of their review of the artifacts, Josh asks her to pick her favorite petroglyph. Katie answers easily, "I prefer the one looking like a spiral. I find it more interesting. I get the sense the maker was trying to express a deeper meaning. I just can't make out what."

A little to the north, along the beach is a derelict fishing boat, canted to one side. Katie exclaims, "Let's explore the cool boat."

Within minutes, they are alongside the broken, wooden craft. Two spars tilt forward and to one side, giving the derelict a rakish look. Josh is the first to speak; "I imagine this was someone's dream at one time." He fingers the lettering on the bow of the boat. "It was called the Tillicum. I wonder what happened."

Katie responds, "It looks as if it was trying to escape from the ocean and collapsed as it made it partway up the shore."

When they finish with the beach, Josh calls Blackie to him and fastens his leash before the couple returns to Mildred's home. They drive to the Stikine Inn, near the post office on the north end of town. Instead of leaving Blackie in the jeep, Josh ties his leash to an exterior sign in a grassy swale out of reach of the street.

Inside, the hostess seats the couple where they can view the entrance to the harbor. When they are alone, Josh inquires, "Do you feel like a drink with dinner?"

"Yes, I prefer red wine."

While they are having dinner, they watch a Native Alaskan woman talk to the waves and sky along the pier in front of the restaurant. With feathers in her hair and a long gown trailing on the ground, Katie finds her fascinating. Not able to hear her words, Katie and Josh make up her dialogue. They guess the woman is displeased with the elements–perhaps more rain is desired. After a bit, the woman leaves.

Later, partway through dinner, the woman comes into the restaurant and confronts Josh in a low and melodious voice, "Blackie tells me he doesn't like being tied up to the post. He is worried about Silver Jack. He worries he might be in trouble."

Josh is caught by surprise, but recovers after a couple of seconds. "Ma'am, I assure you Jack is fine. He should be returning soon from Ketchikan."

Faster than her entrance, the apparition turns and abandons the restaurant, leaving the couple speechless in her wake. Katie is the first to say anything, "Do you know her?"

Josh shakes his head; "I've never met her before tonight. I wonder how she knew Blackie was with me."

Katie smiles, "Blackie must have told her. Or she watched you tie him to the post."

"Makes sense."

Josh pays for dinner, and they walk outside and get Blackie. Katie looks around unsuccessfully, hoping to spot the Native woman. The evening light is fading as she turns to Josh, "I'd like to go back to my room. I've got an early start in the morning."

On the way back to the lodge, Katie thanks Josh for dinner and the tour of the petroglyphs. When they get to the lodge, she leads the way to the dock. Unlocking the storage compartment on her boat, she presents Josh with the bear skull. "I found this and thought you might want to have it for your classroom."

He responds, "Are you kidding. This specimen is in excellent shape. It has all its teeth and the organic material is removed." Josh gives Katie a quick hug, careful not to crush the skull against her clothing.

Carrying the skull, Josh places it on the floorboard of his rig. After admonishing Blackie to leave the skull alone, Josh insists on walking Katie to her room. At her door, she turns and gives Josh a peck on the cheek. "Good night. Tonight was wonderful. Next time, it's my turn to buy."

Chapter 44: Intrusion

Blackie joins me in the front seat as I drive back to my apartment. Along the way, I reflect on my day. Packed, it started with Jack's ransacked boat, a wonderful afternoon spent with Anne and Emily, and dinner and a kiss from Katie.

When I left Colorado I was alone, hurt, and discouraged. I wasn't sure I would ever find another girl to replace Kaeli. Out of the blue, I am pursuing two fascinating women at the same time. It certainly feels better, although it's pretty scary to be in the process of starting a relationship instead of ending one.

My concern, how to tell which woman to go after? At this initial stage, I could lose one without realizing it. Conversely, eventually I will need to make a choice and live with the outcome. I wish it all didn't have to be so complicated.

I turn into the street leading to my apartment. I stop in front, open my car door and step out. As soon as both feet hit the ground, Blackie jumps past me and rushes onto the front porch, barking fiercely.

Concerned, I run to the front door and find it ajar. Jerking it open, I hear my back door slam. As I take in my front room, I realize my apartment has been trashed. Blackie growls, and I grab him by the collar when he lunges past me into the apartment. I flip on the light switch and head for the kitchen to find a flashlight.

With my flashlight in one hand and Blackie's collar in the other, I kick open the back door. Flashing the light around the backyard, I find it empty. Anyone fleeing my apartment is probably long gone. I consider releasing the growling Blackie into the darkness, but reject the idea as too risky. As brave as Blackie might be, he wouldn't stand a chance against a bullet. Jack might get over a trashed boat; I doubt he would forgive me if anything happened to Blackie. Reluctantly, I pull him back inside.

I consider calling the police station to report finding my apartment vandalized. Detective Alex will certainly have piercing questions; ones I might not want to answer. Before placing the call, I inventory my losses. If I'm not missing any valuables, it might be worth it to skip the call.

I try to ascertain how the intruder got into my apartment. My back door opens outward, and I find the doorknob is locked with the bolt extended. The door also won't close, because it's sprung. Someone grabbed the doorknob and jerked the door open. Without a deadbolt for added protection, the only thing holding the door closed is the doorknob bolt extending through a metal strike plate attached to the frame. Like many doors in old buildings, this one fits poorly. A determined man, or anyone with a crowbar, could open this door with little trouble.

Darn, I should have installed a deadbolt when I first got the apartment. I will need to fix the door and install additional security hardware. I should probably get something for the front door, too. Afterwards, maybe I should get a dog. On second thought, maybe I should get a viscous one to guard my apartment whenever I leave. It couldn't hurt. All I need is a Blackie clone.

Chapter 45: Partners

Silver Jack follows Church Street through the darkened town, headed for Josh's apartment. He's excited to be linking up with Blackie and getting Josh up to speed on his successful trip to Ketchikan. As Church Street arcs through town at a slight incline one block uphill from Front Street, he avoids the steep climb up to Josh's apartment he normally has to follow from the marina. The street is well lit and has sidewalks along most of the course through town.

There is little traffic. On weeknights, like this one, most of the town's businesses, with the exception of bars, have been closed for hours. Despite the fact there is no one to see him, it feels unusual to be walking the streets of Wrangell without Blackie.

He checks his watch; it's almost midnight when he turns into Josh's street. When he reaches the front porch, his boots make a thudding noise on the step, and he is pleased to hear Blackie's familiar bark in response to the sound. Knocking on the door, he calls out to Josh, "What kind of greenhorn would leave his partner standing outside in the cold and wet?"

In a flash, the porch light is turned on, and Josh flings opens the door to great him. "Hi. Wow it's good to see you; you're a sight for sore eyes."

"Feels good to be home. Ketchikan stinks too much for my likes."

Josh envelopes him in a bear hug. "I'm glad you're here, but I've got bad news. Your boat was ransacked last night, and my apartment was torn apart this evening while I was gone." Josh steps back and beckons him inside. "Come on in and check it out. I interrupted whoever it was when I returned home, so my mess isn't as bad as yours."

Unwilling to wait any longer, Blackie rushes up and rubs his muzzle against his hand. "Why, you are such a poor baby." He kneels and rubs Blackie's face with both hands, "Did you miss me?"

"I'll say he did. He's been moping around ever since you left." Josh sits on a nearby chair. "You'd better pay attention to Blackie first. Afterwards I'll show you the mess the intruder or intruders left behind. What happened in Ketchikan?"

Still kneeling and petting Blackie, he replies, "I got a written valuation by a jeweler and filed our claims. Everything went as good as could be expected." He cannot stop the excitement invading him, "Looks like we've got ourselves a couple of real diamond claims."

Josh gestures toward the couch, "Sit down. What happens next?"

"We wait to hear back from the analyses of the diamonds. If they come back positive, we go shopping for a mining outfit with experience in diamonds to become our partner. I heard there is a big diamond strike in Canada, and we might start with that company."

Josh queries, "What would you do with the money?"

"Why, I'd buy a new boat and motor. I'd give part of the profit to help the landless tribes get federal recognition."

"What is that all about?"

Jack moves over to the couch and sits down. "Most of the natives in Alaska got recognition in the 1970s from the federal government. What remains unexplained, the tribes in this area were left out of the deal and didn't get any of their traditional lands. For example, Crittenden Creek used to be part of the lands used by the Katc-uddy. I'm not sure if there are any of them left, but it was a shame they got cheated. It makes sense to pay a share to the legitimate landowner. Can you support me on this?"

"You bet. Maybe there'll be enough I can get married, if I can find the right girl."

Thirty minutes later, Josh shows Jack where the intruder had cut open cleaning supplies in his laundry room and dumped the contents on the floor. "The average thief wouldn't look inside laundry detergent for hidden valuables. This intruder knows we've found diamonds and is looking for us to stash them in a less than obvious place. Fortunately for us, our diamonds are in a safe deposit box at the bank."

Silver Jack looks around at the wreckage. "Whoever was here was prepared to do whatever it takes to get their hands on the diamonds. Make sure you stay alert, I don't want you to get hurt."

"Ditto for you, Jack. Why don't you spend the night here? You can have the couch."

"Oh, don't worry about me. I have Blackie. Thanks, but I believe I'll go home." Before he leaves, they survey the remaining mess. Using Josh's cordless drill, he drills three screws through the door and into the doorframe to secure it.

Ten minutes later, he and Blackie head out into the darkness. "Let's link up tomorrow, Josh. Thanks for the key and the new padlock."

Chapter 46: Ambush

"So, what do you think?" Clay orders a second round for the two men.

"We didn't find squat." Lenn rubs one hand over his forehead. "From what I saw, these guys don't have a clue about mining or filing a claim. But it doesn't square with the other facts." Lenn continues his rant, "Not only that, but they had evidence their diamonds were legit. I can't figure it out; how do they manage to be one step ahead of us at every turn."

"Damn those bastards!" Clay growls and takes a swig from his scotch. "Their claims were recorded first. Curse our luck. Those undeserving jerks are sitting on our bonanza."

Lenn agrees, "We deserve the riches, after all I found them first. I need them a damn sight more than Silver Jack or the schoolteacher. What good would all that money do the old man anyway?"

Sitting back, Lenn stares across the room. "Hey, who is the bitch sitting at the table all by herself?"

Clay guffaws "Go ahead and help yourself. That diseased whore will give herself to anyone for a bottle of Thunderbird." He laughs hoarsely, "On second thought, why waste your time on her. When we get this diamond thing worked out, we can order up the most expensive girls from Seattle and have them all to ourselves."

He contemplates being rich. He could talk Claire into leaving her husband to become his full-time plaything. He'd have the nicest house in town, expensive cars, and vacations. Of course, he'd secure the services of the best whores on the planet. There is no way he would limit himself to one woman, especially if he had loads of money.

Leaning forward, Lenn shares, "I have a plan. I believe once you get a mining claim you need to post a copy at the claim site."

Clay responds diffidently, "Yeah, so what?"

"They will need to head out into the brush again soon. We can catch them coming in, or going out, and finish this once and for all, with no one the wiser."

Clay considers Lenn's proposal and finds promise in the idea. "It could work; if we set a trap for them as they come back along their own trail. We only need to discover where they leave their boat."

"You watch for Silver Jack's departure and alert me when they prepare to leave." Lenn adds, "We can follow them from a distance and catch up with them in the brush."

Clay is aware Lenn plans to kill the old prospector and his young sidekick. At this point, there's no other option. "Okay, unless we can come up with a better plan, we'll go with your idea." He stands up. "I probably should go to work in the morning." He polishes off his last scotch. "What a revolting development."

Chapter 47: Proposition

In my classroom on Monday morning I find it difficult to concentrate on getting ready for the start of school, only six weeks away. It's hard to prep when I'm unsure which classes I'll be teaching. Donning latex gloves I return to cleaning and organizing the chemical storage area, miffed my predecessor left it in such a mess.

While I am on my knees, working to remove expired chemicals from one of the cabinets, Bert and Eunice stop by. Bert leans on a counter, "How are things going?"

I choose to be candid; "I'm a little frustrated. I don't know for sure what I'll be teaching." I stand and stretch my legs, "I'm also pretty sore from a hiking trip I took on the mainland."

Both of them give me concerned looks. Eunice warns me, "People get mauled by bears every year. It wasn't long ago a woman was mauled by a brown bear over near Berg Bay. It's twenty miles from here by boat."

I feel as if I need to reassure them I was in good hands. "Oh. I didn't go alone; I went with an old prospector named Silver Jack."

Eunice scratches her head, "It doesn't sound safe to me." Her eyes look worried. "If you keep this up, we'd better warn Mr. Pearson to start looking for a backup science teacher."

"Eunice, the most dangerous thing I encountered on the trip was devil's club." I show them my scratched arms. "Why, there's a greater chance to get mugged in the parking lot outside than there is to be mauled by a bear."

Eunice gets a determined look. "I can tell you young man,

you are going to get yourself killed messing around with Mother Nature. Didn't you get hypothermia within forty-eight hours of arriving in Wrangell? Whenever you think you're going out in the brush, you come and talk to me first. I'll straighten you out."

I'm touched by her concern for my safety. Bert and Eunice stick around for a couple of minutes longer, asking if I need help with my cleaning project. Casually, Eunice mentions another teacher is working in a room in the adjoining wing, in case I'm interested in introducing myself. When they leave, they promise to bring me more trash containers.

I take this opportunity to meet at least one other teacher at the high school and go over to introduce myself. At the hub of the school, I cross to the other academic wing and walk down the hall.

A classroom door is open and the lights are on. I stick my head in the room and look around. "Hello, is anybody home?"

A rotund woman, in a florid-print dress stands up, and walks around a cluttered desk. In a clipped manner she addresses me, "How may I help you?"

"I'd like to introduce myself. I'm Josh, and I'm the new science teacher. Bert and Eunice told me another teacher was in the building, so I came over to say hi."

The woman inclines her head, "Welcome to Wrangell High, Josh. I'm Mrs. Johnson, and I try to teach art to the poor unfortunate children on this island. I've been here for nearly thirty years."

"Interesting." In an attempt to draw her out, I point to the paintings hanging around the room, "Are these yours?"

"Oh, yes. Let me show you my latest masterpiece. I'm quite proud of it. You wouldn't believe all the accolades I receive from my students. Each of them is honored I'm here to provide them with such exquisite instruction."

Mrs. Johnson stops in front of a massive canvas. The most prominent aspects of the piece are swirls of purple and royal blue. Randomly, thin yellow and red lines originate in the background and float off to nowhere in particular, ending with a flourish of black.

I'm confounded by her work. Awkwardly, I stammer, "I–I see. This is an amazing piece. I don't know what to say."

Mrs. Johnson claps her hands together enthusiastically.

"That's the reaction I was hoping for. My students will love it. My students always choose my piece as their favorite in our annual art show. In fact, I always win unanimously. It's a track record I've had for twenty-five years. Let me show you last year's winning entry."

We move to the back of the classroom, and I find myself staring at a piece of lopsided pottery. Remarkably, it's painted in purple and royal blue, sporting several thin lines of yellow and red ending in black flourishes.

I glance around the airy room, it's well lit but I don't find any examples of student art. "I was hoping to look at student art. Do you have any I might review?"

"Oh, no, my students rarely show their art. They prefer looking at mine as much as possible. I do have several pieces I helped students with, if you'd prefer to look at those." Mrs. Johnson leads the way into her supply room, and I follow her into the messiest storage area I've ever observed in a school. It makes the chemical storage area next to my classroom look as if it were an operating room by comparison. Scattered everywhere in disorderly piles is every kind of art material one can imagine. Most look to be ruined, due to the way they have been shoved aside without care or thought. Inside, she opens a cabinet and withdraws several canvasses. I peer over her massive shoulder and find a stack of pictures all bearing a remarkable resemblance to the two in the classroom.

"By the way, Mrs. Johnson, I've met one of your former students. Her name is Anne, and she works down at the café."

Mrs. Johnson leans forward, showing me more of her ample cleavage than I care to notice. "Oh, yes, I remember her. The poor creature had a bit of talent, but she refused to take any direction. I'm afraid her best hope is to find a job as a graphic artist doing posters for community events." As if to emphasize the difference between their levels of talent, Mrs. Johnson spreads her arms, one high and one low, causing one great breast to rise and the other to fall.

Trying with difficulty to maintain eye contact with Mrs. Johnson, instead of staring into her bosom, I am appalled at her behavior. Her comments regarding a former student are inappropriate. One of my pet peeves, a teacher should praise in public, criticize in private. My interpretation of private did not include her sharing her negative comments with me.

"I've reviewed her recent work. Perhaps you judge her too harshly." I struggle to retain my composure as my anger at this incompetent teacher rises to the surface.

"Au contraire, I worked with her for four years and not an iota of improvement came forth, despite my personal attention to her apparent deficits." Mrs. Johnson inserts one ham-sized fist inside the neckline of her dress, and shortens one of her bra straps with a judicious tug. I try not to be aware of the undulation this causes in the entire northern hemisphere of her torso.

Unable to control my anger any longer, I snap at my new colleague. "Your assessment of Anne's work is colored by your own failures, Mrs. Johnson. I can tell you she has a remarkable talent. As a fellow teacher, I find your behavior indefensible. As a person who loves art, I find the damage you have done to border on malpractice." As I talk, my anger flashes white-hot. How could this woman sit here year after year and ruin the future for her students? How could Mr. Pearson allow Mrs. Johnson to perpetrate her abuse on the unsuspecting children of this community?

In the pause following my shocking outburst, Mrs. Johnson's face turns beet red. Her mouth gulps for air. She looks like she is trying to speak, but no sound emits from her thin lips. Finally, she gasps, "Well, I never...."

I cut her off, finished with the woman's arrogance and disdain for her students, "Mrs. Johnson, I am going to try to undo the damage you have done. I've sent pieces of Anne's work for professional appraisal. If the results come back positive, I intend to take this information to the Principal. You're a fraud. I hope you do the honorable thing and resign or retire. Good day."

I spin around and leave the art storage room. On my way out of the classroom my heels thunder against the floor. Out in the hallway, the sound echoes ahead of me in the empty corridor.

I rebuke myself. What kind of idiot would take on a veteran teacher at a first meeting and insult their professional ethics as well as their talent in their chosen field? What was I thinking? My words cannot be misconstrued; I will never be able to smooth over this incident. What have I done? Maybe I should pray Mr. Pearson needs a science teacher more than he needs a harmonious school. Perhaps I'll be lucky and everyone will applaud me for confronting a bad teacher. Not much chance of that happening.

Back in my classroom, I call it a day. After all, I'm not making progress in prepping for my classes or cleaning up the chemical storage room, so I might as well enjoy the summer afternoon.

On my way down the front steps of the school, I notice a blue BMW Roadster in the parking lot. As I near it, the woman from the bank lobby steps gracefully out of the car. She is wearing a rouge, ruffle-trim jacket and charcoal wool pants. The wool pants fit her like skin, and I notice a gap at the point of her crotch where her shapely legs meet her pelvis. Her red hair is tied with a black ribbon. As I move to step past the car, she holds up her hand, "Excuse me; do you work in this building?"

I smile at her, eager to be helpful. "Yes I do. Can I help you?"

"I hope so." Her eyes appraise me from beneath her lowered lashes. She poses, one hand on her hip and the other on the top of the driver's side door. She looks over her shoulder toward the building. "I have permission to put up a poster advertising a charity dance in the window near the front door. Can you let me in the building?"

It's my aim to please. Nothing could be more important to me. I will myself not to stare at her shapely ass, trim waist, and cantilevered bosom, as she walks away from me and opens the passenger side of the car. "I have a key, and I'd be glad to let you in. Can I help you carry anything?"

She smiles at me, "I will carry the poster. But you can carry the tape for me."

I walk up beside her and get a whiff of her expensive perfume. When she straightens up with her supplies, I find we are standing close together. "My name is Claire. What's yours?" Claire hands me the roll of tape and our fingers touch. She doesn't let go right away, so our hands stay in contact.

I don't make any effort to end the connection either, but sadly our fingers break apart when I respond. "Forgive me. I should have introduced myself. My name is Josh Campbell, and I teach science here at the high school."

"I know who you are. I made inquiries after I saw you in the bank lobby." Claire caresses my face; "I thought a handsome fella like you might show a girl a good time."

I enjoy the caress. However, Claire's eyes bother me. The sensuality expressed by the rest of her body doesn't impact her eyes in any way. She places one hand on my arm and rotates closer to me. She whispers into my ear, "Josh. I don't waste words or time. I want you, and you want me. I've noticed how you watch me. Give me your phone number, and I'll call you when I can get away from my husband. You won't regret it."

I consider her offer. I place one hand behind her trim waist, resting it lightly at the top of her firm, athletic ass. I pull her incrementally closer. Looking down into her open lips, her white teeth are flawless. I can feel her breath against my face.

"It would be my pleasure to give you my number, Claire."

"You won't regret it," she whispers, "and neither will I." Claire laughs, a lilting musical laughter, slightly off-key at the end. "I hoped you and I could find something in common. Do you need a pen?"

I nod my head, and she pulls a gold pen and a notepad out of her purse. As I'm writing my phone number, I manage to force out a question of my own. "Can I get your number, too?"

"Don't be silly, Josh. I mentioned I was married. How would it look if my husband answered the phone? Let's get this poster hung up."

I follow Claire up the stairs, trying hard not to stare at her butt as she mounts the steps. At the main door to the school, I unlock it and hold it open for her to enter. Without talking, we collaborate on hanging the poster. I tear off pieces of tape, while Claire uses them to secure the poster to the window. She manages to rub her butt into my groin in the process, and I choose not to shy away from the contact. I'm reminded by my reaction, it has been weeks since I've been with a woman.

"Josh, look for me at the dance. It's this Wednesday night at the Nolan Center, and all the funds go to my favorite charity, so invite your friends and come ready to dance with me."

Claire exits the school and descends the steps to her BMW. I follow, feeling a little like a puppy being left behind. She opens her car door and smiles seductively at me. "I'm glad you came to Wrangell, Josh. This place is rustic and can be pretty dull. I can make it exciting for you. In fact, I can make it exhilarating. Don't let me down when I call you." She seats herself in the roadster, pulls back from the curb, and waves, before reversing gear and speeding away.

I stand there for a moment before her aura evaporates and feel foolish. What was I doing, giving my phone number to a married woman wanting to have an affair? This isn't my style or what I'd envisioned when I left Colorado. What would Jack or Anne think of me, if they witnessed my immature behavior? I don't want the answer.

I get in my rig and head for my apartment. Once there, I call information for the mining claim office in Ketchikan. I want to check out a theory, whoever is behind trashing Jack's boat and my apartment learned our names after making contact with that office.

After several attempts, I connect with the claims office, and they confirm Jack filed two claims, one in my name. I also learn another claim was filed later the same day. I ask for the name and address and write them down. I don't recognize the name, but this is no surprise, as I've met so few individuals in Wrangell.

I ponder what to do. I'd spent the previous day, Sunday, on repairs. Looking around at the mess in my apartment, I plan to go to the grocery store to get more cleaning supplies. I might be able to clean up a fair bit of the damage before I need to get ready for my date with Anne.

Chapter 48: Rewards

Claire's father had outfought all challengers to create the largest logging company in Southeast Alaska. His men had been loyal because her father was fiercest. Today, her father's men did her bidding due to the relentless tenacity of will she possessed. In addition, she offered economic stability where none existed in this wet frontier. Because of her efforts, the company had not suffered a single setback, until recently.

Three months ago, the contract with the mill in Ketchikan had been terminated. When the owners' representative repulsed her overtures, she tried coercion. Her sharp demands for a volume discount on the milling charge backfired, and she found herself in the unique position of having to pay a surcharge if she wanted her wood milled. At roughly the same time, the remaining operational mill in the region closed. This left her company with a huge supply of logs in the woods with nowhere to go.

She had analyzed the situation and realized she could not haul her wood farther than Ketchikan and make a profit. She had been counting on a discount from the mill when she placed her bid on the timber nearly a year ago. In the meantime, lumber prices had fallen, and she is the one feeling the squeeze.

None of the options she is working on provide cash fast enough to prevent a catastrophe. Meanwhile, she needs to make payroll and cover the other expenses of continued operation. She is leveraged at her father's bank far past the ratios allowed by the banking regulators. She'd offered discounted shares of the company to most of her father's old business partners, but not one has stepped forward to invest. Claire understands if the right person looks under the edge of the circus tent, her business will collapse, creating a thud heard all over Alaska. She vows to do everything in her power to prevent the disintegration of her father's company.

Today, she will contact the owners of the mill that closed in Wrangell three years ago. With her persuasion, her bank will loan them sufficient funds to reopen, especially if they hold a lucrative contract with her company. The signing bonus she will insist be included will solve her cash flow needs.

With funding secure, one hurdle would remain, getting permits to open the mill. It could take weeks to get the necessary approval, and safety officials will likely demand capital improvements so the facility will meet current codes. She'll have to use her influence judiciously to clear these hurdles. Overall, the plan might work, but she will need to devote much time and energy to it.

As she considers how she will reward herself for succeeding, Claire recalls the new science teacher. He looks like he belongs in Alaska. He is big, handsome, and smart but no match for her. No man ever could be. She looks in the mirror and examines her cleavage with a critical eye. She resolves to bed him, before he discovers her husband is the Principal. Normally, she would toy with him for a while, just for the sport. But she doesn't have time to play, not this time. She will hook Josh first; whatever he finds out later will no longer matter.

She has a talent for reading men. It helps her talk men like the bank manager into doing what they don't want to do and make it look as if it is their idea. Josh will be no exception. Leaving her office, she toys with ideas to ensnare Josh. Maybe she can use him to get rid of Clay, when the time is right.

Chapter 49: Chagrined

Emily reads aloud, “The Princess of India was beautiful, kind, and intelligent.” Anne listens; it’s a daily ritual. She reads aloud to Anne for at least ten minutes before listening as Anne reads. Each reader gets to select her own reading material. The listener must pay attention and ask at least one relevant question at the end. Anne started using this strategy when her daughter fell behind in reading during third grade and found it helped with reading fluency and comprehension.

It being one of Anne’s days off from work, when reading time is finished, she runs errands. Emily opts to stay home, so she can continue reading. Anne sets off alone and notices Josh’s SUV when she pulls into the parking lot in front of the hardware store. She finds Josh waiting in the checkout line.

Josh greets her, “I’m glad to run into you. I didn’t get a chance to ask you if you wanted to bring Emily along to dinner this evening. What’s your preference?”

Ann is struck by his thoughtfulness. She had hoped he planned to include Emily. Because he hadn’t been clear the other day, she’d prepped Emily not to be disappointed if she didn’t get to go. “Emily would like to come, too. She hates to be left out.”

“It will be fun. By the way, I sent the drawing you gave me to a friend of mine who works in the admissions office at an art and design college.”

Stiffening, Anne withdraws, “My work isn’t that good.”

“Not True. David called to tell me if you have more drawings of this caliber in your portfolio, you could get into any art college in the country."

Anne isn't sure how to respond. She had always hoped her work might be good, but the lone expert on the topic, Mrs. Johnson, had held the opposite opinion. Josh is affirming her artistic skills are worthy of further training. Feeling off balance, Anne takes a deep breath, "I'm not sure what good the information does me. I can't afford to go to college."

"That's not the point. There are lots of ways to study art and develop your talent. The most expensive part is the materials you'll need. My friend David will help with advice. Think of it as having a mentor who can help you bring out the talent you already have." Josh reaches for her hand; "I wouldn't have sent your work to David if I hadn't believed in you. You have a lot to offer the art world. Anyway, your talent deserves to be shared."

Anne is comforted by Josh's confidence. It's nice to have an advocate. This is not a feeling she's experienced in a long time.

Out of the blue, Josh blurts out, "Check out the sign in the window. There is a charity dance this Wednesday night. You work the following morning, but would you consider going with me?" He looks like a little boy, "I don't know many people in Wrangell, and you could help me out. What do you say?"

Anne finds Josh's striking blue eyes and infectious grin difficult to resist. "Okay, I'll go with you. But you have to promise to get me home before my carriage turns into a pumpkin."

Somberly, Josh nods his head, "I agree to your terms."

To regain her composure, Anne glances around the store and notices Josh's shopping cart is full of cleaning supplies and repair tools. "Why are you buying so many things?"

"My apartment was vandalized, and I'm going to spend time this afternoon repairing damaged furniture and cleaning up the mess."

"Can I help?" Anne is curious and concerned. As far as she knew, nothing like this has ever happened in town.

"You don't have to help. I can handle this."

"Oh no, I insist. I have a few things to pick up around town and I'll be right over." It's Anne's turn to smile, "But I can't help you if you don't tell me where you live."

Josh provides directions, “Go south on Church Street. Turn left on Bennett and I’m the last apartment in the complex on the left side of the street.”

Anne stops at the grocery store. She calls Emily to inform her she’ll be home later, reminding her daughter to call with any emergency. She returns books to the library before going to Josh’s apartment.

Pulling into the parking place beside his Subaru, she notices the area in front of his apartment is tidy. Anne knocks on his door, and Josh opens it for her. “Hi. Come on in. I apologize for the mess, it doesn’t always look this way.”

Looking around the apartment, some organization is evident in the living room and bedroom. His laundry room is a total mess. Soap, fabric softener, and bleach are all dumped together on the floor. The kitchen is the same, where the contents of his cupboards are strewn on the floor as well. Anne puts on rubber gloves. “I’ll start in the kitchen. If you fix the broken drawers, I’ll work on the rest of this stuff.”

Anne sorts the items on the floor into piles. Many can be salvaged, such as cans of food, from those needing to be tossed in the garbage because the packaging is torn.

She asks the question that has been on her mind since Josh first told her his apartment had been vandalized, “Do you have any idea why this happened?”

“I’m not sure. Jack’s boat was ransacked the night before my apartment was trashed. I suspect claim jumpers.”

“What do you mean, claim jumpers?”

“Do you remember, when I told you Jack and I found interesting minerals? These were diamonds. But while we were at the claim site, someone shot at us. We didn’t stick around to find out who was doing the shooting.”

Anne finds herself mesmerized by this story. “Why didn’t you tell me earlier? Being shot at is pretty significant.” Anne asks the obvious follow up question, “Did you tell the police?”

“No.” Josh squirms, “When we got back it was late, and then Jack left. It didn’t cross my mind. I did call the police to report Jack’s boat being ransacked.”

Anne considers his situation. “Is it possible you were at someone else’s claim?”

“Not likely. We saw no sign of people being at this site before us. In addition, Jack was able to file on this location without any trouble. I was curious if there was a competing claim, so earlier today I called the mining office in Ketchikan and learned there was an attempted filing on the same spot after our claims were filed.” Josh lifts an eyebrow, “Who is Clay Foster?”

Anne shivers. The Harbormaster always made her feel creepy. She didn’t like the way the man kept looking at her whenever he came into the restaurant. He made her feel dirty. “Clay Foster is the Harbormaster. He’s taller than you, thin, and wiry.”

Josh looks chagrined. “It’s the same man I met at the post office last Friday when I had Blackie with me.” After a pause, he asks, “Can I excuse myself for a short while? I want to report this new information to Jack. Maybe you should go home, and I’ll pick you up later at your place.”

Not about to be left out, Anne states, “I insist on going with you.” Anne contemplates the hazards connected with Josh. She pulls off her rubber gloves and reaches for her jacket; this is one time she is glad Emily is home, safely reading her book.

Chapter 50: Disappointed

Katie is fueling her boat at the dock across from the marina. Starting at first light, she had surveyed the eastern shore of Etolin Island in an area only a few miles from the marina. Returning to Wrangell mid-afternoon, she made a snap decision to knock off for the rest of the day. After all, she has been working long hours at least six days a week since she started her new job. Perhaps she could give Josh a call and talk him into going out for dinner.

She checks the oil in both the outboard and her trolling motor. Satisfied everything is working properly, she hops back onto the dock. In the office, she pays the bill and tucks her receipt in her record book. She casts off from the dock and slowly motors past the marina.

Katie feels an adrenaline rush when she spots Josh. Turning her boat around, she notices Josh is not alone. Reversing, she moves further away, aiming toward her own dock at the southern end of the harbor. Grabbing her binoculars, she picks up the magnified image of a woman through the viewer and grimaces when she observes her to be young and attractive. With a growing sense of shock and dread, she continues to slip through the harbor. A cold chill washes over her as a tear of disappointment stings her hot cheek.

Chapter 51: Knowledge

Silver Jack is cleaning the deck of his boat, when Blackie uses his "we have a visitor" bark. He looks up from his work to find Josh and Anne coming down the floating dock. Both look apprehensive.

He waits until they get close, "Come aboard. Blackie and I were hoping for company." He pulls out folding chairs, opening one for Anne and hands another to Josh.

Josh and Anne bring him up to date, including Clay's attempt to file a claim.

"Excuse me, I'm forgetting my manners. Would either of you care for a drink?" Silver Jack pulls root beer out of his cooler and offers one to each. He watches as Josh removes Anne's bottle cap for her before removing his own. He enjoys the two young people together, not because they make a fine looking pair, but because he is aware of the wounds they both carry.

After a short discussion, the prospector says, "At this point we know one thing Clay doesn't."

"What would that be?" Josh crosses his arms and leans back in his chair.

"Why, he doesn't suspect we know he's after our claim." Silver Jack stands up, and paces along his deck, "The next move is up to us."

Chapter 52: Friends

I drive Anne back to my apartment. She laughs when I tell her about my first night in Wrangell. I arrived late and the deserted town looked like a setting for a twilight zone episode. Her laugh sounds magical to me. I'm amazed this wonderful, kind woman is sitting in my car. Her jet black hair accents her cream colored skin in a way I find more than lovely. "What time would you like me to pick you up for dinner?"

She turns; her green eyes deep and impenetrable. "What about six o'clock?"

"That's good for me. I thought perhaps we'd go to Zak's Café. There aren't many choices in town other than taverns. How does it sound?"

"You're right. We don't have many choices. I've never been to Zak's, but I hear they have pretty good burgers."

Back at my apartment, I follow Anne as she goes to the driver's side of her truck. "I'm sorry I worried you with the whole claim jumping thing. It's something I've found myself in. I feel as if I owe it to Jack to see it through."

Anne looks up at me. This time there is no smile and no dimples, but her green eyes are soft. She places one hand on my arm, "I worry about you."

I step closer and lower my face. Before I can make contact with her lips, Anne rocks forward and kisses me. The brush of her lips is like an electric shock. It's over so quickly; I wonder if I imagine it happening. Anne pivots and ducks inside her truck. I step back, my face flushing red. I stand, waving goodbye as she pulls away and heads down the street.

Not sure whether I should feel ecstatic or foolish, I go into my apartment and clean up for my date with the girls.

#

Dinner at Zak's turns out better than I could hope. We have the dining room to ourselves. Anne joins me in a glass of draft beer with dinner. She looks amazing, and my eyes remain on her. I remember the electric kiss we'd shared earlier and wonder if I will be lucky enough to get another. Emily is impressed with the surroundings and the novelty of being served in a restaurant. Clearly, she and her mother don't eat out often.

During our meal, Emily is bold enough to ask, "Why did you move here?"

I want to give a simple answer but speak from my heart, "I wanted to get away from Colorado and start a new life. I had no idea what was here or even if I'd like it. At the time, it didn't matter."

Emily takes a bite of lasagna, "Will you stay?"

I feel uncomfortable, as if I've been put on the spot. "I've only been here a month, so I'm still getting used to it. I'll stay until I finish the school year because I have a contract."

My answer satisfies Emily enough she changes to a less difficult topic, "What do you like so far?"

Without hesitating I respond, "I enjoy the friends I've made and having the wilderness right on my doorstep."

Anne looks at me, and I sense she's ready to say something important. However, the comment doesn't come before Emily speaks up, "We're your friends, right?"

I smile at Emily. Watching Anne out of the corner of my eye, I nod. "You bet you are. I couldn't ask for better friends than you." Time to change the subject, "By the way, have you been practicing on your bike? I was kind of hoping we could all go for a ride together, maybe on one of your days off."

Later, I take the pair home. Watching Anne sit nearby in the passenger seat nearly drives me mad. I can smell her perfume and catch the flash of her eyes when we pass under each streetlight. I want to reach for her hand or take her in my arms. Instead, I restrain myself, unsure what to do but certain Anne isn't ready for displays of affection in front of Emily.

My prediction turns out to be accurate when I walk the girls to the front door of their apartment. Anne's green eyes are lively, but the body language and talk stay firmly on neutral ground. I wish them good night and drive back to my empty apartment.

Chapter 53: Trap

Clay is sick of Lenn's whining. Even his second double-scotch isn't helping. He is also annoyed at the furtive way Lenn glances around the Marine Bar while he's talking. To Clay, the moron looks guilty and draws attention unnecessarily. Lenn continues, "I'm not sure how much longer I can string Sealaska Corporation along. They might be getting suspicious regarding the reports I've been sending in. I would quit and get them off my back, but I need cash. Pretty soon I'll have to pay rent again and the place I'm staying in is a dump."

Deciding to clamp down on Lenn, Clay lets him have it, "Listen champ. This is the way it's got to be for a bit longer. Until we get rid of our competition, you need to lie low." He takes a deep breath and works to keep the edge out of his voice, "I haven't been sitting around. I've been keeping an eye on Silver Jack. So far, all he's done is buy a lot of dog food. I've been hanging out at the marina so much the entire staff is nervous, wondering what I'm doing there."

Lenn repeats himself for the third time; "We should get more diamonds while we wait for him to show up at the claim. We're going to need the money, and they have to come back and stake their claim. They'd be walking into our trap."

"You fool! That's where they'd expect to find us. But if we jump them along their trail, they'll never be expecting it." Clay runs his fingers through his hair. "We're sticking with the original plan. As soon as the old prospector leaves, we'll follow him over to Crittenden Creek and finish him off. No one will learn he's missing for a couple of weeks. By then, they'll think the bears got him."

Lenn spits on the floor. "Fuck it. Aren't there ways to speed this up?"

Shaking his head, Clay responds, "I haven't come-up with anything. I don't believe the old man will head over there until we get a high enough tide he can get up the river. As far as I can tell, it won't be for a couple of days." He glances around the room and lowers his voice, "But I'll watch him anyway in case he heads out sooner. We want to catch up with him along the river if we can."

Lenn picks up his glass, "I'll drink to that."

Chapter 54: Conflicted

Silver Jack is repairing his stove when he spots Josh arriving. He opens his cabin door and greets the young man, "Come aboard and make yourself at home."

Josh sits on the edge of the boat petting Blackie. Silver Jack can tell the young man is upset. After waiting for Josh to initiate a conversation with no success, he queries, "What is troubling you son?"

Josh grimaces as if he's in pain, "How do you know when you've found the right woman?"

The prospector almost laughs out loud, but the serious expression on Josh's face aborts his laughter. "I'm not the person you should be asking. After all, I've been married seven times and not many of them lasted for more than a few years."

Josh nods his head, "I feel lost. Out of the blue, there are two girls showing interest. How do I pick? What if I make the wrong choice?"

He sits down beside Josh. "I can't be much help. As a friend, I can tell you this. There are two good criteria to consider when it comes to choosing a mate. First, do they treat you well? You can't love a woman long-term, if you don't respect her and she doesn't respect you. The second thing to remember is you have to care about the person you're with. If you don't like them, you won't be able to fake it for a lifetime. I've tried a few times, and it never works."

"I'm taking Anne to the dance tomorrow night. Katie might show up, too. I'm not sure how to keep all these balls in the air."

Josh props his chin in his hands, “I feel as if I’m in a house of cards before it falls apart.”

He mulls over Josh’s comment. “Anne has a daughter. Is that an issue for you?”

Josh sits upright, “Not at all, I like Emily a lot. As much as Anne and Emily are independent and rely on each other for support, it feels as if they are missing something. Maybe I could be what they need.” He sighs, "It could be nice, if it worked out.”

“It helps if you figure out what you want and go after it with passion. Seems to me what you want most of all is to be part of a family.” Silver Jack pauses, “I always strove to get to Alaska and spend the rest of my days hunting, fishing, and prospecting. My compass has always been pointed here. You’ve got to find your bearing and stick to it. It’s the road to happiness in this life.”

Blackie stands, stretches, and licks Josh’s face. The dog can sense the young man’s turmoil. Silver Jack points out, “He’s asking you to take him for a walk.”

Josh gets the lead and takes Blackie over to Chief Shakes Island. Silver Jack worries he’s placed Josh in danger. He understands the young man is a stand up guy, who will try to do the right thing. Unfortunately, Josh could get himself killed. The prospector has been around the block a time or two, and he’s prepared to do what it takes to protect his claim and what he’s earned. He must find a way to keep his partner away from the trouble to come.

He’s aware the Harbormaster has been hanging around for several days. Clay is a lazy, smart-mouth drunk, who gets others to do his dirty jobs for him. He’s watched the Harbormaster make fun of David. The man is a coward, likely to take advantage from a distance. Two men were on the mountain when the shots were fired. Whoever the other guy is, he is worse than Clay. Best to assume this pair is capable of anything.

While cleaning his stove, he comes up with a plan to draw the two men out in the open. He needs to know how far Clay and his partner are willing to go to get what they want. Project finished, he whistles a jaunty tune.

Chapter 55: Embezzlement

Arriving at work, Clay is whistling. Wednesdays are his favorite day of the week for a number of reasons. First, he hands out next week's schedule each Wednesday, and this allows him to give the crappiest details to David. Second, he counts the cash in the safe and makes a deposit at the bank. The major source of cash for the marina is from visiting craft docking overnight. Dockage fees run one dollar per foot of boat length and are higher if the boat wants power and other amenities.

With the average craft running fifty feet in length, a week of collections will amass two to three thousand dollars. Clay has found it easy to skim hundreds each week, with no one the wiser. After all, he is also the auditing officer. No surprise, over the years he has developed a foolproof method to ensure receipts and deposits match.

After returning from the bank, Clay helps himself to a cup of black coffee. It's not as good as scotch, so he adds a shot from the flask in his desk drawer. Using binoculars, he checks on Silver Jack's boat. There's no sign of the codger. That's not unusual; the old coot could be in town or asleep. He shifts the binoculars a bit and looks for the old prospector's skiff. When he can't find it, he walks down the marina. Along the way, he stops several times and engages the locals.

One of them is brash enough to ask, "What's up Harbormaster. You ain't been on the floating dock in five years."

Clay responds to the remark with a biting retort, "That's right Al, neither has your wife. She'd rather spend time with me than come down here with you."

When he arrives at the old prospector's boat, he notes the skiff is indeed gone. Clay scans the harbor fueling station with no luck. He returns to his office trying to look as if he's not in a hurry. He fails miserably and calls Lenn at his apartment. "You'd better get the fuck over here, Silver Jack is gone."

Chapter 56: Lost

On Wednesday, I wake up to waves of water coursing down outside my bedroom window. I roll the covers over my head and snuggle in, but the thought of a cup of black coffee keeps me awake. After a quick workout and breakfast, I do laundry and run errands. It's another wet, gusty day, and I'm glad I can spend it indoors where I'm safe and dry. One of my goals is to get a new lock and deadbolt set for the rear door of my apartment.

Because I need special bits used for installing a doorknob, I head for the hardware store. I'm not impressed when I learn the store doesn't have the tool in stock. The clerk is cheerful, if not too helpful, "We'll have to order it from Seattle; we should have it in a week."

"Does anyone else carry it?" I've stumbled into one of the drawbacks to living in the middle of nowhere.

The clerk scratches his head, "Well, you could probably find it in Ketchikan."

"I won't be taking the ferry to Ketchikan any time soon. I'll order the part. Can you call me when it comes in?"

The rest of my errands go nearly as badly. Frustrated, I stop at the Diamond C for a cup of coffee and a chance to talk to Anne and Emily. I park in the back but before I leave the car, it dawns on me Anne's truck is missing. It's after two o'clock, and Anne and Emily have left work.

On the way back to my apartment, I stop my rig where I can view the harbor. The island is hunkering down to avoid the rain and wind. A lone seagull looks out of place struggling against the westerly. Thick gray clouds make it impossible to see any of the islands to the west. Wrangell is a lost place.

As I get ready for my date with Anne, I recall yesterday's conversation with Jack. I hadn't fully revealed to Jack how shaky my situation has become. In addition to Anne and Katie, tonight I will also have to be on watch for the pheromone intensive Claire. As I struggle with my personal life, my strategy is to strive for balance and keep below the radar. After tonight I will choose one girl to pursue. No more riding the fence for me.

Chapter 57: Control

Speeding northward toward Wrangell, Katie's boat cruises at full throttle, ignoring the choppy waves like a bee heading for its hive. Behind her, the wake spreads out wider and wider until the edges blur away in the distance. With her raincoat fastened against the damp, wet day, she is also protected from the cold, westerly wind buffeting her vessel.

Although her eyes remain alert for drifting logs in her path, Katie is thinking about Josh. She is aware there is a charity dance at the Nolan Center this evening. Should she go, hoping to run into him? What if he's there, but he's with the dark-haired girl she saw in the marina?

Katie is uncertain what to do, and this is unexplored terrain for her. She likes being the one who controls where a relationship with a man will go. She knew she should leave Warren well before she acted on the decision. With Josh, she had the upper hand only to be surprised by the arrival of another woman. Embracing her pique, she plans her retaliation.

Chapter 58: Vulnerable

Silver Jack's outboard motor is cranked up to maximum power, pushing the heavy skiff at six or seven knots. Headed east toward Crittenden Creek, he is grateful to get past Babbler Point without any signs of pursuit. His plan depends on getting out of sight before the Harbormaster realizes he is gone and tries to follow. If Clay and his crony catch up with him on the open water or along the shore, he will have to be ready to fight. He assumes the other men have rifles with scopes. If so, they will have a definite advantage.

If he can get to shore and into the woods, his odds go up. Few have his skill in the deep forest. Being in the woods doesn't eliminate his risk. If the two men learn where he is hiding and come at him from opposite directions, he could be caught in a deadly crossfire.

The day is wet, windy, and cold. White-capped waves run alongside the skiff while he plows eastward. He is wearing his chest-high waders, raincoat, waterproof hat, and leather gloves. After passing Babbler Point, the shoreline curves northward into a bay.

Seeking the best location to drag his skiff out of sight into the nearby woods and brush, he follows the shoreline along the bay. He grounds the aluminum vessel on a rocky section of the bank. Shutting off the motor, he tilts it up out of the way and climbs over the side of the boat.

After getting Blackie away from the skiff, he wades onto the shore and drags the craft, a few inches at a time, up the shore. He wishes Josh were here to help him with this heavy chore. This is the time he's most vulnerable to being discovered, so he doesn't allow himself any breaks while working to get the skiff out of sight. Sedges along the shore are wet and slippery under his feet but also serve to make dragging the skiff a little easier.

Chapter 59: Disgusted

Compelling Lenn to leave the harbor slowly, Clay fumes at being forced to move naturally when all he wants to do with every pore of his body is to speed away. He is diverted when he notices the new fishery biologist arriving at the harbor. He hasn't been introduced, but every male in the region between the ages of sixteen and seventy-six knows the young woman's name and can describe in great detail her obvious physical attributes.

He waves at Katie as she passes, and he is heartened to receive a wave and bright smile in return. He might have to call on the little lady one evening. He notices Lenn watching his face intently when he turns back to scan the water in front of the sled.

Clearing the entrance to the harbor, Clay allows Lenn to accelerate and continue accelerating as they travel north past Point Highfield. By the time they reach the entrance to the Eastern Passage and can view Babbler Point, Lenn's jet outboard is running at thirty knots, skimming over the waves as if they don't exist.

When they near the entrance to Crittenden Creek, Lenn reduces speed. The jet outboard and sled can travel in less than four inches of water. They roar up the shallow river and Lenn keeps to the deepest channel. Several times, the sled bottoms out, but its forward speed and momentum allow it to shoot past each obstruction.

Lenn shuts off the motor below a wide sandbar. "If we want to go any farther, we walk. Even if we drag the sled past this sandbar I'm not sure how much farther we can get."

Clay shares, "There's supposed to be a falls ahead of us.

What I can't figure is how the old man could get farther up the river than us, unless we missed the high tide."

Lenn growls, "We're going to have to wade upriver and find out."

The two men tie the sled to a tree and shoulder their rifles. Clay curses when he steps into the cold river. "Damn, I wish we had waders."

Forty minutes later, after wading past their third turn in the river, the two men stop and scan a long straight stretch. Lenn is disgusted, "I don't see anything. Do you?"

Clay has to agree nothing man-made is in sight. "Let's go back to the skiff, my feet are freezing."

It's easier to travel downstream, and their pace increases. Soon, they reach the skiff and find it high and dry. The tide is lower, so there are more exposed rocks. It takes all their strength and cooperation to drag the sled around and pull it downriver until it floats. Lenn starts the jet outboard and wends his way downriver. At least twice Clay is compelled to go overboard and help push the sled through a shallow stretch.

As they move downriver, Clay watches each bank for signs Silver Jack might have hidden his skiff along the river. His cold, wet feet are miserable. He urges Lenn, "Let's get back to the marina. I forgot to bring scotch."

Chapter 60: Adrift

Behind a rotten log, Silver Jack watches the Harbormaster and his colleague enter the mouth of Crittenden Creek. He's careful to keep the dog lying down and quiet as the sled travels upriver. Using binoculars, he examines the two men and their equipment. Two rifle barrels protrude above the gunwale.

The prospector's memories nag; the second man's lean and wiry look is familiar. He pulls a summer sausage out of his pocket and uses his belt knife to cut the wrapper. He offers the first slice to Blackie, who readily downs the chunk of meat. After giving a second piece to Blackie, he cuts a slice for himself, enjoying the fatty texture. Knowing the protein will recharge him for continued physical activity, he settles back to wait.

#

An hour later, he is alerted to the sled's return by the thrum of the jet outboard echoing downriver. After the two men leave the mouth of the river, Silver Jack continues to watch them as the jet sled heads west toward the airport. To be safe, he waits thirty minutes to be certain they do not return. He glances at his watch and is startled to find it's late afternoon.

Returning to his skiff with Blackie, he scans the Eastern Passage to ensure the Harbormaster is not returning before dragging the craft back to the water. Pulling the skiff is easier since he is going with the shore's incline.

When the skiff is floating, he invites the dog aboard, laughing at the amount of water the hairy animal brings with him.

Fortunately, there is a battery-powered bilge pump connected to a float, which automatically removes excess water. Climbing into the skiff, he pushes away from the bank. Using one of the oars, he paddles to deeper water.

Satisfied he is far enough from the shore for the outboard's propeller to have clearance, he lowers his outboard, squeezes the fuel-line pump three times to increase fuel pressure, and pulls the starter cord. The motor sputters and dies. On the next pull, it comes to life, but he can tell the sound is wrong. Within seconds he realizes the motor is not ejecting water through the indicator outlet near the back so he turns the motor off. Water is required to cool the working parts of the outboard. Without water, permanent damage will occur.

The most common reasons for a water pump failure in an outboard motor are due to either obstruction or a broken or damaged impeller, a propeller-like device needed to force water up to the motor. He prays his problem is an obstruction, because he does not have the parts or tools to replace his impeller.

He paddles back to the shore, where he can stand in the shallow water to work on the motor. He fashions a slender tree whip into a probe so that he can carefully clean the water intake.

Satisfied, he climbs back into the skiff and pushes it out into deeper water. He starts the outboard and is disappointed, but not surprised, when there is no water ejecting from the side.

He shuts the engine down and considers his options. He can only run the motor a few minutes at a time before he ruins it. He could stay at the mouth of Crittenden Creek until a passerby offers help. This is a poor choice; given there are two guys he doesn't want to meet.

His other option is to paddle almost three miles across the Eastern Passage to Wrangell Island. His skiff does not have oarlocks for rowing and is not designed for efficient paddling, due to its width and weight. A heavy crosswind along the passage will push him off course. The final variable is tidal movement should pull him opposite to the wind direction, thus helping him slightly.

He realizes once committed to paddling across the Eastern Passage, he can only use the motor for a few minutes every half hour. He will not be able to stop to rest until he reaches his objective.

Stopping would leave the skiff to the mercy of the wind, which would shove him away from the island. The further he drifts to the east, the farther he will have to paddle, because the eastern shoreline of the island curves southward and away from him.

There is another consideration, the closer he gets to Wrangell Island the more likely a passing boat might provide him assistance, as this is the route taken by anyone traveling around the island. He commits to crossing.

Moving to the front of the skiff, he shifts to the port side, near the deck forming a covered section in the bow. He paddles, experimenting with a stroke to maintain the vector he wants. He settles into a rhythm he can sustain for the long hours ahead. He learns he has to be careful with each stroke or he will bang his hand against the gunwale of the skiff. By leaning over the side of the craft he reduces the chance of this happening but adds to the strain in his shoulders and back.

When his craft emerges from the protection of Babbler Point, stronger winds cause him to work harder. Frequently, he is compelled to move to the starboard side of the skiff to correct his course with several strong strokes. Every half hour he allows himself to run the motor at low speed for three minutes.

Two hours later, he is sure he is no longer making progress against the headwind and the waves. The point on Wrangell Island he is aiming for doesn't get closer and fatigue is taking its toll. He mutters, "There's never valet service when you need it." The sky darkens and the wind picks up. Reaching deep down for his reserves, he increases the pace of his paddling.

Chapter 61: Trapped

We enter the Nolan Center together, with me beaming. Anne looks fantastic, wearing a black dress, high heels, and a tasteful set of pearl earrings. To protect against the evening chill, across her shoulders is a beautiful shawl. The shawl depicts a multi-colored peacock on a black background. I offer her my arm as we pass through the entry, and she gracefully accepts adding two deep dimples to the smile on her face.

A matron who looks as if she hasn't smiled in the last decade stops us. "Tickets are twenty-five dollars." She looks directly at me, "Per person." I get the distinct impression she assumes I haven't the money.

I hand her one hundred dollars. "Please keep the change; it's for a good cause."

I'm surprised when there is no smile as she takes the money from me. "I need identification for you both, if you plan to drink alcohol. The stamp I use on the back of your hand is color coded."

We show her our identification cards and get stamped in green. I turn to Anne, "Green must mean go."

She giggles, "I bet the other color is red, for stop."

I'm decked out in a navy jacket, tan slacks, blue shirt and skinny bolo tie. I don't have much in the way of nice clothes to choose from, but I do try to keep one or two sets for special occasions, like this one. I wasn't sure what to wear for shoes and settled on a pair of nice cowboy boots, as I'd always found them comfortable for dancing. I whisper to Anne, "Remember, I don't know anyone, so please introduce me to folks." I check my jacket and Anne's shawl at the coat check.

The Nolan Center is bright and cheery. The lobby includes a number of intricately carved totems and this evening also provides space for two no-host bars. Dance music flows from the civic center, off the lobby, so I guide Anne in that direction. We enter a spacious room filled with people. The variation in dress is pretty amazing. There are men and women in western clothing, including hats and boots, mixed in with a lot of flannel shirts and blue jeans. Several couples are dancing to a fast western song that ends as we enter the room. Luckily, the following dance is slow, so I invite Anne, "Would you care to dance?" I look into her green eyes and wait for her reply.

"Because this is for a good cause, I can't refuse."

"I like your attitude." I guide Anne and join a dozen other couples on the dance floor. I lead her through the steps and pull her close enough to smell her hair and perfume. Looking down, I catch her green eyes watching me carefully. "What's wrong?"

"Not a thing. I'm wondering if you're genuine."

I respond, "You've got to be kidding. You can't be more cowboy than a guy from Colorado."

"That's not what I meant." She hesitates, while I count steps, and my heart beats. "You're genuinely interested in Emily and me, not just what you can get from us. I wasn't expecting that."

I'm not sure what to say, so I pull her close and kiss her upturned lips. They are sweet, and so is she. The kiss lasts until the end of the dance. When we part, her face is flushed with happiness. My face must be beaming.

As we start our dance, I catch a glimpse of Katie as she turns away into the crowd near the lobby. Certain she caught my intimate embrace, I feel sorry for her as well as guilty. I wanted to get to know her better, and now I understand that cannot happen. It saddens me to have hurt her feelings.

I look into Anne's green eyes and forget the sadness. In a flash, I realize I want to spend the rest of my life with Anne. The reasons are rich, complex, and yet amazingly simple at the same time. I want to be with her more than I want to breathe. Relieved to no longer feel conflicted, I rejoice because I'm a lucky man to be dancing with Anne.

Several dances later, I guide Anne to one of the walls. "Would you care for anything to drink or eat?"

"I thought I saw people with glasses of champagne. We should celebrate. That was a great first kiss." Anne unsuccessfully tries to straighten a lock of hair, which is not out of place until she touches it.

"Wait," I hold both her hands. "I'm counting, and that was actually our second kiss."

"Find the champagne, silly."

I'm about to go; when I spot Claire headed our way. She is decked out for the evening. Her silk blouse is cut low. So low, it reaches her waist. Everything she wears is red with black trim, even her fishnet stockings. As she walks, she reminds me of making love, every move revealed by the tailored wardrobe. She obviously revels in the impact she has on everyone in the room.

"Hi. Josh. Did you miss me?" Claire stops in front of me, ignoring Anne. Her lips part slightly, and her pose conveys sensuality and more than a hint of wickedness.

"I don't know what you mean." I take a deep breath, preparing for the worst.

Claire turns and speaks to Anne. "I thought he'd be glad to see me again. Men don't think the same way we do." Claire glances around and makes an obvious point of spotting a man across the room, "Excuse me; I'm soliciting for the Food Bank."

I turn to Anne, "Let's find champagne."

As we walk, she gives me a curious look. "I thought you said you didn't know anybody in town."

I feel defensive, "I met her at the high school a couple of days ago. She was trying to put up charity posters and the building was locked. I let her in, and that's how we met."

Anne looks over her shoulder at Claire, who is in animated conversation with a well dressed, elderly man. "I hope she doesn't give Mr. Clarke a heart attack. He's a nice man." She turns and looks directly at me, "Claire is married to Mr. Pearson, the Principal of the High School."

My steps falter, and I'm stunned into silence. I was aware Claire was married, but it never dawned on me she might be married to my boss. I feel sick, realizing how close I've come to committing an indiscretion similar to Kaeli's. Sheepishly, I respond, "Wow, that's a mismatch."

As we skirt the room, we come to Katie, and I'm forced to introduce her to Anne. Katie and Anne shake hands, but I can tell their faces are frozen into forced smiles. I feel awkward, but we get through the tense moment with no outburst from either side. I get another look from Anne that tells me she would like to ask me how I met Katie. It feels awkward between us. I'm not sure how to deal with this, other than to change the subject.

Another dance starts, and Katie accepts an offer to dance from a tall man in a cowboy hat. She flashes him one of her bright smiles, and I wince mentally. I doubt I'll be getting one of her smiles any time soon. I take solace as the man is missing at least one of his teeth.

Before we enter the lobby, Anne stops me and introduces me to a stocky man, clearly he's First Peoples heritage, with a head of thick silver hair and broad cheekbones. "Josh, this is the most admired man in town. He's the Chief of Police. Chief Ford, this is Josh Campbell, he's the new science teacher."

"Welcome to Wrangell, young man," his voice is deep and strong. "You'll soon learn this is a community where the children look up to and respect their teachers. I hope you will always remember that." He shakes my hand, and I get the sense here is a man who understands a lot about human nature.

"Yes, sir, I'll try." His features remind me of Mildred. I can understand why Anne would describe him as the most popular man in town. He's kind and truly interested in getting to know me. We talk for a few minutes, and he learns I'm new to Alaska.

We separate from the Chief, and Anne introduces me to another man nearly my height and build, but with brown hair tied back into a low ponytail. "Josh this is Chief Ford's son, Charlie. We went to school together, and Charlie is a carver. Mrs. Johnson didn't care for his art in high school either."

I ask, "What kind of carving do you do? Silver Jack told me there were Native Alaskan carvers in the area. Are you one of them?"

"I do a little carving," Charlie's voice is nearly as deep as his father's. "In fact, I'm working on a totem pole over on Prince of Wales Island. It's an Alaskan Cedar that Silver Jack fell for me. I've got plans to turn it into a full-sized totem. No one has made one in years."

"Fascinating. How is your project going?"

"Frankly, it isn't going so well. I can't find the flow for the traditional patterns. My carvings always turn out too realistic, maybe because I'm half Indian."

We talk with Charlie for a few more minutes and learn he has been accepted at Seattle Art Institute and will leave in a few weeks. Finally, we break away and make for the lobby; my goal is to toast Anne with a glass of champagne, then find a way to repeat the wonderful kiss we shared earlier.

The cash bars are crowded, so I suggest Anne wait while I go through the line to get our drinks. When I return with the champagne, I find she has moved close to the dancing and is talking to Claire. As I get close, I overhear Claire tell Anne, "I can't wait to get him into my bed again, you're a lucky girl." Shocked, I stop walking and watch horrified as Anne bursts into tears and rushes away toward the ladies' room at the far end of the civic center.

Sick to my stomach, I confront Claire, "What did you tell Anne?" My anger rises, and I maintain control, barely, as I try to assess what happened.

Claire pouts, "It was nothing. I told her if she wants you, she is going to have to work for it." She arches her back, which has the effect of lifting her breasts, barely contained by their silk prisons. Her rebellious eyes look directly into mine, "I want you, and I won't let anything get in my way."

I step backward; convinced Claire believes this to be true. My anger wants to lash out, but instead I respond in the calmest voice and coolest tone I can muster. "Excuse me, Claire; I have unfinished business." I turn and walk toward the ladies' room, ditching the full glasses of champagne on a counter near the kitchen.

When I get to the bathroom door, I'm uncertain what to do. I glance around and find no one watching, so I knock and enter. Anne is at the sink, trying to repair the makeup on her face. Before I can speak, she blurts out, "I never want to see you again."

I want to close my eyes to blot out the pained look on her face, but I can't take my eyes away. She is abject, destroyed by my alleged betrayal. I can identify with her emotion; after all, I had gone through the same ordeal less than two months ago. I try to speak, "Anne, let me..."

She cuts me off, "I don't want to hear any stories or excuses. I want to go home." Tears continue streaming down her cheeks. I want to step closer and hold her, but I sense any attempt to get physical will be rebuffed.

"Anne, nothing has happened. Claire is lying to you." Even as I say it, I realize how implausible I sound. I wish Anne could know the truth, so all this pain will go away, and we could go back to the happiness we felt moments ago. A woman enters the bathroom, spots the tableau at the sink and quietly leaves. "Anne, let me take you home so we can finish this conversation in private."

"You won't need to take me home. I've called for a cab. It should already be waiting for me outside." Anne straightens, "I had hoped you were different. You were so genuine, I started to believe in myself again." Her green eyes well up with tears once more. She holds a tissue to each eye to catch her tears. "I'm not sure what to tell Emily. She'll be heartbroken." Anne picks up her purse and strides to the door. "Please don't call me."

I follow her out into the hallway and find a line of waiting ladies. Obviously, the woman who entered earlier had stopped traffic, waiting for us to leave. My eyes are moist with my own tears, as I follow Anne to the checkout to pick up her shawl. "Anne, please wait. I don't want it to end like this."

At the exit, Anne turns and confronts me. Angry and poised, she stands tall. It makes me proud, watching her use all her strength to address the hurt I've dealt her. "It's over Josh. Don't make this tougher by trying to hang on. It was a nice try, but I don't need the drama. I'm sorry it didn't work out." Anne hands me a slip of paper. "Oh, by the way," her tone dead, "Claire gave me this." With a sharp intake of breath, I recognize it as my handwriting, this is the phone number I'd given to Claire.

I follow Anne into the wet night, hopeless as she climbs into one of the town's rusty cabs and drives away. She turns and watches me but doesn't wave. I feel miserable, lost and angry.

As I'm standing there, exposed to the biting chill of the evening, I notice Jack and Blackie approaching. I kneel down and Blackie licks my face. I'm glad for the diversion so Jack won't notice my eyes are red. I ask, "What are you up to?"

"Step around the building. I've got a lot to tell you." Jack looks tired, so I go along. Besides, I'm curious.

The lea of the building provides modest protection from the wind and rain. Jack stops Blackie; "I had a hunch if I left the harbor I'd be followed. I hid by the mouth of Crittenden Creek and waited. Sure enough, the Harbormaster and another fellow showed up and were looking for me. They had rifles, and it looked as if they meant business. After they left, I tried to come back, but I had trouble with my outboard."

I ask the obvious question, "How did you get back?"

"I paddled across the Eastern Passage, and hoofed it to the end of the road running past the airport, and walked back from there. I'm pretty bushed. I can admit it." Jack looks like he needs to sit down. "I'm not going to my boat tonight. Can I get a ride over to Mildred's after the dance is over?"

"I'd be happy to run you over there. First, I've got to talk to someone inside. Can you give me few minutes?"

Jack leans against the building. "What if we wait at your apartment until you're finished."

I laugh, and the sound rings hollow in my ears. I had been hoping to get Anne to come to my apartment for a little while before I took her home. There is no chance this will happen after tonight. "Sure, Jack. I'd be happy to run you to my place and let you in."

"No need for it. Blackie and I can walk over there. It's only a few blocks. We do need the key."

I nod, "Okay." I hold out my key ring after removing the car key. "The silver key is the one. I'll be home shortly. There are blankets in the closet next to the front door, and you can use the couch until I get there." I pause, "You'll find stuff to eat in the kitchen, including dog food. Help yourself to anything you find."

Back in the lobby, I bail my jacket from the check stand and put it on to warm up. My anger has turned into a slow burn that will not go out. I buy a beer at the cash bar and take a big slug. This night started so well. How did it turn to shit so fast?

Standing at the edge of the lobby, the dance floor is packed with couples. All of them are oblivious to my pain and anger. Along one wall is a row of tables, piled with silent auction items. I pace the length of one table, scanning the items for sale, while also watching the dance floor for Claire. Within minutes, I notice Katie dancing with a tall man. I'm so focused on her; it takes me a few minutes to realize she is dancing with Clay, the Harbormaster. I almost choke and nearly spew beer onto the floor.

As I stand there, watching Katie, I realize my every move is being watched by a gaggle of ladies in the kitchen. One of them is the woman who entered the restroom while I was talking to Anne. I turn my back on the watching ladies. I'm sure our story will spread through the community faster than an earthquake. I feel worse, realizing Anne will bear this burden much more than I.

My beer is empty so I buy another. I'm halfway through it when Principal Pearson nears. It takes an extreme effort for me to visualize my boss as Claire's husband. What could the two possibly have in common?

"I have to talk to you, Mr. Campbell. I've received a serious complaint from Mrs. Johnson. I can't say much here, but you're not making a good first impression. Meet me in my office, on Friday morning at nine o'clock."

I mumble, "Okay," before he leaves me alone. I look around. It feels as if everyone within ten steps has overheard Mr. Pearson, although it's unlikely. I feel trapped. There is no one I can ask to dance. Claire isn't in sight. Mr. Pearson occupies the corner of the room near the band, and the far end of the room is too close to the ladies in the kitchen for my comfort. To make matters worse, the band is playing a slow dance, and Clay and Katie are glued together on the dance floor.

Finishing my beer, I hear Claire's voice behind me. "They make a handsome couple, don't they?"

I turn to face Claire. "What's the matter, haven't caused enough trouble for one evening?" I sound petulant, even to myself.

Claire smiles at me. Again I notice the smile is beautiful, but the eyes remain hard, untouched by any emotion I can detect. Behind her, Katie is making preparations to leave with Clay. She flashes him one of her dazzling smiles, and it cuts me to the quick. I can tell I'm the furthest thing from her mind at this moment. I feel battered and bewildered.

Stepping closer, Claire places her hands on my arms. Her nearly unfettered, erect nipples graze my chest. "I can make everything better. You won't regret this night." Her thigh tantalizes my groin. "Not if you come with me."

PART 4: THE WAY TO KOKNUK FLATS

Chapter 62: Alone

Thunder wakes Mildred from a sound sleep. Startled, she sits up in bed and realizes the booming originates at her front door. She glances at her clock. It's nearly midnight. Slipping out of bed, she dons her robe as she walks through the semi-darkness to her kitchen. She doesn't hesitate but opens her front door, not surprised at all to find Jack and Blackie on the porch.

"Can I shelter here for the night? It's not safe for me to go back to the boat."

"Why, of course. Is something wrong?"

Before he answers, Jack turns and waves to a car parked in the driveway. Over his shoulder, Mildred watches Josh's SUV pulling away. Jack peels off his jacket as he steps through the doorway.

"There's more to the story. Josh and I found diamonds over on the mainland, but we were shot at while we were there. We hurried back, and I went to Ketchikan and filed our claims. Since then, both his apartment and my boat have been trashed and searched." He hangs his jacket on peg near the door and sits down on a bench inside the kitchen to remove his boots.

"Today I went over to the mainland and hid. The Harbormaster and another man followed me. They were packing rifles, and they looked ready to use them. Coming home my outboard motor failed, and I had to paddle back. They're watching my boat, so I want to stay away from it for awhile."

As Blackie walks past her to take up his usual position near her wood stove, Mildred closes the door to the porch. Unsettled by his news she fusses, "Why did you put yourself in danger?"

He stands and stretches. Dismissive, he tells her, "It would have been an even fight. I wasn't planning on having to paddle home."

Mildred can tell by the way Jack talks he must be worn out. "You look and sound exhausted. Would you care for a hot bath?" She is surprised when he nods his head, knowing how secretive he can be.

"It would be very nice. I have a lot of sore muscles that would benefit from a hot soak."

"I'll go run hot water for you." She starts the water running in her tub and lays out a bath towel, washcloth, bar of soap, and shampoo. She drags her dead husband's robe out of the back of the closet and lays it across the washbasin, where Jack can't miss finding it.

When she returns to the kitchen, Mildred directs Jack, "Put your dirty clothes outside the bathroom door, and I'll wash them for you." She hesitates, "It's late, but have you had anything to eat?"

"I made myself a sandwich over at Josh's apartment. I wouldn't mind a hot drink though."

Mildred smiles, "I can fix you up with hot chocolate or tea. Which would you prefer?"

He looks at her and his dark brown eyes are so serious, they remind her of her brother. "I'll go with the hot chocolate. Thank you, I'm sorry I woke you up in the middle of the night."

"Under the circumstances, I'm glad you did."

Mildred waits in her kitchen, while Jack soaks in the bath. She fills her teakettle with tap water and places it on her gas stove. Next she heats water so it will be ready to make his drink when Jack returns. Placing a piece of leftover turkey on a plate, she offers it to Blackie. She's not surprised the meat evaporates in several gulps.

Fifteen minutes later, Jack enters the kitchen, dressed in the robe she left for him. His long silver hair is combed back away from his face. "I had to get out before I fell asleep in the tub." He laughs and adds, "It took all my willpower. I sure appreciate you taking such good care of me."

Mildred pours hot water into two cups already holding cocoa mix. She hands one mug to Jack, "Stir this before you drink it." She pats him on the arm. "Let's go sit in the living room; it's more comfortable than the kitchen." Noticing his bare feet, she stops him. "I don't have any slippers your size, but I do have clean wool socks, will they do?"

"You bet. I pretty much live in wool socks."

Mildred retrieves a pair from the dresser in her bedroom. Returning to the kitchen she leads the way to her living room. Her favorite place, the room is also her workshop where she weaves baskets in the traditional way taught to her by her grandmother.

A sliding window overlooks the beach. Because of the semi-darkness, the crests of wind-driven waves pounding the shore are luminescent. She sits on her couch and smiles to herself as Jack takes his usual spot in the recliner.

In the darkened room, she watches him pull on the wool socks and blow on his chocolate. "I've noticed you have trouble eating or drinking anything hot."

"Yes. I've always been that way. I wonder if it isn't genetic. My father couldn't tolerate hot liquids and at least one of my sons is the same way."

Mildred considers the information. "You could be right about it being genetic. By the way, have you talked to the boys recently?"

"I talk to the two older ones nearly every month. The youngest has moved and nobody has his number." Jack looks contemplative, "The two older ones take turns coming up every summer. Their kids are almost all in college. I have three great-grandchildren."

"I envy you. Harold and I never had children. He wanted to wait until we had enough to support them." Sadly she adds, "It's hard to support a family without steady work." Quickly, before she becomes emotional, Mildred asks, "How is Josh? He was out here the other day looking at the petroglyphs with a young lady who is working for the State of Alaska."

She watches as Jack runs his fingers through his drying hair. "Until tonight, I would have said he was doing fine. He's fallen pretty hard for Anne. You know her; she's the one with the daughter who works at the Diamond C. Apparently, hoity-toity Claire Pearson lied and told Anne that Josh had slept with her."

"What a horrid woman."

"I agree. He's not sure what motivated her to lie, but Anne bought it and left the dance tonight in tears. She told Josh she never wants to talk to him again." He pauses for a moment. "I've watched the two of them together. It's a damn shame. It hurts me to see him in such pain."

Mildred nods her head sadly. "That's the thing about life. Our greatest pleasure and our greatest pain are often connected." She sips her hot chocolate, "I used to believe being young was the best and the worst of times. No one gets to sit on the sidelines. As long as you're alive, you're vulnerable."

Jack leans back in the recliner. Mildred watches him stare out over the surf, his face framed by a soft halo of his silver hair reflecting the light from the nearby street lamp. "You're right. Caring for another person, or creature, makes you vulnerable." He turns and looks at Mildred. His dark brown eyes are soft, as if yearning for something long lost. "I'm finished with being alone."

Chapter 63: Screwing Around

Waiting for Lenn at one thirty in the morning, Clay is not surprised to find the Marine Bar busy, catering to regulars. He orders his usual, not willing to wait for Lenn before getting more scotch. Clay is fuming.

#

His evening had started off well. He'd danced multiple dances with the fishery biologist, and it looked as if he was going to get intimate with the pretty little lady. Sadly, he'd misread Katie and ended up earning a slap on the face before being left in the cold on the sidewalk.

He was fussing over the incident when he'd received a call from Claire. At first he'd thought she was calling him to set up another rendezvous, but no, she wanted to talk business instead. Cursing like a logger, there had been desperation in her voice, too. He didn't understand her motive, so he was surprised when she ordered him to rough up the newcomer.

#

Sitting and staring into his drink, he realizes he isn't opposed to the notion, but he prefers to understand the why of such a thing. Fortuitously, he has his own reasons for getting rid of the young man. He can kill two birds with one stone, earn Claire's gratitude and rid himself of an obstacle to great wealth. It isn't in his best interest to confide Claire's plea with his partner. Whatever reward she provides won't be shared with Lenn.

Amused, Clay watches as Lenn slips into the tavern and slides across the room to his booth. Slouching, Lenn's ferret face is almost below his shoulder blades as he slinks onto the opposite bench.

Lenn spits out his report, "The fucker never came back. I waited three hours in the cold for nothing." He sits back and shucks his stocking cap off his head, revealing thin, red hair.

Clay points out, "The old man disappears for days at a time. Nobody gives his absences a second thought. We all laughed at him and even bet money he would never find anything. I can't tell you how many years I've won that New Year bet."

"Yeah, well I'm not laughing." Lenn snorts, "I'd give my left nut to figure out how he gave us the slip."

Finishing his scotch, Clay lowers his voice, "I've been thinking it over. I have an idea. Let's go look at the maps in my office."

"I haven't had a drink yet." Lenn looks around for a waitress, so he can place an order.

Clay throws change on the table, "Save yourself a few bucks. I've got a bottle in my desk." He stands up, "Let's go."

In his office, Clay breaks out his scotch and pours it two fingers deep into two tumblers. Playing the host, he tells Lenn, "If you want ice cubes, you'll find them in the lunch room."

Lenn salutes Clay with his glass, "No thanks. Straight suits me tonight. Now, where is this map you were talking about?"

Pulling out a thin sheet of plywood from behind a filing cabinet, Clay responds, "I have a map of the island. Thankfully, it also shows the surrounding area." He squints at the map, "Here's the mouth of Crittenden Creek."

Lenn peers closely, "It looks as if there's a bay to the west of the river mouth. Does it connect?"

Shaking his head, Clay answers, "Not that I'm aware of. But I suppose Silver Jack's trail starts over there. Maybe we should go back tomorrow and find out."

Lenn smirks; it sends a shiver up Clay's neck. "We're running out of time. We need to wrap this fucking thing up. I say we find the old prospector and take care of him. If the other fellow isn't with him, we come back to town and make sure he has an accident."

Lenn straightens up and takes a hefty slug from his glass. "I'm tired of screwing around. Let's finish this!"

Chapter 64: A Little Hike

My alarm goes off. I groan, roll over, and punch the disable button. I'm desperate to cover my head and go back to sleep. Unfortunately, I'd agreed last night to meet Jack at Mildred's, so we can retrieve his skiff and get it back to Wrangell. I force myself to stagger out of bed before I give in to the allure of its warmth and comfort. I feel sick, not due to the beer I drank last night, but because I may never be right with Anne.

After crawling into jeans and a sweater, I pull on my hiking boots. I carry my old army jacket, wool stocking cap, and leather gloves out to the jeep and toss them into the back seat, sure that later I'll need the outerwear.

My intermittent wipers deal with the dampness I encounter on the drive north through town. Passing the ferry terminal, I read one or two of the cute slogans sported by the B&B on the corner. Each trip past the two-story building I discover more knickknacks, signs, or trinkets on display. They're an interesting diversion.

The streets are wet, and the thin layer of water acts like a weak mirror, reflecting ghostlike images of the scenery ahead. I arrive at Mildred's and a moment of uncertainty hits me. What if they aren't awake? Before I can reach the front porch, Mildred opens the door for me. She smiles and takes me by the arm; "You're in time for breakfast." She lifts my spirits. How wonderful it feels to be expected and welcomed.

Blackie greets me as I enter the kitchen, so I stop and pet him, grateful again to be included without question by this circle of friends. Jack is sitting at the kitchen table, wearing a black robe and gray wool socks. His silver hair is disheveled, and it looks as if he just got up.

"Good morning, Jack." I'm not sure where I should sit at Mildred's kitchen table, so I lean against the wall near her wood stove.

Jack gestures at one of the kitchen chairs, "Good morning to you. Pull up a chair and eat breakfast. We wouldn't want you to get weak. Are you ready for a little hike?"

I sit down as directed. Mildred hands me a mug of hot, black coffee. I look into Jack's twinkling, brown eyes and respond, "As I recall, the last little hike you took me on lasted eight days."

He gives me a hurt look, "Count yourself lucky. Thanks to your Subaru, we get to ride to the end of the road instead of walking from here."

Mildred serves a wonderful breakfast of eggs, hash browns, and bacon, so I chow down. I watch the interaction between Jack and Mildred, and the thought crosses my mind the two might be a couple. I know Mildred has been widowed for a while. My bet is she's twenty years younger than Jack.

Despite the incongruity of their ages, subtle gestures of kindness and intimacy pass between the two of them. I sit back gruntled, getting comfortable with my cup of black coffee and the idea my two friends have an emotional connection.

"Why are you smiling?" Jack jabs my forearm with two fingers. His walnut brown eyes make a sharp contrast to his silver eyebrows. The scene in Mildred's kitchen leaves me feeling good, despite my own difficulties.

Jack gets up and retrieves the coffee pot, filling everyone's cup with the hot, strong drink.

"Do you have any cream?" I ask.

Mildred retrieves canned milk and offers it to me.

"You should drink it straight," Jack intones, "that way it will grow hair on your chest."

"You've seen my chest, it's hairy enough already."

"Don't argue with me boy. I taught you everything I know, and you still don't know nothing."

I laugh heartily at the self-deprecating words. I lift my coffee cup in salute, "Here's to good friends and a great breakfast. Thank you Mildred, you're a wonderful cook." I pick up another piece of bacon from the plate in the center of the table. "What's the secret for this bacon?"

Mildred stops as she passes from the stove to the table and hugs me. "I cook the bacon at the lowest heat for almost an hour until it gets to the stage before it turns crisp. Slow cooking is what makes the flavor stand out."

I savor the last bite of bacon. "Wow, pretty amazing. This will be the ideal against which I'll measure all the bacon I eat for the rest of my life. Where did you learn this?"

"Oh, I picked up this trick from my grandmother. She always tried to treat us special when we came home from boarding school."

My interest is piqued, "Wait, did you go to the Wrangell Institute?"

Mildred runs her hand through the hair on her temple. I get the sudden impression of a young girl, but it vanishes in a flash. "Yes. My brother and I both came to this boarding school. That's how I ended up in Wrangell. Most of my family lives on Prince of Wales Island, west of here nearly four hours by boat."

I pause, not wanting to open any painful memories. "Do you mind talking about it?"

"No, I don't mind. It was a long time ago and a part of my life I'll never forget. I went to the boarding school first. It took me months to get used to the idea I couldn't be with my family except during the summer. They changed my name to Mildred, because no one could use an Indian name.

My little brother joined the school a couple of years later, and they changed his name to Dan." Mildred smiles at me, "He's the Chief of Police here in town. The transition was a little easier on him, as I was there to help him."

Mildred looks out the kitchen window toward the beach. "We were whipped if we spoke anything other than English. I warned Dan, but one day he slipped at school and spoke in Tlingit. That night, the two biggest boys whipped him with their belts. I had to stand by helpless and watch as they did it. They always chose the two biggest boys to do the whipping, so later no one would try to retaliate against them. Dan was five at the time. He claims he doesn't remember the event, but I can't get it out of my head. It made a big impression on me, because I felt so helpless. I couldn't even protect my little brother."

She continues, "We all did chores, even the little ones. School was hard, and the rules were strict. When I was in high school, I went to work for a family in town. There's where I met Harold, my late husband. He was a mechanic in the cannery, and we got married as soon as I graduated. I was sixteen."

I wait at the kitchen table, drinking coffee with Mildred, while Jack leaves us to get dressed. "I met the Chief of Police last night. He reminds me of you. Now I understand why."

"Lots of families were broken apart by the boarding school system. Our people say it will take two generations to rebalance and create the kind of connection between the young and their elders we once had."

Mildred clears her throat; "I heard you had a rough time at the dance last night. I'm sorry."

It's my turn to look out the kitchen window and watch the surf. I think of Anne and the wonder of the kiss we shared during the dance. "It started well. It just didn't go or end the way I had hoped."

Mildred reaches across the table and takes my hand in hers. Her dark brown eyes are moist; "I will pray you find a way to make it right with your lady. Please let me know if there is anything I can do to help."

After Jack returns, we polish off our coffee, and he leads me outside into the faint, mid-morning mist. "I have a spare outboard motor in Mildred's shed. Its low horsepower, but it should work to get me here, although it will be slow going."

We load the outboard, Jack's rifle, four apples, and two candy bars into the back of the Subaru. With a wave goodbye to Mildred, we climb into my rig for a quick drive west past the airport. Jack directs me to continue following Airport Road as it loops back toward town. We drive three-quarters of a mile past the airport complex and turn left on Spear Road, which skirts the southern end of the runway before it turns and enters the woods. From this point, the road parallels the shoreline of the Eastern Passage.

Jack rubs an eyebrow, "We should find a time when we can go back to our claim and set our claim stakes. The schedule looks good for Saturday. The tide will be high enough, and we should be gone less than a week if we travel light and fast."

"I could make it work. What supplies do we bring? Don't we need equipment from your boat?"

"Yes. I've been chewing on it. We'll need to get a few things from there before we go. Maybe we can meet early tomorrow morning at the marina and go get what we need. With any luck we should be in and out before Clay even knows what happened."

The road crosses a creek and climbs over a low ridge. Through occasional gaps in the trees, I spot the water. After a mile, the paved road ends, and we travel on a gravel road. Half a mile farther, we come to the end of the road. I park the SUV on one edge of the wide spot designed to be a turnaround for vehicles.

We each stuff a couple of apples and a candy bar into our jacket pockets. I'm thankful I brought warm clothes. It isn't raining, but the brush is wet. Jack hands me the rifle and grabs the outboard, hoisting it onto one shoulder. "We can take turns carrying the motor. The skiff is nearly a mile from the end of the road."

I follow Blackie as Jack leads the way through the woods downhill toward the shore. I consider ways two men might share carrying the outboard, but can't envision a strategy that will work well in the rough and uneven terrain.

Fifteen minutes later, Jack helps hoist the motor onto my shoulder and provides instruction. "If you place the flat piece below the motor on your shoulder and lay your arm over the end with the propeller, the weight of the engine behind your shoulder will act as a counterbalance."

To my surprise, the strategy works well. I can keep my balance easily as I hike, and the weight is centered so I do not have to strain to carry the load. I chug along, striving to keep my mind off the weight of the outboard as time creeps.

Near the shore Jack's trail is easy to follow. I stagger along a bar, loose rocks slipping away under my feet as I claw my way up a steep bank. My shoulder, back, and legs burn with the effort. Finally, Jack calls a halt, and I am thankful when he takes the burden from me.

I get one more turn at carrying the motor before we reach the skiff. Bending over the stern, Jack disconnects the malfunctioning outboard motor and sets it in the bottom of the craft. The new motor is put in place and hooked up to the fuel line. I hold my breath, watching him reef on the pull cord three times before the motor fires and chugs to a slow start. Oil smoke from the exhaust floats over the water and drifts away into the trees along the shore.

He points, “Untie the skiff and toss the rope into the boat for me, please.” I comply and try to hand the rifle over to Jack. “No, you keep it. There’s not much chance you’ll run into a bear on the way back, but I’d feel better if you keep the rifle.”

I’m reluctant, “What if you run into Clay and his partner on your way around Point Highfield?”

“I doubt if they’ll do anything in broad daylight. Nobody in his right mind will try anything out in the open where anybody could be watching. Plus, without Blackie, this skiff looks like a thousand others. You take him back with you. He’s better protection against a bear than the gun.”

I set the rifle against a boulder and get ready to push Jack out into deeper water. “Where do you want to meet?”

“Let’s meet at Mildred’s. I need your help getting the skiff out of sight and above the high-tide mark. Afterwards it would be nice if you’d run me into town, so I can pick up a new impeller for my outboard.” He sits down in the stern and signals for me to push him away.

I call Blackie to me as Jack turns and heads west along the shore. As I look north, I can make out the general area where Jack and I have claims that hopefully will turn into a diamond mine in the near future. I wonder if we are clinging to a dream that will evaporate when our specimens are evaluated.

I sit on a rock and pull out my candy bar and share it with Blackie. Blackie moves close and I put an arm over his shoulder and scratch him behind one ear. His warmth is a tangible thing on this isolated shore, and it both comforts me and makes me ache for the loss of Anne’s respect and affection.

Grateful for Blackie’s company, I rise, check to ensure I am leaving nothing behind, and move along the trail toward my rig. The dog grabs the lead, and it heartens me to be out in the beautiful Alaskan wilderness with the magnificent creature as my companion.

Chapter 65: Exposed

Clay watches the shoreline as Lenn traces the edge of the bay near Crittenden Creek from west to east. The day is damp, but visibility is good; and the high clouds make it possible to view the top of the mountains on the mainland. Clay spots a disturbed area along the bank. He snaps at Lenn, "Stop, this is it."

Lenn grounds the sled on the shore, shuts off the jet outboard, and Clay steps over the side into the shallow water.

"Hand me the rifle, will ya? I don't want to stumble into a fight and be empty handed."

Lenn joins him carrying his own rifle, and the two men follow drag marks and bent sedges up a shallow rise.

The two men follow boot tracks and paw prints in the sand. Lenn points to the east, "I bet it's not far through there to the river. He must have hid where he could watch us."

Clay curses, angry with himself for missing the old man. "At least he didn't open fire on us. We were pretty exposed, and he'd have had quite an advantage. We've got to figure out a way to come up behind the old fart when he isn't expecting us."

Looking disgusted, Lenn retorts, "We need to find a way to permanently stop him. He has to come back to his boat eventually, and when he does, I'll be waiting."

Chapter 66: The Push

On the way into town, Silver Jack gets a surprise question from Josh. The young man points to a man pressure-washing the side of his house. "What's he doing?"

Silver Jack laughs, "He's washing the mold off of his house. It's common in this wet climate for it to grow almost everywhere, and it's tough. If you don't pressure wash it off periodically, it takes over. In fact, you'll also notice quite a few roofs with moss growing on them. People pressure-wash those, too."

He waits patiently while Josh considers the information. "Aren't there chemicals you can use to keep the moss killed off?"

The prospector responds, "There is, most roofs have a zinc or copper strip along the roofline. Every time it rains a trace goes down the roof and the chemicals kill the moss. Unfortunately, it's not really safe for the environment, and they stopped making the product."

At the Bay Company store Mildred; Blackie, and Silver Jack disembark from Josh's vehicle. Silver Jack sticks his head inside the cab of the jeep and whispers to Josh. "Can you meet me in the morning at six thirty at Chief Shakes Island? We can pick up the equipment we need from the boat, and you can run me back to Mildred's house." When Josh nods his head in agreement, he continues, "If I can't get the part I need for my outboard motor, we may have to reschedule our trip. I'll let you know before tomorrow if I don't get it working."

Back on the sidewalk, the couple wave goodbye to Josh. Silver Jack turns to Mildred. "I'll meet you at the café in twenty minutes. That'll put us there an hour before Anne's shift is over."

Inside the Bay Company, he waits for Clarence to finish serving another customer. When it's his turn, he asks if the parts he needs are available.

"You're lucky this time, Jack. I've got a water pump rebuild kit that fits your outboard, and it's in stock. Otherwise, you'd have to wait a week for it to come from Ketchikan. If you want, I can order another one for backup. The kits are fifty dollars, including shipping."

The prospector ponders the situation; "I'll take my chances without the backup parts. I'll take my five horsepower motor along in case I break down again."

With his rebuild kit in hand; Blackie and Silver Jack walk north along Front Street to the Diamond C. He ties the dog up behind the restaurant instead of in the usual location near the building. Inside, he finds a table with a view allowing him to watch Blackie.

Anne arrives with a cup of black coffee, and Emily brings the menu. "Hi, Jack. You haven't been here for a few days."

Smiling, he responds, "I got stuck over on the mainland when my outboard motor broke down. I had to paddle back." He accepts the menu from Emily. "I'm going to need another menu. There will be two of us for lunch." He is saddened to catch the quick flash of concern on the faces of both Anne and Emily. "Not to worry," he says, "It isn't Josh who's joining me." The relieved looks on their faces sadden him even more.

Within a few minutes, Mildred arrives and takes up the chair beside him at the table. He realigns his silverware with the red and white squares on the plastic tablecloth. "Did you find what you were looking for at the craft store?"

"Yes, I did." Mildred looks anxious, "Has Anne said anything?"

"Not yet, but when she thought Josh might be joining me, the body language was potent. This doesn't look promising."

Within a minute, Emily joins them at their table. She looks so serious and official in her uniform, Jack nearly laughs at her. Emily greets Mildred by name. He doesn't find this unusual, since everyone in town knows Mildred through her work at the Post Office.

Mildred orders a salad, and Jack orders a burger with fries. When Emily leaves the table, Mildred leans over and confides, "This may be awkward. Are you sure there isn't another way?"

He nods his head in agreement, "I've tried to come up with one. But I owe it to the boy to do what I can. It may not help, but I'm going to say my piece anyway." He pauses for a moment, "Most of my life I wasn't one to tempt fate by meddling in affairs of the heart. Now I think of it, fate never done me any favors, and maybe it's time he got a solid left-hook to the jaw."

When their lunch arrives, its fortuitous Anne brings the meals alone. He clears his throat, "Anne. You've known me for a long time, and I've always been one who likes to tease. Right now, I'm not teasing. I need you to know Josh is telling you the truth." Unsure if he should go on, he hesitates. Aching for his friend, he takes a deep breath and finishes his speech, "Claire lied to you. I don't know why."

Anne looks stricken, her face is tight, and her hands clench and unclench as she stands by the table. She turns and faces him. "I don't want to talk about it. It's over, and I want to be left alone. I find it despicable he sent you to harass me."

Speechless, he's not able to find an adequate response to her words and the emotion behind them. As Anne turns to go, Mildred speaks up, "Anne, Josh didn't send us. We came on our own, because we care. We care about both of you. If not today, I hope eventually you will realize we're not your enemies." Anne retreats behind the counter, shoulders hunched, it's apparent she's upset by the conversation. Retreating to the kitchen, she leaves Emily alone in the serving area.

The prospector tugs at his hat, "My plan backfired."

Mildred picks up a fork. She gives him a funny look. "You didn't expect her to sit down and tell us she was ready to forgive Josh, did you?"

"Not really..."

Mildred plays with her salad; "Anne will have to work this out for herself. You've given her a different point of view to chew on. It might be the push she needs to rethink her relationship with Josh."

Chapter 67: Wolf-cry

It's a few minutes after six o'clock, and the morning is cold with no clouds. I try to recall if there's been a morning without clouds in the month I've been in Wrangell, and I come away unsuccessful. I skip breakfast because I hope Mildred will cook us another scrumptious meal after we arrive with Jack's gear.

I need to meet with Mr. Pearson at nine o'clock. Although I'm not looking forward to the encounter, I'm ready to get it over with and have the issues out in the open. As much as I need the money this job represents to tide me over for the year, I'm confident I can find another position if I'm willing to relocate. Maybe losing this job is fate. Without Anne, I will have little desire to stay in Wrangell.

As I stand on my porch, wondering if it's too soon to go to the marina to link up with Jack, I hear a shot, which echoes from the harbor below me. The sound isn't loud but it concerns me nonetheless. I imagine Jack might have arrived before me and run into Clay or his partner.

I unlock my rig, jerk open the door, and jump inside. I pull out of my driveway, headed for the marina with brio. Along the way, my concern increases. What if something has gone horribly wrong, and Jack is involved in an altercation? I will never forgive myself if I'm not there when he needs my help.

Within two minutes, I arrive at the dock and park in the first open stall. As I'm getting out of the jeep, I spot Blackie running on Chief Shakes Island. Relieved, I follow the raised walkway to the famous island in the middle of the marina. The tide is the lowest I can remember.

The raised walkway has a slight curve at the beginning but straightens as it connects with the island. As I complete the curve, I spy a dark mass sprawled on the lawn ahead. From a distance, it could be a torso and legs.

Fearful this might be Jack, I run forward and catch a glimpse of Blackie running into the brush on the southeast side of the islet. In front of me, on the grass, is a man I have never met. I step back, because his throat is ripped asunder. Blood saturates everything, including the grass around his body. I spy a pistol in his lifeless right hand. Pointed at the ceremonial lodge, it radiates evil.

I'm in shock at the sight in front of me, my image of the island as a sanctuary shattered forever. This death is recent, violent, and swift. The man's face is contorted into a rictus of horror. Blood seeps into the grass around his neck. It dawns on me; this man's throat was probably ripped open by Blackie's fangs. A shudder runs down my spine.

I wonder about Jack and the shot I heard earlier. Turning, I stagger across the lawn, past the totem poles, mountain ash, cottonwood sentinels, and ceremonial lodge to the far end of the islet. This is the area where Blackie vanished.

I call out, "Blackie, come here boy." I hear the dog's whine and push my way into the tall reeds and thicket of brush surrounding the cultivated part of the island. Three steps into the thicket, and I stumble. Glancing down, I find Jack and Blackie in a nest formed by sedge.

I kneel next to Jack. He is holding his chest with both hands. Blood oozes through his fingers. His white beard is flecked with dark blood. Blackie lies beside him, licking Jack's face and whining.

Jack spots me and turns his head with great effort. His silver hair falls across his face, obstructing his eyes. "Thank god you're here. Promise me you'll take care of Blackie for me."

I fight to blink back tears as I realize what he means by this request. "I'd be honored to do this for you, but you're going to survive this."

It looks to me as if he's trying to hold his chest together, without much success. His breathing is ragged, and it impacts his speech, so I am forced to lean close to hear his words. "Remember,

I'm headed west of north. Watch for me along the trail."

Unconsciously, I stroke his face in an attempt to comfort him. "You wait here. I'll call for help and be right back. I promise."

I force myself to jerk upright, away from Jack. I look at my cell phone; as usual there is no reception. I glance down at the face I've come to know as well as my own and repeat, "I'll be right back."

Spinning, I leap onto the lawn in one powerful bound. I sprint past the dead man with the pistol and thunder along the walkway back to the pier. Turning left in the parking lot, I cross the dock and jump onto the ramp outside the marina office. I fling open the door and run inside. Standing behind the counter, I find David, who is startled by my sudden entry.

I slide to a stop and blurt out my information in a rush, "Jack's been shot! He's on the far side of Chief Shakes Island and needs help. Call 9-1-1. I'm going back to give him first aid until the ambulance comes."

Without waiting for a response, I grab a roll of paper towels on the desk and leave, letting the office door slam shut behind me. By the time I hit the end of the walkway to the island, my lungs and legs are burning. I jet across the walkway. Reaching the grass, I hear Blackie's forlorn howl, coming from the far end of the island.

The wolf-cry is the saddest sound I've ever heard, the wail lilts higher and higher, ending in a pure note that will haunt me forever. Within seconds of it's ending, I find myself beside the magnificent creature and his dead master. Silver Jack looks peaceful in death. I kneel beside him again and reach for his carotid artery, confirming there is no pulse. With my cheek near his mouth, I pause and hope for evidence of breathing. There is none.

I close my hot eyes, trying to blot out the image of my friend. I rock back on my heels and wish I could join my voice with Blackie's. I shake uncontrollably as a sense of complete loss envelopes me.

Chapter 68: Not Alone

Katie is fueling her boat when she hears the wolf howl emanating from Chief Shakes Island. She realizes it might be Blackie. As she continues fueling, she watches an ambulance arrive at the dock. Within two minutes more people arrive including a police car, followed by another.

Finished refueling, she pays for her purchases and runs her skiff deeper into the harbor. She motors around the marina pushing the posted speed limit, moving closer to the south end of Chief Shakes Island, so she can view what is happening. As she turns into the east side of the marina, behind the island, she notices a group of men in the brush below the knoll.

She recognizes Blackie's midnight black shape on the edge of the bank with Josh sitting nearby, his head in his hands. Without hesitation she runs the bow of her vessel aground. Climbing over the side, she wades through the shallow water, pushes through the tall reeds and walks up to Josh.

When she is a couple of steps away, Josh raises his head, giving her a wan smile. Tears are streaming down his face, and his eyes are red and puffy. He wipes the corners of his eyes with bloody hands, creating streaks of red on his face. "Hi Katie, I have the worst news. Silver Jack is dead." He pauses and with great difficulty adds, "I wasn't here when he needed me."

She sits down alongside him and gives him a long hug. His chest is thick, and she's unable to reach around him with her embrace. She doesn't know what to say, so she remains quiet. Her instinct tells her there is no answer she can give him that will matter.

The best she can do is to provide a little comfort, while the officials nearby complete their work. She is certain Josh's opportunity to be alone with his own thoughts will end soon enough.

She turns her head, looking past Josh's shoulder to watch Blackie, who is in his own version of shock. A short rope is attached to his collar, the other end wrapped around Josh's thigh. Lying with his head stretched out between the paws of his front legs, the dog's brown eyes carry the same pain she can see in Josh's.

She tilts her head, making gentle contact with Josh's temple. She tightens her grip on his chest. "I'm so sorry. Is there anything I can do to help?"

Josh sobs once. In a hoarse whisper he tells her, "I should have been holding him when he died. Instead I was running for help, and he died all alone." She lifts her head to look at Josh. Hot tears flood his face; he shakes his head, sharing one last piece of information. "No, he wasn't alone. Blackie was with him. He must have been comforted by that."

Chapter 69: Wrench

A clatter of falling dishes elicits a curse from the kitchen. The cook is in a bad mood today. Standing beside the cash register, Anne looks into the kitchen to check on the cook. The young girl working as the café's dishwasher hadn't shown up this morning. The backlog of dirty dishes is at crises level.

All morning long, as much as she dared, Anne left Emily to wait on the customers and slipped into the kitchen to help the cook. Fortunately, the café was equipped with a commercial-grade dishwashing station, but it didn't operate itself. Dishes, silverware, and cups all needed to be rinsed, stacked onto trays, run through the dishwasher and auto drying station before being returned to use. Each step took a few minutes, but required attention. Unfortunately, in the short-handed café, extra time had been non-existent all day.

To make matters worse, she knew lower customer service in the waiting room would translate into fewer or lower tips. Work harder and get less. Some days were like that, and you had to take them in stride. For every high there needs to be a low to compensate. It made her remember Josh. The relationship had caught her by surprise. The upswing was fast and wonderful, but she is left with a heartache that won't go away no matter how she tries to forget.

A young man enters the café and sits beside Ernie. She arrives with a coffee cup and at his nod, pours him a mug full of the steaming hot liquid. Ernie asks her for a refill so she tops off his mug, too.

"Thank you." The young man turns to Ernie, "There's a big

commotion down at the marina. I saw the ambulance and several police cars but couldn't get close enough to get a look at what was going on. Have you heard anything?"

Ernie tips his Semper Fi cap back on his head. "No, I haven't heard a thing. Did you go into the marina office?"

Anne is rooted to the floor unable to move. She pauses, wiping the counter, hoping to learn more.

The young man continues, "Yeah, I was there. David told me a fella came into the office and had him call for help. It sounded like the old prospector who lives in the marina got himself shot!"

It's Ernie's turn to get a frozen look on his bearded face. He asks the question Anne is afraid to ask, "You don't mean Silver Jack do you?"

"Yes, that's the name he used. Later I heard two men were found dead, but nobody knows the second guy."

Anne feels her gut wrench. Two men dead, one of them Silver Jack, could the other man be Josh?

Chapter 70: Questions

From behind his desk, the Police Chief is larger and more intimidating today. I'm seated in his modest office, wearing my bloody clothes. Behind the Chief, the harbor and a panoramic sweep of the waters to the west of Wrangell are visible. On the corner of the wooden desk is a nameplate with 'Chief Dan Ford' etched into a brass faceplate.

The office isn't cluttered, but it isn't neat either. In addition to the Chief's antique, oak office chair, two oak chairs face the desk. Oak bookshelves with glass fronts and a brass pole lamp complete the furniture in the room.

Blackie is lying at my feet near a stain on the linoleum floor. The dog is looking to me to be the leader of our torn apart pack. I feel like a mess, and I'm worried Blackie may be euthanized.

Detective Alex is seated in the chair nearest to me. He looks grim. In his lap are an orange prison jump suit and a pair of disposable slippers like the ones handed out in hospitals.

The Police Chief leans forward, causing his oak chair to complain. His voice is gravel, "We are doing everything we can to solve the murders on Chief Shakes Island. I need to ensure we are thorough so we don't overlook anything.

"I hope you can appreciate we are going to ask you a lot of questions. Everything you say or do will come under close scrutiny. Before we start the questioning, we're going to need to collect the evidence on your body. We need to take samples of the blood on your hands and face."

The Chief's glare is withering. "We're confiscating your

clothes as evidence. We'll inventory all your personal items and give you a receipt for them."

A weight crushes me and steals my breath. I squirm in my seat, and my left hand betrays me with a twitch.

The lamp on the Chief's desk flickers in sympathy. "Do you have any questions?"

I look at the Chief, "Do you know who the other man was?"

The Chief gives me a puzzled look. "That's not the kind of questions I have in mind." Sternly he addresses me again, "Do you have questions about the process?"

Unthinkingly, I revert to my military training when faced by implacable authority. "No sir."

"I need to read you your Miranda Rights." The Chief reads them carefully, and I listen intently to the ubiquitous recital. "Do you understand?"

"Yes, I do. I don't need an attorney present to tell you the truth."

"Great. You're here because two men died violently this morning and you're the only suspect we have. Detective Alex will take you to a room and take pictures of you wearing the clothing you have on. He will give you a plastic evidence bag, and I want you to put all your clothes into it except your underwear. We're going to put you in a temporary jail uniform, but you're not under arrest. We'll put all your valuables in another bag and you'll bring them back here for questioning. Afterwards we'll make a decision regarding what happens."

I nod my head in agreement. "What of Blackie? I'd recommend letting him stay with me."

The Chief leans back in his chair. "That's a pretty unusual request." He gives me a direct look; "I could have him taken to the pound while we sort this out."

My stomach sinks, the best I can come up with on the spot is, "I'm not sure your pound is set up for anything like him."

The Chief scratches his head. "Okay, he stays with you. We'll take him one step at a time, too."

Standing, I lead Blackie as we follow Detective Alex down a narrow hallway to a room with no windows, one small table, and a chair. He closes the door behind us and places the jumpsuit and slippers on the table. Using a digital camera, he snaps a series of pictures. He also takes close-ups of my bloody hands and face. Finally, he hands me a bag for my clothes, so I peel off my dirty clothing and place them one at time inside the bag. At his direction, I place my watch, keys, and wallet inside another plastic bag, which I keep.

When we are finished, Detective Alex invites me to put on the jumpsuit and slippers and leads me to a restroom. "You should take advantage of this opportunity. Questioning could last a while." He leans against the far wall, "Don't wash your hands, for obvious reasons." He waits in the restroom as I empty my bladder and together we return to the Chief's office. The room is empty.

I sit with my bag of valuables in my lap, while Blackie sits at my feet. The detective asks me to complete and sign an NCR form listing the contents inside the clothes bag. One copy is placed inside the bag, one is returned to me, and the original goes on the Chief's desk. Uncertain what to do with my copy; I stuff it inside the bag with my valuables. I watch Detective Alex seal and label the bag with my clothes.

We wait for a few minutes, and the Chief returns with another officer. "This is Officer Chak. He's going to take swipes from each hand and your face where we can observe traces of blood. Sit quiet, this shouldn't take long."

Numbly, I comply as the officer completes the assigned task. He is meticulous, and I almost feel clean when he finishes. It takes more than thirty minutes for him to get all the samples and label them. Everything goes into a plastic bag, including a copy of a form signed by all the officers present. I assume this type of control is necessary in case I might challenge the authenticity of the evidence.

The Chief looks at me, "We're going to need a lock of Blackie's hair and swab from his mouth."

The thought of Officer Chak drawing near Blackie with scissors or a swab frightens me. "Perhaps you should let me do it, if you want to keep your fingers."

I get no satisfaction from the relief in everyone's eyes. It's evident to me Blackie's life hangs in the balance.

I take the scissors offered by the policeman and gently bend over and pat Blackie on his shoulder. With one hand I gingerly snip hair along his mane, gathering a dozen specimens an inch long with the hand I've been using to stroke his fur. The dog ignores the procedure, trusting me to keep him safe.

I go down on one knee alongside Blackie. With the swab in one hand, I gently scratch him behind the ears with my other hand. I allow him to smell the back of my hand, the one holding the swab. I know he can smell Jack's blood, but my presence calms him. I bend lower and put my face close to his. He lifts his head and licks my face, trying to comfort me. I stroke the side of his face and slip the end of the swab inside his cheek. In a second, the task is done, and I give him a big hug, to hide my relief and to thank him for being so cooperative.

When Officer Chak leaves, the Chief tells me the questioning will be videotaped. This doesn't surprise me. He's intelligent and thorough. I wonder what he will think when he's heard my story.

We all settle back into our respective positions. The first question comes from the Chief. "Are you aware of any biting incidents by Blackie?"

I try being flip, "He doesn't like bears."

I get a cold stare from the Chief, "Come on, the beast must have had conflicts with people. Did Jack ever beat him?"

My teeth grind, "So far as I know Blackie always won at poker."

"Okay kid, let's start over. Tell me your version of what happened this morning. In your own words, tell me everything."

When I complete my recitation, a series of detailed follow-up questions force me to go back over every step of the morning. As I answer, I recognize the process is designed to accomplish several purposes. First, these questions will elicit a greater degree of detail from me. Second, any contradiction with my first telling will be used to assess if I am fabricating information or making things up. I am also aware they are designed to throw me off balance and wear me down. Despite understanding the technique being used on me, I remain frustrated by the glacial questioning.

Detective Alex, "What is the name of the man you found at

the end of the walkway?"

Chief Dan, "Did you recognize the man you saw lying on the ground?"

For the sixth time I answer, "No!" to a variation of the question regarding the unknown dead man. Finally, I rub my forehead in frustration. "Look, I don't know who he was. But I can tell you a potential motive for Jack's death."

Chief Dan, "Answer the question. Did you ever talk to the man?"

"Listen Chief," I redirect with exasperation, "Last week we filed claims in Ketchikan on a diamond strike over on the mainland. Since then, both Jack's boat and my apartment have been ransacked, and he's been followed. He's spent the last two nights staying with a friend out of town, because he thought he was being watched. If you find who's after the diamonds, you'll find the killer."

My comments are met with a great deal of skepticism. I'm compelled to tell a longer story, covering how I met Jack and agreed to go out prospecting with him. I relate how we found the diamonds and the shooting incident on the mountain. I also describe our flight out of the wilderness and tell what I know of Jack's trip to Ketchikan. To finish, I report finding out the Harbormaster had a competing claim and how Clay and the unknown man with him had followed Jack over to the mainland. "The dead man may have been Clay's partner, but I've never met him, so I can't be sure."

Another hour of questions parses every bit of information out of me. I've missed breakfast and it's well past lunch. I call the question, "Look, I realize I've given you a lot of unsubstantiated information. Is there anything I can do to convince you I'm telling the truth?"

Detective Alex and the Chief exchange glances. The Chief fixes his eyes on me, "You're right. We're going to need time to verify your claims. We're letting you go, but with several restrictions. Don't leave town or try to make any arrangements to do so. I want you to keep Blackie on a leash and don't leave him alone anywhere, except in your apartment or your car."

The Chief pauses before continuing, "I want the diamond specimens as evidence. If you concur, Detective Alex will run you home so you can shower and change into your own clothing. He'll then take you to the bank so you can withdraw the diamonds and come back here to enter them into evidence."

I swallow, not wanting to release the diamonds, but this act of good faith would add credibility to my story. "I agree."

"Good." The Chief gives me a stern look, "I want to be clear this doesn't establish your ownership of these diamonds."

At my apartment, Detective Alex checks out the broken door, while I take Blackie for a walk around my backyard so he can go to the bathroom. Coldly he asks, "How come you didn't report the break-in?"

I don't hesitate. "I was afraid I'd have to tell you about the diamonds, and Jack wasn't here to be part of the sharing. I wish I had done so. Maybe he'd be alive."

I order Blackie to lie down in the living room as Detective Alex makes a note of our conversation before settling down to wait in his patrol car for me as I shower and change. I want to linger under the hot water, letting the heat sink into my bones, but I can't allow myself the pleasure with a policeman waiting for me.

My growling stomach reminds me I've eaten nothing all day; so on my way out the door, I grab an apple to eat on my ride to the bank. I also snag a paper towel I can use to keep the fruit's juice from dripping on my clothing.

After retrieving the diamonds, we return to the police station. The building is one block uphill from Front Street, near the center of town. Back in the Chief's office I hand over the zip-lock bags. "There should be fifty-two specimens. Jack also left three with a gemologist in Ketchikan. The man confirmed the three he examined were diamonds, and he's supposed to get back to Jack with an appraisal. Jack hasn't received it yet."

The Chief offers me a seat. Reluctantly, I take the interrogation chair again. Blackie lies down at my feet and places his head between his paws.

The Chief points at the specimens, saying, "I'm going to give you a receipt for these. Remember, this step doesn't establish ownership. We'll also take a series of photos of the stones and give you copies. These are intended to help both of us prove the owner or owners get back what belongs to them without question."

I bristle at the implication I'm not one of the owners. Ignoring his unsettling comment, I focus on my own concerns, "Chief, do you know anyone with contact information for his kin?"

"Yes, I believe I do. In any case, we're working on it." He settles into his chair, as Detective Alex remains standing. "I promised to share about the dead man. His name is Jason Boggs, and he's from Ketchikan. He's the gemologist Jack visited on his trip to file your claims. His presence here in Wrangell should indicate the value of these specimens."

Chapter 71: To Do

Chief Dan orders Detective Alex to take Josh and Blackie to the marina, where Josh's car is parked. "If Mr. Campbell will permit it, I want you to take pictures of the interior of his vehicle." Dan knows he doesn't have to ask Alex to do a thorough search; the man would never miss such an opportunity.

He is not surprised when Josh agrees to comply with his request to search his vehicle. His gut tells him the young man is telling what he believes to be the truth. The Chief fixates on Blackie's powerful jaws as the animal flows out of the room. Dan is unable to control a shudder. What must it feel like to have your throat ripped open?

He considers what he knows of the case at hand. Silver Jack must have been letting Blackie go for a run when the jeweler from Ketchikan confronted him at the tribal sanctuary. The confrontation ended with Jason Boggs shooting the old prospector. The jeweler most likely was leaving when Blackie overtook the man and ripped out his throat.

He hadn't shared with Josh the jeweler had been carrying two rough diamonds or that he had spent the night in the Hungry Beaver Hotel across the street. These clues support his hypothesis the jeweler had been waiting for Jack, and the confrontation was no accidental meeting. The discrepancy in the number of diamonds the old prospector left with the jeweler causes Dan to wonder; a wrong number or does one missing point to something significant?

He is intrigued by Josh's theory that the dead man was a partner to the Harbormaster. It didn't line up, since the jeweler hadn't arrived in the area soon enough to be involved in the gun fight at the mountain lake.

Dan organizes his work by making a list of all the facts needing to be checked. One of the items to be verified is the recent travel plans of the deceased. He creates another list labeled "Leads" to keep track of his ideas. Finally he creates a list of "Suspects." He puts Jason Boggs and Blackie on his list. Reluctantly he adds both Josh's name as well as Clay Foster. After a moment's pause, he adds "Harbormaster's Partner" below Clay's name.

On his "To Do" list is a reminder to watch Josh Campbell's movements. He turns over all the evidence and facts again in his mind, trying without success to identify the key bit of information eluding him.

Pulling himself away from the brainstorming exercise, he reaches for the phone. He has two calls he doesn't want to make. First, he will call the Ketchikan police department and ask them to identify and visit Jason Boggs' family in Ketchikan and inform them of his murder. Dan will also need to remind his counterpart he will not be able to release the body until a complete autopsy and forensics exam has been completed. He should ask the Ketchikan homicide unit to gather information on Jason, his finances, his movements, and his phone records.

Afterwards, he will call Mildred and tell her of Jack's death. He suspects she might have contact information for Jack's family. Unfortunately, she will be heartbroken by news of his untimely death. Dan has been aware for a while Jack has been his sister's lover. Perhaps she can provide corroboration to Josh's fantastic story.

Chapter 72: Next Move

Clay is annoyed Silver Jack has eluded him several days in a row. Today his goal is to figure out where the old fart is hiding, so he and Lenn can develop a plan to get rid of him. He drives past a parked police car and pulls into his usual spot behind the marina office.

Getting out of his vehicle, he can tell something is going on at Chief Shakes Island. He enters through the back door and wends his way to the front of the building. David is behind the counter and jerks upright when Clay enters the room.

Flicking his head at the island, Clay asks, "What the fuck is going on over there?"

David nervously strokes his thin beard, "Cops are all over the place. They won't let anybody go over there. Silver Jack's been shot, and his body is in the brush on the far side of the island. There's another dead guy, too; but I don't know what happened to him. He's lying on the grass past the end of the walkway."

Turning away from David to hide his satisfaction, a sudden thought hits Clay and he turns back. "Is it possible the other man might be the teacher whose been hanging out with Silver Jack?"

"No, Josh found Silver Jack, and he came running over here to have me call the ambulance." Without pausing David continues, "My guess is the old prospector was dead by the time the ambulance got here, because they never moved him, as best I can tell."

Clay doesn't try to hide his disappointment from David. Let him wonder about its source. "Where's the school teacher?"

"I saw him leave with the Chief of Police an hour ago."

In his office, Clay sits and props one foot on the corner of his desk. He calls Lenn. “I have good news. Silver Jack is dead. Meet me at the Marine Bar at six p.m. I can fill you in on events, and we can plan our next move.”

Chapter 73: You and Me

I depart the police station with Detective Alex and Blackie. In the parking lot the First Peoples woman who talked to me when I was on my date with Katie confronts me. "You should have listened to Blackie's warning."

I stammer out, "What did you say?" My words are wasted, as the woman is already several yards away moving at a fast pace. I watch her hair and bright eagle feather flutter along behind her.

Confounded by her statement, I pull open the rear door to Detective Alex's Bronco and urge Blackie inside. I climb into the front passenger seat for the short trip back to the marina. Jack's death is starting to become real to me, as I realize he won't be waiting at his boat for me to visit. My world has changed forever.

"I'd like to check in on Jack's boat from time to time, until his family arrives, and they make arrangements to take care of it. Will it be a problem?"

Detective Alex's answer is not what I expect. "I'll be searching the boat after I finish with your car. If you're worried about the bilge pumps, I'll check them when I do my search. If there's a problem, I'll come back every day and check on it." As an after thought he sternly adds, "Under no circumstances are you to go near his boat. Is that clear?"

Contrite, I respond, "If you run into a problem you can't figure out, feel free to give me a call."

Detective Alex searches my SUV and takes pictures of the interior. When I am released, I load up Blackie and head back to my apartment. I glance at my watch. It's after 2 p.m. I'm exhausted, but

I need to make several phone calls before I can address my issues.

My first call is to Mildred. She is crying when she answers the phone, so I figure out she must already know Jack is dead. Regardless, I must make sure, "Mildred, I have terrible news."

Mildred sobs into the phone. I can barely make out her words when she tells me, "Jack is dead. My brother called thirty minutes ago to get phone numbers for his sons. Dan told me you might call."

I relive my last minutes with Jack. I wish I could find a way to share them with Mildred. I wipe a tear from the corner of my eye before I continue. "I have Blackie. He asked me to take care of him." I pause, giving my voice a chance to steady, "Of course I said yes."

Mildred's voice strengthens, "You're a good friend. I know he always worried what would happen to Blackie if he died. Your agreeing to take care of him must have given him a lot of comfort. Thank you."

"Mildred, I have to take care of a few things. Can I come over tomorrow or Sunday and visit for awhile?"

"Of course, why don't you come over Sunday for lunch? I have to work tomorrow. It will be nice to talk."

After trying Mr. Pearson at the office without success, I look him up in the phonebook and catch him at home. I'm relieved when Claire isn't the one to answer. I explain why I had been unable to make my morning appointment.

His response is tepid, "I see. Well, it's highly unusual. Can you meet me in my office in fifteen minutes? I'd like to get this over."

I take Blackie for a quick walk in the backyard before leaving him in my apartment. I arrive at the high school prepared for the worst. Based on how my day has started, I have little faith it will improve.

Mr. Pearson is seated behind his desk, which is wide, at least twice the size of the desk in the Police Chief's office. I am spending too much time on the wrong side of desks owned by people of authority. Speaking in his rapid-fire manner, I watch Mr. Pearson's hair jiggle. "Mr. Campbell. I can't have you pissing-off the other teachers. It's too hard to find good replacements."

I stand up, "Mr. Pearson, I won't run away from this issue.

We all need to focus on what is best for the children of this community. Give me hope this travesty isn't going to continue." Realizing belatedly I might be too much on the defensive, I sink down into my chair.

Mr. Pearson waits for me to be seated before continuing, "I agree with you. Mrs. Johnson is an awful teacher, but I've been working on this for months, and I can share she will retire at the end of this year. Be patient and help me find a qualified replacement. If we don't find one, Mrs. Johnson will be back. Trust me to take care of this and do not confront anyone else about his or her teaching ability. Do I make myself perfectly clear?"

"Yes sir." I am unprepared for the meeting to be over this fast. I absorb his words. "You're aware how bad she is?"

Mr. Pearson gives me a wry look, "I know almost everything happening in this building. Give me enough time, and I'll learn the rest." He crosses his arms and leans back in his chair. "I also hear a lot about what happens in this town. I happen to believe Anne is a wonderful girl who deserves a chance at happiness."

#

All the way back to my apartment I remain puzzled by Mr. Pearson. How did he know of Anne and me? Was he up on Anne breaking off our relationship? Was he aware his wife had been making passes at me? Why didn't he fire me when he had the chance?

I continue to ponder these questions as I enter the living room. Blackie greets me, so I sit on the couch to pet him. I remember I need to call Anne and tell her of Jack's death, so I dial her number. I exhale slowly to calm my anxiety.

The phone rings twice before Anne answers, "Hello."

"Hi, this is Josh. I was calling to find out if you heard the news that Jack is dead."

Her voice sounds strained, "Yes. But I heard there were two men dead. I'm glad to hear your voice. I wasn't sure you were Okay."

"I'm fine." My hopes and spirits lift a tiny bit, "But I would like to talk to you if I could. Can you come over?"

Anne sighs into the phone, "Listen, I understand how upset

you must be because of Jack's death. I've told you before. I wish you well, but I don't want to have anything more to do with you. Please try to understand and don't call me again, it's too upsetting."

I pause; my disappointment turning into awareness she will not relent, no matter how I might plead my case. "Good bye then. I promise not to bother you." I slowly hang up the phone. The silence of the room surrounds me like a heavy cloud.

I call Blackie up onto the couch beside me, and he obliges. When he lies down next to me, I lean back and stroke behind his ears. The tactile experience of petting Blackie's thick, double-coat of fur is soothing. He turns his head, and I watch the dark pupil of one eye swimming in the middle of his chocolate iris.

"It's you and me. I can tell you one thing; I'm not leaving this time."

He nods his head as if in understanding, and we sit quietly together well into the evening.

Chapter 74: More

Early Saturday afternoon, Chief Dan is in his office with a cup of black coffee, reviewing what his team has learned in the last thirty hours.

Mildred had been a fount of information, although none of it was first-hand evidence. She knew Josh and Jack had filed claims, was aware of the shooting incident on the mainland, as well as Jack's concerns about being followed by the Harbormaster and his red-haired partner. The most unbelievable part of the tale was the diamonds. He never expected the old man to find anything valuable.

Late yesterday, he had learned the pistol carried by the jeweler had been purchased five years earlier and registered in the man's name. The fingerprints on the revolver matched those of the jeweler, and he had powder residue on his right hand. One cartridge had been fired, so Dan concludes Blackie surprised the jeweler as he ran for the walkway.

The manner of death in both cases is obvious, but preliminary autopsy results will not be available until the middle of the week. Powder burns were found on Silver Jack's skin and clothing near the bullet's entrance wound indicating the two men had been standing close together when the shot was fired. Lab results for powder burns and powder marks should be available in a few days. DNA results for the blood samples taken from Josh and the saliva sample from Blackie wouldn't return for a couple of weeks.

Jason Boggs had been packing a cell phone. The call history portion of his phone showed conversations with his family in

Ketchikan as well as an incoming call from a phone in San Francisco. This might warrant another discussion with a colleague in that jurisdiction, or it might be a dead-end. At least, he would need to find out who called and, if possible, the purpose of the conversation.

#

Dan reviews his "To Do" list. He will ask Detective Alex to research Jason Boggs' travel to confirm the suspect's arrival in Wrangell and check phone records for the Hungry Beaver Hotel, in case the jeweler made any calls from his room. He adds "Interview Clay Foster" to his list. It made sense to figure out who the Harbormaster's partner might be. He'd assign Detective Alex to get statements from David and Clay confirming their whereabouts at the time of the shooting. He makes a note so he will not forget to instruct Detective Alex to conduct the interviews separately. Additional information could often be learned from one's friends and colleagues, who often know more than you think about your business.

There is a knock at his door, so he looks up as Detective Alex enters, cap in hand. "Hi, Chief, may I come in?" he asks belatedly.

Dan smiles and waives at one of the chairs, "Help yourself, what have you learned this morning?"

Detective Alex flips open his notebook, "We've swept the entire tribal sanctuary for evidence. So far, we've determined the shooting must have happened right at the edge of the island. The impact threw Silver Jack off the grassy portion and into the rushes where we found him. The leash for the dog was on the grass; it looked as if he must have dropped it as he was shot. We dusted the metal parts for finger prints." He pauses as if to gather his thoughts, "There wasn't much there that was usable, maybe a partial thumbprint."

He looks up and Dan can tell there is a hint of excitement in the young detective's expression. "I found paperwork on Silver Jack's boat. There's a receipt for three diamond specimens. The receipt is signed by Jason Boggs."

Dan nods his head, "I find it interesting one of the diamonds is missing. What else have you got?"

"I have the inventory of the possessions on both corpses. I found notes on a scrap of paper in one of Mr. Boggs' pockets. There is a listing for a San Francisco phone number and nearby is the word 'chameleon'."

Dan can't help but envision tiny reptiles changing skin color. "What do you suppose it means?"

Detective Alex is grinning, "I was stumped most of the morning, until I realized the note was in the same pocket with the two diamond specimens. I had a hunch so I googled 'chameleon diamonds'. You won't imagine what I found."

Dan makes a sudden connection, "I suppose you're going to tell me there are diamonds that change color?"

"You've got it Chief," Detective Alex's voice trembles. He rushes into his next comment, "However, these diamonds are extremely rare. So rare, in fact, collectors own them all. From what I was able to learn, each one sells for anywhere from ten grand to upwards of two hundred fifty thousand dollars."

Dan sighs, "Good work. That might come in handy to help prove motive. I couldn't figure out why anyone would shoot the old man."

Detective Alex purses his lips, "I wonder if Boggs wasn't trying to get his hands on more specimens."

Dan lets the silence stretch out; giving the detective's words a chance to settle. "I wonder if he wasn't trying to keep the specimens Silver Jack already gave him." In a flash of insight, Dan realizes he might be able to find the missing diamond. He straightens up in his chair. "Find out who owns the San Francisco phone number and get an address. Check postal records to find out if Mr. Boggs shipped an insured package to there. If you get a match, get on the horn to San Francisco and get a search warrant. My bet is the two diamonds in his pocket are standard diamonds, and the one he shipped to San Francisco for analysis was one of these chameleon diamonds."

Detective Alex looks down at his shoes. Dan isn't used to having the young man refuse to follow instruction. "What's the matter?"

Detective Alex gives him a direct look. “I’ve got more information Chief, and you’re going to want to hear this before I go.”

Dan stifles his impatience, “Okay, out with it, what’s so important it can’t wait?”

“I got a call at daybreak regarding a body found along the Stikine. I didn’t want to wake you so I went out and secured the scene myself. The condition of the body was poor, indicating to me it has been there for a while. I believe it’s the body of the other member of the Sealaska research crew.” Detective Alex checks his notes, “And get this boss, I found this in his pocket.”

Chief Dan looks at Alex’s hand and notices he is holding a transparent stone. It looks like one of the rough diamonds Josh turned over to the police. Beyond his control, the hair rises along the back of his neck.

Chapter 75: Battery

My classroom is silent and grows slowly darker, until I am forced to turn on additional lights. It's after 10 p.m., and I'm logged into my computer preparing a lab assignment for a basic chemistry class. While I am working, I hear a scraping noise outside. I glance out the classroom windows and can make out tree boughs moving in the breeze, so I chock the sound up to the wind.

My students will need sufficient information to be successful at setting up the experiment properly and then observe and record the results. To make sure I leave nothing out, I replicate the experiment and wait for the reaction to be complete. I record my own results and plot them before comparing them to the example shown in the teacher's edition.

I stretch my arms over my head and yawn. I realize I'm hungry and tired. Blackie has been waiting at my apartment for me to return for almost six hours, so I call it quits for the night. I put away my equipment and notes, and then turn out the lights. I make my way down the darkened hallway to the back door of the high school.

Outside, I push the door closed, waiting for an audible click before I turn to go. I'm standing in a weak circle of light produced by a yellow light bulb over the doorway. With my back to the steps, I hear a scrape behind me in the darkness. Frightened, I step to my left and spin around to face what is on the steps. I sense a dark silhouette moving toward me.

In a second, I realize something is being swung toward my head as a club-like object flashes through the beam of light.

Instinctively, I hurl myself sideways off the steps and into the darkness to my right. A flash of pain erupts in my head as the club glances off my temple.

For a second, I hang over the darkness, and then I crash into juniper bushes below the steps, shoulder first. The momentum and sloped ground cause me to flip over onto the lawn, sliding over the wet grass toward the sidewalk in the parking lot.

The juniper bushes leave sharp scratches on my face, arms, and legs. My shoulder is numb from the fall and my head hurts like hell. Despite these challenges, I stagger to my feet and lurch toward the parking lot. Adrenaline is pumping through my system, and I feel sick to my stomach.

Away from the building, the light improves, and two men are racing down the steps toward me. One is packing a club and the other is bare handed. I realize I'm in no condition to outrun anyone, so I stop in the middle of the parking lot and confront my assailants. "What the hell do you want?" I'm tired of running, mad, and sore. I want a piece of these two men. They won't take me down running away.

Silently, the pair closes in on my position. They circle me, so I charge the man with the club. Before he can get the club into position to complete a swing, I'm inside his reach, I plant my right foot and unleash a powerful right-hook, snapping his head back. Blood spurts from his lips, and I hear the satisfying crunch of at least one broken tooth. My next punch is a fast uppercut to his solar plexus. I'm hoping to knock his breath out, in an attempt to buy myself a few precious seconds to disable the second man.

I spin away to my right, hoping I have enough time to foil the second man's attack to my unprotected back. I almost make it, when a swift blow to the back of my knee brings me flopping to the ground. I crash to my left shoulder and roll swiftly away.

A boot skims a burning line across my face, and I grab for it with both hands. Luckily, I manage to hang on long enough to deliver a counter-kick to the man's testicles, using all the force I can muster. He collapses across my legs, vomiting. Before I can free my legs, the man with the club returns, delivering a boot to my ribs. Thankfully, he no longer has his club, but his follow-up kick connects solidly, and I hear and feel several ribs snap.

The pain is excruciating, but it inspires me to jerk my legs free of the downed man. I embrace the pain and roll away from the kicks now being aimed at my head. I roll again to avoid another kick and find myself wedged against the curb of the parking lot.

Unable to get away, I watch as the boot arcs toward my chest. I deflect the kick with my arm but it connects painfully and a loud snap announces the breaking of at least one bone. I nearly black out as my arm hangs limp beside me. I feel helpless, unable to defend against another attack. I am without hope, as my assailant lines up for a serious kick to my head.

"Hold it right there, mister, or I'll blow you to hell!" I watch as the Police Chief steps into the faint light, "Put your goddamn hands over your head."

Chapter 76: Medicine

Sunday is the last working day in what is an impossibly long week for Anne.

#

On Wednesday, she had gone to the dance with Josh, and it had been wonderful at first. By the end of the evening, she was wishing she had never met Josh Campbell. She had felt deceived in a personal way, just when she was beginning to have a bit of control in her life. Part of her could have dealt with the betrayal, if Josh would not have also lied to her. Then Jack and Mildred came to her work and challenged her about the veracity of Claire's claim. The following day Jack was dead, and she feared for Josh's life. She was grateful to learn Josh was untouched, but she couldn't allow herself to forgive him or trust him.

To make matters worse, Emily had taken to acting out in unexpected ways. On Saturday she had refused to go to work, and Anne knew working at the café was her absolute favorite thing to do. Anne suspected Emily was trying to punish her for breaking up with Josh. From what Anne could gather, Emily disagreed with her position and had chosen to accept he was telling the truth. As the days had gone by, Anne's belief in anything regarding the matter had undergone a slow transition. Yet, Anne was reluctant to admit she might be the one who was wrong.

Last night, she had found herself making sketches of Josh. She had torn the offending paper to pieces and thrown it away in the garbage. She had been nagged for several days by a question that haunted her. What if he had been telling the truth, and it was Claire who had lied to her?

The hedonistic woman had never shown any friendship to Anne. But what could be a rational explanation for her to lie? This was the crux of the problem for Anne. Without provocation, why would Claire lie? This line of thinking had sustained her position for the last several days. Today it was being upset by a more powerful question. Why would she trust Claire over Josh? In particular, why would she do so, when she's in love with him?

#

By nine in the morning, the breakfast crowd is thinning out. Anne spots Ernie on his way up the ramp to the restaurant, sporting his usual Semper Fi ball cap along with a new flannel shirt. He takes his place at the end of the counter, "Good morning. Where's Emily?"

Anne blushes at the question about her daughter. "Emily chose to stay home today. I'm flying solo. Would you care for a cup of coffee?"

Ernie nods his head. He scratches his beard as she pours coffee, "I was over at the barbershop and picked up a piece of gossip you might want to hear."

Anne smiles, responding in as pleasant a tone as she can muster, "I'm not much for gossip."

He crosses his thick arms, "You'll want to hear this. The Police Chief arrested two guys last night, who were in the process of beating the new schoolteacher to death. The young man is in the hospital, but nobody knows if he's going to make it."

Anne is rooted to the floor, barely able to breathe. She places the hot coffee pot on the counter; afraid she might spill it. "Are you talking about Josh Campbell?"

Ernie reaches across the counter and picks up her hand. "Yes, I am. You get on over to the hospital and check on the young man. I'll help Darcy as best I can until you get back, so don't you come back here until you find out if he's going to be okay."

Anne flees into the kitchen and asks Darcy for permission to leave.

"I heard Ernie. The man is loud enough to scare a moose. No

wonder gossip spreads fast in this town. You run along, I can handle it as long as you're back for the lunch crowd."

In her pickup, Anne fights back tears, afraid of what she might learn at the hospital. The trip is a blur, but the five blocks to the hospital take an eternity. In the parking lot, she pulls into the first available space, not wanting to waste a second searching for a place to park. She enters the hospital, approaching the front desk. Behind the counter is a slender receptionist with curly, black hair and freckles all over her face. Anne recognizes her as an occasional customer of the café but can't recall her name.

"Hi, I'm looking for a patient. His name is Josh Campbell. Can you direct me to his room, please?"

It takes a couple of minutes for the receptionist to look up the information. "He's in intensive care. You can't go in there unless you're related."

Anne assumes a relaxed expression, "Oh that won't be a problem. Can you tell me the room number?"

The receptionist smiles as she answers, "He's in room two thirty."

By the time Anne gets to intensive care, she has rehearsed at least three lies to gain entrance. Opportunely, when she nears the unit, an orderly is backing out of the swinging double doors guiding a portable x-ray unit. He doesn't say a word as she slips through the doors before they close.

Inside, afraid to ask for directions she finds the first room number and explores. Within two minutes she is outside his room.

Pausing, Anne listens to find out if he is alone. Hearing no sound, she enters his room and finds it in semi-darkness. She walks close to the bed but can't make out his features. She is leaning forward, trying to determine if it's indeed Josh, when the lights to the room flip on.

An elderly nurse with salt-and-pepper hair enters the room. "I thought I saw you come in. Have you come to find out how he's doing?"

Anne blushes, "Why, yes. I heard he was hurt. Is he going to make it?"

The nurse turns to the bed and checks the vital signs of her patient. "I'm sure he'll be as good as new in a few weeks. He has several broken ribs. The x-rays show he almost had a punctured lung. Both bones in his lower right arm are broken, and he received a couple of heavy blows to his head. There was also concern about internal bleeding, so we've had him under observation all night. He has numerous cuts, scrapes, and bruises all over his body. Lucky he's in such good physical condition. Not many people can handle so many traumas and be conscious. The night crew sedated him and patched him up."

The nurse turns and appraises Anne. "My name is Kelly. Why don't you sit in the chair and make yourself comfortable. He should wake up soon. You can do me a favor and alert me when he starts to rouse. Look for me at the nursing station down the hall."

Anne is relieved Josh will survive. "Okay, I will. Thank you for your help." She holds out her hand, "My name is Anne."

Kelly smiles as she completes the handshake, "Nice to meet you. Can I get you anything?"

Anne shakes her head, "No thank you. I'll be fine."

She pulls a chair up to Josh's bed and tries to wait. She examines his face. Large, purple and black bruises corrupt his features. Asleep, he looks lifeless, and the thought she might have lost him plucks at her heart. She picks up his unwrapped left hand and strokes it gently. She is overwhelmed by her feelings, why does everything have to be so complicated? She's conflicted to be here after spending the last week refusing to talk to him.

A young man comes into the room. "Hi, I'm Detective Alex. The Chief asked me to check on Josh. He was worried about him."

"Hello, I'm Anne. I work at the Diamond C. What happened last night?"

Detective Alex makes a face, "The Chief was checking on leads related to a recent murder case and saw the vehicle of a suspect parked near the high school. When he got out of his rig to investigate, he walked around the building and found two guys assaulting Mr. Campbell. One of them remains in the hospital this morning, but he has a guard on his room. The other suspect had to have emergency repairs last night by a dentist, and he's in our jail."

"Did they kill Silver Jack?"

"I can't say. But they are going to have a tough time convincing anybody they weren't trying to kill Mr. Campbell. They were using a baseball bat and in the process of kicking him to pieces when the Chief stopped them. Actually, the Chief stopped one of them; Josh incapacitated the other guy first."

After Detective Alex leaves, Anne waits for over an hour before Josh shows signs of waking up. As instructed, she seeks Nurse Kelly at the nursing station. When the nurse isn't there, Anne leaves a message for her with another RN. By the time Anne returns to the room, Josh's eyes are open.

Anne doesn't hesitate; in a terse voice she pelts him with her concerns, "Why weren't you more careful? You could have been killed. Why didn't you have someone call me? I didn't know you were hurt until a little while ago." Her fear for Josh's safety finding release, hot tears explode down her cheeks.

Without a word, Josh lifts his left hand and reaches for her. He tries to smile but its lopsided, and she is reminded half his face is purple and badly bruised. He looks as if he has been in a head-on collision with a logging truck. She moves to the other side of the bed, so she can reach his outstretched hand. "Are you okay?"

Josh's jaw moves slowly, and she is forced to lean close to hear his words. "I'm glad you're here."

Anne lifts her head and gazes down at his face. His dark blue eyes are as intense as ever. She squeezes his hand; grateful he is alive. "I'm glad to be here, too."

A look of pain stretches across Josh's features. Anne becomes worried and glances down the hallway to see if the nurse is nearby. He pulls on her hand, and she turns back to look at him. He stammers, "I...I'm sorry. I thought you didn't want me to bother you."

Anne looks at Josh with tenderness. From deep inside her, the words come spilling out, "I was mad at you." She takes a deep breath and continues, "But I was wrong. It took me awhile to realize I should trust the man I love over the words of anyone else." Anne cries as tears well in Josh's eyes. When they run down his cheeks, she kisses him lightly at the corner of each eye. She revels in the hot, salty taste of his tears and the look of happiness on his bruised face.

He croaks, "I love you, too. More than infinity." He winces, and Anne realizes she is putting weight on his chest.

"Are you alright? Did I hurt you?" Anne is horrified she may have injured him.

He rocks his head back and forth on his pillow, "No. I'm fine."

She strokes a lock of his auburn hair. Bandages hide the rest of his thick mane. Anne laughs, "You look like a mummy."

Josh snorts and then winces when a sharp pain takes his breath away. "Ouch." He smiles at her, "No more jokes, not until they give me more pain meds."

Anne leans forward, "How about this for pain." She kisses him on the lips, rolling his lower lip between hers in a slow sensuous caress lingering for a full minute. Anne is lost in the wonderful exultation of her senses and the glorious sensation of being right with Josh.

A cough from the doorway causes her to straighten up. She places one hand over her mouth as she turns to find the nurse smiling. She addresses Anne in a teasing tone, "I was going to try your strategy shortly. I've been told it accelerates recovery. We call it the secret weapon." She reaches for Josh's wrist so she can check his pulse. "Hi Josh, my name is Kelly."

He responds, "Hello. Thank you. I don't remember getting here."

"Oh, about that, you were talking tough when you arrived. The nurse on the shift before me said you had to be sedated before you calmed down." Kelly is carrying a syringe and explains to Josh he has been given a prescription for pain. "I'm going to give you a dose now. This should allow you to sleep for a couple of hours. You push this buzzer whenever the pain starts to get too much. The medicine takes a few minutes to get into your bloodstream, so don't wait until you can't bear it to call me. The doctor will come by after lunch so that will be a good time to find out what she wants you to do next. Do you have any questions?"

Josh struggles to lift his head off the pillow. He tells Kelly, "Thanks. Where are my clothes and stuff?" After completing his sentence, his head drops back to the pillow. He looks exhausted.

"Your clothes were cut off of you and have been thrown

away. You wouldn't be able to reuse them. Everything else should be in the cabinet at the foot of your bed. Now, if you'll excuse me, I'll leave you two lovebirds alone." Turning to Anne, Nurse Kelly tells her, "He should fall asleep in about five minutes."

Anne focuses her attention on Josh, "I have to go back to work. I'll be back later to check on you. Can I get you anything?"

Josh smiles, stretching his bruised face. "Will you call Mildred? I can't make it today for lunch."

Anne nods her head. "Of course, I'll take care of it right away."

"One more thing, can you check the dresser for my keys? I left Blackie in my apartment, and he hasn't been outside since late yesterday."

Anne searches the cabinet. Inside she finds a bag with Josh's valuables, including his wallet and a key holder with several keys. She hands him the key ring, "Is this what you're looking for?"

Anne notices Josh is losing his concentration, an obvious sign the painkiller is taking affect. He hands her the key ring, grasping a silver key between his fingers. "Here's the key to my apartment. I want you to have it."

Certain he is unaware of the obvious double meaning of his words, Anne smiles. "I'll take good care of Blackie. I promise." She seals her promise with another long sensuous kiss. When Josh is asleep, she whispers, "And I'll take good care of you, too, Josh Campbell."

Chapter 77: It Won't Last Long

A few minutes past noon on Sunday, Chief Dan enters the hospital through the emergency room entrance. His first port of call is to check on his nephew, Officer Martin Chak, at his post outside the Harbormaster's room. "How is it going?"

Martin lunges to his feet, "Hi, Chief, the doctor came by, checked on the patient, and signed the release papers."

"Why didn't you use your radio to call me?"

Martin fidgets with the equipment on his belt, "I called it in a minute ago. You must have gotten out of your vehicle already."

Dan gives his nephew a skeptical look, "Okay. That's fine. Come in and witness me reading him his rights."

Inside the room, Dan confronts Clay, "I never expected to have to do this, but I'm arresting you for conspiracy to defraud, assault and battery, and attempted murder. Before you say anything I must inform you of your rights. You have the right to remain silent. Anything you say can and will be used against you in a court of law. You have the right to have an attorney present during questioning. If you cannot afford an attorney, one will be appointed for you. Do you understand these rights?"

Lying in the hospital bed, Clay looks pale and scared. Dan tries to work the man against his partner; "I thought you'd want to know, when we booked Lenn Richards into jail, we found nine rough diamonds among his possessions. It looked to me as if he was pretty glad you weren't present when we found them. I'm no expert, but the street value on those gems might be upwards of thirty thousand dollars."

After arranging for Martin to escort the Harbormaster to jail, Dan seeks out the schoolteacher. Locating the room, Dan enters to find his sister with Josh. He nods in greeting to Mildred and takes up a position at the foot of the hospital bed. "You look quite a bit better than you did last night. I wasn't sure if you were going to make it when I first saw you. You're lucky you had minimal internal bleeding."

Josh lifts his right arm. A cast from his elbow to his fingers covers it. He smiles at Dan. "I want to thank you for showing up when you did. I thought I was a goner for sure."

Dan is curious, "Did you recognize the guys who jumped you?"

Josh gets a faraway look, "It was too dark. I never saw their faces clearly." Josh looks concerned, "Why, did they get away?"

"No, I wondered if you knew them." Dan continues, "You suspected the Harbormaster has a partner. Well one of the guys who jumped you is the Harbormaster. He's the one you took out of action by kicking him in the gonads. He's going to be walking with great care for awhile."

Dan scratches his temple, "His confederate's name is Lenn Richards, and he was the lone survivor of a boating accident on the Stikine a few weeks ago. The Harbormaster is on his way to jail, and he'll probably be booked with assault and battery, attempted murder, and conspiracy to defraud you and Silver Jack out of your diamond claims. In addition to those charges, Richards will also be booked for murder. We no longer believe the death of his two colleagues was an accident. My theory is they found the diamonds before you did, and he killed the other guys because they wanted to report the find to Sealaska."

Josh is dazed by the news, "How did you figure it out?"

Dan becomes serious, "Yesterday, another body was found up the Stikine. In one of the pockets we found rough diamonds. In addition, the Harbormaster and Mr. Richards aren't faithful partners. When I let Clay know we found rough diamonds on his partner, he got madder than hops. It looks like he'd been worried about Richards holding out on him all along. That's when he told me about salvaging the overturned boat on Kadin Island and finding the

Sealaska group's gear hidden in the brush. He even told me the gear is on the island. Apparently, they'd stashed it in the brush again after they ran into you and Silver Jack.

"If it checks out, this could be an open and shut case with the Harbormaster as star witness. Clay will sing plenty, if it will save him from a murder rap."

Josh looks at him intently, "I hate to change the subject, but have you learned why the guy from Ketchikan shot Silver Jack?"

Dan is abashed, "I'm working on it. When we searched the man's body we found two rough diamonds. As you know, Jack had a receipt for three diamonds. I suspect the third diamond is in San Francisco for analysis. I surmise the jeweler learned it was a rare and valuable diamond that changes color. The jeweler needed the money the rare diamond could provide, so he came to Wrangell to get Jack to sell it to him cheap. Failing that, he shot Jack so he could eliminate the need to return the diamond. He didn't realize Blackie would attack him. I bet the jeweler never saw the dog coming."

Josh shakes his head, "I almost wish we'd never found the diamonds."

Mildred intervenes, "Don't even consider it. Yes, Jack always wanted to find something out there, just to prove it to himself." Fidgeting in her chair she continues, "He was a proud man. But he wanted to be outdoors, enjoying nature more than anything else. So although finding valuable minerals might be viewed as a way to validate all those years of effort, for Jack it was the joy of being out there. I can tell you with certainty, his happiness came from being out there as much as possible."

Josh nods his head, "You're right. Why else would he have spent all those years building a trail to a place he had never been?" Josh gets a puzzled look on his face.

Mildred leans forward in her chair, "What's wrong?"

To Dan it looks like Josh is about to cry.

"The last words Jack said to me were, "Watch for me along the trail."

Dan waits for a long minute before breaking the silence in the room. "I hate to bring this up, but if your claims hold up, you and Jack's heirs are going to be sitting on a fortune. In addition, a mining operation of this value is going to have a big impact on this entire region. You're not going to be able to avoid it. You'll be the most sought after man in the territory. You'd better enjoy your anonymity while you can. It won't last long."

Chapter 78: Stalled

Clutching the phone, Claire's hands tremble. She can't comprehend Clay's audacity. Her lover is threatening to reveal their affair and her part in the diamond claim fiasco if she doesn't help him make bail. Sadly, the idiot does not realize her financial wherewithal is so thin she can't help him, even if she wanted to. She doesn't have any cash, and all of her assets are tied up as collateral for loans she can't pay.

Realizing he might follow through if she isn't trying, she begs for forty-eight hours to come up with enough funds. Left with no other option, he reluctantly agrees. After all, if he does report her involvement, it won't help him, and he'll lose his leverage.

She hangs up, distraught and frightened. Clay might reveal she encouraged him to get rid of Josh.

Her recent plan to start a mill in Wrangell is stalled. The city wants pricey safety and pollution controls on the old mill and is asking for needed improvements to nearby streets as a precondition to giving out a permit. To her mind these demands are nothing short of blackmail. Despite her best efforts, no amount of pleading or coercion works.

Claire is scheduled to pay her employees at the end of the week. She is acutely aware she has five days to come up with nearly four hundred thousand dollars. Her bank has frozen her line of credit, and she has no assets left which are not collateralized. No matter where she turns, there is no business solution that will provide her with the cash she needs. In addition, her accountant has left three terse messages demanding she deposit funds to cover payroll on Friday.

She glances at her father's picture, glaring down at her from its position above her desk. She drops her head into her hands as she sobs, "Daddy, forgive me. I've tried everything. I don't know what to do."

Chapter 79: Safe Place

Early Tuesday, I'm sitting on the edge of my hospital bed when Anne and Emily come to help me leave the hospital. I am pleased Anne remembers to bring clothing from my apartment. "Thank you, I appreciate it. I'm getting pretty tired of this hospital gown. They even cut away my underwear."

Anne kisses me as I watch Emily's reaction out of the corner of one eye. She is giggling, and I let go of worries she might resent or disapprove of my feelings for her mother.

"How is Blackie?"

Anne runs her fingers through my hair. I find the gesture comforting. I look into her eyes and glean a suggestion of greater intimacy to come. The thought is both thrilling and satisfying. I can't wait to get Anne into my arms, with nothing to distract us. My train of thought is interrupted by her answer. She leans forward, with her cheek against mine she speaks into my ear, "Blackie is fine. He'll be delighted to be with you. He thinks everyone has abandoned him."

The girls wait while I go into the bathroom and stiffly get dressed. With clothing on, I feel almost human. I open the door and step out into the hospital room. "How do I look?"

Emily squints at me; "You look like you have a tumor on your face."

I smile, "My face feels like it was run over by a train. Can you help me lace up my shoes? I'm finding it difficult to use my right hand."

#

On Wednesday, I pick up Mildred on my way to meet Jack's family at the airport. While we wait, I overhear a conversation between airport security and a passenger. The two know each other and their tone is friendly. The traveler does the accounting for Claire's logging company and reveals, "I'm on my way to Seattle. I don't want to be here when her employees don't get paid."

Jack's sons are recognizable, each built along the same blocky frame that was his trademark. Mildred and I shuttle them to their various lodgings. The eldest son, Walter, invites us to join the family for dinner at the Stikine Inn. We agree to dinner, but I insist on providing transportation. "It will be easier than calling a cab. They aren't reliable."

Between trips, I stop at the Diamond C for lunch and a chance to visit with Anne. She is so lovely I ache. I'm struck by my luck at getting her back into my life after losing her. While I'm in the café, I learn regulators have closed down the bank. The rumors spread like wildfire, but several of them include speculation the logging company is in bankruptcy. I consider the impacts caused by the bank closing and I'm grateful the diamonds are in the custody of the police.

I pick up Anne and Emily before stopping to pick up Mildred for dinner. When we arrive at the restaurant, tables are pulled together to make room for their banquet. As I sit with Anne, Emily, and Mildred nearby, I get a sense of family in a way I have never experienced. Here at this table, the dialogue is rich and lively. Several conversations involve catching up on the activities of children and other family members.

Wine is served with our meal and everyone raises his or her glass in salute as Walter stands to make a toast. "Here's to Jack, beloved father, grandfather, and great grandfather. There's a traditional Irish blessing appropriate for this moment.

May the road rise to meet you
May the wind be always at your back
The sun shine warm upon your face
The rains fall soft upon your fields

And until we meet again,
May God hold you in the hollow of his hand."

We all take a sip of wine in tribute to the man. The words touch me, and I savor how well they fit the man I'd come to know. Soon, the warm patter of conversation fills the room. I ask Mildred if Jack was Irish.

"Probably on his mother's side. He always talked about being Dutch or Swiss and part Indian. "

When one of the brothers asks me to describe how we found the diamonds, the entire table goes silent. I'm a little embarrassed to find myself the center of attention; but I realize this will become an important moment in the life story of this family, so I overcome my hesitation and tell them how Jack saved my life.

"He talked me into going out into the wilderness with him. He'd spotted a volcanic vent from the top of Garnet Mountain and then spent three years, alone except for Blackie, building a trail, making camps, and hauling equipment to get there. It has to be in the roughest, toughest terrain on this continent. To get there, we began by dragging a boat as far upriver as possible, then hiking across miles of muskeg, careful not to make a misstep or we'd sink into the muck. He built Base where the river becomes navigable by canoe. The entire next day we paddled upriver, forcing our way past rapids and logjams.

"When we got to Halfway we found it flooded out, so we had to rebuild it. The next day we carried a week's supply of food and equipment as we hacked our way through brush higher than our head, then crossed more muskeg. After building Jump Off, we climbed thousands of feet, picking our way past cliffs as we hacked our way through even more brush. After four days, we reached our destination. We were exhausted, soaking wet, and cold."

I pause and look around the table; every face is focused on mine. Even the youngest of the great-grandchildren is sitting quietly, waiting. "Everyone around here called him Silver Jack. By the time we'd climbed the mountain together, he allowed me to call him Jack. We found a fault in the earth and followed it into the volcanic vent. The cliffs were eight hundred feet tall and quite sheer. Below us at the bottom of the vent were a jumble of jagged rocks and a beautiful mountain lake.

"We found the diamonds along the face of the cliff in dark ribbons of rock Jack said was Kimberlite. We didn't know for sure what we'd found, but that night back in Jump Off Jack tested the specimens for hardness. We thought we had diamonds, but we couldn't be sure they were valuable or not."

I stop for a sip of water, finding my mouth dry from all the talking. "The following two days we set the boundaries for our claims. No sooner had we finished, than I was nearly shot. Jack fired back, and we left the mountain as fast as we could. We traveled half the night and all the next day to get back to Wrangell. Once there, Jack went to Ketchikan and filed our claims.

We were waiting for analyses of their value, when Jack was killed. Right now, the police have all the specimens as part of their investigation into Jack's death." As I finish, I feel relief from the pain of his departure. I realize here is a safe place to share my feelings for Jack. I gulp, fighting back tears as I tell the family, "His last words were he'd watch for me along the trail. He'll be waiting for all of you, too."

Chapter 80: Recognition

On Friday afternoon, when Jack's family and friends gather together for his funeral services, I learn his body had been shipped to Ketchikan to be cremated. One of the brothers had flown to Ketchikan and returned with his ashes. I silently thank the family for selecting an afternoon schedule for the event, because this makes it possible for Anne to be there with me. I make contact with her green eyes and catch several dimple flashes in a row. I lean over and whisper into her ear, "Thanks for last night; I'll cherish the memory for the rest of my life."

Anne tilts her head and her jet black hair grazes my face. She smiles and in a happy tone responds to me as she squeezes my hand, "I thought it was wonderful, too."

The turnout is heavy. I recognize several members of the police Department including Mildred's brother and Detective Alex. David, from the marina, comes over and shakes my hand, "I'm sure going to miss him. You'll have to bring Blackie to the office every once in a while, so I can give him a treat." I notice David is shy around Anne, politely tipping his hat to her, while squeaking out a weak, "Hello."

From a distance, I spot Katie. She waves at me, but keeps her distance. Standing beside her is Charlie, the wood carver. I wonder if the two are now a couple. A little awkwardly, due to the cast on my arm, Anne intertwines her fingers with mine, and I forget about Katie. I'm nervous, hoping my plans for the next day are successful.

Because there is no casket, the center of the service is a

blow up of the photo I'd taken of Jack near our mining claim. Jack is standing on lichen-decorated rock. Blackie is sitting slightly behind him. The magnificent creature is wearing his pack and on alert facing away from Jack, on guard. In the background is the glacier fading away into the mist. Jack is looking down at me, holding his machete at the ready in one gloved hand. His rifle is held by the barrel, butt on the ground.

In this photo his intense face is framed by his silver beard and his short-brimmed, rain hat. He is wearing a faded, navy-blue vest over a dark-green flannel shirt. His shirt is tucked into his blue jeans, although one shirttail has come loose, hanging down in front of his hip. The cuffs of his blue jeans are rolled, overlapping several inches of his rubber caulk boots.

All in all, in every way, Jack looks like a mountain man. I admit to myself, he's a little past his prime, but none of this lessens his intensity. Ready for anything, he doesn't look eighty years old.

The family makes the gathering a celebration of Jack's colorful life. One of his sons starts off with a story about Jack running over a cougar with his truck on their way to work one morning. Another son told how the family got through many winters by cutting cedar on Forest Service land without permits.

There are lots of hunting and fishing stories told by locals. But friends from Oregon and Washington are also present, and everyone has a tale to tell. Even Anne has a story about Jack. She describes how he always ordered ham, so he would have a treat for Blackie.

When it's my turn I'm nervous and don't know what to say until I start talking. "I remember the afternoon we found the diamonds. We were hiking uphill through steep terrain and hacking our way through the wet brush, one step at a time. Mostly Jack was leading, and I was trying hard to keep up.

"I asked him which direction we were going. I remember he got a strange look in his eye before he told me we were going west of north. Then he explained this is a direction that has always been important to him. I didn't realize at the time he was right, minutes later we stumbled out of the brush and found the diamond strike."

I pause for a second, "He also said it was the course he

followed when he came to Alaska." As I'm talking, I get a sudden idea. "You should know I plan to do everything I can to make his claim a success. In his honor, I propose we call it the Silver Jack Mine."

After the ceremony, Jack's sons ask to meet with me. I'm not surprised, so I take Anne back to her apartment and wait until everyone else has left. At last, Walter and his brothers are the only ones left.

"We understand Dad asked you to look after Blackie?"

"Yes. It was almost the last thing he said to me." I try not to remember the look on Jack's face and the fear that held me.

"We want to thank you for what you did for our dad. If you've had second thoughts about Blackie, we would understand."

I'm stunned, but smile, "This is one request I am anxious to grant. I've always wanted a dog I could take into the wilderness. As far as I'm concerned, Blackie is a perfect fit for me."

Walter and his brothers look relieved. One confesses, "We didn't know how we would get him back to the lower forty-eight, and none of us have a set-up suitable for Blackie. This couldn't have worked out better."

I reassure them, "Don't worry about it for a second. Blackie and I were meant for each other. He even helped save my life when I almost died of hypothermia."

Walter gives me a bear hug. "Good. I'm glad it's settled. We'd also like to discuss becoming your partners in the diamond mine. Are you interested?"

I don't hesitate, "Yes, I'm interested. I don't know a thing about negotiating contacts or royalties. I also have no experience with diamond mines or any other mine for that matter."

The brothers shake my hand. Walter answers, "We don't have much experience in those areas either, so it will be a learning experience for all of us. We enjoyed what you had to say at the service about naming the mine after dad. This way his name will live on as long as the history of the mine lasts."

I have to discuss one important issue. "I have one request. Your dad and I talked about designating part of any profits to support the legal battle to get recognition for the landless tribes in southeast Alaska." I feel nervous, wondering if this issue will sink our partnership before it begins, "Will you join me in supporting this cause?"

The brothers exchange glances, and Walter nods his head, "We agree. If dad wanted to do it, we won't question it."

The youngest brother adds, "Dad taught us many things. A few were useful, many weren't." He chuckles, "But we know he was always inspired by the quality of the journey most of all. Let's make this a journey we will all remember."

Chapter 81: Commitment

I call Mildred, "What did you think of the service for Jack?"

Her voice is strong, "I've thought about it a lot. It was a wonderful tribute to his life. I really liked the picture you shared. It captured his spirit."

"I wondered if I could come over on your day off and have some breakfast. I could pick up some bacon," I add hopefully.

Mildred laughs, "Yes, I'll make you breakfast, dear boy. But you don't have to worry about me being lonely. Remember, the whole town visits me almost every day at the post office. Besides, lots of people have been dropping by to check on me. I've scarcely had a moment to myself since Jack died."

I'm relieved, "I'm glad to hear that. I really miss him and knew that you must be missing him too."

Mildred's voice sounds cheerful, "Company has kept my mind off his death. Anne came out yesterday, and we had tea and cookies. She's a lovely woman."

Now it's my turn to sound cheerful, "I want to thank you for going to the Diamond C with Jack and talking to Anne. It sounds like it really helped her come around."

"I'm not so sure about that. We did have a nice visit. She came to apologize."

I'm surprised, "Why would she apologize. She had every reason to be angry with me."

"She regrets that Jack died before the two of you resolved your trouble."

I pause, "I hadn't thought about it from that perspective. I hope she can let go of any guilt."

"I believe she was able to do so. We had a good cry. I know I felt better afterwards."

I try to move us to another topic, "Thanks to Jack I got to know you. It felt like we were a family. I'm worried that with him gone, we won't have any reason to see each other. That makes me sad."

I hear a sob, "Josh, as you know, I have no children. I always wanted them, but it wasn't in the cards for me. Now I'm an old lady and know it will never happen. Can I adopt you?"

I smile, "I would love to be your son. Mom, when can I come over for breakfast?"

#

I meet Anne and Emily at the library. While they search for books, I sit in one of the soft reading chairs and ponder my future. It was really thoughtful of Anne to apologize to Mildred. What can I do to ease her guilt about Jack's death? Her concern for other's wellbeing is a powerful part of her character. Anne is bright, articulate, helpful, caring, and empathetic. She's a hard worker and doesn't need a lot of things to make her happy. I think about all the girls and women I've known, and only she and Mildred have demonstrated they care more about the wellbeing of friends and family than about their own needs. This trait probably isn't that rare, but it sure has been in my life.

I remember Kaeli, and realize all we had was lust. Everything we did was centered on her needs. It wasn't sufficient for me, and that's why I never asked her to marry. Real love isn't about physical attraction; it's about caring for someone else more than you care about yourself. I can't imagine being happy without Anne as my life partner. The revelation strikes me like a lightning bolt, it shouldn't be this hard to figure out. Perhaps I'm a slow learner. A new fear grabs me, what if Anne doesn't want to make a lifetime commitment? I swallow a lump, there's only one way to find out.

Chapter 82: Racked Out

The jail cell is cramped and cold, with a single, barred window letting in the gray light of morning. To Clay, the cell stinks of urine and feces not quite covered up by the pungent smell of bleach. The bare mattress is soiled and lumpy. It has cigarette burns and sports a six-inch rip down one seam. The stainless steel commode runs water in a constant drip. The sound gets into his brain and picks at him without cease.

The pain in his nuts is even worse. Josh had kicked him like a rutting moose, and the swelling was taking its own sweet time fading away. It hurt to piss, and he walked like a man in shackles. Earlier he had heard the guards snickering when he shuffled back to his cell after visiting the doctor in the exam room.

For the thousandth time, he scans the pealing walls, looking for anything different in the graffiti. Finding none, he glances across the hall at his former partner. Bored and irritated, Clay calls over to the skinny redhead, "Hey, Nancy, I've got a cigarette left. For a blow job, I'll trade you."

Silence mocks him from across the hall. Clay vows to let his words hang in the air between them until Lenn is forced to answer.

He remembers his last call to Claire. The bitch had turned down his request for help with the bail bond. "I don't have any funds right now. I can't help you."

He had been unable to control his anger, "You're forcing me to turn you in. I might be able to get a lighter sentence, if I testify against you."

Claire hadn't minced her words. "I can help you in other

ways, if I stay out of jail. I can't help you if I'm in jail, too. I might not have any money, but I do have influence left. In fact, I can testify you were duped by your partner and didn't know he was planning to harm anybody."

Lenn, the bastard, had squirreled diamonds just as he'd suspected. The asshole deserves to be facing the death sentence for double murder. Alaskans tend not to be lenient about leaving partners to die in the wilderness. Pondering Claire's conversation, he realizes her plan might work. After all, Clay hadn't been anywhere close to the scene of the murders. He might face tough choices about which facts to reveal or hide to make himself look as blameless as possible. It helps that he told the Police Chief about finding the Sealaska equipment on Kadin Island before his arrest.

Trying to find a comfortable position for his swollen balls, Clay rolls over onto his back. If he had a bottle of scotch, he could drown out his sorrows and his pain. Why had he become involved with Lenn Richards? If not, he would have a great paying job and good standing in the community. Instead, he's racked out in this stinking jail cell waiting for the Alaska judicial system to grind him into hamburger.

Clay yells across to Lenn, "Hey, Nancy, want a cigarette?"

Chapter 83: Important Journey

I pat Blackie and watch him smile over his shoulder at me. I remember how I once feared his wolf-like fangs. Blackie is eager to be off and away into the wilderness.

Together, Blackie, Anne, and I stand on a knob west of the airport and watch a charter plane fly west of north toward Petersburg. It's a rare morning, with full sunlight and a few errant clouds. Sunrays glisten off the plane's windows as it floats above the mouth of the Eastern Passage.

I point at the aircraft and tell Anne about the plans for Jack's grandchildren to drop his ashes over Koknuk Flats in the mouth of the Stikine. "He will like that," I muse, "He told me he'd be waiting along the trail. Hope he enjoys the journey."

Beyond the plane are Garnet Mountain and the headwaters of Crittenden Creek. How long will it take, I wonder, to make the diamond mine a reality? I suspect I will get at least one more chance to follow Jack's trail into the wilderness.

I glance past Anne's beautiful profile and look east toward the snowcapped peaks of Canada, marveling at all the pristine country and realizing much of it will remain empty of humanity for decades. Most people are in such a hurry; they only make it to the easy-to-reach portions of this land. In the month I spent with Jack, I learned there is also a way to create deep and rich relationships. I vow never to forget the lesson.

Turning, I take Anne's hands into mine, "Now it's my turn to start an important journey." Stiffly, because of my broken ribs, I get down on one knee. "I talked the Police Chief into releasing the rough diamonds. I'd like to have the best stone made into an engagement ring for you to wear." I swallow hard, trying to keep my composure. I look up into the greenest eyes on the planet. "Anne, I love you with all my heart. Will you marry me?"

About This Book

The descriptions of Wrangell, Ketchikan, and the areas covered in this story are as accurate as the author could make them for the summer of 2007. Some artistic license has been taken with the layout of the high school and the location of the police station. In addition, the harbor expansion is misrepresented, as it's really the construction of a new marina on the southern edge of town along Zimovia Highway.

Silver Jack is based on my father, Jack Hoover. Jack is a prospector, who lives in Wrangell and explored the region around Wrangell extensively. As of the time this writing goes to press Jack is eighty-eight years of age and continues to go into the backcountry for weeks at a time. The camps and trails used by Silver Jack in this story are there and available for anyone brave enough to use them. You may wish to bring along paddles, if you want to use the canoe at Base, since the ones that are there are beyond their useful lives.

Blackie died a few years ago at age sixteen. For a large dog, he lived a long life and was the best trail mate Jack ever knew.

All other characters in this novel are fictional and any similarities with any individual are coincidental.

This book refers to the Five Landless Tribes of Southeast Alaska. Five Alaska Native communities were excluded from the Alaska Native Claims Settlement Act in 1971, which transferred forty-four million acres and more than nine hundred million dollars to thirteen regional Native Corporations and more than two hundred village corporations. It's unexplained why Alaska Natives in Ketchikan, Wrangell, Petersburg, Haines, and Tenakee were not allowed to organize village corporations and receive land under ANCSA. The battle to resolve this oversight continues in Congress.

About The Author

Ken Hoover moved to Southeast Alaska with his wife Kim on their 42-foot catamaran, *Reiki Master*, after retiring as a school superintendent in 2015. They enjoy whale watching, fishing, crabbing, shrimping, and exploring the nearly ten thousand miles of coastline in Southeast Alaska.

Prior to retirement Ken spent many summers in Alaska visiting his father and exploring the area covered in this novel. He grew up in a remote part of the Pacific Northwest part of a logging family and worked as a choker setter, rigging slinger, hook tender (hooker) and timber faller as well as shake splitter in a cedar mill. Because of a low lottery number in 1971 he served in both the National Guard and Regular Army. He started civil service as a secretary and held positions as accountant, radiation health physicist, supervisor and budget analyst. He worked in school districts in both Washington and Colorado and as a financial consultant for school districts and large corporations on educational finance issues.

Ken's hobbies include cabinetry, carving and skiing.

Ken has bachelor and master degrees from The Evergreen State College and a Ph.D. from the University of Washington and has previously coauthored a book with Dr. Brian L. Benzel entitled *The Superintendent and the CFO: Building an Effective Team* published in 2015 by Rowman & Littlefield Publishers. He also writes educational book reviews for AASA's *School Administrator* magazine.

West of North is Ken's first novel. He can be reached at kkhoovers@gmail.com. Watch for him along the trail.

29053646R00214

Made in the USA
San Bernardino, CA
16 March 2019